CAP PARLIER

CAP PARLIER

SAINT GAUDENS PRESS
Wichita, Kansas & Santa Barbara, California

Books by Cap Parlier:
Anod's Seduction
Sacrifice
Anod's Redemption

and with Kevin E. Ready:
TWA 800 - Accident or Incident?

These and other great books available from Saint Gaudens Press
http://www.saintgaudenspress.com   or call toll-free 1-(800) 281-5170

Visit Cap Parlier's Web Site at http://www.parlier.com

Saint Gaudens Press
Post Office Box 91847
Santa Barbara, CA 93190-1847

Saint Gaudens, Saint Gaudens Press and the Winged Liberty colophon
are trademarks of Saint Gaudens Press

ISBN: 0-943039-03-7
Library of Congress Card Number 2004096706

Printed in the United States of America

<u>DEDICATION</u>

This book is dedicated to my wife, Jeanne, and to my family,

friends and precious fans.

Special appreciation is offered to Greta Robertson, Leta

Buresh and John Richard for their generous time, criticism, advice

and friendship. Criticism, like a mirror, shows us how others see you.

Their honest contribution was of considerable value.

Chapter 1

The data instigating the present patrol action offered only a suspicion of danger or menace. It was going to be a long mission. Lieutenant Anod reminded herself of the credo of pilots through the centuries: flight was . . . hours and hours of boredom punctuated with moments of stark terror. They were having a good portion of boredom. She wondered when the terror would come.

To Anod, the magnificence of the stars, galaxies and the myriad of other celestial objects was the most glorious reward for space flight and service to the Society. The sheer splendor around her made the quiet times enjoyable, but distracting. In contrast, the tension of a mission against an unseen, potential adversary made the enjoyment much less pleasurable.

The three sleek, dart like, fighters of Team Three, Saranon Detachment, Kartog Guards, with their human pilots and not so human companions launched on this mission nearly eight hours earlier. Anod knew Captain Zitger with Sarog and Lieutenant Zarrod with Stasok shared her boredom although she found it somewhat difficult to ignore her concern for Zitger.

They had been cloaked for more than two hours. Nothing was out here, Anod kept telling herself. All the current sensor data remained within nominal values for this sector of the galaxy. Even the communications from Saranon Command Center were boring.

They could listen, but they were not permitted to transmit anything. It was one of the punishing realities of waiting for an enemy that might never appear. Along with the cloaking system, every effort would be made to prevent detection by anyone including an adversary. Their ancestors called it, 'waiting in ambush.'

Anod continued her visual scan of the envelope of space around her. Her two teammates, also dispersed around the refueling barge in their own machines, were not visible to her or the sensors of her fighter. The compact array of sensors packed into her sleek, diminutive warbird transformed the enormous variety of data into an efficient set of symbols and icons for display to her. Whether discrete symbols projected before her eyes or spread across the broad panel cockpit display, the images simplified an otherwise complicated amount of information. Anod and her lifelong, mechanical companion, Gorp, used the information for situational awareness, to anticipate any developing condition.

There was good and bad mixed together in their present situation. The good came from the effectiveness of the cloaking capability. They were invisible to everyone. The bad was the corrosive feeling of being alone in the deep vastness of space. Only Gorp offered some semblance of companionship, but he was tucked away behind her and out of sight. Fortunately, on this mission, one human object, the refueling barge, was visible.

The refueling barge, the blocky, underpowered, spacecraft holding the essential fluid of thrust, was still sitting motionless among the three fighters, but alive, at least that's what the pilots called it, as if the inanimate barge was a living entity. The barge had no human operators; however, even rudimentary sensors could determine the vessel was fully functional and active with normal emissions. Anod occasionally reassured herself of this simple truth by observing the emissions registering on her sensor displays. The barge was also boring except for the fact that it was the bait for whoever might be out there with them. It was the stars that continued to capture Anod's attention as the team waited.

During quiet, peaceful moments on patrol, the majesty of the celestial blanket around her highlighted an elegant, delicately woven lace. It was easy for Anod to lose herself in the features of each object before her. Sometimes she used her visual spectrum sensors as a telescope to enhance the image of a particular object. There was always a temptation to reach out with her active sensors to learn more about the objects she saw. However, waiting in the cloaking mode meant taking information in. Nothing should go out unless an emergency developed. Anod had to be content simply listening and watching.

Zarrod was probably dozing, leaving the vigil to Stasok, his android companion, Anod thought. It was always his response to the boredom of waiting. Zitger was probably listening intently to every word received over the tactical communications link and reviewing every bit of information on his displays.

For some strange reason, Anod's thoughts returned to the events prior to the initiation of this mission. "Gorp," she said as if she needed to attract his attention.

"Yes, Anod."

"Did you notice Zitger's distraction prior to launch?"

"No. I was preoccupied with my duties."

Anod never ceased to be amazed by Gorp's lack of inquisitiveness given his extraordinary intelligence, but then again, inquisitiveness was her strong suit. This time she needed to explore her thoughts aloud with Gorp more to fill the void rather than for true consultation. "He kept staring at the scene wall, you know, the Mountain Meadow he likes so much."

"I did not notice."

"He seemed to be a million light-years away." Her mind vividly recalled her leader's absorption in the scene. The sounds, the smells, the view of the scene from Mother Earth were indelibly etched in her memory. It was her favorite scene as well. This time, Zitger seemed lost in the connective scene. It had taken her hand on his shoulder to shake him free of his mesmerized state after several spoken attempts to gain his attention.

"Maybe he had something special on his mind," Gorp offered.

"Maybe," she said softly more to herself than her companion. Anod struggled with trying to guess what it might that distracted him so thoroughly. The distraction was certainly not common with Zitger, or any of the Kartog pilots. Anod took pride in her general awareness of events around her even though she might be concentrating on one task. The warriors called it, survival focus.

"Team Four commencing preparation period," Manok, the omnipresent central computer on Saranon, announced bringing Anod back to the immediate condition.

The simple statement that was heard, but could not be answered, meant at least another two hours of waiting. Zitger's team had been on patrol through their duty cycle plus most of their scheduled sleep cycle. The three human warriors had been permitted to sleep under the watchful concentration of the three android companions, or guardians as they were sometimes called. Lieutenant Anod had only taken a few short, combat naps, as the pilots liked to say.

Anod shifted her weight more out of frustration with inaction rather than discomfort. There was no fun or enjoyment in waiting. Even a routine sub-warp flight was more fun than waiting. Even waiting in the alert room was less burdensome than waiting in the confines of the cockpit alone in deep space, even with the stars all around.

The seldom-heard collision alarm went off in her headset. Something was heading toward her fighter with a projected closest point of approach, or CPA, of less than one kilometer. The object, whatever it was, would soon penetrate her safety volume, and she knew the detected threat triggered the alarm. Anod clearly understood the meaning of the miss distance calculated by the on-board processor using a variable safety volume dependent on an object's mass, velocity and trajectory stability. In this case, the intruder was either very large or very fast.

Anod quickly glanced at the tactical display that illustrated the object's trajectory relative to her fighter. The object had a constant velocity and flight path. Probably just a drifting rock, Anod thought. "What do you think, Gorp?" she asked.

"The range at first detection with a constant velocity and trajectory plus the fact that the object is still beyond optical sensor range would tend to indicate a rock of moderate size," Gorp responded in his usual thorough manner.

"How big?"

"My estimate based on its velocity and typical rock density is 250 plus or minus 75 cubic meters."

"Well, it's got us beat. The CPA looks like 865 meters almost directly overhead descending from right to left." Anod remembered previous experiences not particularly unlike this one. She and Gorp had been through this type of encounter numerous times although none with an object this size. The challenge of close calls rarely failed to energize her sense of adventure, her need to press the limits and test her skills. The downside was always Gorp's reaction to her intentions. It was a game they played together. "What do you say about watching this thing pass right above us?"

"I do not think that is a good idea, Anod."

The young pilot smiled at Gorp's predictably conservative programming. The traditional instructions given to an android dominated his processes and responses despite his long-term exposure to Anod's aggressive and challenging spirit, and intense curiosity. She enjoyed the mental exercise and thrill of overcoming a risk.

"Where's your sense of adventure, Gorp?"

"You are well aware of trajectory variations and the regulations concerning potential foreign object penetration of the exclusionary volume."

Anod shook her head, not so much in disagreement with Gorp's accurate description of the risk, but because of the android's repeated demonstration of his predictability. The mechanical assistants were not able to evaluate the need for the illogical action versus the regulations.

The tactical display projected an intercept with the rock in 3 minutes, 27 seconds. The velocity of the wandering mass was 56,253 kilometers per hour according to the computer which placed it a little over

3,200 kilometers away. The dense rock with its impressive momentum would literally vaporize the tiny fighter upon impact, if it should happen.

"Well, Gorp, I suppose, in this case, I'm fortunate I'm the boss," she said with an irritated edge to her voice. "This fighter is my responsibility and we are going to watch this rock pass right over the nose."

"As you command, Lieutenant Anod." Gorp usually resorted to the use of her rank when he did not agree with his partner.

"This little buster is moving. If that rock was to hit us without our shields, I'm afraid there wouldn't be much left of us or this machine."

"You are quite correct. It is that fact which necessitates the Society regulation on exclusionary volume. As a point of fact, the rock's momentum would produce significant and serious damage to the fighter even with the shields up."

"Thank you, mister know-it-all."

Anod turned off her helmet display to watch this event without the virtual symbols dancing in front of her eyes. She took a quick look at her tactical display. One minute, thirteen seconds. Not much longer now, Anod told herself.

Since the rock was now well within the range of the visual sensors, Anod directed them to lock on to it. The thrill of watching a potentially deadly projectile flash passed her without effect intoxicated her in the otherwise monotonous waiting.

"There it is, Gorp." The volcanic looking mass with its bulges, bubbles, cracks and craters tumbled slowly as it approached the fighter. "It's not a particularly pretty looking rock, is it?"

"No," Gorp responded.

He never was much for aesthetics, Anod chuckled.

The temptation to press the limit coaxed Anod to nudge the fighter closer to the CPA. The normal apprehension of an encounter like this was insufficient to overcome the challenge of testing her skills.

"Is this really necessary?"

Anod ignored the query. "Targeting," she commanded.

"Solution acceptable."

"There is some satisfaction that we could vaporize that rock before it got us, if we wanted."

"You do not intend to shoot, do you?" Gorp asked as he always did.

"That would not be too smart when we are cloaked, would it?"

"The action of engaging while cloaked would not be in accordance with Society regulations."

"Thank you, again, Gorp. Look at that thing. It sure does look like it's going to hit us square on, doesn't it?"

"Yes, it does visually. Trajectory calculations indicate a decreasing CPA passing 377 meters, now."

"I hope Zitger and Zarrod are watching this rock. I've got no way to warn them without breaking the cloak, and I can't find them to do the calculations. Ah, but I am sure their sensors are functioning properly, just as ours are." Gorp did not respond, which intrigued Anod. Her android usually had something to say about almost anything.

The rock filled her tactical display as the automatic magnification held the rock centered in the 80% area of the screen. The symbols projected over it gave Anod a clear indication of the location, speed, mass, and of course CPA. The detailed features of the rock became vividly clear, as it got closer. She looked out the canopy.

"Here it comes. It sure does look a lot bigger than 250 cubic meters."

"The rock is 276.45 cubic meters by my refined calculations."

An anxious twinge bloomed briefly in Anod's mind as the rock grew rapidly in size. Were the calculations really that accurate? She had done this before without consequence. Of course, they are accurate, she reassured herself.

"It's moving quite fast, as well." Her attention was riveted on the rock. In the last fraction of a second, the enormous velocity of the rock turned it into blur, a mere smudge, even to her sensitive eyes. "Swoosh," Anod said to give sound to the silent passage of the massive projectile. "Damn, that was close!"

"I am certain you are correct, Lieutenant Anod."

Anod looked to her left, watching the rock disappear into the blackness of space. Just before it became too small to see, Anod noticed a slight change with the movement of the rock. She quickly looked at her display. The rock's trajectory changed at a point 12 kilometers to the lower left of her fighter. As she moved to look back out to that point, a bright flash from behind her stung her eyes. Fortunately, the flash filters on her helmet visor prevented the intense light from damaging her eyes.

"Oh, my god!" Anod exclaimed fighting with her own emotions and instincts. She instantly checked her tactical and sensor displays, and immediately switched on her helmet display for instant maneuvering information. Only the barge in its quiescent state showed up. Her mind raced through the possibilities. What had happened? Who was it? Were they under attack from an unseen adversary? There was only one possibility. "That must be either Zitger or Zarrod," she said.

A portion of the engine module of a Kartog fighter passed by her canopy.

"Any signs of an ejection pod?"

"No."

"Any signs of life or biological elements?"

"No signs of life, Anod. There are trace elements of biological compounds."

Anod struggled for information. "Can you ID that engine module that passed by us?"

"Not without breaking cloak to examine part numbers, if there are any," Gorp explained devoid of any emotion.

There was not enough to identify which of her two teammates had just died.

The communications channel remained deathly silent. Why wasn't the survivor talking? What was going on? Maybe whoever is left is thinking the same thing I am, Anod thought. The urge to take action grew rapidly within her. Something was wrong, dreadfully wrong, but she could not arrive at an answer or an explanation.

"Gorp, what can you determine from the explosion?"

"The same conclusion I am certain you have arrived at. One of the Team Three fighters has exploded. There is no clear cause. There are some very weak indications of possible weapons fire."

"Weapons!" Anod exclaimed abruptly. She immediately advanced the throttle to move her location. With a potential adversary lurking close-by, sitting still was not a good idea no matter how good the cloaking system was.

"Anod, I said very weak indications. There is not sufficient information to confirm those indications," Gorp added.

"I understand, but we just can't remain stationary, if there is a threat."

"Sensors do not indicate a threat. The energy levels excluding the explosion remain normal."

Her instincts began to take over. Everything - every object, every action - became a threat until it could be proven harmless. Her mind struggled to fill in the blanks her sensors could not.

Anod increased her speed to half impulse. "The rock must be the key," she whispered to herself. There must be something associated with that rock, she thought. She continued to sift through the possibilities as she maneuvered her fighter to intercept the rock that continued to move away.

Anod accomplished the rendezvous quickly. She approached the rock with all her weapons armed and ready. The object could be a disguise for a Yorax interceptor. Slowly she moved around the massive chunk of interstellar matter inspecting every crack and chip of its surface. It definitely appeared to be a simple fragment of primordial debris innocently travelling through space. The rock's trajectory continued precisely constant from the point of deviation.

Anod backed away from the rock. There was one positive way to determine its composition. Actually two ways, Anod told herself. The active probe sensors could determine complete composition. However, if this was an elaborate camouflage technique, it might be able to fool the sensors as well, and the probe would positively identify and locate their fighter. Of course, obliteration with a pulse from her proton cannon would incontrovertibly establish the nature of the rock. Both choices violated the cloak. Anod wanted to call her surviving teammate, but that would also compromise the safety of the mask.

The urge to engage passed as Anod began to see the rock as a harmless object. Why hadn't she heard from her remaining teammate? If Zitger were still alive, he would be taking more aggressive action as the leader. Maybe it was Zitger that perished and Zarrod was out there going through the same thought processes as she was? The need to answer some of her growing list of questions grew rapidly.

The fighter matched the speed of the rock, one kilometer ahead. It still looked like a rock. She checked her displays, again. All parameters remained normal. They were now passing a point 6,500 kilometers from the holding point.

There was no way to know if the other fighter was near the rock, investigating it as they were, or still holding at the refueling barge, wondering what to do next.

"Gorp, do you have any more information? Can you determine what happened?"

"No. There are no further data."

"We're going to have to do something here pretty quick," Anod said, more to herself than her companion.

Anod's mind worked through possibilities, options, and the ever-present rules of engagement. Doubts began to form though they were somewhat faint. The available facts were contradictory. At that moment, she had no reason to question the facts she had, but she knew she did not have all the facts.

"Gorp, there was only one explosion, correct?" she asked hesitantly.

"Yes."

"That means there are two fighters still out here. None of us has broken the cloak. Correct?"

"Correct."

"What the hell happened back there?"

"A logical conclusion cannot be derived," Gorp responded.

"I know that!" Anod shot back. "We need to consider the illogical."

Anod continued to run through the insufficient available information, though she was rapidly approaching a virtually singular non-solution point. An action would have to be taken. She could not sit and wait forever. They would have to abandon the refueling barge and return to Saranon under cloak. Refueling required unmasking. The sooner she made something happen, the better she would feel. Foremost on her mind was the determination of who was still out there with her in the vastness of space.

Her skin tingled with anticipation as she rechecked all her offensive and defensive systems. The fighter was ready. She was ready. Gorp was always ready.

Well, this is it, she told herself.

Anod selected the short range, conventional radio. Saranon would not hear her transmission for days. Her surviving teammate would hear her within a fraction of a second. "Team Three, report," she said with a calm, but quick command. Maybe Zarrod was waiting for a command from her. All her displays indicated no change to the situation around her.

"Communications from a cloaked state are contrary to the rules of engagement," Gorp stated quickly.

"Thank you, Gorp," Anod said sarcastically.

There was no further response.

The silence of space felt ominous. She had seen only one explosion. The dispersal formation precluded elimination of two fighters by one explosion. There had to be another survivor out here somewhere. Why wasn't he answering, she asked herself?

"Gorp, have you detected anything?"

"No."

This was so strange. Why, why, why?

"Would you agree that either Zitger, or Zarrod survived whatever happened back there?"

"The available information indicates a high probability that one of them survived. As long as the cloak is maintained, we have no method of determination."

"Why didn't the survivor, whoever he is, answer my report command?"

"There is no logical explanation. Therefore, there are only illogical, or implausible alternative cause factors."

"Quite right," Anod said, thoroughly frustrated.

What happened? The question haunted her consciousness. All the information available to her and Gorp told her they were alone with only the residue of a high order, intense, thermal event with various knarled bits of what used to be a Kartog Guards fighter.

"Gorp, did you notice any impact damage on the rock? Any indication of an associated explosion as a result of an impact?"

"No. I was concentrating on the sensors."

"I didn't look for impact or explosion damage. Where's the rock?" Anod asked, she looking at her tactical display.

Gorp found it first.

"The rock is now at a range of 876 kilometers, right 11 degrees, plus 3 degrees and opening at 15.63 kilometers per second."

"We need to inspect that rock more closely. I want to see if the rock might have hit one of our fighters." She started to advance the throttle.

"Anod, we are also opening on our station," Gorp added. "Let me remind you of the rules of engagement, specifically, that there are no obvious or definitive indications of hostile action. At this level, the primary mission must override other hypothetical alternatives."

She hesitated. The dilemma within her made Anod reconsider her actions. "You're right." She recognized the sterile logic in Gorp's statement. She could not dispute the reasoning, however, her instincts told her otherwise. The conflict within her was uncomfortable, but she chose to follow Gorp's advice.

The pilot turned to reverse the fighter's course and advanced the throttle to full impulse power. It would take only a few minutes to return to the loiter station.

"Let's keep track of that rock," she said.

"Confirmed."

"What do you think about trying again to raise the survivor?"

"I do not think it wise to violate the rules of engagement."

Lieutenant Anod did not agree with her faithful companion. The fighter approached the refueling barge at the loiter point. Colonel Zortev's caution prior to their launch from Saranon added to her hesitation. The venerable commander had shared his suspicion about the meaning of activity reported by Manok. Anod was torn between the potential of an undetectable adversary and the overwhelming lack of confirmatory or contributory information. She respected Zortev's experience, success and skill although it could provide little assistance in her present situation. There was only one way . . . she had to force the hand.

"Team Three report," Anod said with more confidence this time, but the doubts remained.

She waited. Still no response. The displays remained unchanged. What facts were she missing? There had to be a reason. Could it have been an uncontrolled breach of the plasma reactor?

"What about compromise of the plasma reactor?"

"It is remotely possible, although highly unlikely. There would have most probably been no identifiable remains of the engine pod."

"I suppose you're right," Anod said in growing frustration. "It is possible, though?"

"Yes. There are two remote failure modes that might result in such an event."

Lieutenant Anod simply could not resist the need to establish the status of her other teammate. The mission was compromised at any rate. She needed to compare thoughts and ideas with Zitger or Zarrod to determine if they should abort the mission. Saranon Station would soon detect the explosion and without contact from Team Three would launch a full response.

"Team Three! Zitger, Zarrod, one of you is out there." Anod shouted with mounting frustration.

Her consciousness vanished instantly, engulfed by a brilliant, absolute light. A flash and it was over.

Chapter 2

A general deep ache throughout her body accentuated by numerous local sites of intense pain provided Anod the first awareness of anything. She tried to move each of her extremities one by one. Each attempt was rewarded with an amplification of the pain associated with that particular limb.

What happened? Where am I, she asked herself?

The world was still black for her even though she thought she had regained consciousness. She knew she was lying prone on some relatively soft surface. The air was warm. The telltale indications of higher than normal humidity were present. She struggled to open her eyes. Something covered her face preventing her eyes from opening. The world remained black. The strong pain in her entire head made the task of understanding her situation even more difficult. Anod could not move her arms and could barely move one leg. Breathing was unobstructed although painful to her chest. Her cardiopulmonary rates seemed to be normal; therefore the oxygen content of the atmosphere was within acceptable levels. There was a growing frustration that she could not overcome the pain to move her arms. Anod wanted to feel her face, to feel for the cause of her inability to see. Most of the elements she could think of appeared to be normal, and yet something was definitely wrong.

"Is anybody here?" she called out.

There was no answer. Wherever she was, it was a quiet place. There was a slight echo to her words that meant she was probably in a large room, but there was no response. She couldn't tell from the available information whether she was alone or not. Her intuition told her that she was not. Someone or something had brought her to this place and was attempting to take care of her. There was some comfort in the intangible care shown her. The sense of the environment told her she was definitely not in a place under Society control.

Could the Yorax have her? It was a possibility although not likely since they probably would have killed her rather than try to mend her. In addition, the material covering or restricting her body was of no known medical technology.

Why couldn't she move her limbs? She could not evaluate her anatomy any further without her hands. Anod took a deep breath in preparation for the exertion to move her arms. Bracing herself mentally against the pain, she summoned all her strength and raised her arm up slightly. Her elbow would not bend. The pain shot through her entire body with such intensity she passed out.

The sound of what she thought was a book hitting the floor was the next reality thrust upon the injured Kartog warrior. The pain returned her to awareness, or vice versa, Anod thought. There were no changes in her knowledge of the world around her, or the physical condition of her body, to provide a clue regarding the duration of her unconsciousness. It could have been an hour, a day, a week or longer. The length of the latest episode was not likely to have been very long. The level and breadth of her pain had not changed substantially. What had changed, however, was her respect for the extent of her injuries and the power that this pain had over her body and mind. Anod fully intended to avoid the protection of unconsciousness until she understood her condition more clearly. She knew she needed personal situational awareness.

Her warrior's mind began anew to search all her senses for additional bits of fact that could allay her concerns. The book. The sound of the book hitting the floor. Someone must have dropped it.

"Is anyone there?" Anod repeated her last question. The same words brought back the recollection of the missing span of time.

"Yes, there is."

Her heart rate instantly quickened with the surprise presence of at least another entity. Anod fought to focus all her senses on the assessment of any potential threat. There was virtually nothing she could do about it, even if there was a threat. However, her instincts focused on one objective only – survival.

"Who are you? Where am I? What is wrong with me?"

"Whoa, slow down. First, you need to save your strength. Secondly, we will have plenty of time to talk. I will be most happy to answer all your questions for which I have answers. Do you understand?"

The strong but calm voice of what sounded like a male human seemed to be friendly. "Yes, I understand."

"OK. Let us dispense with the introductions first, if we may. My name is Sebastian Nicholas SanGiocomo. My friends call me, Nick. Who might you be?"

"My name is, Anod." She decided to omit her rank for the moment.

There was a hesitation in the discussion, as if he were waiting for something.

"What is the rest of your name?"

"That is my complete name."

"Now, isn't that strange. You don't have a family name. That does not seem right. Are you afraid of me? Is that why you are withholding the remainder of your name?"

"I am not withholding the remainder of my name. My name is simply, Anod," she answered with some irritation.

"There is no need to become upset. I am just not familiar with humans that have only one name."

Anod did not want to respond to his rebuke. In the discussion about names, her curiosity needed satisfaction. "Why do you have so many names?"

"Now, that's a fair question," Nick began with lightness to his voice. "I suppose the correct answer is tradition. Family as well as given names have always been a part of our heritage."

"Which is your family name and which is your given name?"

"SanGiocomo is my family name, the name of my ancestors."

"Then, Sebastian Nicholas are your given names?"

"Yes."

"Why do you not use your first name?" Anod asked innocently.

A strong, boisterous laugh began his answer. "I don't like my first name and I prefer the contraction of my middle name," Nick answered.

Anod wanted to discuss other subjects and felt compelled to vocalize several of the lightning thoughts racing through her consciousness.

"Am I your prisoner?"

The question brought immediate, boisterous laughter again from her companion. "Absolutely not. You are free to leave right now if you are able," he responded with a tone of amusement. "You were brought here by a friend. You were near death when he found you. You required immediate medical attention which he was not able to provide."

"Thank you."

"Now, to the rest of your questions. You are on a small planet, we call $\theta 27\beta$, since this is the second planet from the $\theta 27$ star."

Anod struggled with her memory to understand the explanation. "I am not familiar with the $\theta 27$ star system," she stated.

Another jovial laugh greeted her words. "We shall have enough time to talk of the astronomy of our location. I need to tell you about your physical condition."

"Please."

"You have multiple broken bones and lacerations, a severe concussion, internal injuries to your kidneys, liver and spleen, and some bad burns over nearly 40% of your body."

"Am I going to recover? Do I have my arms and legs? How long have I been unconscious?"

"Let's slow down, again," he said softly with more patience. "Trust me. I will answer all your questions."

"I am sorry. I just want to know."

"That is perfectly understandable, now, to continue. In my judgment and a few others who are aware of your existence, you will recover fully. None of us know how your burns will heal, but we are optimistic. You have all your limbs. As far as I can tell, you have all your parts. As to your question regarding the duration of your coma, I can only guess. From our best reconstruction of events, you have been in a coma for nearly three weeks." Nick paused to let Anod assimilate the dose of reality his words brought to her. "We don't know what happened to you, but we do know it was violent. You were in an accident or battle of some kind."

Anod's mental defenses went up immediately as she dealt with her confusing memory of the events and the vast gaps of time since she left Saranon. There was no question in her mind; she did not want to talk about the events that led up to her present condition.

"What did happen to you, Miss Anod?"

Her resolve to avoid this topic solidified rapidly. She raced through the facts in her memory in a desperate effort to understand what happened. There were too many conflicting and confusing facts to reconstruct what had happened. Until she had a clear view of events, Anod had no intention of discussing her situation with a stranger, even if he did save her life.

"Never mind. What happened is not important right now. The most important objective is your recovery, one step at a time. Long journeys begin with small steps, I always say," Nick said almost as if he knew the turmoil within his charge.

Anod wanted to change the subject of the conversation with her unseen companion. "Why can't I see?" she asked.

"Well, the answer to that question is simple. You received some burns on your face and eyes. I have wrapped your head and covered your eyes to enhance the healing process."

"Why aren't you using a neurofiber reconstructor, or a tissue regeneration probe?"

"Maybe because I have no idea what they are. I am certain your technology is superior to that which we possess. However, I am afraid that I can only do what is within my capabilities," Nick responded with indignation.

"I did not intend to offend you. It is just that I am not accustomed to these coverings when dealing with wounds."

"No offense taken then. Our technology may not be as advanced as yours, but it does get the job done. I think you are over the worst part of your healing process."

There was a strong urge to change the subject, again. "Will I be able to see soon?" Anod asked.

"You have been here with me 19 periods, that's about 16 Earth days. Our sidereal cycle is a fraction over 20 hours in Earth time. Anyway, your head injuries should be healed sufficiently to give your eyes a try. How is the level of pain?"

Anod clearly noted his reference to Earth. Maybe he was human. She decided to wait for a discussion regarding origins. "The general pain is tolerable. I have a few locations of fairly intense pain when I move."

"For a woman in your condition, the pain is quite understandable. In fact, if I may be so bold, the type and extent of your injuries would have brought many a man down. There are not many people who would be able to survive these injuries, as you have."

"Thank you," she answered although it did not make her feel any better.

"Enough dribble. Are you ready to try your eyes? Do your eyes hurt?" Nick asked.

"Yes. There is no pain associated with my eyes that I am aware of. The general pain throughout my head may be masking the local pain, although I don't think so."

"Well, let's give it a go, then."

Anod heard his steps and felt a tightness rise up within her. The response was a natural product of her heritage. She knew nothing of her companion other than he seemed to be very concerned and caring, was probably human, and had a friendly, mature voice. There was no obvious reason for her to feel threatened excluding, of course, her current vulnerability. Without fellow pilots, weapons, body armor or the other accouterments of her profession, Anod felt defenseless nonetheless.

"Wait just a moment," he said with a pause. "You haven't used your eyes for a long time. I'd better dim the lights."

The personal concern and somewhat absent-mindedness began to relax Anod a little. She listened to his footsteps as he walked some distance away from her. A crude manual switch clicked although there was no indication of any light level change. Black was black. It did seem strange, however, that Nick had to walk across a room to turn off or dim the ambient light level. Anod's curiosity was being tweaked ever so slightly.

"There, that ought to do it," Nick said as he walked back toward her.

Anod knew each of his actions quite well. Her acute hearing picked up every step of his shoes on the floor, the crackling of the cartilage in his joints and the movement of a mechanical switch.

There were no clues available to her senses that this man was a medical technician, other than he possessed a reasonably good appreciation of medical issues.

Anod felt his gentle touch on her head bandages.

"Please let me know if I cause you any pain."

Anod's slight nod conveyed her agreement. There was some level of pain associated with virtually any movement she made including speaking. The simple movement of her head seemed to cause less pain than speaking words.

Her protector, if that was what he was, began to slowly unravel the bandages from around her head. He elected to remove only the outer layer that would expose her eyes. The desire to test her eyes was stronger than the pain she felt.

"I'm trying to be as careful as I can. I apologize if I am causing you any discomfort."

"No need to apologize. You are doing fine."

The unwrapping of the top layer of protective dressing was complete. Anod could still feel patches of soft material over each eye. She did not attempt to remove the cloth or open her eyes.

"I suggest that you keep your eyes closed as I remove both of the patches. I would like to examine your eyes to make sure we should proceed. Do you understand?"

"Yes."

"Very well. Here we go."

Anod felt first the right and then the left patch being removed from her face. The feel of the air on her exposed skin was refreshing. She was tempted to open her eyes. Anod's growing confidence in the knowledge of her protector convinced her to resist the temptation.

"OK, Miss Anod, your skin looks pretty good. You can try to open your eyes."

The room was dark, but there were shapes. The image of her first sight was blurred like it was out of focus. Anod blinked her eyes several times and squinted slightly to control her ocular muscles. Slowly, the world in her immediate vicinity began to increase in clarity. Colors were not particularly identifiable due to the diffuse, dim lighting in the room and the dull pain she felt in both eyes.

The ceiling looked as if the rough surface of naturally fragmented rock. In fact, the portions of the walls she could see were also of the same material. The room appeared to be a chamber of a cave.

Nick! Anod looked to her right to see the dimly lit form of a man watching her from slightly greater than arm's length. The loose fitting and layered clothing hid the shape of his body and all of his skin except his hands and face. His clothing items were monocolor in greens and browns, and appeared to be clean and well made. He was an average height by human standards.

"Nick?" she asked.

"Yes."

His silver speckled, neatly trimmed beard and dishevelled hair along with the creases of his weather beaten skin established him as a man physiologically much older than Anod. There was an attractiveness and sense of inner peace clearly visible in his light blue eyes. Anod smiled although the physical manifestation could only be seen in the expression of her eyes.

"You are not quite what I imagined. Your voice sounds much younger than you appear."

"I'm not quite sure how to take that," Nick responded with a smile. "At least, you are forthright and candid."

Again, Anod felt the strong need to change the subject. "My eyes hurt a little now."

"They should for a short time as your eyes adapt to sight again."

"Would you increase the light intensity gradually?"

"Certainly."

Nick walked over to a round knob on the wall next to the only obvious door. Turning slowly, the ambient light level began to increase.

"Let me know where you want it."

"A little more," she said. "That's good, right there, at least for now. Thank you."

The room did indeed appear to be a chamber of a cave. There were several benches with crude scientific instruments situated at various positions around the room. The contrast of the rough-hewn walls with the properly kept furnishings reflected well on the owner. Every item, whether on a table, the floor or the wall, appeared to be carefully placed. The impression from this simple observation was that Nick was an organized man who was thoughtful of his surroundings.

"Well, what do you think," he asked in obvious reference to her scan of the room.

"This room reflects well on your character, Nick." Anod was reluctant to ask him what he did, or why he was here. She did not want to reopen the subject of occupation or origin.

"Thank you. How are you feeling now?"

"I feel much better now that I can see."

"That is a good sign, I should say."

The need to understand her physical condition was growing. An attempt to raise her head was met with a jolt of pain.

"Here, let me help you."

He picked up a wedge shaped cushion, placed it behind her head, and then slowly raised her head and shoulders. Anod could feel the strength in his arms as he held her upper body in place with one arm and slid the cushion under her with the other arm.

"Thank you."

Anod looked down the length of her body only to see a sheet covering her. From the bulges in the sheet, it was apparent one leg was larger than the other. Both legs were wrapped. She could feel that. It was not clear to her why the size of her legs were different.

"Would you remove the sheet, please, Nick? I'd like to see the rest of my injuries."

Nick did not respond to her request. His averted eyes and fidgeting were definite indications of his uneasiness.

His reaction to her request confused Anod. She could not understand why he appeared to be so uncomfortable. "What is wrong, Nick? Did I say something incorrect?"

"No. It's just that, well, you don't have any clothes on under the sheet."

"I don't understand," Anod responded with genuine confusion.

"In our culture, it is considered inappropriate for women, or men, to be seen naked in front of the opposite gender."

"In my culture, there is no distinction. Clothes are needed for utility, not modesty."

"Doesn't it embarrass you to be seen without clothes?"

"No."

"Well, then, I suppose I should accept that," he said with sarcasm rather than conviction.

"Did you not take my original clothing off, and have you not changed the wrappings on my body while I was unconscious?"

"Well, yes, but that was different. I had to do that and you had no choice. You are conscious, now."

"I still do not understand your concern. A body is just a body."

"Yes, but you are a woman."

"So?"

Anod felt his searching eyes. "Modesty aside, I would, nonetheless, like to see the rest of my injuries," she requested.

Nick reached up to the top of the sheet covering Anod. He continued to look directly into her eyes as he first raised the cover, and then pulled it back to avoid dragging it across her body. The refreshing caress of the air against her skin brought a smile to her face.

"The air feels so good. I am not accustomed to sleeping with material touching my skin," she said casually.

Nick did not respond.

Anod's eyes scanned her body. Contusions and mending lacerations were rather prevalent making her skin appear gnarly and abused, which it was. There was a large, lumpy surfaced, single piece white boot over her left leg from above mid-thigh to the bottom of her foot. Her right foot was wrapped with a large, wide bandage from her knee to include most of her foot. Anod wiggled the exposed toes of her right foot as a physical demonstration that not every part of her body was damaged.

"Can you tell me the reasons for these unusual wrappings?"

The aversion to looking at her body was plainly evident in Nick's expression. The strange contortions of his face, eyes and lips produced a hearty laugh from Anod, which in turn rewarded her with a strong shot of pain in the area of several ribs. She ricocheted between laughing and groaning. Her laughter added to Nick's frustration, awkwardness and sense of inadequacy.

"Why do you laugh at my beliefs?" Nick was becoming angry.

"If you could observe your reaction through my eyes, you would laugh as well. Just as your beliefs tell you not to look upon a naked woman, my beliefs tell me there is no reason not to look. I have grown up with the conviction that the differences in anatomy between a man and a woman are simply the physical diversity of the human species. Differences in musculature, body features and genitalia are no different from variations in hair, skin and eye color. There was no intent to offend you, Nick."

"Your feelings are quite foreign to me. I would like to understand them more. However, I still feel very silly standing here holding this sheet above you." His resentment seemed to be ebbing somewhat.

"Please, Nick, pull the sheet completely off me, if you will. If you desire, turn around to satisfy your sense of propriety and tell me of my injuries," Anod said with more patience in her voice.

"Agreed." Nick closed his eyes as he completed the task. The elderly man turned around to face the wall and side stepped toward her head slightly.

"I would like you to start at either end of my body and describe the type and extent of my injuries," Anod requested.

"As I have indicated, your face and eyes were burned. There must have been a flash fire because the burns were not extensive. Your eyes appear to be completely healed. I think we can take off your head bandages at any time. Your left arm was severely lacerated. It is difficult to explain, but it was something jagged. There are also some burns on your left arm. Your right arm was simply struck very hard. The nerves were traumatized. They should fully recover in time with gradual stimulation of your arm. The indications of internal injury to your viscera were not substantial and have subsided over the last few weeks. Your right knee and ankle were dislocated without collateral damage. Your left leg, however, was seriously damaged. At least three fractures, two of which were compound, have caused serious damage to both neural and vascular structures in your leg."

Nick paused in his description to either continue his assessment or wait for a response from Anod. The young warrior did not want to respond. She was digesting Nick's statement and reflecting upon what she felt and saw for herself.

He raised his head to look at the ceiling as he spoke. "I have answered your question. Now, I would like you to answer a few of my questions."

Nick waited for a response.

Her mental defenses were still active although she was gaining confidence in her protector. Anod wanted to talk with, to discuss with, to confide in Nick, but her heritage as a warrior exhorted restraint.

"I am a warrior. My training cautions me to avoid divulging more than I have to. I need to know more about you and how I came here," Anod stated.

"So, more questions before answers," Nick said with a chuckle.

"I hope you understand my predicament, Nick."

"I do understand more than you are presently aware."

The cryptic response gave Anod reason to be cautious, but still inquisitive. "Thank you. I would like to know more about you, your heritage and more about this planet."

"OK, but first, can I replace your sheet so I can see your eyes and sit down?"

Anod laughed softly as she said, "Yes, yes, of course."

Without turning around, Nick reached toward the foot of the bed to lift the sheet high over his patient. Anod smiled and laughed a little. Satisfied that most of her body was covered, he turned to adjust the sheet neatly over her body.

"Now, what was your question, again?" he asked looking directly into her eyes.

"Tell me more about yourself and why you are here."

"I am a healer for our society. My understanding of Earth culture tells me that I would be called a doctor on the home planet."

"Then you are from Earth," she inquired hesitantly.

"Many, many years ago, nearly 235 Earth years, if my memory serves me. My ancestors were banished from Earth. There were two migrations due to planetary incompatibility until our group came to θ27β some 85 years ago. We have prospered here since that time."

"Your ancestors were banished from Earth?"

"Yes."

"How many people are on this planet?"

"By our last count, we have about 355,000 inhabitants."

"Why have we never heard about this colony?"

"Again, I have no idea why there is no reference. You must be from Earth, then."

"Yes, but no," Anod responded quickly without concern.

"What does that mean?"

"I am a warrior of the Kartog Guards. I am from Earth as you are, although I have never set foot on Earth."

"What was left of the uniform you had on was insufficient to be a positive indication, I assumed you were a fighter of some kind. What is the significance of the Kartog Guards?"

"It is my parent organization, one of ten special units established by the Society to protect its interests in space."

"An elite unit?"

"I suppose some might use that term. The Kartog Guards is one of the oldest space units and seems to get the hardest assignments."

"Then, you must be very good," Nick added, quietly impressed with his guest.

"I suppose," Anod answered. A few moments of silence passed between them. "How did you find me?"

"Well, you were found in a damaged life support capsule with an inoperative beacon. Alexatron happened upon your drifting capsule. There were no active indications of an accident or a battle, just your drifting capsule," Nick recounted.

"Who is Alexatron?"

"He is a friend, a trader. His family has been allowed to visit this colony for many years. Initially, his grandfather resupplied our group during the relocation to θ27β. Over the years, they have been active interplanetary traders."

Nick SanGiocomo's candor and forthrightness helped Anod accepted the reality of her condition. Her curiosity about so many things was difficult to control.

"You mentioned that Alexatron found my survival pod and there was no rescue beacon. Did he receive any communications about the disintegration of, at least, two Kartog fighters?"

"No. He mentioned nothing like that."

"Where did he find my pod?"

"Near the Ambrodigan star," Nick responded.

Anod did not recognize the star's name. It could be the M19 star by another name, but right now, she wanted other types of information. "Have any Society forces, or any other forces for that matter, been looking for me?" The tone of Anod's voice changed as she opened an area of discussion that she was obviously sensitive to.

"We have heard communications about a search around K7 and 2035RU7 for missing warriors. I have assumed that it was you they were looking for. Until I was able to talk to you, I could not know if the search was friendly or hostile. Prudence dictated caution and I have kept you hidden even from my own people. Only myself, Alexatron and a few other close friends know you are here."

"I suppose that since I am the only one in this room, there were no other survivors."

"Alexatron was extremely lucky to find you. To my knowledge, there were no other survivors. Was there another warrior lost?"

"Yes, at least one of my teammates. I do not know which one," she answered with a hint of controlled sadness. "There were three of us and I believe one of the other two was killed in an explosion of his fighter." She paused to let the years of shared experience come vividly back to her. "I also lost my assistant, my friend, my companion, Gorp."

Anod shifted her thinking off the lost friends. She had to continue collecting information in an attempt to understand what happened at M19, what her current situation was, and what actions should be taken?

"Where is $\theta27$ in the galaxy?" asked Anod.

"About 63 light days from Ambrodigan."

"Well, then, Alexatron has hyperlight capability," she concluded. To Anod, this fact meant that the benevolent trader had access to current technology in many areas. He must be extremely resourceful or accepted by the Society. Independent of whom he might be aligned with, Alexatron obviously had not divulged her existence since there were no signs yet of any unwanted visitors to $\theta27\beta$ looking for her.

"Have you seen any sign of the Yorax in this region?"

"An occasional visit just to make sure we don't forget them," answered Nick. "They tend to leave us alone."

Anod wanted to focus on another aspect of her curiosity. Her concern also entailed the continuing assessment of the tactical situation.

"The walls of this room seem to indicate that we are in a rock cave. If that is true, how far are we from the surface?"

"I have been wondering when you would get down to the specifics of your present environment. We are more than 100 meters below the surface with solid carbon matrix rock above us. The entrance is hidden with a labyrinth of tunnels to the inner chambers. I am the only one that lives in this cave, now. So, I think you will agree that you are safe from sensor probes."

"You seem to have an appreciation for military issues. Are you a warrior, also?"

"We have no warriors on this planet," Nick stated with a firmness verging on vehemence.

"Thank you. I appreciate your candid response."

"I have no idea what happened to you in space. Eventually, if I am to help you properly, I will need to know. I hope you understand that," Nick said carefully and quietly. The expression in his eyes and on his face conveyed the sincerity with which the words were spoken.

"Yes, I understand. Likewise, I trust you will appreciate the situation I am in. I must know more about the events that have brought me here."

"Unfortunately, I am nearly depleted of information which would be of value to you."

Anod considered Nick's statement carefully. Somehow she needed to reconstruct the events at M19, she told herself. Something very violent happened and it was certainly not clear why it happened.

"The pain is beginning to increase and I am becoming quite tired. However, I have a few remaining questions." Anod paused to allow for an objection. None came. "Why are you really hiding me?"

The question surprised Nick somewhat, which was to Anod's satisfaction. She needed to test the veracity of his statements. There was actually little she could do as long as she was confined to bed.

"The circumstances of your accident are suspicious. Alexatron was the first to recognize the feeling and he has convinced me. We don't know why you were drifting in space, but there are some elementary facts which lead both of us to believe that you are still in danger."

"What exactly do you mean?"

"Alexatron and I believe that, if certain people were to find out you are alive, they would come for you."

Nick turned to look back directly into her eyes ignoring her lack of bodily covering, then said, "You are in danger. I cannot tell you exactly why I feel this way, however I believe it nonetheless. Maybe together we can combine our facts to determine the substance of my intuitive assessment. Until that time, I would strongly recommend that you allow me to help you heal until you can defend yourself."

Anod wanted desperately to be able to walk out of this room, to see the stars, to feel the heat of day and to see the remains of her fighter. Patience, she cautioned herself, patience. "I do not have much choice at this point. I will accept your generosity and protection. Now, I am afraid I must rest. My mind is becoming foggy with fatigue and pain." Anod regretted instantly speaking the last sentence. It was never wise to convey the condition of a warrior, to reveal that which is not obvious.

Nick nodded his head in consent and he started to leave the room.

He stopped as if he remembered an essential item of information he had forgotten to tell his patient. Walking back to her bedside without a word made Anod wonder what was going to happen.

"I almost forgot. Would you mind if I covered you back up?" Anod shook her head to convey her acceptance. Nick gently returned the sheet over her without looking at her body. "If you need anything while you are resting, just press this little button. It will ring a bell for me. I will be in the next room and will come in an instant. In fact, if I am not in your room, I will be in the next room until you are able to move around," he said with a pleasant smile.

"Thank you, Nick," Anod responded with an equally pleasant and appreciative smile.

"Oh," he paused, "one other item. Would you like some medicine to ease the pain?" he asked.

"No!" exclaimed Anod. She caught herself in the overreaction, calmed her feeling of vulnerability and said, "I am able to deal with the pain mentally. Thank you for your concern." Nick had a strange expression on his face as if he struggled to understand.

"Have a good rest, Miss Anod," he said as he walked toward the door. As he reached the door, he turned the light knob reducing the room lights until the colors began to disappear. He looked over his shoulder as he left the room.

The door began to close behind him and Anod's attention focused directly on it. Her natural suspicion was immediately peaked, to see if her protector would lock her in the room even though she was essentially immobile. He left the door partially open.

Chapter 3

Anod's first non-comatose sleep period after her arrival on θ27β, if that was truly where she was, comingled with the various episodes of pain. Some of the pain was directly associated with her injuries and the primitive medical technology apparently available on this planet. Annoyance would best characterize other less specific pain she attributed to the lack of an isopod, the controlled environment of the personal levitation, suspension chamber. The warrior was not accustomed to the press of her body weight and the rub of cloth against her skin. Every move she made to redistribute her weight brought a clear, unmistakable jolt of pain from one or more sites along her entire body.

Her heritage and training enabled her to successfully fight against the pain through mental domination. Each victorious bout brought the reward of another segment of sleep, however fitful it might be. The process consumed a considerable amount of her metabolic energy. The manifestations of her efforts began to make themselves known as the grumblings of hunger overcame the shoots of pain.

There were no means of telling what time it might be, or how long she had been struggling with this sleep period. A quick scan of the room confirmed what she already knew. There were no windows, clocks or changing light with which to establish the passage of time. The last jab of pain from her left arm mixed with the recognition of her own need for sustenance convinced her to ask for assistance from Nick, her erstwhile benefactor.

Looking for the little button he had shown her took more time than she was pleased with. Eventually, Anod located the button next to her right hand, the only extremity she could reasonably move. The aperiodic fits of pain and the general discomfort of the bed clouded Anod's ability to judge time. The hesitation in the request for assistance from Nick was more out of respect for his time. Had it been 15 minutes or 5 hours since he left the room?

Her analytical mind reached the inevitable conclusion. There was only one way to progress passed this dilemma. Another shot of pain greeted Anod as she reached for and depressed the button.

There was no immediate feedback regarding the functionality of the call button. She waited for a response. Finally, Anod heard some movement in the other room and noticed several waves of a shadow in the light through the door.

Nick entered the room. He was wearing the same clothing he departed in and looked alert. Anod still had no clues on the passage of time.

"Yes, Anod. How are you feeling?"

"I'm still working on the pain, however I think my sense of hunger is rising to the top."

"That is a good sign. I have been sustaining you with intravenous nourishment, which is probably insufficient for your present state of recovery. Let's see if we can find you something to eat. Oh, yes. Would you like medication for the pain?"

"No. I don't need it." The truth was quite to the contrary. She did not want to deaden her other senses and the levels of pain were tolerable. "How long have I been asleep?"

Nick pulled a rather large object from a pocket somewhere inside his clothing. "You have been asleep from nearly eleven hours."

The elapsed time immediately struck Anod adding to her frustration. Her senses and analytical powers were far from the expected, full performance. Her diminished mental and physical abilities contributed to her protracted feeling of vulnerability. This was a condition she did not like very much.

"Your body is still struggling with the recovery from a severe trauma. You should not be overly concerned about the confusion you have."

"Maybe so," she said tersely. "I am not accustomed to this lack of control."

"Well, I'm afraid you will have to accept it for a while longer."

Her frustration gave way to a flash of anger. "I still don't understand why you don't have a tissue regeneration probe. You should be able to heal wounds such as these within minutes, not days or weeks."

"Anod, your frustration is understandable, however this society, on Beta, does not possess that technology," he responded calmly.

"Please excuse my outburst, Nick. My impatience with this protracted healing process is born from a lack of familiarity."

"Accepted," he acknowledged. "The withholding of technology was a condition of the exile. My ancestors were only allowed to take a level of technology required to sustain life. We only have what we have been able to create or acquire from other sources. Some of us are well aware of the fact that our society is fairly primitive compared to life on your Earth." The tone of Nick's statement reflected shades of remorse and regret.

His statement surprised Anod somewhat. The time was not right for a continuation of this discussion. She wanted to know more about the Betan society before probing deeply into the technological background of her hosts. Furthermore, her hunger was still present and unabated.

"Nick, could I get something to eat?"

"Certainly. I apologize for babbling on about meaningless things. I'll make you some broth and porridge."

Anod tried moving her limbs, again. The ever-present pain was not quite as intense as she noticed yesterday. Some of the pain must have been due to the immobility of her joints due to the period of unconsciousness, she concluded. There was definitely some genuine traumatic pain that was unmistakable. Her right arm and leg began to loosen up as she transcended the first shots of pain. As Anod moved her right arm, the pain became more diffuse and less severe.

The distant noise of metal objects coming in contact caught Anod's attention. The faint notes of a human whistle were a presumptive indication of Nick's engrossment with some task.

"Here we go," she heard him say from the other room.

Anod looked toward the partially opened door as Nick walked into her room with a tray. The two bowls on the tray presumably contained hot food as indicated by the wafts of steams rising above them. He set the tray down on a nearby table to assist her in the struggle to reposition her body for the anticipated meal. "Let's get you set up for this sumptuous first meal of your recovery"

Her efforts to move continued to produce shots of pain at the now familiar locations of her anatomy, as well as some new sites.

"Here, here. Let me help, Anod." He used both arms to lift her shoulders. As he held her, Nick reached for several additional cushions on the shelf behind her bed. Placing them behind her torso to create a backrest, he gently released her to rest against the cushions. He carefully raised the fallen sheet and tucked it under her arms recovering her briefed exposed and bruised breasts.

"Thank you, Nick."

"Let's get some food into you," he said.

Hundreds of questions flowed like a mighty river through her consciousness. Anod considered the moment and decided to continue restraining her curiosity until she knew more about her situation and her benefactor.

"It smells good, Nick. What have you prepared?"

"This," he said pointing to the left bowl, "is a porridge made from a combination of native, hybrid grains which are derivatives of oats and rice from Earth, I believe. The other bowl has a broth made from the meat of a Boracki otter. It has exceptional complementary cellular regenerative capability and it tastes great."

Anod was not quite sure what to think. Was he being sarcastic or lighthearted?

Nick placed the tray on a makeshift support in front of Anod. The food tray was close, but not resting on her traumatized body. Sitting on the edge of the bed, he began to feed her the porridge with a spoon.

"You are quite right, Nick. The broth is very tasty. I have never eaten food like this. There is a certain excitement associated with the tastes, textures and temperatures of these foods."

"I'm glad that you enjoy it. Both of these foods will aid the healing process for you."

Nick continued to patiently feed Anod as she discreetly and persistently moved each of her fingers and toes, a hand, a foot in her own contribution to the recovery process. He was well aware of her efforts as she watched the expression on her face change with the passages of pain and the movement of the sheet.

"You seem to be feeling a little better today," he said.

"Yes, I do. My joints and muscles are beginning to work again, and this food is sweet music to my stomach."

"You should make fairly quick progress now, I should think."

"It feels like it to me. Every additional movement brings a reduction in pain with a few notable exceptions. In fact, I'd appreciate your help to try moving around a little."

"It would be my pleasure," Nick responded as he continued to feed her. "You know," he paused to look directly into her eyes, "you are quite an intriguing character for us."

Anod's defenses immediately sprang up.

"You said us. How many people know I am here?"

Nick noticed the reaction in her body as well as her words.

"Easy, Anod. You have not been exposed, yet."

"What do you mean, yet?"

"I mean, as your recovery progresses, we will be less able to conceal your presence."

"You have not answered my original question. How many people know I am here, that I am alive?"

"The number has not changed since your arrival. To the best of my knowledge, only four people, Alexatron, me and two other trusted Betans know that you are alive and that you are here. Why are you so defensive?"

"There are certain questions regarding my predicament which raise my suspicion. Until I am able to answer those questions to my satisfaction, I must ask you to be very protective of my existence."

"Agreed. I would like to know the answers to some of those questions as well," Nick said in deliberate reference to the conditions that brought her to the planet. "I can assure you that I will not intentionally divulge your presence."

"Thank you, Nick. For all I know, there may have been treachery involved with the destruction of my fighter. If so, my presence may place you and your friends in danger. I need to get answers, and if the worst is true, I need to leave here as soon as possible."

"Should we notify your people?"

"No. Well, I should have asked a question first before I answered so hastily. What type of communications capability do you have?"

"Radio."

Anod laughed so hard she triggered several sites of recurrent pain adding groans to the laughter. Nick stopped his efforts to feed Anod and looked at her somewhat in astonishment. "Radio," she choked out through the rolling cycle of pain and laughter. "If we used radio, we would be old by the time I could send a message to and receive an answer from the one person I can trust. Furthermore, everyone within sublight distance would hear the transmission. No, we should not send any messages."

Nick was visibly hurt by the derogatory reference to their antiquated communications equipment. He wanted to let his anger out to counter the humiliation he felt. Instead, he was perceptive enough to recognize the limitations of their exile on this planet.

Anod likewise recognized her *faux pas* immediately. "Nick, I must apologize. I did not mean to offend you. It's just that your group here on this planet has led a very sheltered existence with respect to technology."

"We are well aware of that," he answered tersely.

"Nick, I am truly sorry for my rudeness. In order to make proper decisions, I must understand and appreciate not only my situation and condition, but also the tools available to me. Please do not hold my heritage and the technology I grew up with against me."

"Certainly not! By the same token, please don't hold our technology against us."

Anod's focus changed quickly to a more immediate subject. "Would you help me with the food you have prepared?" Anod could not grasp a better subject to alter the course of the dialogue between them.

Nick did not answer her. After a short hesitation as he appeared to struggle with his emotions, he continued his assistance. With the porridge and broth consumed, he picked the bowls and utensils, and walked to the door.

Anod was partially surprised and partially bewildered by Nick's withdrawal from their interaction.

"Nick, wait," Anod said to his retreating posterior.

He slowed his pace for a few steps as he continued toward the door.

"Nick, please, what did I do to offend you?"

The elder man stopped as if some unseen force had instantly frozen him. Nothing moved, not even his robe responding to the breathing of his chest. Anod did not know what to say, or what might happen. She felt the mercy of her benefactor ebbing from her grasp. After several exceedingly long moments, Nick turned to face Anod still sitting in her bed.

"You are my guest, my patient. I do not have to like you. I am obligated to provide proper medical attention to your wounds. I will do my humble, primitive best to assist your recovery to full health. You are welcome to leave our planet whenever you wish," he said with a calm, resigned voice, but annoyed. He turned again walking toward the door.

Anod chose to let the harsh tension of the moment pass. Time might soothe the hurt feelings. Now was not the time to confront the emotions within her caretaker. He passed through the door pulling it closed behind him in yet another symbol of his frustration with her.

The persistent sense of vulnerability realigned her focus from Nick's emotions to her extrication from this predicament. She had to push herself to get out of the bed, out of this cave and back into space. The urge to move to a neutral battlefield was still present despite the obstacles before her. The warrior spirit within her would not rest.

Her right arm was moving a little easier. The pain was no longer sharp and specific. The hurt was now more like an ache. The muscles in her right arm were weak from disuse, but were still functional. She reached for the edge of the sheet covering her, lifting it away from her right side. It was time to take the next step. She moved to the edge of the bed.

Anod took a good look at her exposed right leg. Several bruises were visible on her thigh, hip and abdomen. The ankle and knee were the principle pain sites. Her right leg was the first limb to leave the confines of the bed. Blood rushed into her leg causing a definite throbbing sensation to confirm her diminished physiological performance.

The left leg and arm were another matter. Her left side must have taken the brunt of the trauma from the breakup of her fighter and ejection from the conflagration, Anod told herself. She reached across her body to lift her left arm into the cradle of her groin. The pain in her left arm provided physical testament to the condition of her arm under the crude bandages. It was difficult to ascertain the precise nature of the injury to the arm, but the pain certainly verified the serious damage Nick indicated. The hard bandage on her left leg was heavy, but not too difficult to move. The pain in her left leg was not as bad as she expected, probably due to the special casing Nick placed around the leg.

As a prelude to the final segment of her movement, Anod moved the sheet to free the remainder of her body. There was a moment of hesitation before Anod moved her left leg off the bed. She anticipated the extra weight of the casing and braced herself against it. The leg fell to the floor with a thud and sent waves of pain reverberating through her body. Anod quickly cursed herself for pushing too fast.

Anod sat on the edge of the bed with both feet resting on the floor. The agony was subsiding back to the dull ache as she noticed the exquisite feeling of air on her back. There was a distinct pleasure in the small accomplishment and the interesting blend of excitement and pain.

With several deep breaths to muster her inner strength, Anod stood using the frame of the bed for support. The throbbing in her legs was waning as she took the first tentative steps of her rehabilitation. The results of the injuries sustained in space were quite apparent as Anod began to slowly move away from the bed. The air in the room was cooler than she thought and felt invigorating on her exposed skin.

This was a painful activity for Anod, but it was an effort that had to occur if she wanted to return to self-sufficiency as quickly as possible.

Each small step was a significant victory for her in the testing process. She needed to know how far she could go. Her joints were still stiff from the immobility of the coma and her coordination was definitely less than acceptable. However, first steps were first steps.

A previously unnoticed mirror on the wall behind her bed gave Anod an additional objective, self-assessment. Slowly, she approached the mirror until she stood in front of it fully erect.

"Wow," she said aloud as she saw her image and the extent of her injuries.

The hard casing on her left leg and the bandages on her right leg and left arm were not new to her eyes. However, they looked different when seen together as part of her whole body. At least her abdomen was relatively free of injury except for a few nearly vanished bruises. The color of her skin seemed to be a little pale to her recollection. This was the first time she saw the bandages on her head. Her face was not too bad. It was still swollen slightly and pinkish in color from the flash burns, but there were no lacerations or major wounds. The cranial bandage covered most of the remainder of her head. Only a small patch of her auburn hair was visible at the top.

Anod turned as far around as her sore neck would allow a view of her posterior. The backside was not too different from the front other than patches of discoloration associated with multiple contusions and some other types of abrasions. She surmised the sores were probably due to the continuous contact with the linen sheets for the last few weeks.

The motion detected in her peripheral vision and the sound of the door opening caught her attention. She turned to face the door standing as tall as she could. The startled expression on his face and in his eyes was confirmation of the surprise Nick felt. His vision moved from the empty bed to Anod standing nearly five meters away along the wall.

"My God, what are you doing out of bed?"

The strength of his words stunned Anod for an instant. She was totally unaccustomed to being spoken to in such a tone. The verbal bludgeoning was amplified by the elation associated with her accomplishment. It was a strange blend of emotions passing through her consciousness as she stood erect and proud.

"I must exercise my body, if I am to recover quickly," she said with firmness.

"You could just as easily refracture your leg as well," he responded sharply.

"It is not as bad as you might think, Nick. There is some pain and throbbing in my legs and left arm when I am standing, but other than that I feel pretty good."

Nick turned away quickly without another word. "If you are going to move around out of bed, will you please wear a robe, or gown, or something?" he asked in a noticeably more subdued tone.

"My apologies once again, Nick. It seems most of the things I take for granted or as a fact of life are offensive to you. Where can I find a robe, or gown, or something?" Anod asked mimicking her host.

"Just a moment."

Anod looked behind once more to see her face and body in the mirror. The body was a little beat up, but she was beginning to feel better. A sense of focus began to return. She was going to recover from the cataclysmic events that brought her here.

The shadow in the doorway presaged Nick's return. He carried an armful of folded clothing over to a table adjacent to the bed. Lifting the top garment from the stack, he offered it to Anod.

"This should do. It is about your size and it is loose fitting."

Anod took the garment. The smooth, soft brown cloth was a type of overlapping robe with large open sleeves. Although a simple garment, the use of only one arm made the donning of the robe difficult. Nick eventually noticed the complication, suppressed his inhibitions and assisted Anod with the robe. He started to button the front on Anod's right side, and then realized she would not be able to reach the top button with her right hand. Looking toward the ceiling, Nick reversed the overlap and buttoned the robe on the left.

Anod looked into his eyes as if to see the man within. There was a silence and stillness between them.

"Thank you for the help, Nick." Anod hesitated continuing her survey. She saw sincerity and compassion in his eyes, which provided a small boost to her confidence in him. "I'd like to ask you two questions."

"Yes."

"First, do you have a cleansing chamber or some way for me to clean my body? And secondly, why does the sight of my body bother you so much?"

"It's just that, well . . . it's just that we consider the human body to be a highly sexual entity, especially the opposite gender. We just . . . no, no." He stopped abruptly turning away from her and started to walk away. He turned back around as if he reconsidered his actions. "Do you understand?"

"No, I do not," Anod answered innocently. "What is sexual?"

This time it was Nick's turn to laugh loudly more it seemed to relieve some inner pressure than to respond to a humorous statement.

"Oh my gosh. Oh my gosh. What do I say? How do I answer that kind of question?" The tone of his voice and his facial expression indicated he was talking to himself rhetorically rather than asking her. "We must have this conversation because it has implications far beyond the question, but not now. Can we discuss this later?"

Anod nodded affirmatively and with some confusion. She did not understand what had just happened. This was such a strange situation.

"Oh, yes, your first question. I don't know what you mean by a cleansing chamber. Maybe that would be a good topic for future conversation as well. Anyway, I presume you're asking about a shower or a bath. There are two methods we use to cleanse our bodies. In your condition, you will have to restrict yourself to a shower until your cast comes off."

"A shower, I presume, means what the name implies. What is the cleansing agent?"

"Water," Nick responded with a chuckle.

"That should suffice."

"Are you able to walk without support?"

Anod started to take a step away from the workbench she had been holding onto. Her step was noticeably unsteady.

"No. I think I can walk with support."

Nick wrapped an arm around her waist and cradled her right arm. Anod noticed immediately that he was strong and solid for his age. "We have to walk to the adjacent room."

"Before we go to this room, would you mind removing the bandage from my head and any others you think appropriate?" Anod asked.

"Certainly."

Nick moved a chair close to Anod and motioned for her to sit. He began to remove her head bandage with care and patience. When her skull was completely free, he examined several locations to ensure proper healing.

"I'd say that your head wounds and burns are looking quite nice."

Without a response from Anod, he moved to her left arm and completely removed the bandage. Anod looked down to see the remnants of the lacerations and burns to her left arm. She tried to move the arm only to be rewarded with strong pain in her joints, but it was moving. As Anod continued to gently exercise her left arm, Nick removed the bandage from her right leg. There were no noticeable injuries to her right leg other than the residual of several bruises around her knee and ankle.

"Yes, indeed, you are healing quite nicely. I am afraid we should leave the cast on your left leg for a little while longer," Nick said as he stood in front of her.

"Agreed," Anod said. "You have done a very good job tending to my wounds, Nick. I am most grateful."

"You are most welcome, Anod. Now, would you like to take a shower?"

Anod smiled at his reference to the shower of water that would clean her body. "Yes, I would." She stood with the support of the chair.

Nick guided Anod toward the opposite end of the room. There was a certain touch of curiosity about the destination since Anod had only seen one door in her earlier survey of the room.

I missed the mirror, so maybe I missed another door as well, she said to herself as they slowly moved toward the far end of the room. Anod still could not see another door. As they approached the far wall, the existence of a portal behind a small curtain became apparent. Anod had noticed the curtain earlier although she assumed it was *le objet d'art* due to its rather ornate embroidery.

Nick pulled the curtain aside revealing a short, narrow passageway leading to a small, dimly lit room. He adjusted his hold on her to follow her through the narrow opening. The small room was definitely a special purpose area probably for cleaning the human body.

"Are you familiar with these fixtures?" Nick asked as he gestured to the various objects in the room.

"No."

Nick looked to his right to begin the explanation. "This is a sink for washing your face and hands. This is the toilet for disposal of bodily waste. And, here is the bidet for cleaning afterward. A bathtub is under this seat panel. This little room is the shower. I am a little uncomfortable with this, but do you need me to explain how to use these?" The reticence in his voice was unmistakable.

Anod thought she understood what each fixture was to be used for, but she did not entirely understand how to use them. It appeared that these were tools for manual cleaning of the body. The cleansing chamber was all she had ever known. The memory of the blue light of the scanner descending down her entire body came back to her in vivid detail as well as the rush of warm, soothing air caressing her body and whisking away any residue.

The tools in this room were as foreign to her as the bed and Nick's aversion to her body. She hesitated to ask Nick for a further explanation considering the earlier friction.

"What I don't understand, I am certain that I can figure out," she said finally.

"Very well," Nick responded with some relief. "I will leave you then. I anticipated this some time ago, so I think everything you need is here," he said motioning toward the small cabinet in the corner. "I will tidy up the other room while you clean. If you need something, please call me."

The Kartog warrior nodded her consent. Nick acknowledged her agreement and started to leave her alone. "Wait. I almost forgot. We must protect the cast from the water."

After several additional questions, the reason for his statement became clear to Anod. The water would adversely affect the casing, and her covered skin would deteriorate due to an inability to dry properly.

The process of covering her cast did not take long. With that task complete, Nick departed, pulling the screen across the passageway.

The new challenge before her again stimulated Anod's curiosity. She experimented with the individual knobs beside the sink faucet and was not particularly surprised to discover hot and cold water. A quick glance to the shower confirmed the existence of similar knobs. Anod hobbled slowly around the room to continue her exploration. There was a slight anticipation associated with using each of these new tools.

Anod reminded herself that challenge and accomplishment, however minute, provided the necessary stimulant to future achievement. This philosophy often overcame the obstacles of life. So many things were new experiences, new challenges, for Anod.

The buttons on her robe were a little more difficult to undo than she expected. Fortunately, there was no timetable, no deadline, and no reason to be in a hurry. In time, Anod was able to remove the robe and place it on one of several hooks along the wall next to the shower.

The process of temperature control for the water spray interested Anod. She enjoyed the simple experimentation.

Slowly, she moved into the shower space that was rather spacious, certainly larger than cleansing chamber she was accustomed to. The occasional shots of pain from one location or another did not seem to bother her. The penetrating warmth of the water began to work its wonders. Anod felt her whole body relax even though she did not feel tense. The process, an experience she had not enjoyed before, was thoroughly engrossing for the warrior. She could feel the pain withdraw from most of her joints allowing an increasing range of motion. This could become addictive, Anod said to herself.

The cleaning bar made her skin smooth, almost slippery. She had not been able to touch her own skin and most of her body for a long time. Life was returning to her body. As her enjoyment of the warm water progressed, her thoughts began to drift to another subject. Why was she on Beta? What happened at M19? Why had this happened to her?

Anod began to remember the search of the 2137M19 star system for the suspected Yorax activity. The other elements of the mission were so routine, cloaking, waiting, boredom, the asteroid, the explosion . . . . The asteroid, she thought, the asteroid was not exactly routine. It was certainly not abnormal, but it was also not routine. She had examined that rock in every way she could while the masking command remained valid. There was nothing unusual about that rock, so why the explosion? Either Zitger or Zarrod had died in that explosion, or maybe one of her teammates was in the same condition she was? Had one of them survived the explosion? Sensors had indicated no identifiable remains other than the residue of the explosion. It had been a complete vaporization of the fighter and its occupants.

What happened out there?

She wanted to think that it was just a freak accident. That particular explanation probably would have been acceptable, except for the destruction of her fighter. Did the Yorax have a new, more powerful tactical system? Could they avoid detection and engage without exposure?

Anod did not like the thoughts running through her brain. Something was dreadfully wrong about the sequence of events near M19, like the possibility of some crazed creature behind a closed door. She returned, in memory, to the sequence, once more. The passage of the asteroid, the explosion, pursuit and search of the asteroid, return to the loiter station, call for the survivor . . . the call for the survivor. Communications. She grasped at the key to the closed door. The transmission, her call-out, was the only time she was exposed. If an adversary had engaged her, it was at that instant when she had been the most vulnerable. If an attack had occurred, where did it come from? How did they, or whoever, know she was there? The questions were confounding as well as frustrating.

There had to have been some foreknowledge by her attacker. If the Yorax had been able to penetrate the cloak, they could have attacked at any time. No, someone knew what to wait for. Who could it be?

Zitger, or Zarrod.

Absolutely not. They were her teammates. They worked together, ate together and slept together for years. Maybe one of the other teams had betrayed them. If that was true, then Zortev and Manok have been compromised. The likelihood of both of them being compromised was next to impossible which brought her back to her teammates. It just could not be true. It must be the Yorax and a new targeting system, or something.

"Are you OK, Anod?" asked Nick from a position out of sight.

"Yes, Nick. I was just enjoying the water." Anod noticed for the first time the thick fog of steam around her.

"You've been in there a long time. I wanted to make sure you did not hurt yourself."

"No, I am just fine. I'll finish shortly. Thank you for your concern."

"You are quite welcome."

Anod checked her body one last time to make sure she was finished. Turning off the water, she reached for the towel. This was the first time in her life she had to wash and dry herself. The cleansing chamber did all the work for her on Saranon. As she dried her body, her thoughts wandered into the region of certain depression. She missed her friends, her environment, the tools of the Society, the isopod, Gorp. "Oh my," she said aloud to herself. Gorp was gone, dead. Her companion of so many years and so many experiences no longer existed. Even though he was a machine, she had always thought of Gorp as a person, as a friend, as a protector.

"I have to think of something else," she again spoke aloud although she was the only listener.

The light of day, I need to see the light of day, she thought. I need to feel the warmth of the light on my face, to feel the wind and breathe fresh air.

The aches and pains had noticeably subsided. Her right arm was nearly normal in function and without pain. Even her left arm and right leg had a substantially improved range of motion without pain. The left arm was definitely not very attractive with minor distortions of the healing wounds, but it was progressing rather well.

Putting her robe on was significantly easier than the removal had been, which was another demonstration of the warm water's therapeutic effect. Anod was able to return to the larger room without support, an effort that gave her some satisfaction.

Nick was working at a bench opposite from her bed. The sheets had been changed and the bed remade. He apparently did not hear her approach him. As she stopped beside him, he turned his head to see her and flashed a demonstrative expression of approval.

"The shower seems to have helped you," he said with a smile.

"Yes, it did," Anod responded. She moved her arms and right leg to provide positive proof.

"I should say so. May I take a closer look?"

Anod nodded her head.

The examination did not take very long, but was reasonably thorough. The most noticeable element was the distinct lack of any aversion in Nick. The curious difference between casual observation and medical examination added to the perplexing traits of this Betan man.

"I must be perfectly candid, you are recovering much faster than I have ever seen with wounds this extensive. Do you have special recuperative powers?"

"No," Anod said with a broad smile. "Not that I know of."

"It certainly is impressive."

"Nick, I would like to get some fresh air," Anod said. "The air in here is very heavy. It feels hard to breathe."

His expression changed instantly as he avoided her eyes. Something happened, Anod realized quickly.

"I don't think that would be a good idea right now," he said looking at the bench without doing anything. "First, it is our night time and there isn't much to see. It will be light in a few hours. However, more seriously, while you were taking your shower, I received a message that the Yorax are looking for you. They referred to you directly, not by name, but there is no question that it is you they are looking for."

Anod considered what her protector had just said. Several questions flashed into her thoughts. She felt the defenses going up again and her vulnerability increasing.

"How did they find out I was here? Where are they? How much time do I have?"

"A Yorax patrol ran across Alexatron's ship. They interrogated him, however, according to Alexatron, they derived no substantive evidence from their questioning. Their scanners may have collected some residues of your presence. Retracing Alexatron's log, they suspect you are alive and on this planet. Fortunately, Alexatron was able to protect your true existence and location. So, they don't know you are with me. They have started a search of the planet. Our population is not particularly supportive of the Yorax, even though they know nothing of your existence. They started their search some distance from here. They have been sweeping the planet with their sensors from orbit. I pray that you do not have any distinguishing features like biological beacons, or unique organic structures that might trigger their sensors."

"No, I don't. When do you think they will reach this area?"

"Tomorrow, or the next day."

"How can I escape to space?"

"You can't," he said regretfully. "We are prohibited from possessing a launch capability as part of our confinement."

"What about Alexatron?"

"What do you mean?"

"Can we get Alexatron to pick me up and return me to the Society?"

"No," was Nick's terse response.

Anod waited for more justification. She could surmise some of the obstacles, but she also knew that will power could overcome a great deal of obstruction. "Why?"

A somewhat frustrated expression passed across Nick's face. "First, the Yorax have indications you are here. They most certainly are watching all traffic to and from Beta. Second, it is not reasonable to ask Alexatron to risk his livelihood, his family and his culture with such a serious threat."

Anod knew he was right and knew there were many other reasons why the idea would not work. She felt some embarrassment over being told about the tactical significance of suspicion and bioscanners. The feeling passed quickly. "What weapons do you have?"

"None of substance. We have mostly physical hand weapons for hunting and tools, and a few laser pistols."

"Do you have a plan?"

"There appears to be only one thing we can do. We must both hide in a special chamber so they cannot detect our existence. That will only cover the short term. The Yorax commander has indicated they will tear the planet apart, piece-by-piece, until they find you. I'm sure they believe that you could not leave the planet."

"You're right. Let's get passed the initial search, then we can work out a better solution," Anod said confidently.

"The best thing right now is for both of us to get some sleep before dawn. We have a little less than three hours," Nick said.

"I feel this need to take some action, but I know you are correct. A rested mind is a quick and focused mind," she acknowledged.

"Do you need anything else, Anod?"

"No."

"Then, I'll awaken you just before the dawn."

He left the room. She moved over to the bed. The feeling of the clean cool sheets felt good on her skin. Sleep came quickly to the warrior despite the impending survival challenge. Her conditioned mind enabled Anod to isolate and compartmentalize life events. It was an acquired technique common to her lineage.

Chapter 4

Anod felt Nick's gentle hand shaking her awake. She did not feel rested as she made a quick survey of the room. The dark chipped walls of the cave gave the room a heavy appearance. This had to be Nick's work room to which he added a bed and various living accouterments either to accommodate her or for his quick use after a long fatiguing day at the several workbenches along the walls. A handful of desk and floor lamps distributed around the room provided the necessary light. Anod was satisfied nothing had changed.

She waited for Nick to leave the room then left the warmth of her bed. Since her joints were a little stiff and painful, she moved each one to ascertain its range of motion and the boundaries of pain. She longed for the soothing and caressing sedation of the hot water, although she knew quite well the first priority had to be the impending threat of the Yorax search. A quick assessment of her injured body made her smile ever so slightly and nod in approval. Her recovery was making good progress, as Nick had said.

The robe Nick had provided was noticeably easier to put on and button than it was previously. The ease of movement was one more positive sign of her recuperation.

Anod felt a tremendous, almost overwhelming thirst for information. Where was her enemy located now? How were their operations being conducted? She knew Nick would probably not have any more information than he had prior to the sleep period, and she felt blind without her sensors and helpless without her weapons.

Adversity creates many things, Anod told herself, although the thought did not provide much comfort.

"Are you dressed?" Nick asked from behind the door.

"Yes."

Nick entered the room carrying two plates. "Here are some bread, berries and water, Anod. It is not an elegant meal, but it will sustain us." Nick handed her one of the plates, and a fairly large container of clear, cold water.

"Thank you, Nick." Her mind continued to race through assessments, alternatives and options. "Do we have any more information than what we had last night?"

"No," he answered with some solemnity. "There have been no more communications, so it is difficult to establish the situation."

"I will feel better if I can perform a simple recce of the area and understand the environment. Would you mind if we did that rather soon?"

"I assume recce means reconnaissance or reconnoiter."

Anod nodded.

"Of course not," Nick responded. "I do not profess to be a tactician. I will trust that part of our survival to you as long as you feel up to it."

Anod smiled slightly as she felt the strength of her instincts returning. "When it comes to survival, there is only yes and no. There is no room for feelings," Anod said to reassure Nick and, to a certain extent, herself. "We have one small advantage among several. We know they are here. They do not know with confidence that I am here. They suspect it, but they do not know."

"I am ready when you are."

"This is a very tasty bread, Nick. Thank you."

"I baked it myself and you are quite welcome."

"Shall we reconnoiter the area?"

"As you wish." He moved toward the door, stopped a few meters short, then turned to her. "Wait! We need to get some real clothes for you. Even though you are a little bigger than I am, some of my clothing should fit you," he said. "Wait here, I'll fetch something appropriate." He left the room.

A strange feeling returned to Anod. She was reminded that she was not on Saranon or within the controlled environment of the Society. She had never been concerned about the size of clothing or personal equipment. The correct sizes were always perfectly provided by Gorp. The central computer understood every detail of her anatomy and physiology more precisely than by anyone else, including herself. Her health was evaluated every day during her suspension in her isopod. There were so many things that she simply took for granted, as part of the reality of life. The realization that humans lived without the benefits of the Society's technology triggered her curiosity, but her questions would have to wait until the danger was past.

Nick returned with a stack of folded clothing. The quantity of clothing indicated either his desire that she wear an enormous amount of items or his indecision on what would be appropriate.

"Let's try some of these," he said.

Anod began to take off her robe, at which point Nick deposited the armful of clothing on the bed.

"I'll leave you for a few minutes while you try these clothes on."

Curiosity continued to play heavily in Anod's consciousness. Was the reserve of this one man indicative of the Betan culture? Why were they so inhibited by simple anatomy? Why were these humans so different from her? The growing questions in her mind brought a certain determination to learn more about this society and what motivated her local protector.

The task of changing attire did not take long. Nick had provided several garments that were loose fitting enough to accommodate her taller frame and the casing on her left leg.

After completing her dressing task, Anod walked awkwardly toward the door. It was now time for her to accomplish the most important immediate goal, establish a good plan to deal with the approaching Yorax.

Nick sat at a table with his back to her as she entered the adjoining room. The walls and dimensions were essentially the same as her room. The contents of the room were somewhat chaotic compared to her recovery room. A small cot with clothing scattered around it occupied one corner. There were several additional workbenches with different pieces of ancient scientific equipment. Nick must have sensed she was present since Anod knew she did not make a sound. He turned to look at her with a startled expression.

"I didn't expect you out here so quickly. You must be feeling much better," he said with a smile growing across his face.

"Yes, I do feel much better. I am still a little sore in places, but everything seems to work. The clothes you provided are quite adequate and I thank you. Now, can we proceed with our recce?"

"Yes, certainly," Nick responded rising from his chair. "It should be light now. If you will follow me . . . ," he said motioning to another doorway.

The route to the exterior meandered somewhat. The rock walls of the rooms, halls and tunnels changed texture and color as they moved away from the original rooms. Nick made a few comments on objects they passed, or the purpose of different locations within the cave network. Pride in the contents of this cave system was evident in each of Nick's statements.

A different character of light became more perceptible. They must be approaching the mouth of the cave Anod surmised. After several additional bends in the tunnel, the exterior environment came into view. Light from the parent star, the characteristic blue tint of a nitrogen-oxygen atmosphere, and the trees all added color and dimension to the world outside the cave. Large green trees in many shapes and types populated the location as far as the eye could see. Anod had seen trees similar to these in pictures, in the scene wall and holographic recreation chambers, but she had never seen the real thing.

There was an innocent fascination associated with the entire sensory content of this place. Sight, smell, hearing and feel were bombarded with substance, with material to expand the horizons of experience. The cool, light wind brought the sounds of birds and other animals, the rustling of the leaves, and the smell of the trees and the soil. It was a rich, hearty smell with many elements most of which Anod did not directly recognize. All she knew for certain was everything was pleasant and peaceful. An inner calm seemed to ride on the stimulation of the senses.

"Well, what do you think of our planet, Anod?"

"It is magnificent. It is probably the most wonderful place I have ever been," she responded as she continued to absorb her surroundings. "I have lived virtually my entire life in a controlled environment with occasional visits to alien planets. Even then, I needed life support. This is simply fantastic."

"We like it. It is pleasant. Our ancestors have told us this planet is the best of Earth. Naturally, we are very protective of this environment. I have not set foot on Earth either, Anod, but I am not sure that I need to as long as we have this place."

Anod's mood changed in an instant. "We will have more time to enjoy this environment later, however, we have a threat which we must contend with. How would you expect the Yorax to arrive and from where?" Her decidedly more serious disposition made Nick stop for a moment.

"From the last report I have, the main search team was in Iskihana which is about 57 kilometers in that direction," he said pointing off to the right front of the cave entrance. "I expect them to use their land scooters."

Anod clearly remembered her threat equipment briefings. The Yorax land scooter carried two individuals and their equipment at speeds up to 200 kilometers per hour in open, flat terrain. A gravity wave converter provided the levitation and propulsion. The limited power storage restricted the duration of free flight the scooters could maintain. Anod knew the scooters would be quite helpful in most of this terrain although they were not capable of climbing angles greater than about fifteen degrees.

Anod's evaluation of the immediate vicinity around Nick's cave categorized the terrain as rocky and mountainous with fairly steep approaches. The Yorax soldiers would not be able to ride their land scooters up to the cave. With the limited assessment, Anod felt confident that they would have to move at least the last half-kilometer on foot.

"I don't think they can get their scooters up here." Anod scanned the trees toward the valley below. "How do you think they will arrive here at the cave?"

Nick considered the question, then answered, "If they don't use the mass transporter from orbit, they will probably come from over there." He motioned to a small clearing in the trees that allowed a clear view of the valley below. "That's the way they came up here the last time."

"How many times have the Yorax been to your cave?"

"Twice."

"Is anything different here other than my presence?"

"No. Everything has been the same for more than five years. Both of their visits," he said sarcastically, "were about a year ago."

"Last night, you mentioned a special chamber. Where is it?"

"It's deep in the cave complex."

"How will it prevent the Yorax from finding us?"

"The small chamber, as well as most of the inner cave structure is solid anthratite. I have a special camouflage cover for the entryway. No known sensors can penetrate the crystalline structure."

Anod's eyes narrowed. She knew he was missing an essential detail. "What about their residue scanners?"

Her fear was confirmed. "What do you mean?"

Anod could feel the tension in her gut and throat. "My God, Nick. The Yorax can detect our odors, our scent, our thermal signatures just like the wolf."

The confusion on his face added to Anod's tightness. Her mind raced through the alternatives.

"What should we do?" asked Nick with the smell of fear on his breath. "Wouldn't it be better for me to be present so they think everything is normal?"

"No, I don't. First, they have probably scanned the area already. In which case, they know there are two humans in this area. Secondly, if they use their damn bioscanner on either of us, they'll either identify me immediately or detect your deceit in hiding me."

A strange pounding sound could be heard in the distance. It was an unusual sound, one that Anod had never heard before. It seemed to emanate from the ground beneath their feet.

"Come, we must go. They are on the way here. According to the signal, they are not taking violent action, yet," Nick stated. He began walking slowly back into the cave.

"Was that some kind of communication?"

"Yes, it is a low frequency rock transmitter similar to seismic shocks. We can send simple messages considerable distances, actually to most locations around the planet. The origin can be quickly determined, if desired. Unless you are touching the surface, you would not be able to detect the sound. The Yorax have departed from my neighbor's dwelling. They live about five kilometers from here. The Yorax are all on their scooters."

"Most ingenuous," Anod responded as her mind considered the consequences of this communications medium.

"We may not be as backward as I am sure you must have thought."

A response did not seem appropriate. The clear air of the exterior had an invigorating effect on Anod. For the first time since she regained consciousness, she had no detectable pain.

"I think we should avail ourselves of the protection of my emergency chamber," Nick said casually glancing at Anod.

"We need to mask our signs," Anod stated as she looked around for possible implements.

"What do you need?"

"Something to fill the air with other particles like dust or mist." Finding a fallen tree branch gave her the tool. She added, ". . . and, something to blur the thermal signature of our footprints. This should do it," she concluded without saying, I hope.

The two humans continued walking backwards for some distance back into the cave with no apparent sense of urgency. Following Anod's lead, Nick picked up another branch as they stirred up a small cloud of dust behind them. Anod knew the crude masking process would not be perfect. Acceptable or adequate were the words that came to her hopeful mind.

They eventually split from their egress route. This was a new part of the cave complex for Anod. Fortunately, her senses of direction, memory and navigation skills were able to keep track of all the changes in their path.

The polished, zigzag edges of a small, precisely cut entryway identified the chamber. A thick, matched door of the same material hung on massive internal hinges. Nick motioned for Anod to enter first while he checked the floor for any traceable signs of their presence. The small chamber of about four meters cube had only one entrance. As soon as Anod was in the room, Nick reached to the side and pulled a fitted slab of anthratite across the entrance. The lines defining the edges of the jagged door virtually disappeared. Anod had to examine the door very carefully to find the edge.

Nick immediately went over to a small device on the only table. It looked like a crude navigation instrument.

"Just as I suspected, they have already entered the cave. Let me see if I can determine how many of the bastards there are." Nick picked up a set of headphones and a writing utensil. He made several marks and calculations over the span of about a minute. "There are about 10 to 15 of them." He continued to listen to the minute sounds propagating through the rock. "There are three distinct types of footsteps." Nick concentrated on the sounds. "That's strange, one of them has a very different characteristic. I haven't heard that type before." Nick paused once again concentrating on the audio indications. "The strange one almost sounds like a human."

"Well, I don't have any experience with rock sound identification, so I won't be of much help to you."

Nick ignored her comment. "It is tempting to take a look," he mused. "I'd like to know what sort of person makes that type of sound."

"Can you tell what they are doing?"

"The best I can determine is, they are performing a routine search of the cave. It does not sound like they are disturbing anything."

"That's good."

The concentration of his face was a sufficient indicator for Anod to be quiet and let him focus on the detection task.

Anod looked around the confined space of the chamber. The two chairs they were sitting on and the table for the rock listening device were the only furniture in the room. Several cushions were stacked in a corner. Shelves along two of the walls contained various foods, water and some medical supplies. This was a room that had been well thought out and used more than once. It must be Nick's form of passive defense against adversaries or predators, which must be why he called it his emergency chamber.

Leaning over, he whispered something that Anod could not quite hear.

"What did you say?" she asked softly into his ear.

"They are right outside the entrance," he said with his mouth at her ear and motioning toward the entryway.

Both of them strained to hear sounds from the far side of the barrier door. There were no discernible sounds detectable even with Anod's sensitive hearing. Nick returned to his headset. At least, they were not ransacking the place, Anod thought.

Evidence. The word flashed into Anod's consciousness like a bomb burst. Was anything identifiable as evidence of her presence? Was their recent occupancy detectable? An entire series of questions shot through her mind as she considered their vulnerability.

Anod felt like a trapped animal with these thoughts at the apex of her awareness. These were not feelings she was familiar with. They were certainly not feelings that made her comfortable. Her instincts told her to fight. Hiding in a small room with an adversary searching the exterior was not the honorable action to be taken in this situation. However, Anod did not move. In fact, she was barely breathing, as though the minute sound of her respiration might be detected by the Yorax patrol.

"They are nearly finished with their search, I would say." Nick looked into her eyes and smiled.

"Can you tell if they have found anything?"

"I don't believe so. They have done very little talking and their motions are still slow and methodical."

Nick returned his concentration to the task of listening to the Yorax patrol. His intensity was noticeable and admirable to Anod. He may not be a trained warrior, but there were the makings of a good warrior, she told herself. His desire for survival was quite apparent, Anod thought.

"It sounds like they are departing. If so, this was not a particularly thorough search. Let me listen to see if I can account for all their troopers departing the cave," Nick said softly. His words seemed to be more to himself than to her, Anod thought.

The Kartog Guards pilot again chose not to respond since she could contribute nothing to the accomplishment of the task.

For some unknown reason, Anod looked down at her left leg and foot. The white casing protecting her mending leg became a huge weight attached to her body. It was at that moment she realized the limitations of her current state. The delayed realization was more a product of her unrestricted, vaunted position as a warrior of the Society than her personal capabilities. A broken leg, even an incident as severe as Nick has indicated, could be totally repaired in a few minutes with the medical technology of the Society. Prolonged recovery was simply not an experience Anod was familiar with. She was certainly not accustomed to limitations on her performance, either mental or physical.

Nick moved perceptibly for the first time after his extended period of intense concentration. "I think I have accounted for all of them. There were 14 by my count," Nick said. He froze in an instant. Something on the headset must have caught his attention. "For a moment, it sounded like they were coming back into the cave."

"We should wait for a period before we leave the protection of this chamber."

"My feelings precisely, Anod. I will listen periodically to see if I can detect any presence."

"Do you have a biological sensor that can detect and classify living elements?"

"No. We don't have that technology either."

"Then, we wait," she said.

Nick removed the headset laying it beside the device on the table. He searched her eyes as if he thought answers could be found. "Why are the Yorax looking for you?" Nick asked as if he just now realized the threat was real and greater than he anticipated. The tone of his question was more in the form of a demand than a request.

"It would seem to be fairly apparent, at this point, that the Yorax perpetrated the attack on my flight at M19. I don't know how they did it, but it appears to be true. They are probably looking for me, to eliminate the last living evidence of their attack," Anod said calmly.

"How many colleagues did you say you had?"

"Two human and three androids."

"Do you suspect they are dead?"

"I am fairly certain one is dead. The explosion was violent and there were no detectable survivors. I believe the others are as well."

"What were you doing to provoke an attack?" Nick asked innocently.

"We did not provoke an attack," Anod responded with conviction. "We were on patrol investigating an energy disturbance in the sector. There was no reason for an attack. This incident was plainly the blatant aggression of the Yorax."

"Are you certain that it was the Yorax that attacked you?"

"No, I am not absolutely certain. I have no conclusive evidence. However, the fact that they are on this planet searching for me is certainly a strong indicator."

"What do you want to do?"

"That's a good question since I seem to be the focus at the moment," Anod responded. She thought for a few seconds then added, "My first objective is to recover to full health without jeopardizing you or your citizens."

"A reasonable objective, it would seem."

"I'd like to ask a few questions, if I may."

"Certainly."

"What form of government do you have and who is your leader?"

"We have a loose confederation council which provides the basic societal structure we need. Our heritage has made us quite suspicious of a strong central government. Our leader, the Prime Minister, is Bradley SanGiocomo, my son."

"Does the possessive, my son, indicate you are linked to this man?"

The puzzled expression on his face lasted only a short time. "Yes, I am his biological father."

The words seemed clear enough to Anod although the implications were absolutely foreign to her. The confusion must have been evident to Nick.

"Father means I contributed to his creation and birth."

Anod knew what the words meant. Eventually, she gave up trying to understand the implications. "You must be a proud father."

"Yes, I am. He is a good man."

Anod's mind jumped to another thought. "How do you move around on the planet?"

"We try not to move around much. This is a bountiful planet and we are dispersed enough so we do not interfere with others. We communicate through various means to understand events, or carry on the community activities we must. Essentially, we have clusters of families who choose to lead simple, agrarian lives."

Anod's frustration with being caged up was starting to wear on her patience. "Why don't you take another listen for our visitors?" she asked somewhat rhetorically. Anod's tactical inquisitiveness needed satisfaction, plus she also wanted time to digest what Nick said.

"Good idea," he responded placing the headset back on his head and facing the listening device.

As Nick concentrated on his acquisition task, Anod considered her situation. Her leg was getting better, or so she thought. The cuts and contusions still were not completely healed, however, except for appearance, she could function. It was the restriction of the leg casing that was the primary limitation at the present time.

There was a strong urge to risk a communication attempt with Saranon or any other Society unit. A Society starship would have the desired effect. Even a couple of fighter flights would occupy the Yorax. The longing to be rescued from the threat of capture was strong. She had to remind herself that she could not depend on rescue. Survival was foremost on her mental list of priorities.

"Where were you?" Nick asked.

"Oh, sorry. I was considering the situation and the options I have."

"I think you were concentrating as much as I was."

"Could you determine anything?"

"I know there is no movement inside the cave complex. The Yorax patrol is continuing their search. It is probably a good assumption that the cave is clear."

"Maybe so, however we should make a couple of additional evaluations to see if we can pick up any stragglers," Anod said with determination.

"What's a straggler?"

Anod smiled in recognition that Nick was definitely not a warrior. "A straggler is someone who stays behind an advancing unit. He could be wounded or injured, or he could be waiting for someone to come out of hiding."

"I see. Then, I suppose you are right."

Nick reached over to the food shelf to retrieve several hard bread crackers. He extended his hand to Anod who declined the offer.

"Do you have any way to ascertain the size of the Yorax force on the planet, or the number and size of the spacecraft they have in the vicinity of the planet?"

"I can try to find out the size of the search team on the surface. However, I have no way to determine the size of the orbital force," Nick responded.

Anod nodded her head in agreement. She would take whatever information Nick could acquire.

He moved several switches on the controller device in a specific sequence. Shortly after Nick completed the switch inputs, Anod felt a peculiar series of thumps in the floor.

"There goes the message. It is not exactly what you asked, but it is the closest I can get within the limits of our rock communicator," Nick said.

"What did the message say?"

"'Number visitors.' The message said, 'Number visitors.' I hope that whoever is listening will recognize that we already know we have visitors and will figure out we are looking for more information. We won't get an accuracy statement, but we should know if there is a large, medium or small group of them on the planet."

"If we know there are more than one team, that information will be sufficient."

"I'll have to keep an ear to the rock, as we say. If we are going to get any information back, it will come in about ten minutes or so."

"How long have we been in here?" Anod asked. She missed the ability to ask the computer or Gorp routine questions relative to status.

"I am not sure. However, I would guess about an hour."

"A patient commander can wait considerably longer than that. They couldn't have enough troopers to deposit stragglers everywhere," Anod thought aloud.

Nick started to say something and stopped with his mouth open. He raised his hand to the headset indicating that he heard sounds that could be significant. He listened intently for several seconds. Anod could feel the reverberation of the rock floor.

"We have an answer. With our crude system, it is difficult to determine the precise meaning of the message. However, the signal probably means they have three teams on the planet." Nick looked directly into Anod's eyes. "I'm sorry we can't provide more information."

"No need to apologize. I believe the answer is three teams. If I was the Yorax commander with a typical security force, I would only deploy three teams to the surface."

"Is that good or bad?"

"I would say that it is good. If our assumptions are true, then this is a routine operation for them. I imagine that it is important for them to find me, but it would not appear that they are convinced I am here."

"Do you still think we should continue to hide you?"

"For the time being, yes."

"Then, so be it," Nick said with emphasis.

"I would like you to know I am extremely grateful for your effort and the risk you have taken on my behalf. You were not asked to take this risk, and I am thankful that you did."

"You are most welcome, Anod. I suspected from the first moment Alexatron told me about your circumstances that you were a good person in a bad situation. I just felt it."

"I hope I am worthy of your feelings."

Nick took off the headset finally laying it on the table. From the expression on his face, his mind had already changed the subject of discussion. "Would you tell me some more about your team and where you came from?" Nick inquired cautiously.

Anod thought for a moment considering his question. "I was the right wing of a three fighter flight of Kartog Guards. My team was one of four flights stationed on the outpost of Saranon in the K7 star system. Our general mission was to protect the interests of the Society in that region of the galaxy."

"What is a right wing?"

"It is a tactical position on the right side of a formation of fighters."

"Does that mean someone else was in charge?"

"Yes. My leader was Captain Zitger. The left wing was Lieutenant Zarrod."

"Were they males?"

Anod thought for an instant that it was a bit odd for him to use the past tense in reference to her teammates. "Yes," she answered with an inquisitive tone. "Why do you ask?"

"Well, I'm not really sure. Do all the females have names that begin with the letter A, and males with the letter Z?"

Anod thought for a moment. "Yes, to the best of my knowledge that observation is correct."

"Why is that?"

"I suppose it is simply tradition. It is certainly the only status I have known."

Nick smiled and then chuckled a bit, immersed in his thoughts. Anod waited, watching him intently. She wondered what was so amusing to him although she hesitated to ask. The expression of anticipation or interest on her face must have inspired him to speak. "Do you find it odd that the names of people establish their gender and in such a dramatic way?"

"Not particularly," Anod answered with some trepidation. "Some cultures utilize a suffix to denote gender. The Society represents people in this manner. It seems quite normal to me."

"I agree, however the A and Z relationship is intriguing. A and Z are the two letters in the English alphabet which are the farthest apart, and yet they are right next to each other in a circle of letters." Nick was noticeably enthralled with his analysis. "I wonder if this relationship is indicative of the relationship between men and women within your society?"

"I'm not sure I understand your question."

"Let me see . . . how should I word this?" Nick thought aloud. "Are men and women in your society treated the same? Do they do the same types of work?"

Anod considered the implications of Nick's question with some dismay. She still wasn't quite sure what he was concerned about. "Yes, of course. There are no differences across gender other than anatomy."

"Surely, there must be some differences. Your leaders, the military, scientists, judges, something must be different."

"There are nine members of our supreme council which is the leadership of our government. Five members are female. About half of our Board of Governors are female." Anod stopped for a moment to look directly into the elder man's eyes. "Why are you so surprised about the equality of our population?"

"Equality is not the correct word. We have equality on Beta, however there is a distinction between the sexes. Our men and women are not prohibited from pursuing any activity. It's just that a natural separation seems to occur along gender lines. Our men and women tend to gravitate toward certain interests."

Anod considered Nick's statement carefully trying to ascertain the direction as well as intent. "There is no identifiable separation of the sexes across all elements of our society. I think great care is taken to ensure gender homogeneity within the population."

Anod's answer intrigued Nick noticeably. He continued to look at her with a strange fascination. No words appeared to be forming within him. His expression was becoming indicative of a thoughtful trance.

Anod's thoughts jumped to another subject.

"Why don't you have another listen for intruders, Nick?"

There was no outward response from her benefactor. Nick simply continued to stare at her, a slightly discernible smile on his face. Anod wondered about the thoughts flowing through his brain.

"Nick, are you all right?" There was still no response. "Nick," she said with a conspicuously louder tone of voice as she reached over to touch his knee. "Are you OK?"

The expression in his eyes changed instantly.

"Sure, sure, I'm quite all right," he finally responded.

"You appeared to be in a trance or dazed."

"I was just thinking about your words and trying to visualize your society. Now, what was it you wanted?"

"I thought you should have another listen for our friends out there."

"Certainly. You are quite right," Nick said as he lifted the headset to his ears.

For the first time since entering this small chamber, Nick sat facing Anod as he listened to the rocks around them. A sense of amusement overcame Anod as she watched the old man's face contort during the listening process. There was a near comical series of expressions passing across his face. She struggled to contain her laughter in recognition of the concentration required to accomplish the task.

After several minutes, Nick looked up to see the humor in Anod's eyes only to realize that he was the source of her glee. A flush of embarrassment flashed across his face. "What is so funny?"

"I must apologize again, Nick. The changing expressions on your face while you were concentrating on your listening were quite simply, humorous."

"I didn't realize I did that," he responded with some levity.

Anod thought it wise to return to the point of concern. "Did you hear anything out there?"

"There was no indication of any intruders in the cave complex. However, one or more stragglers, as you call them, would be undetectable if they remained motionless. I cannot tell if they might be present."

"That's understandable."

"Nevertheless, I did pick up some signals that might indicate the patrol continues to move away."

"I'd say that it's time to see who's out there." Anod rose from the chair and moved slowly toward the entrance.

"Are you sure we should do this? We have enough supplies to stay in here for several days," Nick responded. The hesitation of a cautious man was in his voice.

"Yes, I am sure. It serves no purpose for us to hide like rats in this chamber. We have given the Yorax no quantifiable reason to suspect you or your dwelling. As such, there is no justification to squander valuable personal resources waiting idly on a hunch. The Yorax are quite predictable with their twisted logic."

"Well, then, I must concede to your judgment. I just hope you're right," Nick said with timidity.

Anod began to remove the cover. Nick touched her shoulder. "Allow me, please."

She stood aside as Nick carefully moved the chamber cover away from the entrance. A rush of cool air greeted them from the nearly dark exterior. Nick looked both directions along the passageway then stepped out. Anod followed suit.

Instinct took over and shifted to high intensity. She turned to Nick passing a silent hand signal indicating she wanted to quickly and quietly search the cave for intruders. He acknowledged her signal.

Silently searching a dark cave with a partially immobilized leg provided an additional obstacle to Anod's efficient prosecution of her clearing task. Her breeding, training and inherent skills did not allow the distraction of frustration or anger. The cool, calm, precise methodology of her craft simply took a little longer to complete.

The cave was clear.

"Let's see what's outside, shall we?" asked Anod.

It was dusk, or evening nautical twilight in the terms of the naval heritage of their common past. The air was even cooler outside the cave. The lack of radiant heating from the mother star and the clear skies of the atmosphere around them allowed rapid cooling of the surface. The surrounding spectacle of the stars that the celestial dome above them began to show through the retreating light of day. This was truly a beautiful and peaceful place.

In the fading light, the movement of the trees with the wafting wind reminded Anod of the scene wall that sustained them at her station on Saranon. The unique holographic projection that created a selectable wide variety of four-dimensional scenes complete with sounds and smells gave the remote human servants of the Society a sample of the home world. She also remembered Zitger, Zarrod, Gorp and the other androids as well. The remembrance brought the drain of her loss. Friends, lost in a still unknown fight that she would never physically see again. The vision of their presence, their friendship, would remain indelibly etched in her memory, forever.

Anod looked to her right to see Nick absorbing the beautiful scenery of this place. There was a sense of pleasure that was mysteriously unfamiliar to her. The pleasure was equally present for her benefactor.

The message was clearly written across his face.

"You truly have a beautiful planet, Nick," she said. Her words seemed somehow out of place at this idyllic moment.

He looked over to his guest. A smile grew across his weathered face. "Yes, it is, isn't it."

Chapter 5

A day and part of the next passed since the Yorax searched of the SanGiocomo cave. The intruders continued their quest elsewhere on the planet. The threat to Anod diminished, although it was not eliminated from the realm of concern. Even the planet, or at least the locale, provided the heightened impression of tranquillity.

Nick was due to return soon. He had departed with Anod's concurrence the morning after their unwelcome guests. He had planned to make several visits to neighbors and leaders to ascertain the mood and condition of the people. They both acknowledged the day was rapidly approaching when Anod would need the help of others to achieve her goals.

Exploration of the cave complex and her close surroundings occupied her time during Nick's absence. Exercising her muscles and joints took on obsessive proportions. The confining properties of the casing on her left leg were also becoming both irritating and frustrating. She continued to tell herself, the cast, as Nick called it, had to come off at the first opportunity upon his arrival.

The weather outside the cave remained picturesque and pleasant. A few, small, puffy clouds crossed the sky propelled by a light breeze. The winds also brought the stimulation of odors and fragrances quite new to Anod.

The experience of using all her physical senses was both provocative and enticing. There was a simple enjoyment to this passive activity and a feeling of completeness that was strangely foreign to her. What was it about the sights, sounds, smells and feel of the trees that provided these feelings? Anod could not answer the question, but she could not resist repeatedly asking it, either.

The warmth from θ27 flushed her face and body as she sat on a flat rock near the edge of the forest. Listening to the wind rustling leaves of the trees, and the birds and other animals speaking their melodious tones added to the calm that washed over her. A recurrent thought did pass through her consciousness several times. She could become accustomed to this place quite easily although the powerful undercurrent of duty invariably altered the image.

The crack of a breaking branch brought her instantly back to the focused control of her instincts. It was not a natural sound in the forest. The proximity of the sound added urgency. The cave entrance was too far for her to seek refuge given the limitations of her burdened left leg. The possibility that it could also be a Yorax patrol mixed with the fleeting thought that it might be Nick returning from his trip.

Anod quickly looked for a position of concealment. She needed a defensive position although she had no weapons. Off to the left, away from the approaching steps, a stand of moderate sized coniferous trees grew from the midst of several large boulders. The shadows were dark and the position offered a reasonable view of the clearing in front of the cave.

As quickly as she could, Anod skipped across the intervening ground swinging her disabled leg. The exertion quickened her pulse and breathing.

There could be one or two others although it was impossible to determine absolutely. The approaching steps among the leaves and twigs became more pronounced above the peculiar thumping of her steps. More than one person approached the clearing. Probably two.

The clustered rocks near the grove were solid and quite secure although it did little to relieve her apprehension – a fact that made Anod's awkward movements a little more productive.

She situated herself among the rocks behind two trees. The sounds of the intruders were no longer discernible over the whispers of the wind in the tree branches above her. They were there nonetheless, evident in the lulls of the wind.

Anod worked quickly to control her breathing. The cast on her left leg provided an undeniable aggravation. She struggled to move it out of the way and yet provide some motion in case she needed to defend herself against an aggressor.

The approaching steps were more identifiable, now. The characteristic crunch of leaves, twigs and branches along with the crack of an occasional rock confirmed there were two intruders. Anod longed for her biosensor. The small hand held device would provide her with the genetic identity of the intruders, information that she needed for proper anticipatory decision-making. She did not have access to the weapons that gave her some advantage. It would be simply her cognitive powers over those of the intruders that would protect her. Anod had to assume this threat most likely had weapons, also.

The intruders entered the clearing in front of the cave. Anod could not see them yet, because of the rocks and trees of her hiding place, however their steps indicated they had left the forest. She observed intently although her patience restrained her desire to lean out for a better view.

The muffled sounds of human voices could be heard while the character and words of the voices could not be determined. Shortly thereafter, she saw the intruders. It was Nick with another man. His companion was noticeably younger and larger nearly seven centimeters taller and probably ten to fifteen kilograms heavier than Nick.

They stopped at the entrance to the cave complex. Something concerned them as they discussed what it was in quiet tones. Nick had not provided any indication that he would return with another person. An inherent cautiousness held Anod in her hiding place. She needed some assurance that the situation was acceptable before she exposed herself. It was quite possible that Nick was in a situation of jeopardy as well. However, the man with him was certainly not a Yorax soldier.

"Anod, it's Nick," he shouted into the cave. "Everything is OK. I have a friend with me and we are coming in." The elder man said something to his companion, and then they both started into the cave.

At that moment, Anod instinctively knew she was not in danger. "Wait, I'm out here, Nick," Anod said from the protection of the small grove of trees.

Both men stopped and turned to face the grove. Neither man spoke as they tried to assimilate the words they heard and the location of the speaker.

Anod began the slow process of extrication.

The two men walked slowly toward her as she emerged from the cluster of rocks and trees.

"What were you doing in there?" Nick asked.

"Being cautious. I heard you coming and I could not tell whether you were a Yorax troopers or not."

"I should have thought of that. I'm sorry for the scare."

The lean features of the taller, younger man were a dramatic contrast to the weathered countenance of Nick. His dark, sapphire blue eyes possessed a strange cool fire, a subtle indication of the intensity within. Nick's companion was solidly built with a well-defined musculature evident despite the clothing covering him. He did not appear to be carrying any weapons.

"Oh, my. Please excuse my terrible manners. Anod, this is my son, Bradley James SanGiocomo," Nick said gesturing toward him. "This is Anod whom I have talked so much about," he said motioning toward her.

"I am honored to meet you, James."

"I prefer Bradley if you don't mind," he responded coolly. "It is nice to meet you." The younger man extended his right hand.

A few awkward moments passed until Anod deduced that the extended hand was a greeting that she eventually reciprocated. Bradley reached for her right hand to grasp it, firmly shaking it several times.

"This is a simple greeting among friends. We call it a hand shake," Bradley said.

"Pleasant custom."

"Bradley is the Prime Minister of Beta, the leader of our people. After discussing a couple of general items, I thought it was time for me to acknowledge your presence to our leadership. We believe in the collective solution and the people have a right to know."

Anod nodded her head to indicate that she understood. For some reason, she did not feel like talking.

"Shall we go inside? I am quite thirsty," Nick said.

Anod nodded, again.

She began swinging her left leg as they began to move toward the cave. They started to walk slightly faster, quickly realizing she could not move as fast.

"Would you like me to carry you?" Bradley asked.

Anod looked at him inquisitively. She wondered why he would ask such a thing. "I am quite all right, thank you . . . which reminds me . . . I'd like this casing taken off today, Nick."

"I don't think your leg has healed sufficiently," he responded.

"How will you know unless we check it?"

"Good question. Your other wounds have healed more rapidly than I would have imagined. So, I suppose, your point is well taken. Let me get a drink of water, then we'll see to your leg."

"Very good."

The three of them walked slowly into the cave. Only Nick and Anod spoke with the conversation being benign and pointless. Bradley chose to walk a few steps behind his father and their guest. Eventually, the trio returned to the laboratory that had become Anod's room.

"Anod, would you sit on the chair nearest the workbench?" Nick asked.

The warrior ambled slowly to the designated chair. The support of the chair brought a wave of relaxation that was welcomed and embraced. The younger man continued to remain distant from the conversation and from Anod. She was certain he was still assessing the measure of the woman from another world.

With his thirst satisfied, Nick approached Anod and said, "Let's have a look at that broken leg of yours. First, I must find my plaster cutter. Ah yes, here we go."

Nick started to look for the best place to start the removal process. He tried moving the loose fitting cloth of her pants' leg.

After several attempts to solve the puzzle, he said, "I'm afraid you will have to take your pants off. We'll leave the room unless you need any help."

"Nick, as you know, that is not necessary."

Anod stood to remove her lower garment. Nick turned to avert his eyes while Bradley did not move a muscle. The young leader did not take his eyes off her and remained expressionless. The doffing of her pants did not take long. Anod sat back in the chair.

"Shall we get started here?" Nick asked somewhat rhetorically as he placed the cutter at the upper edge of the leg casing. Anod did not feel a response was warranted or desired.

Several times during the slow, laborious process Anod glanced over to Bradley. His position, posture and expression had not changed. His trim figure leaning against the wall at the foot of her bed with his arms crossed and his cold constant stare made her wonder about his thoughts and intentions. Maybe I should not be so accepting of this man just because he is Nick's son, Anod suggested to herself.

Nick finally completed the cut and began to open the casing. Soon, the skin of her leg could feel the release of pressure. At first, Anod did not move her leg. She simply inspected it as Nick was doing the same. Meeting Bradley's distant, suspicious eyes dampened the expanse of her smile. What was it that made this man so detached? His personality, or at least the impression of his personality, was in such contrast to that of his father. There was something that was a very serious concern to the younger man. His consistent observation of Anod made it quite apparent she was either directly or indirectly entwined in his incertitude.

"That should do it," Nick said finally. "I would say that your body has some miraculous healing powers compared to what I'm used to. Your leg is certainly not completely mended, however it does look pretty good considering how badly it was damaged."

"It feels pretty good," Anod added.

"You might as well stand up and give it a try. Wait . . . first let's move it a little. We ought to check the joints and muscles."

Anod slowly began to move her ankle and knee. Various levels of low-grade pain were evident. Her joints were stiff and somewhat resistive. The still healing wounds provided the most noticeable pain probably from the obvious severity of the damage, Anod told herself.

"It doesn't feel too bad. My muscles and joints are a bit sore," Anod said.

"That's to be expected. Your leg was in really bad shape when you arrived. I wasn't sure I would be able to save it. In fact, I'd say judging from the curative ability of your body that you saved your leg."

Anod stood without putting much weight on her left leg. The slight throbbing at the point of the compound fracture in her femur was further evidence that the healing process was not quite complete. Slowly, she shifted her weight to her left leg until she was standing erect. There was essentially no change. Anod continued to shift her weight left to the point where she could lift her right foot – still no appreciable change in the condition of her left leg.

Anod needed the support of a wall to place one leg and then the other into her pants. She was cautious with her movements to avoid any shock to her left leg.

"This is a good sign, I would say." Anod smiled at Nick.

"Yes, I would agree. See how it feels walking on it," he requested.

She deliberately took short, slow steps. Anod felt somewhat awkward with her gait. The joints of her left leg were not quite fully functional. Normal use of the leg, at least while she was walking, rapidly returned although muscle atrophy was always slow to recover.

"It feels pretty good, Nick."

"Good. Good. I must admit, I have never seen a human being heal so quickly from injuries as severe as yours. Why are you able to recuperate so swiftly?" Nick asked.

"I am not a medical technician. I am not sure I can answer your question. However, it is my understanding that our physiological healing capability has been bred into us over the years."

"Bred! You said bred," Bradley interjected vehemently. "Did you really intend to say this trait was bred into you?"

The strength of his words took Anod by surprise. She looked at him with astonishment. No one spoke. Bradley stood fully erect with both hands on his hips. The fire in his eyes brought an immediate defensive curtain down around Anod. Her mind focused completely on situational assessment and potential reaction options.

Nick eventually shifted his sight from his son to his guest. His eyes asked Anod whether Bradley's question was true.

She slowly moved her head toward Nick without taking her eyes off Bradley. Her mental withdrawal was reactionary and self-protective.

"I'm not sure I should continue this conversation," Anod said finally with a soft, calm tone. She wanted to diffuse the confrontational posture of the younger man. She was also questioning her trust and the wisdom of her openness, until she understood the thoughts of Bradley.

Neither of the men spoke in response. Bradley had not taken his eyes off Anod. He had not even blinked that she could tell. Nick shifted his vision from one to the other trying to understand what was happening and why.

"Anod, please excuse my son. Sometimes his protective nature overrides his manners and hospitality," Nick responded to Anod. Turning toward Bradley, he said, "What do you think you are doing? Anod is a guest in my quarters. If you cannot find it in your heart to treat her as such, you are welcome to leave."

The situation did not appreciably change. The air of confrontation remained.

"Bradley, did you hear me?" Nick asked with a touch of anger in his voice.

Eventually, Bradley took his eyes off Anod and looked at his father.

"Yes, I heard you. There is something that is not right about your guest," Bradley said with a sneer as he referred to Anod.

"Whether there is or not, does not change her status as my guest. She has been through a traumatic event. She is separated from her people. Yes, I suppose there is something different about her, just as there is with each and every human being."

"No, I mean really different, as in, I'm not sure she is human," Bradley responded.

Anod had a slight urge to answer his insult, but she also knew this was best handled between the two men. She did not react in any manner.

"You did not see her when she was brought here," Nick said with intensity and anger. "She is human. I have examined her. I have seen her flesh torn open. I have seen her bones and blood. She is as human as you and me. Yes, she may be different, but that does not make her other than human."

"I want to hear the answer to my question," Bradley said trying to return to the subject of his concern.

Both men looked at Anod as though they expected an answer. Anod chose to say nothing and returned the stare of Bradley.

"Anod, I would like to hear your answer to Bradley's question as well. My curiosity is barely containable." A sense of levity returned to Nick's words.

Anod looked directly into Nick's eyes. "I'm not comfortable talking about my past, my heritage or myself."

"I am sorry, Anod," Nick said calmly, and then his expression turned serious as he looked to the younger man. "Bradley, you will apologize for your rudeness." He looked back to Anod. "Sometimes, he makes me so angry."

The younger man did not respond at first. "I offer my apology," he finally said to Anod. "I should not have reacted with such immaturity. It is just that I have never seen a woman such as you."

Anod looked directly at Bradley. "What does being a woman have anything to do with my abilities, or how you respond to me?"

"Women are not warriors in our culture. Women birth our children and hold the vital responsibility of raising our future generations. Women do not fight in battle," Bradley answered.

Anod did not fully appreciate his answer or understand why she was so offensive to him. His tone changed substantially. The sincerity of his words was disarming.

"In my culture, there is no differentiation by gender. Men and women share common functions and responsibilities."

"Who raises the children?" Bradley asked with indignation surrounding the words.

"I do not want to talk about my people or my society."

"I am famished," Nick said changing the subject. "Are both of you ready to eat?"

"Yes," said Bradley.

"I'm a little hungry. I would like to eat and then take a little walk to exercise my leg."

"Very good," Nick acknowledged.

Anod and Bradley sat on opposite sides of the table. The only audible human sounds were the strange mixture of mumbled words and whistled tune coming from Nick. Anod was aware of the prolonged dwell time of Bradley's stare, although she chose not to return it. She kept her head positioned so that Bradley was continuously within her peripheral vision.

The three of them ate virtually in silence. Nick talked about some of the activities he performed or was involved in over the last few days. The mood was much more subdued and cool than prior to his departure. The situation she found herself in with Bradley present was rapidly becoming untenable. She knew that she could not let down her guard until she understood the motivation behind his barely contained hostility.

Without finishing her portion, Anod thanked Nick for the preparation of the meal and excused herself from the table. She wanted to feel the fresh air, she told her host. The overwhelming urge to exercise her leg was the dominant force within her at the moment. She needed to quickly return to full performance. Neither man followed her nor asked to join her, which was preferable to Anod.

The evening air was cool, clean and rejuvenating. Anod walked around the circumference of the clearing, randomly stopping to listen for possible intruders approaching. When she was satisfied that she was still alone, Anod scanned the sky.

The stars with their infinite beauty and enchantment took on new significance this evening. She began to survey the stars to determine their relative locations. With the spatial relationship of the stars, the process of celestial navigation, or in her case, location, could be determined. Identification of primary and secondary stars escaped Anod's grasp. The reality was positive confirmation that she was not close to Saranon. The patterns were markedly different.

Her left leg began to tell her to slow down. The dull ache in her lower leg grew in intensity. She took the opportunity to sit on a large rock. The respite was partially to take the weight off her leg, but also to exercise her knee and ankle. The capabilities of most of her joints were nearly perfect. The atrophy of her muscles from the immobilization was more of a concern. Stretching and twisting without the full weight of her body on her leg brought a different ache as her muscles slowly began to regain their resiliency.

A light breeze brought the characteristic scents of the forest. The sights and smells of the Betan forest were quite similar to the scene wall on Saranon except more pronounced and dramatic. Nick's abode and its immediate environs possessed an intangible attraction for Anod. However, it was the reality of the stars that continued to draw her away. The inner turmoil was not an emotion familiar to the young warrior.

Anod heard the soft steps in the grass of the clearing behind her. She turned slowly to see Nick approaching her.

"I know he's a bit brash," Nick said as he sat down beside her. "It is a wonderful site, isn't it?"

"I am fascinated by the stimulation of all my senses – a stimulation that is quite full and more complete than what I am accustomed to."

"I have known three planets in my life. Beta is by far the most soothing and hospitable."

"The appreciation for the natural environment of your planet is impressive. However, I want, I need, to return to the Society and my people. I also want to find out what happened to me at M19. This is an internal conflict I am unable to resolve," Anod said with strength and obvious confidence that contradicted her words.

"As I started to say earlier, my son is a bit brash. The trait has been with him for many years. It is probably why he is our leader. Bradley feels a heavy burden trying to protect our way of life without violence. As I'm sure you have guessed, you are an enigma to him."

"I understand," Anod responded. She chose not to talk about what was on her mind. What had she done to offend him? What reason had she provided for him to be suspicious of her?

"Please do not feel unwelcome, Anod. It is quite understandable that you wish to return to your people. We will help you achieve that objective as best we can. While you are here, you are my guest and you will be treated as such. Plus, I have so many questions I want to ask and subjects I wish to talk about." Nick's broad smile was clearly evident even in the dim starlight.

"Thank you, Nick," she said. "Where are the Yorax? What are they doing?"

"Their search continues. As we would expect, they have found nothing because there is nothing to find elsewhere on our planet. They have been respectful up until now, although their searches are unlawful and against our will. There is no way to predict what will happen when they complete their search unsuccessfully," Nick answered.

"The Yorax have been relatively predictable in the past. If they are convinced I am on this planet, I would expect them to increase the intensity of their search. They might conduct a demonstration of force to intimidate the population."

Nick did not speak as he considered her words.

The stars moved across the sky at a perceptible rate that indicated that Beta was roughly the same size as Saranon. The hospitality of the natural atmosphere, vegetation and life was diametrically opposed to the desolation of her barren outpost.

"We shall cross that bridge when we get to it," Nick said.

"Nick, this may be a difficult question, however it is a question I must ask. What do I do about Bradley?"

"Ignore his coarse character for now. He is a very intelligent and capable man. He will warm to you as he gets to know you."

"Something about me bothers him? He does not like me, and unfortunately, I am not sure I should trust him. I sense his hostility and my instincts tell me to avoid him."

"He is simply cautious, Anod. He has a different way of showing it. Just stay neutral for a short time until he can get to know you a little. He will see the goodness in you."

"I will take your advice," Anod said with reluctance in her voice.

Nick stood and began shifting his weight from leg to leg several times. He kicked a rock into the forest. His head hung low as if his neck muscles had lost their strength.

"Anod, I know you don't care for personal questions, but as a scientist, your choice of words at our evening meal absolutely intrigues me."

She looked at him responding without words.

"You used the word, bred, earlier this evening. Please tell me what you meant."

"Not now, Nick. I do not want to talk about myself, nor my culture. We may have common ancestors, however I fully realize fate has separated us many years ago. Now, we are different."

"Would you talk to me sometime soon? My intellectual curiosity is virtually beyond suppression. In our years of exile, we have seen strange creatures and a broad variety of beings. Most of the humans from outside our colony are outcasts of one sort or another. You are the first human from Earth." Nick was clearly absorbed with the anthropological ramifications of the split genetic heritage they possessed.

"Remember, Nick, I have not set foot on Earth either."

"Oh, yes. Yes, yes, I know, but," he paused to collect his thoughts. "You are of the society of Earth."

"In that sense, you are correct. The Society is the collected population of Earth, both on the planet and serving in space."

"What is the society?"

"Nick, I know you mean well, however I also meant what I said. I don't want to talk about my culture right now."

He shifted his weight back and forth again. Anod was quite aware of his nervousness. She wondered about what was making him so uneasy around her for the first time.

"I will respect your wishes, Anod. Although I would like to say, my curiosity and need to learn are driving me crazy."

Anod smiled as she looked directly into his eyes. "Thank you for your honesty. We will talk when it is time."

"Very good," he quickly responded. "Would you like to go back inside to talk to Bradley?"

"Actually, no, I would not. Feel free to return. I'd like to stay out here to enjoy the stars and the ambience of your lovely planet."

"I'm in no hurry to go in, unless you would like to be alone."

Anod shook her head to indicate her ambivalence. Craning her neck to observe the night sky was becoming a pain. "If you will excuse me, I'm going to lie down to look at the stars."

Nick's chuckled in relief. "I think I'll join you."

Both of them lay down on the cool ground. Anod sensed that Nick was still hoping to strike up a meaningful conversation. Her interest was simply not there. Scanning the sky from horizon to horizon yielded several potential waypoint stars. However, the groupings were still not evident.

The brilliance of the stars returned her thoughts to the loss of Gorp, her companion from creation, and Zitger and Zarrod, her compatriots for most of her professional life. The uncertainty of life without the protection and caring of Gorp and Manok brought a new dimension to her life. Anod was simply not accustomed to paying much attention to the little actions and activities of life.

The cool, night air caressed her face drawing out the worries and concerns of her immediate existence. The strange feeling of the uneven, hard ground, the intoxicating smell of the soil beneath her and the gentle fragrances of the forest around her contributed to her interlude.

"Anod, did you hear me?"

"No, I suppose I did not. My mind must have been on other things."

"For a moment there, I thought you had fallen asleep. Anyway, I was asking you what you see looking up at the stars."

"Home. I was born a warrior. I am an instrument for the protection of the Society. My home is among the stars. It is the only home I have known." Anod wanted to say more, but decided against it. The struggle within her continued unabated.

"Don't you feel a kinship with Earth?"

"Yes, I do. However, I have only seen Earth through the scene wall or the holographic chamber. I have never experienced the real, the actual, stimulation of my senses by Earth as I have here on Beta."

"I understand what you mean," Nick responded. He paused staring at the stars and inhaled deeply. "There is a common ground to our experience. You have chosen to do so out of a sense of duty. I have been consigned to the same choice by the conflict of my ancestors. My grandfather was the last of our clan to have stood on the planet Earth."

The term, grandfather, was not familiar to Anod. She surmised the reference applied to Nick's ancestors. "Do you regret your fate, Nick?"

"In some ways, yes. In other ways, no. I know Earth is a part of my past and for that reason, I do regret our banishment. On the other hand, my generation and my son's generation have never known Earth, so it is hard to miss what you do not know." He paused for a moment to collect his words. "This place is home now. I have no desire to leave this planet."

"Do the other citizens of Beta feel the same?"

"Most do, although I have not talked to all of our citizens. Most of us share the acceptance of our fate and all of us love this planet."

The genuine pleasure in his voice did not go unnoticed by Anod. There was an air of pride in the delivery of his words. "That is a good feeling to have, Nick," Anod responded. She wondered about her own feelings. The choice of words she might use to describe Saranon, or the other outposts of her life, would not have quite the same ring to them as the words of Nick SanGiocomo.

The quiet moment allowed Anod to concentrate on another scan of the night sky. Her inability to spatially orient herself with the stars gave her an unsettled, off-balance feeling deep within her soul. The lack of navigational resolution within her ordered mind was not a common state for the Kartog warrior.

Low on the horizon, off to the right, Anod detected an object moving out of plane with the stars. It was quite faint and not particularly distinguishable. In a few more minutes, she would be able to determine the track of the object.

"There," she said pointing to the item of interest. "Do you see that object?"

Nick sat up in hopes of improving his ability to acquire the whatever-it-was thing. Anod could see him shaking his head as he continued his search. "I don't see anything other than stars. Where is it again?"

"Right there." She pointed carefully. The track was clear. It would continue to pass to the right of them, south of their location. "That object may be the Yorax battlecruiser in an equatorial orbit."

"My eyes are still near perfect, and yet, I see nothing," Nick said.

"Yes, that's what it is. I can pick out the shape now. There is only one, so far, and that is a good sign."

Nick ignored the search for the Yorax spacecraft to look at his quest. "Anod, would you allow me to test your eyesight and your other senses, tomorrow?"

"Why?"

"It would appear that you have extraordinary vision. Is this common for your people?"

"Extraordinary implies a level above a known standard. In that sense, no, I have normal vision as far as I know. My visual acuity is similar to my fellow warriors. We certainly do not think of it as extraordinary." Now, Anod's curiosity began to twitch.

"Maybe," he paused. "However, relative to our vision, it does seem to be extraordinary. Would you mind if I tested you?"

"Not at all, Nick. I would be interested to know what you think is extraordinary."

"Thank you. We'll test you tomorrow, or maybe it's today. Are you ready to get some sleep before the light returns?"

The elder man never did indicate he saw the Yorax craft and didn't seem to care. It was now out of sight, anyway.

"Yes, now that you mention it, I guess I am ready to get some rest."

Nick slowly rose to his feet.

Anod noticed a little more pain in her left leg probably due to her overexertion, inactivity and the chill of the night air. Nick offered his hand to assist her.

After a few steps, the muscles and joints began to loosen up and the dull pain began to diminish. The return to the cave was uneventful.

Bradley was not in the rooms they passed through. He is probably asleep in another room somewhere, Anod said to herself. She had to come to grips with his hostility and accept Nick's request for tolerance. The reality did not make her feel any better about the situation. She trusted Nick for some reason and with that trust the warrior in her could relax.

Chapter 6

Anod awakened to the sounds of activity in the next room. Presumably, it was Nick although it could be Bradley. The prospect of the latter did not fill Anod with joyous anticipation.

Sitting on the edge of the bed, Anod ran her hands over every portion of her skin to survey the lingering damage. Most of her body functioned properly although her recovery was not complete. The texture of her skin and the firmness of her muscles were returning. Residual pain, albeit nearly imperceptible, was still present in several of her more damaged extremities. A few more days and some good exercise would vanquish the remnants of her ambush to the past, she told herself.

Bending and stretching her lean, rangy body brought a smile to her face and soul. The movement felt good as a reminder that she was very much alive. She moved through an elaborate series of motions to stress each joint and stretch each muscle. Anod moved her statuesque, unadorned and unencumbered body through a series of intricate motions of a well-ordered traditional martial exercise. Anod always derived pleasure and personal satisfaction from the freedom of her morning exercise.

Despite the slow, deliberate movements, the glistening beads of sweat across her entire body were visual confirmation of the success of her callisthenics. The sensations of the descending perspiration tickled and tingled adding to the invigoration. Anod always enjoyed the wetness and slipperiness of her body during strenuous exertion.

Anod purposefully took extra time in the warm spray of the shower to allow the heat to penetrate deep into her muscles and joints. The therapeutic value had been quickly realized and was now fully utilized. The warmth of the water and the beating rhythm of the coarse spray removed the remaining pain. She was actually beginning to feel good.

The process of dressing took a little additional time in the mood of the moment. As she dressed, Anod listened intently to the sounds from the adjoining room.

There was no talking. The sequences of sound seemed to confirm the estimation of only one person present. The question in Anod's thoughts was one of identity. Was it Nick preparing the first meal, or Bradley performing some other task?

Having completed her dressing task, Anod took a deep breath to cleanse her lungs. She felt the surge of oxygen rush through her body. Confrontation was not what she needed nor wanted to begin a new day. However, postponement was an unproductive abstention of life. Anod walked into the food preparation room.

Nick. It was Nick. She recognized his speckled gray hair instantly.

"Good morning, Nick," she said with the enthusiasm of a fresh beginning and released apprehension.

A shudder through his body demonstrated his surprise. He turned quickly to face Anod. "Oh, you startled me," he said as he took a deep breath to ease his own tension. "Good morning to you, Anod."

"I suppose I should learn to contain my excitement early in the day."

"No, I just wasn't listening to the sounds around me. My mind was on other thoughts."

"What were you thinking about, if I might ask?"

"You."

"What about me?"

"I imagine the best way to state this is," he paused as if he needed to choose his words carefully, "the mystery that surrounds you."

Anod laughed loudly and from deep within her. "I am not mysterious. I'm simply human," she responded with amusement.

"Yes, you are human. However, you are most definitely mysterious. There are so many things that I don't understand and want to know."

The definite and obvious course of this conversation turned Anod's mood. "Where is Bradley?"

"He rose before both of us and left. He should return at any moment," Nick answered. He recognized the change immediately. "I won't bother you with all my questions until you're ready."

"I must understand my situation, Nick. You have been most gracious and caring. I wonder if these traits are limited to you, or do the other inhabitants share them? You have made me feel welcome from the beginning."

"Bradley will warm up to you, as I said yesterday. I am sorry his attitude has made you feel so uncomfortable."

"The environment is not yours to apologize for, Nick. It is what it is. I appreciate your thoughts, though."

"Our population is kind and caring with a reasonable measure of suspicion, Anod. Our ancestors were banished from Earth because of their beliefs and resistance to the direction of the world order. We try to live in peace with all creatures great and small from all corners of the galaxy."

"How do you think they will feel when they learn of my presence?"

"First, there will be some resentment toward me for harboring you without the consent of the people and subjecting our population to the Yorax intrusion. Secondly, they will be skeptical of your purpose for being here and your intentions."

"I guess that's even more of a reason for me to leave as soon as possible."

"No! That is not the message I am trying to send. You are welcomed here and you will be welcomed by the others once they understand the situation."

"Maybe?"

"It is my opinion that the sooner we introduce you, the sooner we will get passed our inherent suspicion."

"I will trust your judgment, once more, Nick."

"Good," he responded quickly and emphatically.

It was apparent he wanted to complete his meal preparations without words. The task did not take long.

"Are you ready for some good food?" he asked.

"Yes, I am," Anod smiled.

There did not appear to be any desire on Nick's part to wait for Bradley to join them. The supposition could mean several things although it was odd considering his earlier comment that his son was expected momentarily. Anod considered whether she should let it pass.

"Isn't Bradley going to join us?" she asked.

"I have no idea. He comes and goes as he pleases. He left a note that indicated that he would be here for early meal. However, I have learned after many years that it is not wise to hold your life waiting for him."

Anod laughed softly at the image of Nick's life stopping cold as he waited for his son. They both laughed although not for the same reason.

Their relationship was slowly beginning to evolve and settle into a level of understanding and implicit communication. In several ways, Nick reminded her of Colonel Zortev whom she had served for most of her professional life. There was a quiet, humble wisdom associated with this elder man.

"Would you mind if I examined your senses?" he asked.

"What kind of tests do you want to do?"

"They are simple, non-intrusive techniques to establish the performance of your physiological sensory capability."

"No, I don't have any objections."

"Good. Let's go into the other room," he said as he walked into Anod's room.

Nick removed several pieces of equipment from various cabinets throughout the room. The unknown items triggered Anod's voracious curiosity. She watched Nick intently as he prepared his test equipment. The purpose and operation of most of the tools were not readily apparent.

The instructions from Nick were simply and direct. The process of testing usually became evident with a cursory visual survey of the apparatus along with the directions from Nick. A distant scientific intercourse between them ensued as the testing proceeded. The elder man provided neither verbal nor non-verbal indications of the progress, or Anod's performance against the test standards. The entire battery of tests took slightly more than 95 minutes to complete and involved each human sense individually, or in combination. The testing process was fascinating to Anod since she had never been tested in this manner before.

The data were fed through a series of cables into a computer processor of some type. Nick sat intently watching the display lights wink at him. Even the characteristics of the computer technology used on Beta were an additional element of interest to Anod. She had never seen a small stand-alone processor like Nick's.

Her attention alternated between the concentration illustrated across Nick's face and reflected in his eyes to the methodical processing of the computer. His intensity or anticipation was at a level similar to the focus he demonstrated while he was using the rockphone during the Yorax search of the cave. There was a certain amount of admiration appropriate for this elder scientist.

The muffled whirr of a motor internal to the computer produced a small strip of paper with a tabulated series of words and numbers.

"Just as I thought," Nick said more to himself than Anod.

The Kartog Guards warrior waited without interfering in his thought process. The longer she waited for Nick to complete his analysis or interpretation, the more her curiosity grew. His facial expression changed several times in conjunction with various groans or grumbles.

"Yes, indeed, Miss Anod, you are an extraordinary human being as I suspected."

"What do you mean?"

"Let me explain these results, this way," he said holding up the strip of paper. "As a scientist for nearly 60 years, I have never seen human sensory performance at these levels. Not even close, I might add."

"What did you find?"

"Every one of your physical senses, sight, hearing, smell, and probably taste and touch, has an unprecedented range and sensitivity. In a couple of areas, you are off the scale." Nick stopped to look at the strip of paper again. "In fact, if I did not know otherwise, I would not recognize these test results as human."

Nick looked directly into Anod's eyes as if to determine her reaction, or search for a confirmation of his findings.

"I don't know what to say," Anod finally responded.

"Well, let me ask you something. Are all of your colleagues similarly equipped?"

It was Anod's turn to search his dark eyes for an indication of his intent. Nick's reference to her as if she was an android puzzled her. Was she losing his trust? Was he becoming more suspicious of her? The questions did not have answers in his eyes.

"Why would you ask the question that way? I am not equipped with anything. You have seen my body, my bones, my blood and my flesh. I am not an android. I am a human being, a simple representative of the human species."

"You may be human, Anod, but you are definitely not simple."

She did not know where this conversation was headed. Her defenses were coming back up. There was a subtle, threatening tone to his words. The reality of her isolation rushed back into her consciousness.

"Tell me, Nick, what is human?"

The expression on Nick's face changed instantly as if his memory had been washed away. "What?"

"What makes someone human?"

The question must have made him think about a subject that had previously been intuitive and unquestioned. "I've never thought about it." He stopped to consider his words. "There must be limits."

"Like what? What makes us human?" Anod repeated.

"Logic. Anatomy. Written communications." Nick paused to

think and Anod gave him the time. "Imagination. Artistic creation. Maybe face-to-face sexual intercourse. I don't really know."

Anod felt a strong need for fresh air, or at least to extricate herself from this uncomfortable situation. She walked toward the door without saying a word to Nick, or looking back at him.

"Where are you going?" Nick asked to her retreating figure.

There was no answer and no hesitation in Anod's movement.

"Anod, please, I meant no harm."

The sounds behind her indicated that the elder man was not following her. She wanted some time alone. Maybe he sensed her need and was willing to comply.

Once outside, the warmth from the parent star combined with the cool, fresh fragrances of the morning air quickly brought an inner calm. Small, puffy clouds moved gracefully across the sky with their unusual spectrum of colors. There was coherence to the diffraction of light by the moisture in the small cloud. The array of changing colors added a delightful complement to the shades of green and brown that was the trees and hills of this region.

Anod did not appreciate the continued close scrutiny. Her physiological characteristics were normal for Earth, the Society and Saranon. These people were descendants of the same ancestors. Why was she so different from them? Why were they so preoccupied with her differences?

The past. The key was the past. Anod searched her memory for bits of related information. There was a reason for the differences. What was it about the Society that was so much different from the organization and functioning of the population of Beta?

Life was certainly more automated within the confines of her previous existence. Humans did what they were good at. Computers and androids did what they were good at. It was a true synergistic relationship, each entity complementing and often amplifying the capabilities of the other. The people of Beta appeared to utilize very little equipment, tools, computers or other enhancements. An obvious dissimilarity that by itself was not a particularly enlightening reality. There had to be something else, something much more dramatic.

Her physiological performance was different. She still did not know how disparate the characteristics were. Nick's reaction to the test results certainly indicated that she was different from them. Anod fought within herself with the facts and perceptions flashing through her thoughts.

She was human just as they were, but she was different. She looked the same although she was not the same. What was it about her past that made her uniquely different from Nick and Bradley?

The sound of a single approaching person truncated the analysis of her past. This time she did not have the urge to hide or run. With her leg free of the restraints of the casing, Anod felt more able to deal with an intruder. She surveyed the entire area for approaches, avenues of egress, should they be needed, and other indicators that would establish her situation. Her confidence was strong as she waited for the visitor. One person eliminated the possibility of the Yorax. They never travelled alone.

Out of the forest, she saw Bradley's head crest over the lip of the rise. He was not the face she wanted to see right now, but she felt more on neutral ground. The smile on his face was a marked contrast to the scowl he displayed yesterday.

"Good morning, Miss Anod," Bradley said with a light, airy voice.

A smile and a pleasant greeting. Why was Bradley so different this morning? "Good morning to you, Bradley," she responded.

"Is my father inside?"

"Yes."

"Very good," he said as he continued into the cave.

Anod watched Nick's son disappear into the cave. A strange cloud of doubt or suspicion, Anod was not sure which it was, descended upon her. The two men had seemingly switched rolls. One was congenial while the other was abrasive. With Bradley entering the cave presumably to talk with his father, Anod wondered if Nick's caustic doubts would affect Bradley's current bright nature.

A quick self-reminder flashed to her. There was no sense worrying about things you can't control. The need to change her condition was becoming strong. She was not accustomed to and did not like being dependent on others she did not know, especially infidels that had been exiled from Earth many years ago.

The neutral ground of space was where she needed to be. Flying a Kartog fighter a short distance from this star system would do the trick, at least to broadcast an emergency distress message and defend herself against an inevitable Yorax response. Time was all she needed. A Society starship would be quickly diverted to her rescue. In fact, knowing Colonel Zortev, there were probably two or three starships searching for her.

"Anod, we really must talk," Nick shouted from the entrance to the cave some 20 meters behind her.

She turned to see both Nick and Bradley standing side by side. The expressions on their faces were virtually identical, passive concentration.

Well, Nick's mood must have won out, she told herself. There were not many options available to her at this particular point in time.

"I know I have been a burden to you since my arrival," Anod said walking toward them. "If you can provide me with a spacecraft, I will be out of your way. Once I return to the Society, I will ensure that you are adequately compensated for your protection of me during my recovery."

Nick chortled a loud and deep laugh. Bradley remained stoic.

"First, we have no spacecraft. Secondly, you are not a burden upon us. And thirdly, we don't want you to leave."

Anod's mood placed a different color on his words. She stood facing them at the entrance to the cave. "Do you mean that I am not free to leave?" she asked with some force. She did not want to seem threatening, however she did want the two men to feel her strength.

"No. No. You are perfectly free to leave, if any of us could figure out how to make it so. Unfortunately, you are suffering the same fate our people have suffered for so many years. Anod, you have been and you will remain our guest. As such, you are free to leave whenever the means for your departure becomes available."

"Thank you."

"Now, we still need to talk. We need to know about who you are and what your presence means to us. Bradley is fairly certain that the Yorax will return. Their next visit may not be so pleasant."

"I would agree with that assessment."

"Can we go inside and talk?" Bradley asked.

"If you don't mind, I would prefer to talk in the fresh air in the shade of a tree," she answered gesturing toward a large, leafy tree.

"So be it," Bradley responded. "I'll get us something to sit on." He looked around. Several segments of tree trunks used for various purposes were scattered around the clearing. Bradley lifted each stump to carry it into the shade of the large tree. His physical strength was evident as he carried the heavy stumps.

With three makeshift stools arranged in a reasonable triangle, Nick motioned for each of them to take a seat. The cool of the shade felt so good to Anod.

It would be Nick who would initiate the discussion. He looked at the dirt in front of him and opened his mouth as if to speak, but no words came out. Having considered the words he wanted to say, he raised his right hand and spoke.

"I would like to begin by saying that we are not your enemy. We are trying to help you as well as protect our people and ourselves. I must add that my scientific curiosity is almost unrestrained. You are a fascinating person whom we would very much like to know better."

Anod acknowledged Nick's statement with a simple nod of her head.

"Let's start from the elementary and work out," Nick continued.

Another simple nod of agreement.

"The test results establish unequivocally that you have extraordinary sensory performance, far beyond anything we have seen or heard of. Do you know why your sensory performance is superior to ours?"

Both men looked at her intently. Anod felt the concentration and focus on her. Were they trying to observe some strange metamorphosis once the facade was removed? They waited patiently for her answer.

"I'm not sure I can explain it properly." Anod hesitated to select the words she wanted to use. Earlier reactions by both Nick and Bradley elicited a certain measure of caution. "I am a genetically engineered or modified clone of my predecessor."

Neither man spoke. Several glances from her to each other passed quickly between them.

"Then, you meant bred as you said yesterday?" Bradley asked.

"Yes."

"Oh my God. I don't believe it. What has our species come to? What will we become?" Nick spoke more to himself than to Anod and his son.

Bradley simply stared at Anod. His expression had turned stone cold and did not change, not even for an eye blink. It was as if he was staring down a wild animal not daring to flinch or look away.

Nick was more animated with his fidgeting and soft mumbling to himself.

Anod was having a difficult time understanding the reaction of the two men to her pronouncement. She did not feel different from them. She possessed the same human characteristics and features. Why were they responding in this manner, she asked herself?

Finally, the scientist in Nick prevailed over the emotional. He returned to the rational, open logic of this avocation.

"You said genetically engineered," he said and waited for a confirmation from Anod. "Does that mean your genetic map was cloned from a predecessor, as you say, and altered in the process?"

The reluctance to answer any more questions along this line was strengthened by her concern for their potential reaction. However, Anod decided to continue since she did not feel particularly threatened although she did feel very alone.

"Essentially, that is correct," she responded.

"You have no mother or father?" asked Bradley.

"If by, mother, you mean someone who nurtured me through youth, my mother, as you call it, is the Society. It has provided everything for me and I serve in recognition of that gift."

"The society, as you call it, cannot be a mother," Bradley said with force and conviction, and some apparent resentment to her choice of words.

Anod recognized immediately the emotional facet to this topic, although she did not understand why it was so emotional. "What is a mother to you, if I may ask?"

"A mother is someone who gives birth to you, nurtures you as you grow and supports you in life," Bradley responded with no less emotion although more controlled and subdued.

"What is birth?" Anod asked innocently.

"I don't believe this," Bradley barked in disgust as he shook his head.

"We owe you an explanation, Anod. However, I must know a few more details if you don't mind." Nick waited for Anod to accept. "I'm not sure how to approach this, so I'll simply jump in. I have an understanding of the principles involved, but I do not understand how this can be done. Can you tell me how the process is done?"

"It is actually quite simple. An extraction of a clean deoxyribonucleic acid string, our genetic blueprint, is analyzed, assessed and, where appropriate, altered through a series of selective enzymatic processes to produce the desired results. The medical technicians are able to correct damage or errors and enhance characteristics."

"Incredible. Absolutely incredible." Nick paused for a moment. "Aren't offspring produced naturally?"

"I'm not sure what you mean. I was produced by a very natural process."

Bradley grunted his repugnance, rose from his stump and walked to the opposite end of the clearing. His back remained toward them.

The father watched his son as if to assess his mood. He turned his attention back to his guest. "Within our culture, offspring or children are produced by a sexual coupling of a man and a woman. The male fertilizes the egg produced by the female. The woman gestates the child in her womb for a period of about 9 months, then gives birth to the child. It is the physiologically as well as biologically natural process."

"I am not familiar with that process. In the Society, intimate contact between humans is forbidden."

"Oh my God. What have we become, indeed?" gasped Nick.

The air of aversion bothered Anod. In a small way, she felt ashamed. The reactions, comments, questions and gestures of both men conveyed their inability to accept Anod's heritage. The emotion slowly began to generate a resistance and defiance within her. They did not understand her or the Society. Why were they responding in this manner? Why was her background so upsetting to them?

Nick was the first to speak. "Why is sex forbidden? What is your society trying to accomplish with that approach?"

"It is the belief of the elders, our populace and the Supreme Council that personal intimacy is a distraction of creative energy and a destructive force within a community."

"Why do you believe that?"

"The order of the Society says that destructive emotions such as jealousy, envy, attractive desire, lust and deceit are born in intimate activity. Destructive emotions deplete the creative capacity of a civilization."

"We have normal sexual activity within our society and I don't think it is destructive. Sexual or physical communication between a man and a woman is one of the major elements that bond families together," Nick said.

"How do you deal with the destructive forces of personal intimacy?" Anod asked.

"We try to establish a positive social environment through traditional marriage, the bonding of a man and a woman, and strict moral standards which discourage aberrations. However, it is an accepted price to pay. All freedoms have a price," Nick responded.

"An interesting justification for your position. The technical performance of the Society is certainly an implicit substantiation of our system."

"Yes, I suppose it is," Nick said.

The perceived impasse halted the conversation for a moment while Anod and Nick looked into to each other's eyes partly to judge sincerity and also to consider the next words each would say.

Bradley broke the stall. Anod look over her shoulder as the younger man walked back toward the triangle of stumps.

"You are telling us that you are forbidden to touch another human being," Bradley said with a strange combination of emphatic statement and complex interrogative.

"No, that is not what I am saying. We are not forbidden to touch another human in the sense of a hug or handshake. The practice of intimate contact is simply not acceptable," Anod answered.

"What kind of world is this?"

"I would like to return to the scientific, if we may," Nick interjected. "How far do your doctors and scientists think they can take this genetic improvement process?"

"Again, I am not a medical technician, however it is my understanding that we are near the limits. The levels of improvement with successive generations have been decreasing. We are in a period where we are adjusting to the changes."

"What do you mean by that, Anod?" Nick's instinctive curiosity was fully involved, again.

"Some of our people are having difficulty accepting the higher sensory performance. They cannot shut off their auditory receptors when they want quiet, for example."

"Yes, you're right," Bradley acknowledged although he had no way to truly know the accuracy of Anod's statement. "I hadn't thought about that part of the problem. Well, then, how are you able to do it?"

"My capabilities are not always switchable, but I have learned to ignore some of the inputs. Selective listening as an example."

"Does everyone get these enhancements?" Bradley asked.

"No. Only the chosen are enhanced." Anod wanted to be honest, and yet she knew her answer was going to produce an adverse reaction. She was right.

"The chosen?" Bradley asked with a sneer in his voice and on his face.

"Who are the chosen?" Nick asked trying to bring some calm to the conversation.

"I'm not sure we should continue this discussion. The changes that have occurred on Earth may not be acceptable to you."

"You are right there," Bradley quickly responded.

"That may be so, Anod, however, it does not change our desire to learn, nor our attempts to understand," Nick added.

A hesitation in responding provided Anod some time to think about her answer. "The chosen are a small segment of the population who are selected by the elders as contributors to the Society as a whole."

"How small of a segment are these chosen, as you call them?" Bradley asked in a more controlled and inquisitive tone.

"About five percent."

"FIVE PERCENT," Bradley shouted at her.

"Yes."

"What does the remainder of the population do?" Bradley asked without the anger of a moment earlier although the touch of revulsion was quite evident.

"The populace does what ever they want to do."

"That doesn't make sense!" Bradley said with a strong tone. "Do you mean they do whatever tasks they want?"

"No. I mean they do whatever they want. If they want to do nothing, they do nothing. If they want to sail the ocean, they sail the ocean."

"Do they work?"

"No."

"How does the Society afford to pay for whatever they want?" Bradley asked with his perpetuated tone of disgust.

"If you mean how are they allowed to follow their desires, it is simply the way of life for the populace."

"I still don't understand," Bradley admitted with a decidedly more inquisitive voice. "Let me see if I can state this in a different way. The majority of your population does not have to work to earn money in order to afford the pleasures they desire."

"You are correct, I believe. First, we don't have money. Second, they do not have to pay for anything."

"This is incredible. You are saying five percent of the population supports the whims of the remainder of your people."

"Correct," Anod responded.

"I can't imagine how that must work," Nick said.

The two men seemed to drift off into their own thoughts as they considered the information Anod provided.

The silence of the moment allowed Anod to consider other changes to their environment. A deep breath of the clean, fresh air relieved some of the growing tension within her.

The rotation of the planet brought the light from the θ27 star more directly upon them. Anod was beginning to get uncomfortably warm. She rose to walk toward the edge of the forest. The robust smell of the tree bark, the dirt under her feet and the myriad of odors on the wind brought further relaxation to the Kartog warrior.

Anod turned to find the two men still in a near trance lost in their own thoughts. "Can we move over to this shady area?" she asked.

Neither man responded. There was no indication either father or son heard her question. Anod waited patiently diverting her attention to several birds performing intricate aerobatic maneuvers over an adjacent outcropping of rocks about 200 meters from Nick's cave.

Bradley was the first to move. The younger man turned to look at Anod. "Certainly. I'll move the stumps," he said.

At least, he could hear me, Anod said to herself.

Bradley lifted his stump and walked toward her. Anod passed him after deciding that she could move her own stump.

"That's OK, Anod, I'll move your stump," he said pleasantly.

Anod did not respond to his offer. She squatted to wrap her arms around the large stump. A quick evaluation of the weight confirmed her visual assessment. The stump would be near her physical lift limits. Without considering her recent injuries, Anod groaned aloud as she lifted the stump. This thing must weigh more than 60 kilograms she told herself. She moved slowly toward the shady area.

"I would have moved that for you, Anod," Bradley said as he approached her.

"Thank you, Bradley," she groaned under the strain. "This is good exercise for me." Anod felt better saying it, although she knew the statement to be less than the absolute truth.

Through her peripheral vision, she saw Bradley tap on his father's shoulder to break his concentration. A gentle hand under his arm helped him rise to his feet. Bradley moved Nick's stump as well. The new spot looked as if it would provide sufficient protection from the heat of the star until the setting time. Anod carefully lowered her stump to the ground near the trunk of a large conifer tree with expansive branches.

The strain on her body from the weight of the stump was quite apparent. She was reasonably confident that she did not damage anything although the muscle fatigue was undeniable. Anod placed her hands on her hips, forced her elbows and shoulder as far back as she could and took a long, deep breath. Holding the air in her lungs, she forced the refreshing air deeper into her lungs. The exhalation brought the expected relief from some of the stress.

Nick returned to a seated position on his stump without the slightest consideration for Bradley's effort on his behalf. His son did not appear to object.

Anod realized the impact her revelations were having on the two men, these descendants of banished humans. There was also recognition on her part of the lack of knowledge she had of these people. The history journals referred to the split of the people of Earth due to cultural differences. Unfortunately, the information relative to this segment of the human species was not extensive. There was no discussion in the journals of the underlying motivations for the split or the background societal stimuli leading up to the split.

Meandering among the trees, Bradley chose to consider his thoughts in a different manner than his father. Nick was the first to return to the conversation.

"What you have told us is staggering to our way of thinking. The implications of these changes are virtually unimaginable," Nick confided.

"Your assessment is understandable considering your isolation from the evolutionary changes which have occurred. Haven't you heard any news of Earth since your split from the Society nearly 200 years ago?" Anod asked.

"There have been very few contacts. The traders that occasionally arrive are fringe characters that like their distance from politics, people and events. To my knowledge, you are the only inhabitant of Earth we have had contact with in my life time."

"That is unfortunate," Anod responded with a calm, subdued voice.

"I suppose. However, we are happy people. We like how our culture has maintained itself."

"The attractions of your way of life are understandable."

"The changes on Earth help me appreciate the reasons for our departure. My wildest imagination could not have provided any anticipation for what you have told us," Nick said.

The detachment of Bradley from the conversation was certainly noticeable. He would disappear into the forest for short periods of time until his wandering brought him back into view. Anod could not comprehend the depth of his turmoil. She had simply spoken words of truth and they were just that – words. The minuscule description of the structure of civilization on Earth presented no threat to these people. Why were they so troubled?

"Why is the information I have given you so difficult for you and Bradley to accept?" Anod asked.

"It is not the information that is hard to accept, it is the implications of that information," Nick responded.

"What do you mean?"

"The elders, whom I presume are your leaders, have decided to alter the natural course of life. In essence, they are tampering with nature." Nick had a stern, determined expression on his face and defiance in his eyes.

"How is our process different from utilizing medicines to eliminate diseases, or using a time warp matrix to alter the time-space continuum?"

"We are talking about living human beings. There is a difference. I'm not sure I can articulate the delicate difference, but there is a difference nonetheless."

Anod evaluated his words although she did not recognize the differences. The society she described was familiar and acceptable to her. She was content and satisfied with her life and had no reason to question the basis of her community. Even, the populace was content, everyone seemed to be quite happy and there was virtually no crime, no crime of any type. The solutions to perennial dilemmas facing complex organizations of free people appeared to be successful and beneficial. Of course, her feelings were based on an inherently limited amount of information. She had never set foot upon the soil of Earth.

"I cannot argue the point since it is a matter of conjecture and supposition," Anod finally answered.

"We shall let it lie, then."

Bradley returned to the triangle of stump stools with purpose in his eyes. He sat down with his back as straight as a rod, his feet and knees spread wide, one hand on his left knee and the other raised pointing toward her.

"You may have extraordinary senses, Anod, but you have no spirit, no emotions. You are simply one step short of a machine," Bradley expounded with some force.

The verbal onslaught by her persistent nemesis did not surprise her anymore. The Kartog Guards warrior had become accustomed to his antagonism. There was an undeniable twinge of resentment toward his lack of understanding and appreciation. None of those emotions had any place within the context of these discussions. Anod chose to ignore Bradley's statement. She turned her attention to Nick who remained contemplative.

"What have you got to say for yourself?" Bradley continued.

"There is no purposeful response," she said simply.

"Let me ask you this, what is the purpose of the majority of your population? Why do they exist, if they contribute nothing?" Bradley asked.

"Their purpose is to enjoy life. They are perfectly content in that roll. The Society asks nothing of them and expects nothing in return."

"That is no way to live a life, without purpose. Pleasure is not purpose," Bradley stated.

"Let's change the subject, please," Nick interjected. "I'd like to return to the scientific line of discussion."

Bradley turned away from his father and their guest. Anod nodded her head in agreement. Nick clasped his hands with his elbows on his knees as he leaned toward Anod.

"You stated earlier that you are a clone from a predecessor and that you were started from elemental DNA."

Anod nodded again.

"From the molecular level, how were you matured? How did you grow? Were you placed in a surrogate or some other medium?"

"The gestation process is actually quite simple. An artificial womb in created and suspended in amniotic fluid. All nutritive and neurological functions are completely provided. The growth process is completely and continuously monitored for potential complications although they are extremely rare."

"This may seem a bit foolish, but how are you born? How do you make the transition to breathing air and self-sufficiency?" Nick asked.

"When gestation is complete, as determine by a complex set of biological parameters, the infant is simply removed from the sac. Normal life functions are initiated and maturation continues."

"You say that so matter of factly, Anod. Who raises you? Who nurtures you? Who teaches you?"

"Our early growth is supervised by an android specifically configured for each individual," Anod responded.

"An android!" Bradley shouted. "An android! How can a machine raise a human being properly? This is insane, absolutely, pathologically insane."

Anod maintained her calm, controlled demeanor. "Actually, it is quite logical. My android was with me from my beginning until he perished in the explosion. Androids are consistent, dependable, faithful, loyal and ever watchful. Gorp, my android, was a good friend, a confidant. He was always there to help when I needed him. Our androids are meticulous teachers, patient and persevering. If you did not know they were machines or didn't watch them too closely, you would not know they were androids."

The younger man's discomfort with Anod's cultural background was still quite apparent. He could only shake his head in disbelief and mumble unintelligible words.

"Fascinating," Nick said aloud. "Thoroughly and unequivocally fascinating." His eyes were directly on Anod, however he was not talking to her.

Anod felt a peculiar sensation as if she was a small insect under the bright light of a microscope. During her entire life, she had never been exposed to unbridled curiosity. Most of the questions were certainly logical although the reactions of the two Betans were puzzling. The provocative facet to these discussions was the questions she was beginning to ask herself. It was an interesting feeling even though she was not accustomed to or appreciative of the singular focus and persistent scrutiny of these two citizens of Beta.

The conversation seemed to be driving Nick and Bradley deeper into their own thoughts. Their internal analyses of the information presented to them were taking more and more concentration. Nick was the first to return to Anod.

"What you have said is, you are grown artificially as a clone and raised to adulthood by an android. You have not suckled nor been touched by a mother, a human being who cared for you."

It was not clear to Anod whether Nick was making a statement to her trying to elicit a response, or simply talking aloud. Somewhat in her own defense, since it was the prevalent emotion, she decided on the former assessment.

"In general, you are correct. I'm not sure what suckle means with respect to human beings. It is not a word I am familiar. However, we are not forbidden to touch other humans and we are touched. It is more in friendship that we touch than any other basis."

"Let me sort through this. First, suckle is how a newborn infant child feeds at the breast of its mother. We feel quite strongly that it is an essential process of human growth and maturation. Second, we also feel physical contact between humans, from simple to intimate, is intrinsic to proper development." Nick's tone was calm and confident – almost soothing.

"With that explanation, I will say you are correct in your assessment. To the best of my knowledge, I did not suckle at a woman's breast, although I think I am an example that it is not an essential element of growth."

"Point taken. I do not agree that a lack of human contact during development is acceptable, but point taken." He paused to gather his words. "My thoughts are so intertwined, I am having difficulty deciding where to start."

Anod waited for her host.

The light of θ27 was beginning to fade. Virtually the entire daylight period had been spent in these discussions. The word, inquisition, popped into Anod's thoughts although the conversation was certainly not adversarial or deleterious.

Bradley remained lost in his own thoughts. There were some slight signs that he was aware of the conversation going on around him. He chose to remain within himself and not participate.

While she waited admiring the intricate colors of the fading light against the clouds above, Anod considered her own questions. Questions that she did not have answers to.

Why were these people so sensitive to the process of growth on Earth? Why do they find my life so revolting? Anod tried to recall some of the memories of her youth. The remembrance was good, pleasant and comfortable. There was nothing to be ashamed of as they were implicitly communicating. Her youth was rich and rewarding with stimulating discussions, experiences and events. Why do they object? It simply did not make sense.

The brief descriptions the two men provided certainly did not convey a better culture or way of life. Beta was definitely not utopia although there were attractions. The pleasure of the environment in all its glory was a refreshing, enjoyable element of this place.

The light of distant stars was slowly burning through the dimming atmosphere. The two men were still lost in thought. Anod could only guess about the process of consideration that continued within them. The response of her body to insufficient nourishment was undeniable. The temperature of the cooling atmosphere was equally incontrovertible.

"Excuse me, Nick and Bradley," she waited for their eyes to indicate attention. "We are in the night period and we have also not eaten since the dawn. Shall we return to the cave? I would like to feed my body."

Neither man responded at first. There was an immediate question, Anod asked herself, whether they actually heard what she said. Nick was the first to react.

"You are absolutely correct, Anod. I lost track of time. Let us get something to eat." He turned to his son. "Are you agreed, Bradley?" The younger man's responses were characteristic of a person rebounding from a trance. Slow steps of awareness became obvious in the diminishing light.

"Certainly. Yes. Let's go in," Bradley said finally.

With that answer, all three people rose from their stumps to walk into the cave. No words passed between them. Anod still could not understand why these two distant relatives of Earth were having such apparent difficulty accepting life on the planet as it was now. The purposeful logic and order to life seemed so easy to accept despite the fact it was her heritage, not theirs.

The words that passed between them for the remainder of the evening were simple, not provocative, and ordinary expressions of hospitality. The mood of the two men was slowly returning to the jovial, lighter side. A sense of fun was returning to the conversation.

Nick and Bradley eventually drifted into a conversation of routine domestic matters. At first, the words were interesting from the perspective of a limited view of local activities. The purpose and direction were not evident and Anod soon lost her curiosity.

"Thank you, Nick, for another delicious meal. Now, if you both will excuse me, I would like to enter a sleep period," Anod said.

"Certainly," Bradley responded.

"Yes, absolutely. You are quite welcome, Anod," Nick stated. "I would like to thank you for talking to us. We may not show much gratitude, however we are grateful. We also may not agree with the changes on Earth, but we appreciate your candor and openness."

"I agree," Bradley added.

"You are quite welcome," Anod answered. There was no desire to continue the questions. "I will see you in the morning."

"Have a good night sleep," Bradley said.

His cordiality was somewhat baffling to Anod considering the reactions the younger man displayed most of the day. She was appreciative nonetheless.

"Thank you," she acknowledged.

Anod rose from the table and departed to her adjoining room. She partially closed the door behind her, not thinking it might be necessary to close it entirely.

The privacy of her separate room brought a relaxation she had not felt until her arrival on this planet. In all her years with Zitger and Zarrod, as well as others, Anod had never experienced this growing need to be alone. The intense questions and conversation of the last few days were enervating in a primitive way although they were forcing her toward her own contemplation.

The attraction of a hot shower added to her feelings of relief. This was her time. The process of removing the weight of her clothing had its own element of relief. All the periods of personal time with her Guard comrades never elicited this response. The conflict was frustrating and yet invigorating. Full of life, one might say.

A short knock on the door drew her back from the freedom of her own thoughts.

"Yes," Anod acknowledged.

"Anod, I had one question I wanted to ask before you sleep," Bradley asked.

"Enter," she said.

The door opened allowing the Betan leader to come into the room. He stopped with a jolt.

"Excuse me, I did not realize you were not dressed," he said with some embarrassment as he averted his eyes. "I will leave."

"There is no reason to leave nor be embarrassed. I was preparing to clean my body. What is your question?"

"Very well. If you are not embarrassed, then I shall not be embarrassed." Bradley raised his head, stood tall and looked Anod directly in the eyes. "Would you object to meeting several members of our governing council, tomorrow?"

Bradley stood like a statue, stiff and motionless. Anod was slightly more animated as she moved in a strange combination of stretching movements. As he waited for her to consider his question, he began to loosen his rigid muscles.

Anod stopped her motion, stood straight and direct with her feet about shoulder width apart and both hands resting on her hips. "That decision belongs to you, Bradley. You and Nick are the best judge of the interests of your people. To answer your question, I have no objection."

"Very good," he acknowledged with a nod of his head. Bradley took a step back and started to turn. He froze in mid-movement turning back to face Anod. "Aren't you the least uneasy with a man looking at you totally naked?"

This had all been explained to his father. Obviously, they had not talked about the differences in propriety. "Your customs are a bit foreign to me. In our culture, there is nothing to be ashamed of with respect to the human body. We use clothing for practical reasons. Skin doesn't protect you from the elements and it doesn't have pockets." Both of them laughed. "So, no, I am not embarrassed, ashamed or uneasy. My body is essentially the same as any other female, and not appreciably different from yours. There is no reason to hide it."

He stood motionless looking at her as though a scene wall or some other figure of interest captivated him.

"Is there anything else I may help you with, Bradley?"

The Betan leader shook his head as if he had been dazed. "Ah, no. I think that was it," he acknowledged. "I will see you in the morning, then."

"Yes, you will," Anod said with a smile. "Good night, Bradley."

"Good night," he answered as he turned and left the room without hesitation.

Anod stood still for a moment as she considered the strange exchange with Bradley. The Betan attitudes toward the human body still were too confusing to be even remotely understood. Maybe in time, Anod told herself.

Chapter 7

A dull, distant crackling attracted Anod to the mouth of the cave. It was still early in the morning and the others continued their slumber. The dim light from around the last corner was not consistent with the time of day. A strange and intriguing image greeted Anod as she passed the final turn.

The crackling had gradually become a muffled roar. Sheets of liquid were falling across the mouth of the cave. She stood back avoiding the splash zone since she was not familiar with this phenomenon. Nick was not available to ask for an explanation. The drops from an unseen source pummelled the ground as far as she could see. The torrent of liquid across the cave entrance made visibility of the exterior sporadic and difficult.

Slowly, Anod began to analyze the changes she was observing. Cautiously, she placed her hand in the falling liquid. Her hand did not tingle, or show signs of a reaction. The liquid was cool and thin as she moved her fingers to judge the consistency. The smell was not distinguishable even to her heightened senses. Anod continued her methodical evaluation of the liquid, eventually touching her tongue and then her lips to the moisture on her hand. There was no taste. She waited to feel a reaction, some indication of toxicity or danger. After waiting for any response, she cupped her hand to collect more of the liquid to repeat the process with a larger quantity. The same result was derived. There was no apparent danger. She strained to see where the liquid was emanating. The source was not apparent. A thick layer of dark clouds covered the entire sky. Anod thought she could see drops falling all over the ground in the clearing. This liquid must be coming from the clouds, she acknowledged to herself.

Anod searched her memory for information related to this phenomenon. In time, she was jolted by her realization. Rain, this must be rain; water that condenses and falls from the atmosphere.

She burst through the shimmering sheet of water into the clearing beyond. The ground was soft and yielded beneath her feet. Water rushed down the face of the mountain above the cave creating a small waterfall. She stood ankle deep in the water that moved swiftly around her legs as the drops fell upon her entire body.

Raising her arms to present the palms of her hands to the falling rain, she tilted her head back to feel the rain on her face. This was like a natural, atmospheric shower, a colossal version of the personal shower she had grown to appreciate. She could feel the stream of cool water rolling down her body between her breasts and along her spine. The water was gradually collecting in her boots. A surge of energy began to swell within her.

Her body gradually took on a jovial animation. Her feet moved in a random, but intricate pattern of steps swirling about in the flowing water. With her arms outstretched and palms held up to the falling rain, Anod knew she could pass for a primitive human dancing to her rain god, or a crazy woman possessed by some strange force.

Laughter, hearty and robust, mixed with the muffled sounds of her feet sloshing in the water. Occasionally, she would shriek or yell an unintelligible, but somehow appropriate set of sounds, in a vocalization of the joy within her. Anod had simply never felt rain upon her face. The sensations brought jubilation and an almost juvenile exuberance.

After a series of her shouts, Anod thought she heard a voice. Stopping, she looked around her. There was no immediate evidence of another human. She could not hear the voice among the clamor of the rain. Was she dreaming of a missing teammate or was there a hidden observer? Confirmation came a short time later.

Among the mixed sounds of the crackling rain and gurgling shallow stream around her, Anod heard the muffled sound of her name from behind the waterfall. It must be Nick or Bradley. She walked calmly, in distinct contrast to her strange dancing, toward the entrance to the cave.

The singular form of Bradley SanGiocomo stood behind the fall. He shouted at her, but she could only understand a few of the words. The weight of the water from the fall crashed down upon her as she reentered the cave. She didn't remember the impression of weight when she had departed the cave.

Anod smiled broadly with water dripping from her entire body as she said, "Good morning, Bradley. I've just been enjoying your rain."

"You continue to amaze me, Anod," he said returning her smile. "I take it you have never experienced rain."

"You are most correct. A truly unique atmospheric phenomenon."

"I suppose I never really thought about rain in that way." His eyes said he had something else to say. "Have you lived your entire life in a controlled environment?"

"Yes, I have. The majority of my life has been spent in space in the service of the Society."

"Well, then, I am glad you can enjoy our rain."

"Thank you."

Was Bradley trying to soothe the turmoil of yesterday? Anod sensed his lack of approval through his averted eyes. She surmised, he was having difficulty talking to an adult human who was completely soaked and was dancing in the rain.

"As we discussed last night, I would like you to meet other members of our governing council."

"As you wish. I am ready. Where do we meet them?"

"First, I think it would be wise for you to change into some dry clothing. Second, we should eat something before we travel, plus we need to wait for the rain to stop. And third, my father is still asleep and I'd like to wait for him to join us," Bradley said calmly without looking at Anod.

The peculiarities of the Betan culture continued to baffle her. Why do these people possess all of these confining customs or conventions? Aversion to the human anatomy? Societal structure by gender? Narrow definitions of pleasure? Why are these people so restricted?

"Does my wetness offend you, Bradley?"

"No," he answered. "It's just not something adults do."

"Why?"

"Playing in the rain is something our children do and they grow out of it, I suppose."

"Doesn't the rain bring you pleasure, much like the personal shower does?" she asked with persistence and curiosity.

"I never really thought of it that way, either," he responded. "Playing in the rain means you get wet which, in turn, means you have to change clothes. It seems like a waste of time."

"Interesting logic," Anod said. "Then, I will change clothes as you ask and we shall proceed with your plan."

"Good."

The return to her living quarters was embellished with a brief explanation of the composition of the governing council and the individuals she would meet. Anod listened intently as Bradley described members along with their individual as well as collective anticipated reaction to her presence. She recognized there would be difficulty due to Nick's protracted non-disclosure of her presence, however Bradley presented them as logical and reasonable people. They would probably come to quickly understand the underlying justification for withholding her presence.

By the time they were ready to begin their journey, the rain had stopped. A trickle of the waterfall was still present, however the gaps were sufficient to allow them to enter the clearing without getting wet. The ground was still soft although not as mushy as it was during the rain. The light and radiant warmth of θ27 were beginning to reach the surface through small breaks in the clouds.

For the first time, Anod descended the slope of the mountain leaving behind the boundary of the clearing at Nick SanGiocomo's cave. The scent of the trees and other vegetation wet from the recent rain was heavy and strong. The animal life in the forest was abundant with a wide variety of small to large creatures, some walked and ran while others flew with wings. Even the sounds of the forest enthralled Anod.

They crossed several streams and a small river at the bottom of the valley. Finally, Anod saw some evidence that other people inhabited this planet beside Nick and his son.

A small trestle supported a covered platform waystation in front of them. A long, linear, dark, semi-circular object with rectangular holes cut across the bottom extended passed the elevated platform. The dark object was a long, straight, cupped channel about 3.5 meters wide, set on top of a series of tall posts, and occupied a straight swath in the forest that stretched as far as the eye could see in either direction. This must be their principle means of conveyance, Anod reasoned. The platform was large enough to shelter 10 to 20 people from the weather with seats and other amenities. There would be no justification for a waystation such as this to serve only two people. Anod wondered where the other people might be who would use this facility.

This morning, there were no other inhabitants waiting for transportation. They passed under the raised half pipe guideway to ascend a short set of stairs to the waystation platform.

Anod continued to assess the area. She did not like the idea of standing on an elevated platform without easy egress when there was no positive method of identifying the possible occupants of an approaching transport vehicle.

"Anod, you do not have to worry about passengers on the train. You appear just like any other woman on this planet. You look like one of us," Bradley said.

"You understand my concern for traps," she responded.

"Your profession makes you very suspicious," Nick added more as an observation than a statement.

"My suspicions keep me alive. I must be prepared for any possibility. I try never to underestimate my adversaries."

"A logical trait for a warrior," Bradley said. "If anyone wants to talk to you, I would suggest you point to your throat to indicate you cannot talk."

Anod smiled in recognition of his concerns, pointed to her throat and nodded in agreement. Everyone laughed at her gesture and facial expression. She continued to scan the groups of majestic trees on both sides of the rails. Excluding the birds and other animals that crisscrossed the rail clearing, there were no other signs of life.

A very high pitch shrills coming from some distance to the right announced the approaching transport vehicle. Anod looked off toward the break in the trees. Neither of the two men heard the sound, or maybe they were ignoring the sound. The frequency of the sound was decreasing, probably an indication of deceleration.

A short time later, her eyes caught the first motion of the vehicle as it approached. She could definitely tell it was slowing now, judging from the closure rate, somewhere in the neighborhood of 200 kilometers per hour and decreasing, Anod calculated. Compared with the current and previous sounds, the vehicle was probably capable of at least 500 kilometers per hour.

The highly polished, aerodynamically shaped, metallic vehicle rode slightly above the rails. Probably magnetic interactive propulsion, Anod said to herself, archaic but efficient. Several torsos could be seen in the windows although most of the two cars appeared to be empty.

"We have our own technology," Bradley said to Anod. "The train is levitated and propelled by controlled interaction between the magnetic field of the planet and the induced fields of the rails and the cars."

"Very interesting," Anod answered without acknowledging her earlier unassisted assessment.

"We are proud of our train system," Bradley said.

The train stopped precisely positioned beside the waystation platform. Anod quickly surveyed the entire vehicle. None of the passengers had the characteristic tortured, leathery skin of the Yorax that was a welcomed observation. The riders all appeared to be human and none seemed to be hostile or threatening.

The doors opened, no one debarked and the three of them boarded.

Anod quickly noted there did not appear to be an operator that was another interesting feature. The seats were widely spaced with armrests and high back headrests. They walked between the separated, three abreast seats to the rear of the last car where three adjacent seats were open. The chairs were comfortable and supportive. The doors closed.

A mechanical sounding voice announced their departure. "The train will be departing SanGiocomo Station momentarily. Please secure all carry-on items in the space below your chair." The voice paused. "Prepare for acceleration." The voice paused again. Anod wondered why the voice needed to announce the acceleration of the train. The answer did not take long to present itself.

As she looked across the car to Nick and Bradley, the train began to move. The motion was smooth and quiet. The force of acceleration began to build rapidly and exponentially, Anod estimated. The Betans did not have anti-gravity devices or related technology, which explained the need to withstand the forces of acceleration. It also partially explained why these people were not able to easily escape the planet's gravity to the freedom of space.

There was a slight aerodynamic noise of the air passing the exterior associated with the velocity of the train, but other than that, it was a very quiet and soft ride. The attainment of cruise velocity did not take long. When the acceleration nulled, Anod estimated their speed to be nearly 170 meters per second, or about 600 kilometers per hour.

The near-field objects were simply a mass of indistinguishable colors. The change in terrain and vegetation soon allowed her to see far-field objects. The predominate vegetation consisted of thick stands of various types and sizes of trees. Occasional buildings provided signs of other inhabitation.

The contrast of the train's technology with the rest of Beta sparked the obvious question. "This technology," Anod said waving her hand around the interior and looking at Nick, "does not seem consistent with the societal limitations you talked about a few days ago."

"Well, yes, I suppose it does," Nick responded. "It was a condition of exile, not existence. We developed the technology we felt we needed. The train and rockphone communications systems are examples."

"Approaching Sloan Waystation. Prepare for deceleration," the mechanical voice stated. With the announcement, each of their chairs slowly turned until they were facing aft. The deceleration utilized a similar profile as the earlier companion acceleration. Anod now understood completely why the cars of the train were furnished the way they were, and why there was a necessity for large, uncompensated accelerations and decelerations. The transportation system needed to cover large distances and yet make multiple stops. More importantly, the Betans did not have anti-gravity technology that could negate the force of acceleration.

They had passed several stations as indicated by the flashes by the windows without stopping which probably meant there was a signalling system for passengers awaiting pick-up. An intriguing system, Anod mused.

"Arriving at Sloan Waystation," the voice proclaimed. With the announcement, the chairs turned forward prior to reaching the stopping point.

The area of Sloan Waystation was flatter and more agrarian than Nick's forest region. There were also more buildings scattered about in a dispersed, small village.

Two people, a man and a woman, boarded the train. The stop did not take long. The train repeated the necessary announcements and they were soon on their way.

They had been riding the train for a little more than two hours making several stops to take on and off load passengers when Nick leaned across to Anod. Although the speed of the vehicle prevented a good evaluation of the terrain, the changes were quite evident. The mountains and forests gradually changed to rolling hills, and then flat open fields many of which were surrounded by lines of trees. The blending of the colors smeared across the windows like paint on some large dynamic canvas was fascinating enough for Anod.

"This is our stop," he said simply.

"Approaching Providence Waystation," the voice announced. The faithful mechanical servant droned the remainder of the preparatory statements out.

The village of Providence was the largest collection of buildings Anod had seen on the planet. The elapsed time of their journey by train was about a quarter hour short of three hours. The total distance from Nick's cave was probably close to 1500 kilometers. The terrain of the village was essentially level with only slight undulations. Portions of a large river could be seen through the spaces between buildings. The largest structure visible from the train was about four layers high, maybe 20 meters.

The quantity of people in Providence was also the largest Anod had seen, yet. Their attire was distinct and quite varied. The males wore boots, pants, shirts or small robes and often had hats adorning their heads. The clothing of the females was markedly different. Anod had never seen people wearing long flowing garments very much like robes. You could not see their legs or much of their bodies although the general contours established some features of their anatomy.

The train stopped. Several other passengers including Anod and the two SanGiocomos rose to disembark. It was close to midday. The air was noticeably warmer than when they had boarded the train. Some of the temperature change was due to the time of day, but most of the change was probably due to the altitude difference between the two locations.

The entire feeling of the environment was also different. As they descended to the ground below and began to walk through the town, Anod could feel the heaviness of the air. She could smell the dustiness with an odor less sweet than the trees. There was also a new mixture of fragrances, some of them were pleasant and some were quite offensive.

Anod followed Bradley and Nick as they moved among the people. The recognition and gestures of respect provided some impression of Bradley's status within the community. Most of the people passing by acknowledged his presence. Hand motions and words of support were common. Neither Bradley nor Nick offered any explanation of what was happening, where they were going, or what to expect. Anod surmised, based on their earlier discussions, they were probably going to some governmental or community meeting place to be introduced to the other leaders.

Walking felt good. Her anonymity, in contrast to Bradley's popularity, added to her enjoyment. The people were not concerned about her, in fact, most of them did not seem to even notice her. Absorbing the diversity and stark contrasts between the human features and dress of these people contributed to Anod's enthusiasm for the journey and this planet.

Without a sign of his intentions, Bradley stopped. Nick happened to be looking away from his son at that moment resulting in several additional steps. Anod, from her position a half step behind the two men, stopped with Bradley. The expression of intensity on Bradley's face puzzled Anod. He looked both directions, up and down the street, several times. What was he looking for? People continued to move in both directions along the street. It wasn't the presence of other individuals. It must be something specific.

Satisfied the undisclosed threat was not present, Bradley motioned for Anod and Nick to enter a small, nondescript store. The building was apparently an informal meeting place serving food and beverages. Tables and chairs were randomly placed around the room. A long, waist high counter occupied one side of the room and appeared to be a serving place. The establishment was modestly attended. Bradley greeted several of the patrons as well as the proprietor as he led them through the door at the rear of the service room. They ascended a small, spiral staircase at the far corner of the storeroom-office room behind the front area.

Several men and a couple of women occupied another large room above the serving room. The occupants stopped talking and looked toward the stairs as the trio entered the room. Anod could see the questions in their eyes, their body motions, and the gestures of the new people she was about to meet.

Introductions confirmed her presumption. The men and women in the room comprised the Betan leadership council. The peculiar meeting place was not explained although it quickly became clear that caution and some secrecy determined their actions. With the greetings and cordiality satisfied, it was time for the council to gain a better impression and closer understanding of their visitor. Bradley and Nick decided not to directly participate in the discussions.

They all sat around a large table furnished with containers of water. Bradley sat at one end of the table while Anod was asked to sit in the middle of one side. Nick decided to sit in one of several chairs placed along the wall opposite from Anod. He wanted to see Anod and be within her sight.

A man introduced as Henry, who appeared to be the oldest person in the room, began the specific questioning.

"Why did you come to our planet?" he asked.

"I was on a patrol near the star, 2137M19. For reasons I do not know, my fighter was destroyed in what I believe was an ambush. The last thing I remember was the bright light of the explosion that consumed my fighter. Fortunately, my ejection capsule provided sufficient life support. The next thing I remember was regaining consciousness in Nick's cave."

"Mister SanGiocomo," Henry addressed Nick, "what was the length of time between the explosion and her return from consciousness?"

Nick shifted his seated position and looked directly at Henry, then at the other council members. "We have no way to determine the duration exactly. I believe she was in a concussion trauma induced coma for twenty days plus or minus three or four days. Based on the information from Alexatron, Anod was probably adrift for three days, enroute with Alexatron for five days and under my care for the remainder of the time."

"Was her identity or the origin of her ejection capsule determinable at the time of her rescue?" One of the two women, the one introduced as Betsy, asked.

"No. It was clear she was some kind of a warrior, but there were no distinguishing features or identification," Nick said.

"Why did Alexatron bring her here?" Betsy continued. "Why didn't he turn her over to the Earth authorities?"

"He told me that he intercepted her capsule adrift while enroute to Quadritrix. As I'm sure you are aware, Alexatron is not particularly popular with the Earthlings. He also knew she was severely injured and in need of immediate medical attention. My medical examination confirmed his assessment," Nick responded.

"Anod, Nick and Bradley have told us some of your background. Would you please tell us about the characteristics of your birth, your youth and the societal structure on Earth?" Henry asked in an almost apologetic tone.

Anod hesitated to answer as she searched the council to determine the potential for conflict. The memory of Bradley's reaction to her revelations did not encourage her response. Nick, undoubtedly sensed Anod's reluctance, provided a preface, and reassured Anod. There was an air of trust to the discussion. It helped to convince Anod to open up to these people.

Anod proceeded to explain the process of cloning new humans from genetic traces and the correction of any deficiencies and the specific improvement of certain physiological traits. The logic behind the technique as well as the ethics of the practice were common themes to a large part of the discussion.

Reliance on biocybernetics, cyborgs, androids and other robotics were of particular interest to these distant relatives. Anod was not ashamed of her heritage despite the occasional derogatory remark. In fact, there was an element of pride in what the Society has been able to accomplish. Questions came at a staccato pace that prevented her from asking questions in return. She wanted a better explanation of the obsession with parentage and the birth process. From the little information she was able to glean from their remarks, their method of procreation was inefficient and probabilistic.

The structure of the Society also attracted considerable inquisitiveness. It was difficult, if not impossible, for the Betans to imagine five percent of the people supporting the entire population. It was even more difficult for them to understand how the considerable majority could possibly be happy and content not doing anything constructive. Anod was careful to describe, in as much detail as she could and as she understood from history, the transition of the people of Earth into one common community under one leadership with the recognition of unanimity of purpose and common goals. In essence, everyone was able to do what they wanted. There were no obstacles to happiness. However, there was a price to pay for utopia.

The price was acceptance of rule of Societal Law. Aberrant and deviant behavior was simply not tolerated. Anod recalled her history education in recounting the series of anthropological experiments in the late 21st century to excise detrimental human traits and suppress divisive societal characteristics. Greed, jealousy, envy, deceit, among others were severely punished through a variety of non-injurious processes. Poverty, hunger, disease, and ignorance were also largely eliminated with the broad application of advanced communicative and computational technology along with the exceptional efficiency of robotics.

The demand for human labor had diminished substantially below the size of the population. The transition period was a turbulent and violent segment of Earth history. The solution was recognition of the needs of the human population in comparison to the requirement for high productivity, manufacturing capabilities.

The character of the questions from some of the leaders and the verbal as well as expressive communication between them provided a positive sign regarding acceptance by some and rejection by others. It was also clear that the majority opinion was shaping up with a serious concern about Anod and her cultural heritage as a threat to their desired way of life.

Nick remained seated against the wall opposite from Anod and did not speak other than to answer informational questions from several council members. Even Bradley, seated at the table with the other leaders, did not participate in the discussion except for providing an occasional procedural statement. Although they did not ask questions, their presence did seem to have a balancing effect. Anod was thankful for their involvement even if it was essentially non-participative.

"What are your intentions, Miss Anod?" Betsy asked.

"I would like to leave this planet and return to Saranon without endangering your people," Anod answered. While her response was generally truthful, there was a growing attraction of this planet although she did not feel particularly welcome here.

"It is clear . . . ." A person bounding up the stairs interrupted Henry's statement.

A young adult male struggled to catch his breath having run some distance to this conference room. He was unarmed although his large muscular frame certainly indicated his potential for physical power. His blond hair, blue eyes and light brown skin gave him a healthy appearance.

"The Yorax," he said gasping for air. "They're back," the young man struggled to catch his breath. "There's a twelve man patrol coming up the street." His chest heaved. "They are not searching any other buildings, and," again a pause for air, "I think they are coming here."

The words and actions of the group conveyed the recognition of the threat.

"Calm. Please." Bradley tried to provide some order. "Considering the circumstances, this meeting is concluded. Proceed along your assigned egress routes. I will contact you once the situation is resolved."

There were no discernible responses other than the retreating figures of most of the Betan council. Bradley and Nick did not leave. Anod did not perceive a reason to run, so she stayed as well. Bradley proceeded to the window overlooking the street where Anod joined him.

"They aren't that close yet," Bradley stated.

"Are they coming from both directions?" Anod asked.

"No. The young man's location was to the north, which is near the train station. There has been no warning from any other direction. I would assume the Yorax are investigating non-specific leads since they did not materialize near the store."

Anod knew what she would do in this situation, but she decided to let Bradley lead since he was more familiar with the local environment and the Yorax were not an immediate threat. "What do you want to do?"

"Let's see what they will do," Bradley answered. While there was a sense of urgency in the other council members as they departed, Bradley remained calm and calculating. "Father, you will not be able to move as fast as Anod and me. I would suggest that you begin your journey back to the cave."

Anod was immediately impressed.

Nick nodded his agreement and departed.

Bradley continued his vigil at the window concentrating on the street to the left. Anod continued to scan both directions as well as the rooftops along as much of the street as she could see.

"There's the first of them," he said.

Anod looked left to the street below. The distinctive brown scaly body armor and the threatening shaped communicator helmets of the Yorax identified the intruders immediately. Somehow the peculiar battle dress was nearly palatable when compared to the gnarly bodies, ink black eyes and deep yellow, pointed teeth of the underlying creatures.

They were moving fast along both sides of the street. Their presence cleared the populace off the roadway. The patrol was looking for something with several of them using hand scanners to search the immediate environs of the street. Drawn weapons provided the positive indication of their readiness.

Anod felt vulnerable although she did not feel threatened just yet. However, being unarmed against a superior armed patrol was not her idea of a beneficial situation.

The street below was nearly void of people as the patrol continued to approach. The Kartog pilot rapidly scanned every position she could see. The patrol in the street was the only sign of a threat. Anod looked back to the left.

"Oh my god," she gasped as she staggered backward several steps. It was as if she had been hit be some unseen enormous force. The expression of shock and surprise on her face produced an understandable and immediate reaction in Bradley. He rapidly looked from Anod to the street in successive jerks in a desperate attempt to assimilate what was happening.

"What? What is it? What do you see?" Bradley nearly shouted with a new excitement in his voice.

"Oh my god," Anod repeated as she continued to intently watch the approaching patrol.

"Anod, for God's sake, what do you see? What is down there?"

The initial shock quickly disappeared to be replaced by the ice-cold determination of a warrior about to do battle.

"Down there. In the middle of the Yorax patrol. Do you see the human?" she asked.

"Yes."

"That was my team leader. His name is Zitger," Anod said with noticeable anger in her voice. "He is not a prisoner. Does he look like a prisoner to you?"

"No."

They continued to watch the patrol and especially the human among them. He was dressed in a strange set of segmented body armor plates, carried a LASER pistol and wore a headset for communications. Zitger talked to the Yorax leader several times as they moved.

"He betrayed us," Anod snarled. "He killed Zarrod, Stasok and Gorp, and nearly killed me." Anger grew within her.

"How do you know he is not a prisoner?" Bradley asked her reflecting his inability to discern the subtlety.

"First, the Yorax never patrol with prisoners. Any prisoner they desire to keep alive, they immediately transport to their battlecruiser in space. Most captives, they kill. Second, do you see the Yorax captain walking next to him?"

Bradley nodded.

"If you look closely, they are walking side by side and carrying on a conversation as equals. The Yorax, especially their leaders, would never allow that discussion with a captive," Anod said.

A deluge of questions, concerns and contingencies rolled through the consciousness. She considered a variety of potential actions while both of them concentrated on the street below and the approaching patrol. Anod watched her former leader with intensity, each moment providing further confirmation of her initial assessment.

"It does not appear they know we are here, or they would have quickly focused on this tavern. They continue to scan."

"Don't relax too soon, Bradley. It is a common ruse among predators. When an approach is difficult, let your prey think they have not been seen." She paused to take a deep breath to relieve the building tension. "We have no weapons to defend ourselves as much as I would enjoy avenging Zarrod's murder. Regrettably, I think we must withdraw to avoid remaining too long in the snare."

"I will acquiesce to your skills, Anod. Come, we will depart together. We must take a long, circuitous route out of the city."

The Betan moved quickly through a door at the rear of the room. Once outside, they were on the roof of the tavern shielded from view of the streets by other buildings. Bradley moved quickly across a series of roofs passing several access doors. His movements were almost catlike as Anod observed and appreciated his nimble agility in spite of his size.

After approximately 300 meters along the tops of the buildings, Bradley moved through a particular nondescript door, down a series of stairs and into the basement of what appeared to be some type of office building. A quick check of the immediate environs confirmed their solitude upon which a large tool shelf was moved aside revealing a tunnel behind it.

The tunnel actually began a complex maze of tunnels specifically designed to confuse and disorient any intruder. There was a renewed appreciation for the ingenuity of these exiled humans. Bradley moved through the series of chambers and tunnels with a deft skill born in recognition of their limitations as well as their capabilities.

Distances were exceptionally difficult to judge in the limited light and paucity of metrics. To the best of her ability, Anod estimated several kilometers of travel although it was not clear what the net distance from the tavern might be.

During their egress from the tavern and the meeting, Anod's thoughts continued to be jerked back to the scene she had so recently left. The sight of Zitger among the Yorax and obviously aiding them in their search for her was now indelibly etched into her memory. Why did he do this? Why did he betray his own people? Why did he become a murderer? Thoughts of Zarrod, the youngest warrior of Team Three, also filled her thoughts.

Hundreds of possible explanations rushed through her brain. The vast majority of them were devastating and demoralizing in their consequence. However, the questions of cause were questions to which there were no answers within her reach.

Anod could feel the seductive grasp of rage nibbling at her thoughts. It would be so easy to give into the siren's call and unleash that rage on her tormentors. Fortunately for her safety and that of her companion, the cool logic of a practiced tactician remained dominant. Anod told herself repeatedly as if she fought against the tide that rage, anger and revenge were debilitating emotions that clouded the logical mind. Nonetheless, the attraction was strong and required active resistance.

They eventually stopped near an indistinguishable door that was essentially identical to virtually every other door they passed since entering the tunnel complex. Bradley still did not speak. He did not look at Anod although she studied his face and eyes transmitting his concentration. Anod listened for movement within the tunnels. There was only the almost imperceptible ebb and flow of their breathing.

Undoubtedly satisfied the tunnels were clear, Bradley gave Anod an approving nod and opened the door. They entered a small room lit only by the dimmed light of the handlight Bradley carried. Another door opposite from their entrance was obviously the next action. However, Bradley stopped to peer out several very small windows in the far walls to ensure the exterior of the room was safe for their exit. Anod chose not to look, trusting the judgment of Bradley in this particular situation.

Again, satisfied no danger was present, they entered a modest room furnished as a personal residence with chairs, a table, a bed and a food preparation area. There was only one window covered by a thick cloth. First, Bradley and then Anod moved the cloth slightly to view the exterior.

It was evening twilight, which meant they had spent over two hours moving through the cave complex. The room appeared to be built into a small cave or cusp in the rock. A mixture of small groves of trees and farm fields occupied the visible terrain beyond the small dwelling. A twinge of disorientation plucked at Anod's conscious thought. She tried to visualize the city, or what she knew of it, relative to the terrain she observed from the train as they entered the city. She did not recall hills or other rock formations. The distances they travelled in the cave complex could not have been that great. Given a little more time, the Kartog warrior would regain her sense of location.

Bradley finally turned to look her in the eye. "We'll have to spend the night here, I'm afraid."

"Very well," Anod answered. "Where are we?"

"We are presently about 2.5 kilometers from the center of town and nearly a kilometer from the edge of Providence," he responded.

"Whose dwelling is this?"

"It is a community safe house, one of many associated with the tunnel egress system," Bradley answered.

The interlaced tunnel system and the sense of community impressed Anod. "The tunnel complex and your use of it is quite superb."

"Thank you. As a non-violent people, we do pride ourselves on passive defense techniques we have developed."

"Understandable." Anod thought for a moment while Bradley considered the near future. "Why don't we continue our egress to your father's cave?"

"For the next 15 kilometers, it is open country with few hiding places. If we happen to be caught moving in this area, we would have nowhere to go for protection. A shuttle vehicle passes by near here every morning moving people to a train station eight kilometers from this place. From there, we will utilize the train to return you to the mountains."

"Return me? Where will you go?"

"I will go with you until you are safe, then I must return to Providence. I must attend to the affairs of state."

"So, then, we shall spend the night here?" she mused.

"We have food and drink, and we are safe."

The discussion between them during the meal centered on the events of the day. Their words and tone were formed more in the manner of a mutual debriefing than a commiseration on Anod's betrayal by Zitger and Bradley's continued vulnerability.

Anod tried not to think of Zarrod and Gorp, and their uncalled for demise. She felt a level of need to grieve for her companions that she had not fully felt until the realization associated with Zitger's appearance. Her young friend as well as her lifelong companion did not even have a chance to defend themselves, and she barely escaped with her own life.

Bradley continued to talk in an almost abstract way that seemed to be intended more to fill a void than pass for constructive discourse. Anod's thoughts drifted in and out of awareness.

The earlier burst of anger and retribution within her began to subside, replaced by calm resiliency. Although the character of her motives was irrevocably changed by Zitger's appearance, the need to determine why persisted. Occasionally, the idea of simply confronting Zitger temporarily occurred to her as she sorted through alternatives and options.

"Anod, are you listening to me," Bradley said finally breaking through her concentration.

"Actually, Bradley, you caught me," she answered. "I've been thinking about the options I have available."

"Why I? Aren't we in this thing together?"

"My apologies. Yes, it is we. However, it is gradually becoming obvious to me that it is in the best interests of you and your people if I leave Beta. As long as I am on your planet and among your people, there is the potential for discovery and eventual punishment for harboring me."

"You may be right, but I do not agree with your conclusion." He stopped his response to look around the room. "I believe it is a nice night out. Let's go outside, enjoy the stars and talk."

Anod nodded her consent. He turned out the only light, which was dim already. Once outside, the awesome light show of the galactic umbrella took hold of their awareness, at least for a few moments.

"The wonderment of space and celestial phenomena never ceases to consume me," Bradley said.

Anod was not quite so quick to appreciate the stars above. She concentrated on a methodical scan of the immediate environment and eventually the visible terrain for any threatening signs. There were no unusual sights, sounds or smells detectable by her. Satisfied they were safe, she turned her head to the stars.

"I keep forgetting the inherent suspicion of a warrior drives your actions," Bradley observed. "For that, I am thankful you are here. I suppose I am a little too trusting sometimes."

"It is simply my instinctive response, Bradley. My sixth sense, or the little voice that talks to me within, has kept me alive up until now. Some people call it intuition, however it is nonetheless real. Intuition must be fed scraps of data to fuel the fires of evaluation." She shifted her eyes from him to the array of lights above them. "Yes, you are most definitely correct. The stars are magnificent."

"At times such as these," Bradley continued, "I often can feel the hope that I see in the stars. With a display like this, you cannot resist the sense of adventure, the sense of the future, and hope for tomorrow. On a quiet, peaceful night with the array of galactic stars above, I feel the future," Bradley said with some emotion in his voice. He stood still and did not speak as if he wanted his previous words to fully dissipate before speaking again. "I think you are a part of the reason for this sensation I feel."

Anod looked into his eyes. The sincerity was evident and undeniable. "Why do you say that? I have brought you nothing but trouble."

"You cannot look at just the surface. I think I see much deeper into you. There are elements of you that are quite strange and alien to me and to our community, and yet there is a quality about you, we cannot ignore."

"I don't understand, Bradley. I am just a simple human."

"You are so wrong," he responded. The Betan leader took a few steps away from her, shifted his weight from leg to leg several times, turned and moved back to her. Bradley crouched down, picked up a small stick to make some marks in the dim starlit soil. "You are a natural leader with a calm, inner confidence. Although I am not comfortable with your birthright and heritage, I am becoming accustomed to your character."

"I appreciate your candor, Bradley," she said. "There is also much more to me than you have seen."

"I'm sure there is," he answered quickly. "Here I have been babbling on and you are not particularly talkative. Is something wrong?"

"You are correct. I don't feel like talking much. I have some mental adjustments to make after seeing Captain Zitger with the Yorax." Anod did not like stating this specific segment of reality, but felt she owed her honesty to Bradley. In actuality, she wanted to devoid her thoughts of the traitor who once was her friend.

"Your withdrawal is understandable, Anod. Maybe I should be quiet and leave you to your thoughts."

The caring tone of his voice conveyed the subtle change continuing in the son of Sebastian Nicholas SanGiocomo. Anod liked the change. She could feel her internal defenses lowering ever so gradually.

"Thank you, Bradley."

He nodded his head in acknowledgment. "We have a long day tomorrow. We should get some rest while we can."

"Agreed."

They both returned to the small dwelling set in the rock. After rechecking the window, Bradley turned on the dim light. He moved around the room in a random fashion cleaning up a few dishes and shifting the positions of several objects. It was not clear to Anod what the purpose of this activity was. Whatever the purpose was, it did not particularly matter to Anod. The sanctuary of sleep beckoned her.

She hesitated in her preparations for sleep, wondering if she should acquiesce in the Betan customs. Her mood and thoughts removed her latent concern. Anod continued to remove her clothing.

Bradley did not seem to notice Anod undressing, or climbing into bed. Somehow, it did not matter to her. As she began to drift into sleep, Anod felt a need to check the room one last time.

The light was out and the room was quite dark although the ambient light of the exterior gave her just enough to see shapes. At first, she could not see the Betan leader. Her heart rate quickened slightly. Then, she noticed him lying on several small cushions along the exterior wall. He reclined with all his clothes on including his boots, and stared at the ceiling.

"Bradley, you do not have to be so uncomfortable sleeping on the floor," she said. His head turned toward her. "This bed is big enough for both of us to get a good night's sleep."

He averted his eyes. "Thank you, but I cannot," he answered softly, but with conviction.

"Your customs are so strange to me. I do not understand why you must be uncomfortable when there is room for both of us, and this is a good bed."

"Unmarried men and women do not stay in the same room, let alone the same bed."

"I still do not understand," she said.

"The bed is where a man and a woman make love," he responded.

"What is, make love?"

"Have sex. Make babies," Bradley said with some aggravation.

"I am not concerned about such things. If you choose to be uncomfortable because I am a woman and you are a man, then so be it. Your prim manners are your concern. This is a good bed and you are welcome to join me in a good night's sleep."

Bradley did not move initially. He continued to stare at the ceiling. Eventually, the practical need for restful sleep overcame his demure behavior.

As he started to get into bed beside her, he realized he should take off some clothing. Removing his boots, overvest, trousers and shirt, he lay down stiffly beside Anod with his undergarments on. With his legs straight and his arms tight along his torso, he lay on his back and continued to stare at the ceiling. Anod could only smile.

Chapter 8

The sound of movement outside the room awakened Anod first. The low level of yellow light indicated the time near dawn. The sound was a soft, crunching sequence characteristic of steps on a thin, crusty surface. The steps were slow and deliberate although there were not many.

Bradley was in essentially the same position he had been when they entered their sleep cycle. His muscles were relaxed, but his limbs were straight as if wrapped up by some invisible material. Anod considered climbing over him to investigate the sounds. They did not seem threatening, but she also did not want to be caught in a defenseless position.

She touched his shoulder. "Bradley, wake up. It sounds like we have a visitor," she whispered to him. There was a short delay, and then his eyes opened. He looked over to see Anod raised on one elbow looking at him.

"What? What is it?"

"Listen."

A noticeable change in his alertness and concentration flashed across his face. At first, he did not move. As soon as he heard the exterior sounds, he rolled onto his right side and rose onto his right elbow as well.

Three steps were all it took to get the Betan leader out of bed and to the window. Anod decided to follow behind him. He noticed her rising from the bed and turned to see her standing beside him. Bradley staggered a few steps away. Confusion and frustration replaced concentration in his eyes. He shifted his eyes rapidly between the window and Anod's unadorned form moving toward the chair holding her clothes.

Anod dressed quickly without looking at her companion. By the time she was ready, he was at the window.

Still looking out the window, Bradley finally said, "It is only a cow grazing at the edge of the clearing."

"A cow? Is that an animal?"

Bradley laughed aloud breaking some of his tension. "I keep forgetting you are unfamiliar with rural life. Yes, a cow is a domestic animal bred for milk and meat."

"I see," Anod responded realizing that he must think she was a bit backward, not knowing about domestic animals. There was no point in reminding him that the Society's replicators could produce milk, any of its byproducts and meat without sacrificing the cow's life. The rhetorical question of who was more backward did enter her thoughts, but was not transformed into audible words.

"We should eat and be on our way," he said as he moved away from the window. He walked to the storeroom to gather up some food for a quick meal as well as for their impending journey.

Anod could no longer resist the desire to open the conversation. "Bradley, I'm not going to bite you. It seems I must continually apologize for offending your modesty. It is quite a dilemma."

Initially, he did not respond in any manner. It was not clear he had heard her words.

"Did you hear me?"

Bradley nodded his head. "I heard you. I suppose it was my turn to be lost in thought."

"What were you thinking?"

Several moments passed. "My father told me about your immodesty, Anod. It does not offend me, however your lack of attire did surprise me, somewhat."

"Your father tried to explain the Betan sense of propriety. I still do not understand why your culture insists on looking at the human form as something other than a physical manifestation to be admired," she stated. "I was too tired last night to discuss it, or be concerned about it. I am accustomed to the freedom of an isopod for fatigue recovery. On this planet, I find it quite hard to obtain an efficient, thorough sleep cycle. Freedom from the confines of clothing seems to be the closest I can reach to the recuperative power of an isopod."

"You are our guest. I will do my utmost to make your stay as comfortable as possible," he said. There was a peculiar mixture of respect and revulsion in his voice. "Now, we must be on our way."

Anod's assentation to both the change of subject and the need for their departure was provided with a slight nod of her head.

The bright light of the parent star was just crowning over the distant treeline. The air was cool and invigorating. They had to walk along narrow, dirt paths through cultivated fields for a little more than a kilometer to board a circuit shuttle. The tree lined, dirt roads provided boundaries for the multi-colored, varied texture of the many farm fields along the way. The deep rich aroma of the soil was intoxicating and unfamiliar to the Society pilot. She was now living scenes she had only read about in books of history and fiction.

They stopped at a moderate size, multi-purpose building beside a wide paved roadway. Bradley told her this was the shuttle waystation that served many needs for the local community. This location was the hub for these people with its small store, local communications and governance as well as transportation building. During the brief delay until the next shuttle, Anod took the opportunity to walk around the various areas to observe the local activity. No one seemed to notice her other than normal cordiality afforded a visitor to the building. Bradley also enjoyed some anonymity. Very few of the local citizens recognized him and those who did, conveyed their recognition with their eyes and maybe a nod of the head.

The shuttle arrived on schedule. The vehicle was quite boxy with seats for a driver and ten passengers plus limited baggage space. It used a series of wheels to move along the roadway. The mechanical features of the machine interested Anod although she did not want to draw attention to herself with unusual curiosity about a common transport vehicle.

Only two passengers occupied the shuttle. They were Betans, a man and a woman who appeared to be together. Anod and Bradley were the only passengers boarding at this location.

The speed of the shuttle was substantially slower than the train, probably because of the unprotected access to the roadway by any creature. The ride was smooth and quite comfortable, much to the surprise of Anod. It was relatively easy for her to push aside the difficulties of her situation as she enjoyed the passing scenery.

Several stops were made along the route. Bradley informed her the shuttle was the only public transport for the rural populace. They would ride to the nearest train station for their return to SanGiocomo Waystation. The distance to reach the train along this route was about 100 kilometers. They would take the train initially away from SanGiocomo. The plan also called for them to switch rail lines twice in order to approach SanGiocomo Waystation from the opposite direction from Providence.

The shuttle arrived at Seymour Waystation near mid-morning. Several buildings in addition to the train platform signified a larger local community than the small village at the beginning of their road journey. Bradley confirmed the assessment telling Anod about the farm products exchange located at this junction. Private dwellings were also sprinkled among the other public functional structures. There were also more people sitting, talking, walking and working in this little community. Seymour was the largest village other than Providence she had seen. It was not large and sprawling, but it was a respectable size. Approximately one thousand inhabitants, Anod estimated.

The printed schedule on the entry wall of the train platform told them the delay for the next train was 42 minutes.

"Can we walk through the town, Bradley?"

He shrugged his shoulders and said, "I don't see why not."

Seymour was an interesting place. Noticeably more rugged and rough edged than Providence. The majority of the people displayed obvious signs they were farmers as well as other manual laborers. These people definitely used their bodies, hands, legs and backs, to perform their work. The air of joviality observed in Providence was replaced by stern resoluteness in Seymour. It was not an unhappy town. It was a town of focused purpose.

The little shops lining the streets were a kaleidoscope of different foods including baked goods, candies, a wide variety of meats and meat products, and vegetables and fruits of bountiful quantities and types. Some of the grown foods were new to Anod.

The replicator foods she was accustomed to were still based on known samples. The computers could not produce what they did not know.

"Shall we stop at this cafe to get a bite to eat before we board the train?" Bradley asked.

"That sounds like a good idea. I am feeling somewhat hungry." She smiled at Bradley who in turn returned the friendly gesture. "It is a feeling I had never experienced until I came here."

"You were never hungry?"

"No. Manok is very thorough with the care and feeding of the humans under his charge."

Bradley chose a table outside in the patio adjoining the street. It was a pleasant day.

"Who is Manok?"

"He is the central computer who supervises the routine activities of my detachment on Saranon."

"You call a computer, he." Bradley said with a touch of indignation.

"Certainly. In his own way, Manok is a living organism. He is confined to the boundaries of his neural networks, but he has conscious thought."

"Incredible."

An attractive young woman dressed in a long garment draped over her modest body appeared with small cards. Anod was able to recognize the descriptions of several prepared foods. She quickly deduced the cards must provide the choices of meals prepared by this eating establishment.

Anod listened to Bradley order, then she asked for a bowl of porridge with fruit and some tea.

Bradley smiled at her conveying his appraisal that she handled the new situation quite well.

As the woman departed presumably to the food preparation area, the Betan leader returned to his questions. His eyes brightened and his smile grew with self approval.

"If I didn't miss something, it is interesting that the computer's name is Manok. A name beginning with the letter M, a letter in the middle of the English alphabet, midway between A's for females and Z's for males," he stated with noticeable pride of insight.

"Your observation is partially correct," Anod responded. "While you are correct about our human names, the computers and other mechanicals have names beginning with letters between males and females."

"I thought you said you were raised along the lines there were no differences between the sexes," Bradley said with marked curiosity.

"That's true. However, despite our culture, there are differences. I have breasts. Males have a penis. Anatomical differences do still exist. There are also personality differences. Each of us is still unique. We may be clones from our predecessors, but we are still unique by education and experience. We grow *from* our predecessors, not *as* our predecessors."

"Interesting. Very interesting," were the only words he said. Bradley stared at his folded hands resting on the table. There was no reason to disturb his thinking since there were enough sights around them for her to absorb.

The woman returned with their requested food dishes. The arrival of their meals did not bring Bradley out of his thoughtful trance, at first. The young server glanced questioningly at Bradley as she completed her presentation. She gave Anod a strange look to indicate she thought something was wrong with him, then departed shaking her head in disbelief.

Bradley returned to reality. "Ah, the food has arrived."

"You were somewhere far away."

"Well, I guess I was. My imagination occasionally gets a grip on me especially when I listen to you describe life on Earth."

Anod chose not to respond and continued eating. The intonation on the spoken words from Bradley and Nick regarding Earth made her feel like an alien, a stranger among her own neighbors. The Betans, from what Nick had told her, were descendants from the same people. They had the same fundamental genetic blueprint.

"I know you're tiring of all our questions about Earth, but we are so curious about the changes that have occurred since our historical split. If you will permit me, can I ask you a few more questions?"

She nodded her consent.

"You mentioned the other day, the relationship between your elite and the general populace. If you, as a member of the elite, are a clone, are all of the general populace clones, as well?"

Anod considered how she wanted to answer the question. "The answer, in broad terms, is yes, they are clones just as I am. However, I must add that a portion of the population chooses to live beyond the law. They are not."

"Why would an individual want to be a clone, or the converse, why would someone choose to live beyond the law, whatever that means?"

"The benefits of society are afforded to those who live by the laws. If they refrain from sex and ancient reproduction, they are completely taken care of and are provided satisfaction and contentment."

"Why did Earth choose this way of living over the natural processes?" The sincere curiosity in his voice provided an air of innocence.

"The plain and simple fact, as I understand our history, is the rampant population growth in the late 20th and early 21st centuries dramatically exceeded our ability to support and sustain the people, or relocate them to the other inhabitable planets within the home solar system. The cycles of famine increased in frequency and severity despite the best efforts of the fractious governments, at the time."

"I think I am beginning to understand, to see the picture. The changes were for survival." Bradley's words were spoken more to himself than Anod. His eyes had lost focus as he began to drift into his meditative state. He did not get there.

Out of her peripheral vision, Anod spotted two men walking toward them with intense concentration . . . on her. Their appearance, they were both armed with old LASER rifles, triggered the appropriate response within her. She nudged Bradley under the table. His return was slow, much too slow for the rate of approach of the two men. Conscious of the rapidly changing events, Anod kicked him trying not to be too obvious. She did not want the two rogues to become reactive.

As Bradley's eyes focused on her, he instantly recognized the message being communicated, but initially did not know where the object of her attention was located. A slight movement of her eyes in the direction of the advancing threat provided him the information he needed. His recognition coincided with their arrival at the cafe table. The change of expression on Bradley's face established the seriousness of the threat.

They were dressed in similar fashion although not the same. Their attire was marked by high boots, loose trousers, drab shirts and peculiar jackets with unusual pads affixed to specific positions, over the shoulders and chest, and the upper and lower arms. They both wore dark eye protectors obscuring Anod's ability to evaluate the signs that were always in the eyes. The most notable feature other than the LASER rifles was their lack of cleanliness. Not one spot on them appeared to be clean.

"What can I do for you, gentlemen?" Bradley asked the two men trying to be neutral and cordial.

The two men were definitely not like the other citizens she had observed to date. They must be outlaws, or some other type of brigand, Anod concluded.

"We want the woman," the man on the right said.

The statement confirmed her assessment and initiated a more specific and urgent evaluation. Nasal bridge, temple lobe, neck were all exposed. The chest, solar plexus had limited vulnerability due to the unknown nature of the jacket pads. Groin and knees were exposed. They were both within striking distance and good targets. To ensure neutralization of the rifles without risk of injury to bystanders, she needed to be standing approximately between them.

"Why are you interested in my wife?" Bradley stated more than asked.

"She's not your wife, man. She's the alien the Yorax are looking for." The man on the right continued to do the talking.

Bradley laughed. Good touch, Anod said to herself.

"I am afraid you are mistaken and I suggest you leave us alone," Bradley used a stern voice.

"Well, I'm afraid you're not in much of a position to argue, now are you?" the man on the left said as he brought his rifle to bear on Bradley.

"Wait. Do not harm him. Whatever you want with me . . . I'll go with you, just don't injure him." Anod said as she stood.

They both backed up slightly, obviously threatened by her rise from the table. Anod surmised they had information, probably from the Yorax and more specifically from Zitger, regarding her martial arts skills of which they were about to get a superb demonstration.

The rifles pointed directly at her, now.

"I'll go with you, just don't hurt him," Anod repeated as she moved slowly toward them with her hands held palms out about shoulder height.

The two men made a fundamental tactical mistake. They did not fully evaluate the environment of this engagement. The man on the left backed into a table that made a loud scrapping noise. First, the man on the left and then the other looked back to see what caused the disturbance.

In a flash that startled everyone who saw it, Anod swung her right leg in a large, calculated arc hitting both rifles in sequence near the grip stock. As intended, both weapons were extracted from the hands of their owners and flew through the air landing in the laps of two stunned onlookers.

The surprised expression on the face of both antagonists did not prevent the next rapid sequence of events.

In a majestic contortion of her body, Anod, virtually simultaneously, struck one man's anterior leg just above the knee resulting in an audible crack, and a swift blow with the side of her clinched fist slightly above the right ear and eye of the other man. Both of the rogues fell to the ground with one unconscious and the other screaming in agony.

The dull pain in her left leg from the twisting action of her movements as well as in her left elbow brought back a not so subtle reminder of her recent injuries and incomplete recovery. Anod moved slowly to straddle the chest of the still conscious man. He stopped screaming undoubtedly because her movement toward him presented a much more grave threat to his well-being than his broken knee.

"Who sent you here?" she asked looking down at the man prostrate beneath her.

"Don't hurt me any more. Please, don't hurt me anymore," he said.

"I will not touch you as long as you answer my questions," Anod said with a strong, forceful voice. "Now, who sent you here?"

"Nobody sent us."

Anod placed one hand on his shoulder as if to stabilize her target

and raised her other hand like the cocked hammer of an ancient pistol.
"Wait! Wait! I'm telling you the truth. No one sent us here."

"Then, why did you interrupt our meal?"

"A human with the Yorax has offered 1,000 gold pieces for your capture."

"Who do you think I am?"

"You are Anod, a warrior, a lieutenant in the Kartog Guards."

She did not change her expression, nor move a muscle as she continued her questioning.

"Who was the human with the Yorax?"

"He never told us, but the Yorax called him, General Zitger."

The statement did not surprise Anod although it did disappoint her. Essentially, the words confirmed her assessment from yesterday afternoon. Anod stood up and moved away from the man.

Turning to Bradley, she said, "We need to go. Is there any way we can keep these two ruffians from talking to anyone for a few days?"

"No," he said. "There isn't a constabulary in this region."

"Then, I'm afraid we must take the risk. Let's pull them inside so they are unable to witness our departure."

The two men were dragged into a front corner of the cafe building with one of them crying about the intense pain in his leg. No one attempted to resist the move although it was apparent the proprietor was not pleased. A simple verbal warning to the conscious man, not to follow them, elicited an enthusiastic agreement.

Anod walked toward the door with Bradley following her, froze prior to the entryway and considered the consequences of what they were about to do. Without looking at her companion, or discussing her decision with him, she returned to the two prostrate men striking each of them with a sharp blow to the nasal bridge. Fragments of their cranium penetrated the cerebral cortex killing them instantly. Anod checked both men for the lack of carotid arterial pulse to confirm their deaths.

The leader of the Betan people stood in shock with his mouth dropped open. He did not believe what he had just witnessed which made him an accomplice to the murder of two men. Anod stopped directly in front of him to whisper a simple statement of the result and a directive. At first, Bradley did not respond although he looked directly into her eyes.

Anod touched both shoulders then said, "Bradley, it is up to you. These people must understand the gravity of the events they have witnessed."

Eventually, nodding his head in agreement, he turned to the proprietor and the three patrons. "Citizens, I am Prime Minister SanGiocomo. You have witnessed the execution of two traitors who threatened the safety and security of our people. I will contact the constabulary in Providence to investigate this incident and remove the bodies. Please remain here to provide the authorities with your observations. They should be here within an hour or so. Thank you."

No one moved including Anod. Bradley walked to the counter and asked the proprietor for his communicator which he was promptly provided. The call to the chief of state security was brief and direct. He did not precondition the man to the desired outcome. A simple statement regarding the demise of the two men was all that he said. The care with which he spoke was the only protection they had from exposure to the Yorax. The people needed to feel they were not threatened.

Bradley performed his task exceptionally well.

They left the cafe walking calmly, but quickly to the train station. Bradley did not speak to her, or look at her. As they approached the stairs leading to the loading platform, the train arrived. Several people debarked at Seymour Waystation and an approximately equal number boarded the train. Bradley and Anod passed through the doors as they closed behind them.

Once the train began to move, Bradley spoke with a whispered voice and tears welling up in his eyes. "Why did you kill those two men? They were no longer a threat to you."

Calmly, Anod looked directly into his eyes and said softly, "They would have eventually passed the information back to Zitger and the Yorax. They would tell them not only I was alive and on this planet, but I was in the company of the leader of the Betan people. In addition to the fact that I would be compromised, retribution against you, your people and your planet, for harboring me, would have been swift, pervasive and violent. It is the way of the Yorax. In the light of your passivity, the risk was far too great, so I took the only action possible. I deeply regret taking their lives. There simply was no other choice."

The effect of her words on Bradley was obvious and effective. Slowly, he resigned himself to the reality of her statement.

Gradually, Bradley regained his composure and logical thinking. They spent the remainder of daylight covering their tracks. They changed trains three times resulting in a strange circuitous journey across a substantial portion of the planet.

They arrived at SanGiocomo Waystation two hours after the end of evening twilight. As the only two humans on board, neither of them was particularly concerned about being seen. The walk up the slope to Nick's cave was slow due to Bradley's caution about the darkness and inability to see. Anod's exceptional night vision did not comfort him much. The movement through the trees to the clearing in front of the cave took nearly three times as long as it did during daylight. Starlight and the dim light from the interior of the cave illuminated the clearing sufficiently for Bradley to feel comfortable.

"Anod, sit with me here before we go in. I would like to talk to you in the quiet of the night air."

Without answering, she chose one of the stump chairs near the edge of the clearing and sat down.

He looked directly at her as he sat down on the opposite chair. "As tragic as the loss of life is, I am convinced you made the correct decision. However, I must warn you, further transgressions against Betan custom will not be tolerated. You cannot unilaterally decide to take the life of a Betan citizen."

"I understand what you have asked," Anod said. "I know you would not have agreed. I made the mistake of assuming there was a security organization immediately available under your jurisdiction. I had hoped we could rely on them to keep the hoodlums silent. When I realized they would not be under control for some time, I acted in the only way I could. I could have eliminated them with my first blows, but I did not. I had no intention of violating your laws."

"I understand. Please try not to do it again."

Anod nodded her consent. Other topics were on her mind. "The incident today is even more of a reason I must leave this planet. My presence continues to place your people at increasing risk."

"You have no way to leave."

"I must find a way."

"Alexatron or any of the other traders do not visit on a regular basis. Maybe we could lure one of the Yorax interceptors to the surface and capture it for you."

"That would not work," she responded deflating his enthusiasm. "The Yorax utilize a similar genetic identification process to the Society. They would recognize a human at the controls and engage the vessel immediately."

"Can you think of anything?"

"No. With the Yorax so close, we can't risk communications. Even if one of the traders were to visit, I'm not certain I could get passed the Yorax battlecruiser or its interceptors."

Bradley did not speak again. He simply looked at her with the soft light illuminating the white skin of her face.

"You are an amazing woman, Anod. I am thankful fate brought you to this planet. It seems every moment I am around you I see a new facet of your character. I have never known a woman, let alone a human, with your depth."

"Thank you, Bradley." Anod did not know what else to say. A fundamental change over the last two days was evident. She was beginning to like Bradley. The turbulence and shots of adrenaline over the last two days exhausted the Kartog warrior. "Aren't you tired?" she asked.

"I suppose I am, but I have found I enjoy your company," he responded. "There is a freedom about you, I can't put into words – and the contrasts – the contrasts are so dramatic. You don't appear physically strong and yet you are more powerful than most men. You are gentle and quiet, and then you can . . ."

"I am not a killer, Bradley, if that is what you were thinking," she said. "My task in life is to protect life, to nurture life and not to interfere with the natural course of events. This mandate does join with my training. The term we use is, justifiable force. There simply was no other choice." Anod still felt a need to defend her actions.

"Yes. Yes. It's just I find myself seeing what I want to see." Bradley briefly drifted off probably to consider his words. "Do you have bounty hunters or lawlessness on Earth?"

"To my knowledge, there is no reason for bounty hunters. The stimuli for crimes are, for the most part, eliminated by the allowances for personal satisfaction and fulfilment. There are those who rebel against the system simply because there is a system. Some deviation is tolerated although any effects on other humans or any living creature are not accepted."

"What do you do with those who choose to rebel? Kill them, or banish them to some distant planet?"

"No, Bradley, we are not a violent people by nature. The deviants are isolated in remote colonies on Earth, or they are given the choice to leave. This arrangement has provided immense stability for the people of Earth. The vast majority of the population lives in harmony and enjoys life."

"I don't know about harmony and enjoyment without physical contact, without sex," he said more to himself than to Anod.

Anod considered Bradley's statement for a few moments. "We have harmony and enjoyment without sex."

"Maybe, but there can't be as many facets to life as there is with it."

"The Society does not share your opinion."

It was Bradley's turn to ponder the words and imagine their meaning. "I suppose when you refer to rebels as you mentioned earlier, there are those who defy the prohibition on sex."

"I suppose."

"Do they banish citizens for having sex?"

"If they violate the law, yes," Anod answered without conviction. Her fascination with the anthropology of the Betans was growing although the physical element intrigued her. "Why do you have this obsession with intimate contact?"

"I wouldn't call it an obsession. The bonding that occurs between a man and a woman through their physical union is incomparable to the best of my knowledge."

Anod could sense the sincerity in his voice. It was not an experience that she was familiar with, nor did she have any desire to find out. She did have many more questions, however. "How do you deal with the negatives of that connection?"

"Like what?"

"Possessiveness. Jealousy. Anger. Severe mood swings."

"For someone who has not experienced love, I'm not sure I understand where you acquired these opinions. Nevertheless, you have been indoctrinated well. The detrimental emotions are the price we must pay for the enjoyment. Sex to me is a celebration of life. It is also our method, the natural method, of procreation. It is the penultimate means of non-verbal communication when it works. I can't tell you it works all the time, but when it does, it is incredibly majestic."

"You didn't answer my question," Anod said bluntly.

"I suppose I didn't. We discourage the bad elements of sex through societal pressure," he said calmly. "We also punish detrimental behavior although we are not proud of that. We eliminate the cause factors of deviant behavior by emphasizing strong family connections. We have also tried to lift the stigma associated with sex which was prevalent in our distant past."

"I'm not sure I understand all that in light of your near revulsion of the human body," she said with a certain innocence.

"You do know how to cut right to the bone," he responded. "It is not revulsion, Anod. We tend to associate the naked human form in sexual terms. We do appreciate the human body almost to the point of reverence, however the sexual organs are just that - sexual."

"Interesting." Anod looked away from Bradley to the stars around them. The longing within her was still present. The environment on this planet was peaceful and soothing despite the threat from the Yorax and now the bounty hunters, but space was where her heart was. She wondered how many more Betans had been convinced to try to capture her for a reward.

"Have you thought about trying it?" Bradley asked returning her to the topic.

"No. Intimate contact is not something that interests me," she responded softly although it was not an entirely true statement. There was a measure of curiosity about this element of major difference between their two cultures.

"Don't you wonder what you are missing?"

"No."

Bradley did not speak. He just looked at her. There was an unusual expression on his face, one she had not seen before. The mask of darkness provided the impression of anonymity for Bradley. The superior night vision of a Kartog warrior was not something he was thinking of, at the moment. There was a hunger in his eyes.

"Maybe we should go in. We both need some sleep," Bradley said.

"I agree."

Bradley stood with her, and then moved toward her stopping within arms reach. Anod did not know his intentions. He stood in front of her looking at her with a need to say something. She waited for him to speak.

Her peripheral vision saw both of his hands rise. He touched the skin of her face. The light, delicate touch seemed more to appreciate the texture of her skin and the contour of her face. Holding her head gently, he leaned forward to touch his lips to hers. There was a strange electricity between them, an energy Anod had never felt before.

The Betan leader drew back from her, releasing her head. He stood very still. "I needed to do that. I hope you didn't mind."

There was a strong feeling of vulnerability, of being disarmed by his touch. She also did not know how to react, or what to say. Anod stood equally still waiting for the next surprise.

Stepping aside, Bradley took her elbow in his hand to lead her to the cave entrance. Acquiescence seemed like the appropriate thing to do.

The temperature rose noticeably as they walked further into the cave. There was a subtle sense of domesticity. Nick was slow to recognize their presence that did not give Anod a particularly good feeling. No early detection system increased their vulnerability.

After the usual greetings, they sat around the table with a hot cup of tea. Father and son talked about the events of the last two days. Bradley made an obvious attempt to avoid discussion of the swift result of Anod's judgment. The words he spoke possessed a certain element of pride, maybe even admiration. There was no question Bradley was impressed with the capabilities of their guest.

The comparison of experiences was interesting and, in a strange way, entertaining. Anod chose not to contribute to the conversation as her thoughts kept returning to her most recent new experience on θ27β. The forbidding nature of the incident did not lessen its impact. Another human had never touched lips with her before. It was simply not an act accepted within the Society. There was no purpose, no meaning to that form of conduct, although the impression was similar to the sensations she felt hearing the wind in the trees, smelling the intoxicating scents and seeing the glorious colors of the trees moving in the light wind. Something was different, unexpected, about Bradley's initiated contact with her.

"What do you think, Anod?" Bradley's simple question, forcefully delivered, separated her from the thoughts she was considering.

"About what?"

"Just as I thought, you definitely weren't with us," Bradley said with the lightness of a chuckle to his voice. "My father and I were discussing possible courses of action from here. He feels we should stay here. I am not so sure. Do you have an opinion?"

Anod looked at both men and then at her hands resting on the table. "I cannot stay here. I need the freedom of space to defend myself, but I cannot do it alone against an Yorax battlecruiser." She stopped to evaluate her words.

Many images passed through her thoughts as the two men waited patiently for her to continue. The recurrent nightmarish image of the systematic destruction of the beautiful and tranquil Beta along with its caring inhabitants was not acceptable.

Satisfied and confident in her own assessment, she continued, "It is only a matter of time until the Yorax positively establish my presence on this planet. Once they have sufficient evidence, they will methodically destroy the planet in their efforts to find me. I am the only survivor who can testify to Zitger's treachery and betrayal. If I am able to alert the Society, the response against the Yorax would crush them. They will do everything to prevent that."

"We understand that, Anod. However, we cannot simply give up. What do you want us to do?" Nick asked.

"I must find another defensive position that does not jeopardize either of you," she answered. Both men looked at each other as they communicated, non-verbally, about the next move.

Nick was the first to speak. "There is another cave, higher in the mountains, about four hours from here. The place has adequate supplies and is remote from everyone. It is an abandoned hunting lodge from many years ago when we searched for wildlife. That cave is also excavated out of solid anthratite. With the proper screen, you would be safe from the Yorax sensors."

"I must return to Providence." Bradley said. "First, we must close the investigation into the incident at Seymour Waystation. Second, I must obtain a clear consensus on our approach to this situation. The best thing for all of us, right now, is your disappearance, Anod."

"Very well. I will leave first thing in the morning."

"I will take you up there," Bradley offered.

Anod nodded her consent.

The thought of hiding was not highest on her list of actions to be taken. However, Anod regretted taking the lives of the two bounty hunters at Seymour even though it was the only obvious choice. She resigned herself to the less desirable course of action. "Will I have access to any weapons?"

Bradley lowered his head looking at some undefined spot on the table in front of him. Her question was not one he really wanted to answer.

As the younger SanGiocomo considered his response, Nick rose from the table to clean some dishes and separate himself from the issue. There was a slight flash of thankfulness he did not share the responsibilities of state with his son.

"There are no weapons up there. However, I will arrange for one of our most trusted young security men to bring you several weapons for your defense. His name is, Otis Greenstreet. He's an intelligent, capable young man about your height, maybe a little shorter, although he is about 20 kilograms heavier than you. He has black, curly hair with dark skin. He will be wearing a full brim, red hat. I will tell him your name, but I will not tell him who you are or why you will be at, High Cave, simply that you require a few selected weapons. There should be no problems."

"That sounds reasonable," Anod said with a firm, decisive tone. She wanted to convey a simple impression her destiny was still in her hands. "How long do you think I should remain at this high cave?"

"The duration depends on many factors. The most significant is the resolution of the Seymour investigation and the actions of the Yorax. I should think a few days to a couple of weeks. I will do my best to keep you informed, but do not expect daily information."

A simple head nod acknowledged her acceptance of Bradley's estimate.

Chapter 9

Anod and Bradley began their journey through a part of the forest Anod had not seen before. The whispering of the wind in the trees and the new complex scents of the soil and vegetation of this portion of the forest were stimulating and pleasurable to the Kartog warrior. Everyday, she was exposed to new sensory experiences. The intoxication of simple physical pleasure with whatever senses might be involved was new and thoroughly enveloping for the young pilot. Her sterile, high efficiency world did not recognize the need for this type of satisfaction. The more she was exposed to, the more she wanted to experience. The smile on her face was becoming virtually permanent. Anod liked Beta. It was a pleasant place.

The two travellers did not talk much during the hike partly due to the exertion of the climb, but mostly due to the thoughts within each of them. They crossed several streams that contained cold, sweet water, clear as crystal. Even the sounds of the forest were soothing. The few words spoken on the ascent were focused on observation and acknowledgment of the uniqueness of the forest. The creatures of the forest from tiny insects to large mammals were bountiful. The variety of life added to Anod's enjoyment.

Bradley began to stop more frequently to permit better listening than to rest. High Cave must be near, as indicated by the additional caution. Anod smiled to herself in recognition of Bradley's unpolished tactical skills. He seemed to be improving. Without discussion, both of them agreed implicitly there were no detectable threats. Bradley checked a small cave entrance near a tiny stream had to be their destination. Bradley motioned for her to remain near the entrance while he completed a peripheral area search to ensure they were alone.

"Everything seems to be in order," he reported on his return.

There was no need to respond other than a simple head nod.

"Shall we go in and see what shape the place is in?"

Again, she answered with a gesture.

This cave was quite a bit smaller than Nick's abode. Anod had to stoop slightly to avoid hitting her head on the surrounding rock. A barrier was a small door recessed back about three meters from the mouth of the cave. Several overcenter latches kept the door closed and the animals out of the cave. The entrance of the cave in front of the door had been used several different times by various animals for protection from the elements.

The interior of the cave was surprisingly dry which made the temperature feel more moderate than cool. Several chambers had been excavated. The smaller chamber was the storeroom containing a bountiful supply of various preserved foodstuffs. The other room was a simple living area with two moderate size beds, several dissimilar chairs and a good size table. Anod recognized immediately the lack of routine human facilities that meant she would take another step away from the physical care she was accustomed to from Manok and his minions. Life continued to be a glorious adventure, she told herself.

"Everything appears to be in order here," Bradley said after his survey of the cave. "Will you be OK, here?"

"Certainly," Anod responded. "I shall be quite comfortable." She was not entirely convinced of the veracity of her own statement although she knew there was no need to criticize the hospitality.

As a good host, Bradley methodically briefed Anod on all the provisions, utensils, tools, limited amenities and an overview of the surrounding area. He was careful to describe the use of the entryway-blocking screen for protection from sensor intrusion. Several cautions were also provided regarding the wildlife and vulnerabilities of the area. In many ways, Anod was satisfied she would be safe, once she had some weapons, and she would be quite comfortable.

"I shall leave you to the pleasures of the forest. As I said last night, I will make arrangements for one of our trusted young men to bring you several weapons and to check on you. Don't expect him for a few days. It will take me the rest of the day to get down the mountain and travel to Providence. I will make sure he brings a message to you regarding my assessment of the situation. Does that sound reasonable?"

Bradley stood about one meter from her, but the expression in his eyes conveyed the concern and caring he felt for her. She knew he was not the same man she met at Nick's cave nearly two weeks earlier.

"I shall be quite all right, I should think," Anod responded. "Good luck in Providence and safe journey. As we say, godspeed and following winds."

"Ah, a historical phrase from our collective past. Thank you, Anod." Bradley moved toward her and kissed her on the cheek.

Anod liked the warmth of his touch.

The Betan leader turned and walked quickly away without another word. Anod watched his departure until he neared the top of the rise. Then, she pretended not to look as he stole one last glance of her as he crossed the crest of the ridgeline.

The next several days and nights were spent performing a complete inventory of the interior provisions and equipment, and a thorough survey of the surrounding terrain, vegetation and lighting effects from the θ27 star.

The provisioning was precisely as described by Nick and Bradley. The quantity and variety of food stockage were exceptional. Anod estimated that she could sustain a solo existence for about three months with normal usage and more than five months with sparing use. Supplementation of the food stores with indigenous editable fruits, plants and animals could stretch her sustenance virtually indefinitely. There was some comfort in this assessment.

The cave was situated quite well from a tactical defense perspective. There were no other signs of inhabitants or even human presence within one kilometer. The process took her two days to complete due to the extra attention she devoted to the likely avenues of approach into the area. The combination of the inherent isolation of the site and the anthratite composition of the cave walls provided confidence in addition to the comfort. She knew she would be safe and healthy at High Cave.

Nonetheless, her impatience drove her to produce several primitive weapons. The set of fire hardened spears and wooden throwing stars along with the assortment of knives provided at the cave gave her an adequate capability against threatening animals. The rudimentary weapons would not be much help against LASER rifles or other modern weapons, but they were better than nothing. Any weapon in the hands of an expert, determined, professional warrior was not something that should be underestimated. Anod's practice with her new weapons continued each day, but after several days, she was confident with the capabilities and limitations of each instrument. Regardless, the arrival of more capable weapons would be a welcome moment.

If there was a detractor to High Cave accommodations, it would be the lack of facilities. There was no water, either hot or cold, inside the cave. She had to carry the water from the stream for drinking and cooking. The single entity Anod missed the most was the hot shower she had become accustomed to at Nick's cave. Cleansing her body after the day's work was accomplished at a small waterfall and pool upstream from the cave.

The adjustment to the cold water of the stream took several days. Anod tried several different methods of entry into the water. She settled on a quick dive into the pool, then she would climb several rocks to a convenient submerged rock ledge under the waterfall. Standing under the cascading water invigorated and stimulated her entire body. The energy of the falling water, even though it was cold, made her scalp tingle and her skin ripple with a chilly wave. Her spectrum of physical sensations continued to broaden.

Fortunately for Anod, the air was relatively warm. The short walk back to the cave was an intriguing mixture of the coolness of her skin and the caress of the warm air. Her body except her hair dried and she returned to her normal body temperature by the time she reached the cave.

The solitude of High Cave also allowed sufficient time for recollection and consideration of her thoughts and dreams. Anod knew there was an impact on her life from her experiences on Beta. During the quiet moments, especially in the evenings, she recalled the events since Colonel Zortev first indicated Manok had found an anomaly. She remembered with anger the betrayal and ambush in space, and the death of her friend and comrade. Eventually, Anod worked her way to more pleasant memories. The peculiarities and customs of these distant cousins from Earth were a humorous topic she still did not fully appreciate nor understand. It was the touching of lips with Bradley that occupied the most time within her thoughts. The sensations and nondescript feelings were new, different and intriguing to the young woman of the Society unaccustomed to physical and emotional stimulation.

The new feelings were helping her realize and appreciate the characteristics of her own body and soul. These were experiences that were unfamiliar to her under the protection and watchful eye of Manok and the Society. There was no resentment to the protection, simply expansive curiosity about additional dimensions or facets to her life.

The fifth day ended quiet and peaceful. Anod harbored some concern about the messenger to be sent by Bradley who had not arrived, yet. Was he all right? Had the Yorax discovered the truth? Was a new conflict in the offing? She still felt comfortable although the lack of information regarding the situation in Providence added to her sense of vulnerability.

Life must continue.

Anod decided she would make a short night patrol of the approaches from SanGiocomo Waystation after her afternoon waterfall shower and evening meal. The starlight in the early night sky would be more than adequate for her movements through the forest.

The light from the θ27 star was low on the horizon with about two hours of daylight remaining as she walked the 200 meters upstream to the fall. She was lost in her thoughts within the sounds of the falling water and the envelopment of the spray to be aware of the new set of eyes watching her.

It was not until she walked slowly back to the cave that her sixth sense told her something was different. Anod froze in a semi-crouched position, like a cat ready to pounce on a mouse, in order to eliminate any extraneous sounds. She methodically scanned the entire visible horizon around her. All her senses were on edge as she concentrated on detection and identification of the source of her concern. During her second sweep of the area, she instantly turned toward a movement detected near the boundary of her peripheral vision.

A young man was in the process of emerging from behind several small bushes near a large, old tree. The full brimmed, deep red hat, just as Bradley had described, was the most obvious clue as to the identity of the visitor. Anod did not move as the man began to slowly walk toward her. She noticed immediately the LASER rifle slung over his shoulder as well as the pack on his back. He made no threatening motions. The young man's dark, chocolate brown skin, short, curly black hair and slight smile enabled Anod to conclude he was probably the messenger promised by Bradley.

As he approached the far side of the stream, he stopped and said, "You must be, Miss Anod. My name is, Otis Greenstreet. I bring a message from Bradley SanGiocomo."

Anod did not answer. She stood erect and faced young Otis. The assessment continued. There was not even a twinge of embarrassment in his eyes or face, as she stood completely nude before him. He was indeed shorter, about five centimeters, than she was and solidly built. His carriage indicated a well-trained and capable warrior.

"May I come across?" he asked motioning to the stream between them.

Anod did not answer immediately. She wanted to see how he

would react to her lack of cooperation. The slight smile remained on his face exposing his pure white teeth providing a deep contrast with his dark skin. Anod motioned for him to cross as she walked toward the cave. He followed a few meters behind her.

Without speaking to Otis Greenstreet, Anod dressed to arrest the chill she began to feel. She motioned toward the pitcher of water on the table.

"Please," he responded.

After a quick drink to quench their thirst, Anod sat at the table and Otis followed sitting across from her.

Anod decided it was time to speak. "You indicated you brought a message from Bradley."

Otis reached inside his tunic to extract a sealed letter and handed it to her. Anod opened the seal and read quickly.

She was relieved to learn the Yorax had not discovered her presence. In fact, they were not even aware of the incident at Seymour Waystation. With the investigation essentially complete, Bradley deemed it necessary to confide in the Commander of Security with regard to her background and existence. The leadership council, initially angry over Anod's unilateral action at Seymour, quickly understood the regrettable reality. The letter also provided a brief description of young Otis.

Otis Greenstreet was a family friend and a martial arts enthusiast. Well educated, intelligent and decisive were words Bradley used to describe him. The most important item was simply, Bradley trusted Otis.

"Thank you for the message, Otis. I was beginning to wonder what was happening in Providence," Anod said putting the letter down.

"Mister SanGiocomo wanted to make sure he fully understood the situation."

"Are the Yorax still patrolling the planet?"

"Yes. There is a certain sign of frustration, but they appear to be quite tenacious."

"It is their nature, I'm afraid. You brought some weapons for me," Anod said changing the subject.

"As requested, I brought a LASER rifle, a couple of magnetronic pistols and a hand sensor."

"Thank you."

"Bradley wanted me to ask you about your feelings regarding High Cave, the area, the food and other provisions."

"Everything is quite satisfactory."

A lull in the conversation permitted Anod to retrieve a bowl of fruit she picked earlier in the day. Anod could feel his eyes. There was something different about this man, she thought. Anod could not classify her feelings. He watched every move she made.

"May I ask you a question?"

Anod nodded her consent.

"Weren't you embarrassed standing in front of me without your clothes?"

"No. Why should I be?" Anod responded withholding her true feelings. Her irritation, although well concealed, grew each time she confronted Betan prudishness regarding human anatomy.

"Well, all the women I have known would never be outside without clothing and would run for cover if someone saw her without clothes."

"Were you embarrassed by my nakedness?" Anod asked with purposeful determination.

"Well, no, I suppose I wasn't. You are a very beautiful woman and I liked what I saw."

Anod could sense the appreciation in his voice. Yes, this man was definitely different.

"Why weren't you embarrassed as other men on Beta seem to be?" she asked.

"A very good question. My parents gave me a keen appreciation of the human form. They are both artists. I have always found the female form very attractive."

The conversation with Otis that evening was stimulating and enjoyable. In so many ways, the young man was self-assured, confident, as well as intellectually stimulating and yet curious in an innocent fashion. There was more laughter and joviality than she had experienced in many years.

Otis turned serious. "I heard about what happened at Seymour Waystation. I am impressed with your prowess."

"You should not be impressed. It was an unfortunate incident that might have compromised your entire planet. Furthermore, the loss of life should never be taken lightly."

"Yes, I agree. However, when you filter out the tragic side, your ability to deal with two armed men, both of whom were larger than you, with such swiftness and decisiveness is admirable."

"Violence should never be admired."

"I won't argue the point. I am simply acknowledging your martial arts skills. I am an aficionado of martial arts."

Anod did not like the new direction of the conversation. It reminded her of the dark side of human nature although it was certainly an environment in which she was accustomed to working. It also reminded her of death. The demise of the two bounty hunters was not something she wanted in the forefront of her memory.

"Would you teach me some of your techniques?"

"Maybe later," she answered. "Right now, I want to enter my sleep cycle. I must rise early tomorrow. If I am not here when you rise, please help yourself to the food and have a safe journey back." Anod hesitated for a moment. "Tell Bradley, I am healthy and safe."

"I will do as you wish."

Anod rose from the table, checked the door to the cave including placing the sensor screen across the entrance and prepared for sleep. Otis followed her lead. She noticed him checking her as if to gauge his own actions.

As she moved to lie on her bed, Otis said softly, "Wait. Please." He walked toward her. "You are a most fascinating woman. I sincerely hope I am able to know you better."

A simple nod acknowledged his compliment. The expression in his eyes and on his face spoke of more thoughts rumbling through his brain. She waited for him to speak.

Young Otis Greenstreet didn't speak. He leaned forward to touch his lips to hers. There was feeling and emotion in his lips similar to the sensations she felt when Bradley had performed the same action. This was different, however. Otis reached up to touch her bare breast. His touch and caress were soft and gentle, actually appreciative. Anod felt a kind of internal electricity shoot through her body. She also felt her nipples rise to his touch producing a comparable pain and pleasure to that she felt under the waterfall. The rapid changes in her body were alien to her and much too overwhelming.

Anod placed her hand on his chest and drew back from him. The feelings intoxicated and intrigued her in a similar, but different, way as the forest sensations. However, she did not like being so near to a loss of control.

Otis lowered his eyes and his head. "I hope I did not offend you, Miss Anod."

"No, Otis, you didn't offend me. These are just feelings I am not familiar with, and I must understand them."

"You have never kissed, or made love?"

"If your actions are called kissing, yes, I have. Bradley kissed me before I left for High Cave. However, kissing, as you call it, is not something we do among my people. I do not know what making love means."

It was Otis' turn to recognize her innocence.

"Then, you are missing so much of what life is all about," he said with a broad smile and a twinkle in his eyes.

"Maybe so, but I am also tired. Good night, Otis."

His brightness vanished in an instant with her words and the realization the night's discussions were over.

As part of her routine at High Cave, Anod moved silently among the trees at morning twilight. She completed her perimeter check without detecting any alterations. For some reason, she did not want to talk to Otis before he left. She positioned herself among a small stand of trees and bushes on the high ground behind the cave entrance to observe his departure.

Otis did not emerge from the cave for nearly an hour. He was either a late riser, or he waited as long as he could for her return. Anod decided it was probably the latter since he spent a few long moments scanning the entire area probably for signs of her.

Most likely convinced she was not in the immediate area, nor would she return soon, young Otis Greenstreet departed toward SanGiocomo Waystation.

Anod moved carefully and quietly through the forest at a considerable distance behind and to the flank of Otis' path. There was a strange combination of repulsion and attraction to the handsome young man. It was nice to watch his movements from the anonymity of distance.

Occasionally, he stopped to listen and look around him as if he was still searching for her. His actions brought a smile to Anod's face.

Life in the mountains continued to be peaceful as well as stimulating. Anod enjoyed watching the variety of animals and especially the birds. She missed the freedom of flight, even if it was only within the atmosphere. Despite her enjoyment of the environment and all the elements that populated the area, Anod knew the deficiency she felt and was reminded by the apparent effortless soaring of a majestic bird above the trees. There was some solace in her acknowledgment of the eventuality. She would again realize the freedom of flight, it was simply a matter of time and patience.

The professional side of her character was also exercised during the several days since the visit of Otis Greenstreet. Anod practiced with each of her knew weapons through several different potential scenarios. Her learning curve with unfamiliar weapons was particularly steep, as it usually was. The Kartog warrior was satisfied with her proficiency after four sessions over two days. The addition of a hand sensor to her figurative toolbox was a welcome complement to her exceptional physiological sensory capabilities. The device, in essence, increased the range of her senses in a manner of speaking. It also provided other information not detectable by human senses. Her only sensor targets were the animals of the forest. There was a certain dimension of fun associated with combining her senses with the data from the inanimate device.

On this day, as she moved quietly through the forest and its bountiful vegetation, her hearing first detected the sound that was not characteristic to the forest. Anod listened intently in her effort to identify the source of the sound before she was able to see it. The task did not take long.

The distinct crackle of crushing leaves and the occasional snap of a small twig coupled with the low frequency rhythm established the source as an approaching human. The hand sensor confirmed her assessment. The source was a single, human male walking in the direction of High Cave. The data along with her senses led Anod to the conclusion another courier was enroute to deliver a message from Providence. Was it Otis again, or Bradley maybe? Could her visitor by a new person?

Anod began the slow, cautious, methodical process of stalking her target. The challenge, since she did not feel threatened based on her assessment, was to approach the quarry to within striking distance without being detected. Carefully placed steps for short distances of five to ten meters on an intercept vector made her appear like a large cat moving through the forest.

The process took slightly less than ten minutes for her to be approximately twenty meters from her intruder when she recognized her visitor was, Otis, as she suspected. His movements were not particularly cautious which indicated that he did not feel threatened either.

Anod quickly scanned the entire detectable horizon to establish the lack of unwanted trailers or other visitors. The age-old technique of using an innocent vanguard to open the door and put the house at ease was known as, 'trailing the target.' Despite Otis' failure to exercise prudence during his ingress to High Cave, Anod knew she had to be certain Otis was not followed. To her satisfaction, they were alone.

The game continued as Anod positioned herself on the near high ground overlooking the cave and the stream. Otis proceeded down to the stream.

"Anod, it's Otis," he called out to announce his arrival.

He crossed the stream and entered the cave as he repeated his announcement. It took only a few seconds for Otis to reappear. He stood a couple of meters from the entrance to the cave and looked around the entire area. Observation was a unidirectional endeavor for the two humans. Anod wanted to wait for an appropriate time to join her visitor. Waiting was better than letting Otis know she had been watching him.

The proper moment presented itself when Otis reentered the cave probably to wait for her to return. Anod quickly moved out of her observation position and descended the hill. Their meeting occurred as she was crossing the stream.

"I guess you were out walking," Otis said.

"Yes, I was. Welcome back, Otis."

They walked into the cave to sit at the table. Each of them took some water to compensate for the dehydration endemic to high altitude living. Several pieces of fruit were also a pleasant addition to the liquid.

"Has everything been OK since my last visit?"

"Certainly. Quite nice, actually."

"Good. I bring greetings from the Prime Minister and the Leadership Council."

Anod smiled and nodded her head.

"They have asked me to convey to you the goal of the Council. They have decided to protect you, until you are able to carry out your desires."

"That is welcome news."

"The Yorax activity on the planet has diminished substantially. Everyone feels they are discouraged and may be getting ready to leave."

"The Yorax do not get discouraged," Anod said bluntly. "They may be preparing to depart, but it is not in their nature to become discouraged."

Many words passed between them as Otis explained the situation in Providence and the other bits of information relative to the action of the Yorax. Anod asked specific questions regarding the lone human among the Yorax, the betrayer of her people and the murderer of her friends.

Zitger remained elusive. Otis had never seen him although he had heard the stories of his existence. Most of the Yorax patrols were the typical size of ten troopers plus or minus a few. None of their actions over the past week or two had been threatening, or even aggressive. The assessment of the Council was the Yorax were convinced their prey was not on the planet, but their orders required them to continue the search. The preponderance of information provided by Otis seemed to indicate a complacency, or lack of commitment toward the search.

The reduced intensity bought some breathing room for Anod. Concern for survival was no longer the immediate, or even the primary issue. If the Yorax ever departed this planet and this region of space, Anod knew she would be able to eventually determine how to leave the planet and return to Saranon, or at least the Society.

Words moved across the table and throughout the room with the buzz of a swarm of honeybees. The two humans took advantage of the several hours remaining of the afternoon to discuss a wide variety of topics. Otis asked many questions as a schoolboy might ask his professor for the wisdom of her experience. Anod continued to probe for additional information on the situation and mood of the people beyond the environs of High Cave. Laughter was the most common sound and enjoyment was the most prevalent emotion.

"The light of θ27 is waning for this day," Anod said. "I would like to take my shower, if you will excuse me." The loose reference to the waterfall as a domestic device was a recognition on her part of the image associated with the word.

"If you object, I will understand, but may I join you?" Otis asked.

"If you wish."

Otis took his direction from his host as they doffed their clothing and headed to the fall. The young Betan had to take several plunges into the pool in what seemed to be a loosing effort to dampen his excitement. The physical male manifestation possessed no special significance to Anod, other than being a uniquely male physiological response similar to the prominent erection of a female's nipples, the reasons for which she did not understand nor particularly care.

For the most part, Anod was blithely unaware of the young man's predicament. She dismissed the repeated dives into the pool as a simple desire to enjoy the water. Each time he emerged from the pool, she could not help noticing the shine of his dark chocolate skin and the bulges and ripples of his bountiful muscles. Anod enjoyed watching him move as he used the rocks and ledges to leave the pool and return to the waterfall. The definition of his muscles was sufficient for each movement to be exquisitely illustrated by the contraction and relaxation of the complex muscle groups of his body.

There was little conversation mainly due to the dominant sounds of the waterfall, but also due to Otis' repeated rapid departures. Anod did not need words to realize the attraction Otis felt for her. To the Kartog warrior, the attraction was among friends, people who enjoy each other's company.

"I've had enough," Anod exclaimed. "You're welcome to continue." she said as she dove into the pool and swam underwater toward the downstream end of the pool.

By the time Otis returned to the cave, Anod was already dressed in her loose shirt, overvest, pants and boots. The common attire of the Betan mountain people offered immediate warmth. Otis dressed quickly although he was not entirely dry. The wetness just did not seem to matter.

"You are so open, free and candid with your thoughts and experiences," Otis said as his expression turned more serious. "If I am becoming too personal, please tell me, it's none of my business."

"I'm not sure what you mean, Otis."

"Well, it's too difficult to explain, so . . . well . . . maybe I should just say it."

"That sounds like a good idea," Anod responded with a slight chuckle.

"You said during my first visit that you did not know about making love."

Anod nodded her agreement.

"I am very attracted to you, Miss Anod. You are one of the most incredible women, one of the most incredible people, I have ever known."

"Thank you, Otis. I enjoy your companionship as well."

"Miss Anod, what I feel is different from friends. I want to make love with you." The seriousness of his tone conveyed the intensity and earnestness of his feelings.

"If I knew what you were talking about, I could more properly offer my answer, or my help." The tone of his words raised the first alarm within her. Anod suspected the implications of his words were contrary to Society law.

"A man and woman making love is the closest two people can become. It is, in my opinion, the highest form of human communications."

Otis paused as if his words were somewhat lost on a woman who had only recently been kissed for the first time. "Maybe I should just show you."

Anod did not respond to his suggestion. She did not encourage, nor discourage him. The anxiety of a trapped animal best described Anod's feelings. The mixture of her compelling need for some space to think with her inherent curiosity to absorb more experience regarding this culture tortured her thoughts. He said, 'the closest two people could get.' There was considerable room for interpretation of her visions. "What exactly do you mean by, closest?"

"Well, I'm not quite sure how to explain it. It's the kind of question a child asks his parents. I think it would be better to show you. It will make more sense once you've felt it."

What could possibly be too difficult to explain with words? Maybe he meant something other than the images running through her head. Maybe it wouldn't hurt anything or violate any rules. She reluctantly nodded her head to feed her curiosity.

Several of the light sources were extinguished although there was certainly sufficient light to see the sincere expression on his face as he stood over her. He reached down to lift her shoulders indicating he wanted her to stand. Otis held her head in both hands as he kissed her lightly. Strangely, she felt herself respond to the warmth, softness and feeling of his lips. His hands moved slowly removing her clothing as he continued to kiss her lips, cheeks and neck.

At first, she resisted his initiative. Her training and education told her his intentions did not seem to be consistent with Society law. Anod wanted to stop, she considered a more physical, resistive response, but she could not resolve the conflict between the tutelage of her youth and morays of her people, and her basic curiosity that possessed her. Maybe she wouldn't violate any rules. After all, being naked was not particularly unusual, or even out of the ordinary.

Anod liked the sensations she was feeling. His hands slid down her shoulders and arms until they touched her breasts. Ever so gently, he enveloped her breasts caressing the curves and feeling her nipples respond to his touch. She had never had anyone touch her like that. His touch was not just a touch. She felt more. A caring, appreciative feeling passed through his fingertips into the core of body and soul. The remainder of her resistance seemed to evaporate as the need to learn more occupied her mind.

The electrified sensations shooting through her body were intriguing, frightening, painful and pleasurable. Anod thought her knees would buckle when he firmly squeezed one of her nipples. The peculiar sensation in her groin was seductive and intoxicating producing warm waves that rolled over her body. Anod wondered how the touch of this man could possibly cause such luscious physical responses. Were these feelings within her, untapped all along, or were they the product of some magical properties of his hands and fingers? The sensations and emotions were overwhelming in a good way, and yet they scared her as well. The changes within her body were new. The throbbing in her chest, the ache in her lower abdomen and the wetness between her legs were all sensations that were totally alien to her.

He broke his fondling only long enough to complete her disrobing as well as his own. Otis drew her body close to him so the heat of their bodies combined to draw small beads of sweat over them. He caressed the twin globes of her posterior with a delicate, appreciative, light sliding of his hands.

Anod could feel the rivulets of perspiration descending her body and mingling with his. The moisture made their bodies slip and slide like well-oiled machinery. She could also feel a hard object pressed tightly between them. There was a strong element of curiosity about the changes she was experiencing. At just that moment, she felt him move his right hand to the small patch of hair between her legs. His touch remained light and gentle as he probed the folds of her flesh. With an involuntary movement that surprised her, Anod moved her legs slightly further apart only to feel his finger enter her. The gasp from her lungs was as much the result of her astonishment as it was the pleasure of her acceptance of him. Anod pulled away instantly. The images in her mind never came close to this. No one, human or android, had ever touched her like that, been inside her body. There was no question in her mind about the prohibition of such intimacy.

Shock, concern and fear filled his eyes. "Did I hurt you?"

"No."

"What happen? Why did you pull away? Didn't it feel good? Haven't you ever felt that before?"

Anod considered whether to answer his questions as she tried to find her own answers. It was too much. Society law clearly forbade intimate contact. While she might be able to rationalize his touch and his kiss, a finger inside her body could not be rationalized with the intent of

Society law. It was not right. "It is not permitted."

"What? You mean making a connection with you is not allowed?"

"Yes."

"That's incredible. It is what men and women are supposed to do. They are made to be close. Why else would a man have a penis that fits so naturally and perfectly in a woman's vagina?" There was a flash of surprise in his eyes as if he had said something he shouldn't have spoken. "I'm sorry I didn't mean to be so frank."

"No apology necessary. Is that what you were going to do?"

"It was the direction we were headed."

Anod knew unequivocally it was wrong. She struggled to think about the law and even harder to remember what the punishment was for such violations. As hard as she tried, the price for transgression of the intimacy laws did not come back to her. However, she also knew his logic did make sense. Why did males have a penis that changed size so dramatically? She had seen men, her compatriots, with erections many times, but she had never associated the rigid, protruding male member with the cavity between her legs. Maybe there was truth to his statement. Maybe that was why men and women were structured the way they were. Her thoughts returned to sheer pleasure of his touch. It did feel good, she admitted to herself. Almost as good as flying among the stars. She could not deny the pleasure. There were no laws against pleasure. Anod knew she could recite the essence of the law even if she could not remember the exact words. But, why? Why did the Society really have the intimacy laws? There was a dominant measure of discovery that kept coming back to her. These were feelings she had never felt and she liked them. She wanted to feel more. Maybe one experience like a low pass over the surface of a moon would not compromise her. Maybe it would be OK, not hurt her.

Otis must have sensed the thoughts within her. "Do you want to continue? Do you want to experience making love?" he asked with some trepidation, but obvious sincerity.

"I don't know. Part of me does and part of me knows I shouldn't, I can't."

"What does you heart tell you?"

"I don't know. I've lived my life on the strength of my brain, my logic, not my heart."

"Maybe it is time to listen to you heart."

"Maybe."

"So, what does your heart tell you?"

The thoughts were new, different, seductive and confusing. She was in new territory. She had no experience base to help her resolve the questions. Maybe she should listen to her heart, trust the feelings.

"Well?"

His chiseled body and deep brown color were impressive in a most artistic sense. She wanted to feel his touch, to answer the wealth of questions about what the sensations meant. What was the connection?

"I don't know."

"Maybe we shouldn't then?"

"I just don't know, Otis. You are a nice man. I enjoyed your touch, your gentleness. I have so many more questions than I have answers. I just don't know."

Otis stood before her calmly and innocently as he waited patiently for her to reach her own decision without any pressure from him.

"I should think one time would not hurt," Anod responded with a slight smile and less than full confidence.

"Are you sure?"

"No, I'm not, but I'm willing to try."

Otis moved toward her. Her body seemed to melt into his as his arms enveloped her. Ever so slowly, Otis began to kiss her again. The feelings returned quickly. Anod herself sought his lips, encouraged his touch, felt his muscles with her fingertips.

Reaching down to her knees, Otis lifted her like a feather. With extraordinary dexterity and strength, he balanced on one leg and used the other to pull back the covers of her bed. Lowering her gently to the bed, he moved with the precision and grace of a big cat to lie next to her.

Events were moving much too fast for Anod. She was without question in territory that was wholly foreign to her. She had no experiences to rely on. A voice within her told her to slow down; she did not know what was going to happen next. And yet, Anod was not able to stop. She wanted, she needed, to know what was on the other side.

Otis gently moved her knees apart as he moved between them. Anod watched with an almost detached curiosity as he entered her body. An audible groan emerged from her in recognition of the slight pain she felt and the intense pleasure that mixed with it. Ever so slowly, he pushed deeper into her. Anod felt every millimeter of him gradually fill her up like some strange missing puzzle piece. They were joined together as one. The motions of their bodies blended as each complemented the other.

Anod amazed herself more by the reactions and responses of her own body than she was by Otis and the feelings associated with their union. The sensations saturated her thoughts and awareness.

Anod found her body responding in ways beyond her control. Her state of being frightened her. Everything in her life was centered on control. She took great pride in her mastery of events. This situation was like none other in her entire existence. Anod resented the sense of irresistible abandon, and yet she was sucked further into the whirlpool of passion that was a vast unknown region. There was no resistance available to her. She hated it and she loved it. But, worst of all to her consciousness, she found herself needing it.

They moved together changing positions numerous times to find new angles and sensations, to expose new portions of anatomy to the access of their touch. There were no words between them, simply the message of touch. The heat of their athleticism, enthusiasm and enjoyment became unbearable.

Otis' motion took on a new urgency, simultaneous with a strange tingling feeling originating at the point of their union and spread rapidly throughout her entire body. The changing waves of these sensations overwhelmed her. The panting groans from her chest increased in frequency and volume along with the surge of the hot wave building quickly deep within her body and soul.

The wave crested and crashed down upon her with a violence that shook her entire body. The shudders of ecstasy joined with an enraptured scream of pleasure.

Shortly after the hot, rolling waves of pleasure engulfed her, Anod felt every muscle in Otis' body become as rigid as steel. He shook like a great building quivering from the force of tectonic shifting of its rock footing. Soft, imperceptible growls, almost like murmurs, were restrained within him.

The urgency of their breathing absorbed both of them as they collapsed into each other's arms. They lay together still joined as fatigue overcame both of them. Recovery was slow and coupled with a gradual descent into sleep.

In the semi-conscious state approaching deep sleep, Anod thought she heard Otis whisper, "I love you." A subconscious smile passed over her.

Chapter 10

The bright, distinct beams of light from θ27 sprinkled and danced across the forest floor on this clear, crisp day. Anod could hear the insects moving among the leaves beneath her. The birds flew in different patterns through the trees. Several species simply soared on the light wind above the trees as a celebration of flight, while others darted among the vegetation scooping up the various insects detected by their refined senses.

Occasionally, a small cloud rolled and tumbled in a languid and yet purposeful procession above the broken canopy of trees. There was an attractive fascination about the motion of the clouds. The scientific element of her education taught her considerable knowledge about the vast variety of clouds observed throughout the universe. Even though Anod had never set foot on Earth nor observed the clouds of the Earth atmosphere, she knew the clouds above her were quite similar.

This was the first day since her arrival at High Cave she decided just to relax and enjoy nature without performing any of her usual duties. Anod lay on the forest floor with her arms and legs spread wide like a pinwheel. The light reflected off the leaves of the trees flickering like tiny beacons scattered all around.

The sounds and the scents of the forest were an accentuation of the visual images around her. The birds were the most vocal with an almost symphonic melody of soft chirps to loud screams. There was a definite rhythm to the forest.

Anod lay so still for such a long time, several different mammals cautiously worked their way toward her to investigate the strange addition to their forest. The wondrous enjoyment within her had to be carefully contained to avoid frightening them. A large racoon, a small yearling deer and a solo but menacing wolf each sniffed her body with their cold wet noses sending slight tremors through her. Without knowing what the animals would do, there was a certain tension to allow for an instant reaction, if need be, although none was required.

Between visits from the local residents, Anod's thoughts continued to review events in a random order. The topic most often passing through her consciousness was Otis Greenstreet and the episode of five nights ago.

The warmth of pleasure and enjoyment remained vividly with her, but there was an underlying fear as well. The dark side of her thoughts was much like a primitive person faced with the ritualistic power of demon spirits. There was a foreboding to the sensations she felt. Uncontrollable forces were being unleashed never to be contained again. Her heritage, although not instructive in the communications of human intimacy, presented her with established limits that were now far behind her. Anod was alone upon the sea of personal discovery. The contrast between her sense of transgression and her feelings of desire for the new experiences spanned the full spectrum from the deepest black to the most brilliant white. Anod felt something was wrong, and yet she also felt the dawning of a new era.

It was an hour or so after midday when Bradley arrived alone. He passed a little more than 200 meters from her recumbent position.

Anod waited until she recognized him, then called out. "Bradley, I'm over here."

The Betan leader stopped to look toward the sound of her voice. It took several seconds for him to see her and only after she raised her torso resting on her elbows. The broad smile on his face vanished in a flash to be replaced with a mysterious expression near terror. Bradley sprang toward her running as fast as he could.

"Are you OK? What happened? Did anyone hurt you?" he fired the questions expressing his concern.

Anod laughed loudly as she assured him. "I'm quite all right. In fact, I don't think I've ever been better."

"You gave me quite a start seeing you lying on the ground out here."

"I am sorry if I scared you, but I was simply enjoying the expanse of nature around me," she responded. "This is not an activity I have been able to enjoy before."

"Maybe I should join you, then," he said as he lay down on his back beside her. "I don't get to do this very often either."

Anod could hear his breathing as his body struggled to dissipate the adrenaline squeezed into his cardiovascular system. His actions certainly illustrated his personal concern for her well-being that made Anod feel even better inside. It was good to have friends, especially new friends.

"I thought I would bring the good news myself," Bradley said. "The Yorax have departed finally. Fortunately, they were not able to find any evidence of your existence. They left behind an array of remote sensors that I believe we have completely located and identified. We still need to be careful, but the situation looks considerably better."

"That is good news, Bradley. How is the Seymour investigation going?"

"It has been concluded. The incident was determined to be justifiable homicide. I met, along with the security people, with the witnesses at Seymour. I believe everyone is completely satisfied although very few people know who you are and why the events were justifiable."

"That is also good news."

Bradley rolled toward her so he was resting on one elbow. Anod did not move other than to roll her head slightly to look directly into his caring eyes.

"I've come to take you down from the mountain. If you are ready, we can leave promptly for my father's home. We shall have dinner with him."

"I am quite ready. I think I should close up High Cave, and then we can go, if that's OK."

"Absolutely."

They rose together and walked to the cave. He chattered like a schoolboy about the events of the last couple of weeks. Bradley was obviously proud of his accomplishments as well as the beneficial turn of events.

Returning High Cave to essentially its original condition did not take much time. They began the journey to Nick's cave at about mid-afternoon. The walk would take less time since it was downhill. Barring any unexpected delays, they expected to arrive at Nick's domicile around sunset. Earthlings, regardless of their ancestry, still used Earth astronomical terms. The $\theta27$ star was not the Sun and yet they referred to the day-night terminus as sunset.

The discussion enroute was a stop and start amplification of the activities of the Yorax and the actions of the Betan people. The issue of communications was raised several times during the journey. Anod was quite aware of the conflict mounting within her soul between the excitement of this planet and its people, and the yearning to be with her long time friends. There was also the smoldering fire of retribution for Zitger's betrayal of Team Three. The need to set things right was strong.

The descent from High Cave took even less time than expected. They arrived at the clearing prior to sunset to find Nick sitting outside observing the clouds and the intricate colors sprayed across the sky.

Upon seeing his son and their guest, Nick rose from his seat and walked quickly toward them. "Anod, it is so good to see you again," he said as he embraced her and kissed her on both cheeks.

"It is good to see you again, Nick."

"How did it go up in the high country?" Nick asked.

"My stay at High Cave was very relaxing despite the lack of communications. I enjoyed the exposure to nature."

"That's good. We were concerned about you since things are a bit primitive up there."

"I had no problems. It took me a few tries to get used to the cold water of the fall, but even that became enjoyable."

"How was your health up there?" Nick continued his questioning.

"My health was great. The mountain air seems to have a therapeutic value for both the body and soul. I have only one concern," Anod said as she hesitated for a moment. "A few days ago I began bleeding between my legs for some unknown reason."

The expression on Nick's face immediately changed to the stern expression of neutral concentration. Even Bradley's smile vanished as he listened intently.

"Did you injure yourself?" Nick asked.

"No."

"Did you do anything different, or unusual?"

Anod thought for a moment with an innocence of *naïveté*, then said, "The only thing unusual for me was, Otis Greenstreet and I made love, as he called it."

"What!" Bradley exclaimed verging on anger. His eyes turned from concern to rage in a flash.

"Bradley, please. Leave us, now," Nick commanded.

Bradley looked disapprovingly at his father, but did not argue. He turned and walked off down the hill as if he were leaving for the train waystation.

Nick cleared his throat. He shifted his weight several times which was a clear sign of his uneasiness with this situation.

Anod did not understand what was happening or why, other than she was probably experiencing first hand the other emotions associated with human intimacy.

He cleared his throat again as he struggled with words. "You say, you and young Greenstreet . . . uhhmmm . . . you and Otis made love."

"Yes."

"How long ago was that?" Nick asked trying to be detached.

"That was five days ago."

"When did the bleeding start?"

"Yesterday."

"Do you have any pain in your lower abdominal region?"

"None."

"Have you had a menstrual cycle?"

"I'm afraid I don't know what that is, Nick."

The older man finally smiled with a combination of a huge burden being lifted and acknowledgment of a profound discovery. "Have you ever bled like that before?"

"No."

"They must have suppressed your menstrual cycle," he said more to himself than to Anod as he looked at his feet. Then, he spoke gently to her eyes. "They must have given you some drug to suppress your reproductive system. Now that you've been separated from that process, your reproductive system is returning to normal functionality."

Anod did not respond. Her mind raced through all of the retrievable information in her memory.

Nick explained the entire human reproductive cycle and related physiological effects with her. Actually, she listened mostly although she did ask an occasional question.

Nick suggested an examination to determine the validity of his diagnosis. Much to Nick's chagrin, but not his surprise, Anod submitted to his examination without the slightest modesty. The diagnosis was correct.

The changes in her life from the controlled environment of the Society never seemed to stop rushing at her. Some of the changes were more difficult to handle than others. This was one of those changes. The realization that the Society regulated her body as well as her environment was not a comfortable thought.

"Well, at least you're not pregnant."

"You mean . . . you think I can become pregnant?" Anod asked with a curious, inquisitive tone.

"I believe so."

"Then, why was Bradley so upset?"

"Anod, my dear," Nick said more as a father than a medical technician. "Bradley cares for you a great deal. In fact, I think he loves you. Making love is a very special activity between a man and a woman. I suppose he thought that was his place."

"What does that mean, his place?" Anod did not like the sound of the words, or the image the words created within her soul.

"He wanted to be the first to make love to you, I suspect," Nick answered with some solemnity in his voice.

The ensuing discussion regarding the nuances and subtleties of human emotions enlightened and perplexed Anod. Terms like desire, monogamy, lust, virginity and fidelity were explained in detail with Anod's barrage of questions adding to the expanse of the conversation.

"Maybe I should take the liberty to tell you a little more about my son," Nick said waiting for a sign of agreement from Anod. "He was, and still is, a very intelligent and ambitious person, but there are several events which have affected his life." He hesitated to choose his words. "Bradley was very close to his mother, as I was. She was a high-spirited, dynamic woman. Unfortunately, she was killed when he was 12 years old by a marauding band of Feretonin bandits."

Anod lowered her head slightly to say, "I am terribly sorry."

Nick acknowledged her condolence and continued. "He worked hard to learn the basic skills of a fighter although I struggled to dampen his vengeful vigor. I believe, as our people do, violence simply brings more violence. As he matured, he learned to control his desire for retribution. However, the loss of his mother at such a critical time in his life left a permanent scar."

Another momentary pause enveloped Nick as he collected the necessary words. "The other significant event was the loss of his young wife and newborn child. This was many years ago although sometimes he acts as if it happened yesterday. He had already assumed a leadership role within our Council and was responsible for security. His wife, Mary, was nearing her birthing time when some unexpected crisis, I can't remember what it was, called him away. Bradley thought he could take care of the situation and return in time. That was not to be the case. Despite the best attempts of some of our medical experts, Mary died as a result of a rare complication and the newborn boy died a few days later from unknown causes before Bradley could return to them. He has never forgiven himself for either loss."

"The loss of people close to you is very difficult to deal with. However, death is part of life. He should not blame himself for events which were beyond his control," Anod said with softness in her voice.

"Of course, you are right, but that does not change his feelings."

Anod looked around remembering that Bradley had walked off into the forest. She could not detect any sign of him. Nick quickly recognized the effort.

"He will return when he is ready. Maybe we should get something to eat?"

"Certainly," Anod answered without enthusiasm. "Do you think we should look for Bradley?" she asked earnestly.

"No. He is off by himself, probably down by the river, if I were to guess. He wants time to think."

Bradley did not return to his father's cave that night. Quiet thoughts intruded on the pleasure of conversation with Nick. Curiosity as well as an unexplainable stroke of empathy mixed with her concern for Bradley. Anod wanted to know more about his thoughts and the reasons for his anger.

The following day was spent observing Nick as he experimented with several new devices he had been working on. A strange mixture of medical, personal and communications devices were distributed on the various benches in the rooms of his laboratory. Nick was a medical doctor by education, training and profession although he was a research scientist by avocation.

Anod admired the depth of his personality and capabilities. The impressive number of facets to Nick's character was on balance with the sheer power of technology within the Society. The Betans could not do as much as the Society, but they were more fully dimensioned individuals.

Conversations throughout the day sprang from topic to topic as Nick and Anod compared thoughts and observations. Each learned from the other. There was a lightness, an airiness, to the words that passed between them, whether the subject of the moment was a physiological detail, a computer application problem, or appreciation of the flavors of various fruits. Anod enjoyed talking to Nick. He was simply fun to be around.

Late in the light of day, as Anod reclined against a tree watching nature's myriad of activities around her, Bradley returned to his birthplace.

"Anod, I must apologize for my rude departure. I simply needed time to think," he said as he approached her. His mood was calm and pleasant.

"There is no need to apologize, Bradley. We all need time to think sometimes."

"Have you enjoyed your first day back?"

"I most certainly have. It is a genuine treat being around your father. He is an extremely interesting man."

"I would agree although he does have trouble with focus sometimes," Bradley said with a laugh toward his absent father.

The image of Bradley's departure slipped casually back into her thoughts. Anod debated with her conscience whether she should ask him to explain his reasons. Curiosity defeated courtesy.

"Why did you leave so abruptly, yesterday?"

His expression changed from jovial to serious in an instant. She recognized the precarious nature of the topic for Bradley. The struggle with acknowledgment and the decision to discuss the subject was quite obvious on his face and in his eyes. Anod felt the raw edge of regret for broaching what was obviously a sensitive subject for Bradley.

"By discussing my reasons, I must also admit to you the frailties and vulnerabilities of our emotions, of my emotions." Bradley stopped with his eyes on the ground between them allowing time for him to compose his sentences. He raised his head to look directly into Anod's waiting eyes. "You are a very special woman. We have been blessed with your presence. Despite our disagreements, I have become quite attached to you. I recognize that I have assumed too much and taken too much for granted with respect to your feelings."

Bradley paused again, breaking eye contact probably to sort through the next block of words. Anod did not speak or move, and continued to wait patiently for him to vocalize his thoughts.

"I regret that Otis took advantage of your innocence," he continued. "I believe physical love between a man and a woman is special and unique. It is also the process of procreation. The incident with Otis brought back a few too many memories of earlier losses. I simply felt it was happening again."

His eyes remained on her as if to ask, what do you think? Anod considered whether to mention Nick's offering of information about his past, but thought better of it. She could feel the sincerity and emotion still floating around them even though the words had passed.

"Did my contact with Otis spoil our relationship?"

"No, not unless we want it to."

"I have not lost anything. I am still the same person. In fact, I suspect I may be a better person from the experience. Otis is a very nice young man. I appreciated his company and his humanity. There is nothing for me to be ashamed of."

Bradley looked like a little boy caught in the act of some

mischievousness. He again stared at the ground between them and kicked a few stones across the ground.

The specter of forbidding returned to her like a bolt of lightning. The physical act with Otis at High Cave was not accepted behavior for a Kartog warrior, male or female. The recognition of her violation was strong within her, but the conflict with the blossoming of her human heritage was also changing her thinking.

"I wanted to be your first lover," he said without looking at her. There was a tone of embarrassment in his voice.

Such timidity for a leader was strange and foreign to Anod. And yet, the contrast seemed to make him even more human. Maybe these were characteristics she would just have to get used to.

"Bradley, my feelings for you have not changed. I am not entirely certain what all these emotions mean, but they are undeniable. They are not something I am accustomed to. I care for you very much."

His mood changed as he raised his head to look into her eyes. Without speaking, he stepped toward her. Their lips touched in a momentary kiss between a man and a woman.

"Maybe I should say hello to my father."

"That sounds like an excellent idea to me," Anod responded with a bubbly tone. She wanted to keep the mood of the moment moving toward the upbeat and positive side.

As growing friends, their talks invariably intertwined history with life on Beta. Nick recounted their history from the banishment of his ancestors from Earth, initially to a colony on Mars. Then, as the population of Earth began to migrate further into the solar system, they were pushed farther and farther away from Earth. He described the odyssey in significantly more detail than he had several weeks earlier.

There was a definite fascination, for Anod, listening to the history of these people. The hardships they endured. The incessant movement that forced them farther away from Earth as punishment for their dissension. An air of persecution was delicately woven into the meaning of the constructed sentences. Resentment did not flutter into his words like an uninvited wasp. The balance Nick maintained between the difficulties of the past and the accomplishments of the present impressed Anod.

Nick also spoke with considerable praise about the incalculable value of the series of macrobiological and ecosystemic experiments that began in the late 20th century on Earth. Fortunately for the Betans, some of the principle architects of those early efforts were among the banished.

Additional infusions of knowledge, several different times during the early years, helped them adapt rapidly to new environments.

The two previous planetary experiments prior to arrival on Beta had been failures. In both cases, the basic natural environment had been too immature and the imported organisms did not possess a broad enough adaptability. In those cases, a balanced ecosystem was never achieved. Luckily, $\theta27\beta$ was a mature, ecologically stable planet that was able to easily accept the additional organisms carried by the pioneers.

"For a group of people prohibited to have spacecraft, you sure were a nomadic group," Anod observed with a slight chuckle.

"We had help initially from the Earth Coalition. Later, we were fortunate enough to run across several benevolent traders who were willing to help," Nick explained.

"You've been on Beta for the last 75 years?"

"A little less than that, actually."

"Then, Bradley was born here," she said looking at Nick. "Were you born here also, Nick?"

"No. I was born on Garundar in the Gammalulon System. My wife, Sara, and I did not immigrate to Beta until about 50 years ago. Bradley was born right here in this cave, in the next room, actually."

"I've been to Garundar. It is not a nice place," Anod added.

"We tried hard to make it a better place, but we were all glad to leave that forsaken planet."

"From what you've told me," she said smiling to both Nick and Bradley, "life on Beta has been pretty challenging as well."

"The early years were difficult. Eventually, Sara and I felt good enough about the situation and our progress to bring a new life into this world." Nick grinned at Bradley and reached across the table to ruffle his hair. "I think we're here to stay this time."

The relationship between father and son was noticeably different from any relationship she had experienced. Something was missing in her life as pieces of a puzzle lost in a move. The attachment between two human beings represented by Nick and Bradley was one of the missing pieces, Anod was now convinced.

Nick was the first to recognize and acknowledge the late hour. "I'm turning in," he said as he rose from the table.

The inquisitive expression on Anod's face undoubtedly prompted Bradley to say, "It means he's going to bed. It's a phrase from our mutual distant past, I might add."

Recognition also came to Anod. They joined Nick rising from the table. Bradley hesitated. Anod thought he had something else he wanted to say. He moved slowly toward her.

"I'm glad you're here," he said. "I hope you'll have a good night's sleep." He leaned forward to kiss her on the cheek.

Anod liked the feelings she had around him now much better than when she first met him. Reaching up with both hands, Anod gently gripped his head and pulled him toward her. She kissed him with a growing demonstration of the fires of passion kindled earlier within her. Bradley wrapped his arms around her body drawing her even closer. The sensations deep within her, similar to that evening with Otis Greenstreet, came flooding back into her. Anod liked the electricity surging through every nerve in her body.

Bradley stopped abruptly growing stiff next to her. "I can't," he said. "Not yet. I'll see you in the morning." He started to walk away.

"Did I do something wrong?" she asked innocently.

"No. You did absolute nothing wrong, Anod. The problem is within me," he admitted. After a brief moment for thought, he said, "Please, have a good night's sleep. Everything will be OK, just give me a little time."

Anod nodded her agreement.

Anod was not aware of any scheduled or even planned activities the next morning. She woke early, but did not rise. It was easy to drift in and out of semi-consciousness between sleep and alertness. The smoothness of the sheets were one of the small, new pleasures Anod discovered, or more properly, been exposed to since her arrival on Beta.

Her thoughts meandered among the short spans of dozing. The broad variety of the images came and went through her consciousness. Last night's kiss; the speed of the trains; the mass of people in Providence; Bradley's volatility toward her heritage; the sensations with Otis; they were all around her. Gradually, the thoughts occupied more of her sagacity until eventually she recognized the futility of extending her time in bed.

Nick moved through his usual routine when she got up without concern for the languid routine of the others in his home. Anod chose to eat some fruit and a little bread instead of preparing a fuller meal.

"Where's Bradley?" she asked Nick.

"I think he's still sleeping," he answered without looking up from his workbench.

This morning's project was another electronic circuit board being modified to accomplish some different task. There was a certain affinity with this old form of inanimate calculation and decision-making. The Society's vast computer systems used a hybrid molecular circuitry taking advantage of the unique properties of electrons and photons as well as magnetism. There was an element of enjoyment in seeing how old technology performed similar tasks.

Noticing the time, Anod suggested, "Maybe I should check on Bradley."

"You didn't stay up too much later than I did last night, did you?"

"No."

"Then, it might be a good idea to check on him. It is unusual for him to sleep in."

Anod checked his room and established his absence. "He's not there," Anod reported.

"Then, he's probably off trying to complete some action or another." Although hospitable enough, Nick's concentration was on the task before him, not conversation.

Anod thought she would take a little walk through the forest to see if she could discover some new creature or scene to add to her experience.

Despite the serenity of the Betan forest, the conflicts in her life began to crowd her conscious thoughts. Why did she never touch her own skin before her arrival on this planet? The touch of her hands provided an inner appreciation and its own form of pleasure. She liked the feel of her skin, the curves of her body, the softness of her breasts. Even the scars dotted around her body could not spoil the pleasure of her own touch. The little differences seemed to occupy the greatest time. The isopod versus the bed. The cleaning chamber versus the shower. The replicator versus human prepared foods. Anod found herself thinking of the possibility of combining the effortlessness and thoroughness of the Society's bodily cleaning station with the enjoyment of the Betan water shower. The best of both worlds, Anod thought. It might not be practical, but it was an attractive idea, the combination of efficiency and pleasure. However, it was the big items that were the most troublesome.

Her asexual, focused, unemotional life as a protector of the Society was now in almost mortal combat with the pleasurable, multi-dimensional emotional character of the banished earthlings. Anod enjoyed, or rather was learning to enjoy, the pleasures of being human. The downside of her existence on Beta was the irrepressible feeling that she was trapped, or hobbled. The yearning to travel among the stars was and would remain strong within her, but the satisfaction of her need was virtually impossible without the higher technology of the Society, or even the Yorax. Anod liked the Betans, Nick and Bradley SanGiocomo, and Otis Greenstreet, as well as her other acquaintances. Juxtaposed with these feelings was the reality that she also missed the professional discussions with her comrades on Saranon or on a passing Society Starship.

There just did not seem to be any path or method available to her for blending the best of both worlds. It was an attractive idea although there was always the risk of contamination of one or both worlds in the process of assimilation. Nonetheless, the idea had merit.

By the time she returned to Nick's cave, the light of day was rapidly dwindling with the spin of the planet away from the life-giving star. Bradley had returned sometime earlier. Both men were seated at the table talking and casually eating. Their discussion occupied the preponderance of their attention. Anod could hear an occasional word or phrase as she moved toward the eating area.

The conversation was actually a debate. They were rationalizing their respective views on whether to show Anod something, some object. Anod knew without hearing all the words, the discussion was not meant for her participation or consumption. Her respect for her benefactor outweighed her curiosity.

"Hello, I'm back," she said loudly with a melodious, almost singing tone. She was still about ten meters from the room, but they needed time to recompose their conversation, or end it. They chose the latter.

"We're in here, Anod," Bradley said first.

Speaking as she approached the eating area, she said, "I hope you had as glorious of a day as I have had." She completed her sentence as she entered the well-lit room. Her eyes required a few moments to adjust to the increased intensity.

"I've been walking through the forest enjoying the plants and animals, the water and the air. You have such a magnificent planet."

"I'm glad you like it," Nick said sounding somewhat distant although trying to be cordial.

The three of them exchanged descriptions, observations and impressions of the flora and fauna of Beta as well as other planets within their mutual experience. It was clear to Anod they were not ready to talk about the sensitive topic and Anod left it that way. Not one thread of controversial, sensitive or even serious conversation arose this evening.

Bradley was the first to fold having given up his protracted struggle with fatigue. He excused himself wishing his father and Anod a peaceful and pleasant night's sleep. There was no kiss this night, not even an attempt, probably in deference to the presence of his father, Anod surmised. The reason was unclear. The fact was disappointing.

It did not take Nick much longer, before he too needed to retire for his rest. Anod was left with the solace of her own thoughts that quickly led her to the shower and bed. She considered going to Bradley since she longed to feel his touch. Her intrusion would not be fair, she concluded. Anod quickly released her thoughts to enter the rejuvenating sanctuary of sleep.

Anod found the note on the table near a large bowl of fruit and a freshly baked loaf of bread. It was a simple message to inform her of an unspecified errand that required both of them to attend to. They intended to return around nightfall.

The note, coupled with the private words apparently about her the previous night and their unusual departure without an explanation, began to raise her suspicions. The process was as natural as the stars. When one item is found out of place, it is noted. When two items are found out of place, there is a reason.

Anod decided, since she had the day to herself, maybe it was time to analyze Nick's little projects.

As a precaution against the possibility of surprise, Anod carefully arranged a band of dry leaves near the entrance of the cave. She took great care to make the arrangement look natural. The slightest crackle of someone stepping on the leaves would be heard.

Satisfied she would have some warning, Anod quickly set upon the task of inventorying and assessing Nick's projects. There was no emotion as she methodically worked her way through his laboratory.

Anod's survey lasted several hours. The singularly impressive variety of projects included medical instruments and devices, astronomical image processors, and a complex signal processor for the subterranean rock communicator. They were all hand made, personal tributes to the mind of their creator.

Of more significance was the file of printed messages from the rock communicator. Most of the messages were routine, simple, governmental communiqués sent to and recorded by Nick SanGiocomo for his son, the Prime Minister. The messages to Bradley were the first reference to his title as the leader of the Betan people. Prime Minister Bradley James SanGiocomo had a certain ring to it.

Sprinkled among the routine dispatches were several cryptic notes about unnecessary exposure to a controversial piece of equipment. Two of the messages alluded to 'our guest.' Even without direct linkage to Anod, it was easy to assume that she was 'the guest' the Council was referring to. The sensitivity of the item was quite apparent based on the coded names, the lack of other related information and the strong words regarding consequences. There was one message in the entire file that made Anod run up the remaining defensive elements of her psyche.

Possible reasons for events of the last few weeks began to make some sense. The image formed in her mind regarding her presence as an open wound for these people. She was a threat to their way of life. Several members of the council wanted to negotiate with the Yorax to avoid any future conflict. One positive indication was Bradley's political position defending her recovery and safe passage.

Anod closed the file, satisfied she had extracted every fragment of information she could from the messages. She walked to the mouth of the cave. Her rudimentary warning system was still intact. Anod's mind continued to churn through all the information she acquired during her survey.

There were still too many variables to eliminate most of the alternatives to arrive at a conclusion. The turmoil her presence brought to this planet and the leadership of its people had a foreboding nature to it. An inevitability of her compromise seemed to be quite clear. The confining feeling of caged animal returned to her, again. She felt like an eagle with a broken wing unable to use all its capabilities to defend herself from a predator.

True to the note they left that morning, Nick and Bradley arrived shortly after sunset. Anod was sitting under the leafy branches of a tree near the edge of the clearing watching the color changes of a disappearing star. She heard their approach a good ten minutes before they emerged from the forest. They did not notice Anod sitting in the shadows.

"Welcome back," Anod said from her seat.

Both men stopped their discussion as well as their walk turning toward her.

"Are you out here enjoying our sunset?" Nick asked with lightness to his words.

"Yes," she answered succinctly. There was coldness to her voice. "I have had an enjoyable day." The words had no emotion.

They both glanced over their shoulders in the direction of θ27. Bradley walked toward Anod as Nick continued to absorb and enjoy the mixture of colors painted across the sky.

"What did you do today?" Bradley asked.

"Just relaxed." Anod did not feel particularly talkative.

She searched their eyes, expressions, body motions and words for clues to what might be happening, or about to happen.

"Is something wrong, Anod?" Bradley asked.

Should she confront the situation, she asked herself? Both men displayed concern in their eyes. Why did they save and protect her? Do they have ulterior motives? Is she supposed to serve some other devious purpose? So many things did not match up.

"Where did you go today?" she asked with a slight smile trying to mask her suspicion.

"We had a meeting in a small town several thousand kilometers from here," Bradley responded.

"What was the meeting about?"

Their expressions changed. The immediacy of the questions brought winds of distrust. Bradley continued to do the talking. "Anod, we had a special meeting of the Leadership Council." He stopped for a moment as if he tried to decide what to say, or how to say it. "We have decided to take a very big risk for our people. There is serious concern your presence will continue to place our planet and people in jeopardy." He continued to look directly into her eyes although he did not speak.

"What do you want me to do?"

"Tomorrow, I will take you to our meeting place. We have decided to show you one of our most sensitive secrets. We are trusting you to respect our wishes and conditions," he said.

"What are they?" There was no point in agreeing to conditions without knowing the situation and consequences.

Bradley methodically detailed the litany of conditions required for her access to the secret place. The prerequisites were understandable and acceptable especially since she considered herself an outsider. The most intriguing condition was that the unnamed property would remain under the control of the Betan Leadership Council. The property. Maybe they were talking about the device mentioned in a couple of the cryptic messages in Nick's file.

"Agreed," Anod simply stated.

"Before I give you any more information, I must impress upon you . . . well . . . I should say . . . well . . . we are trusting you with our safety," Bradley said with considerable solemnity and reservation.

Anod did not answer for a short time. The seriousness of the moment warranted a hesitation. With equal gravity, she said, "I have no problem with that. I just hope you are not going to ask me to compromise my beliefs."

A short, choppy laugh answered her response. Bradley smiled. "We are not going to ask you to compromise your beliefs. We are going to show you a damaged Yorax interceptor."

"What!"

Both men nodded their heads as Bradley continued. "Nearly five years ago, the interceptor was discovered abandoned, drifting in space. It was brought here by one of our trusted merchant traders."

"Alexatron," Nick added.

"Is the craft flyable?"

"We do not know," Bradley answered.

"I believe it is with some repairs," Nick offered. "There is some battle damage mostly to structure although there is also some specific damage to the ship's circuitry."

"Why haven't you tried to fly it?"

"First, as we talked about earlier, our culture formed under a prohibition from space travel. We have simply chosen as a people not to undertake such activity," Bradley said. "Second, we don't have any pilots."

"I can handle the last part," she stated confidently. "Why are you now willing to take this risk?"

"We have not failed to notice your sense of confinement. We acknowledge that you may feel like a prisoner on Beta, and your heart is in space," Bradley said.

Anod surmised that the craft was hidden in a cave of antratite to shield it from probing sensors. She turned her attention to another concern. "Could it also be that you want me to leave?"

Again, a serious, focused expression returned to Bradley's face. "There are those among the Council who want you to leave. They are convinced your presence is an ominous threat to our people."

Her defenses lowered slightly as she absorbed his sincerity. "And some of them are right," Anod answered. "As long as the Yorax hunt for me, my presence is a threat."

Bradley's eyes changed expression with his thoughts. "Let's go inside. It's starting to cool off quickly."

Both men intertwined comments on the area where the craft was stored and where Bradley would take her tomorrow. It was another mountainous region in the opposite direction from Providence. The journey would take about five hours by train. Over 2,000 kilometers, Anod told herself, trying to visualize distance, geography and spatial relationships. They would plan to stay at the site for several days to allow Anod sufficient time for inspection and evaluation of the interceptor.

The elder SanGiocomo eventually gave up the effort to remain involved and excused himself.

The conversation between Anod and Bradley slowly began to meander through unrelated topics like the weather, the growth of Providence as the center of Betan government, and the sensory stimulation of the mountain air. Occasionally, Anod's thoughts recalled the sharp contrast between the earlier, near hostile reaction of Nick's son to the now, effervescent, jubilant nature of the man sitting across the table.

The pace of talking diminished gradually until there were noticeable periods of silence. Anod stood and said good night. Bradley's expression changed quickly with his eyes saying, do not leave, I want to say more.

A delicate kiss with their eyes amplifying the message momentarily joined them. Bradley hesitated for several heartbeats then he pulled her whole body toward him. They kissed more deeply than she had ever experienced. She could feel his caress across her back and shoulders. The mysterious electricity she felt with Otis began to flow through her body. Anod was not quite sure what to do about it, but she was certain she wanted the feelings to continue.

Bradley stopped his caress and drew back from her slightly although he did not release her. Anod wondered if he still had some misgivings about her, or reticence because of her union with Otis Greenstreet.

"Anod, you mean a great deal to me. You are a very special woman. I want our relationship to grow. I just don't want to move too fast, to rush things."

"I share your feelings, Bradley."

"I will say, good night, then," he said softly kissing her lightly. "I'll see you in the morning. Have a good night's sleep."

"Thank you. Good night to you."

Anod watched him leave the room, but she wanted to ask him to stay. These relationships were so new to her. She was not confident she knew or could feel the right thing to do.

As she neared the envelopment of sleep, her sixth sense told her something was different. Opening her eyes, she saw the form of a man silhouetted by the dim light from the door behind him.

The silhouette was deep black and solid. The size and shape of the form were clearly those of a mature man wearing a long robe. Despite her superior vision, she could not see any features of the man that might enable recognition. Anod thought the visitor was Bradley, however the lack of recognition tightened her muscles.

Anod raised herself on one elbow as an initial step to any move she might have to make and as a sign she was aware of his presence. The combination sheet and comforter still covered her body.

"I was wondering whether you were awake." The voice confirmed the visitor as Bradley. He did not move.

"I am," Anod answered without indicating her concern.

"Can we talk for a little while?"

"If you wish."

Bradley walked, step by step, toward her bed. His motions were strangely protracted as if he was walking on a thin layer of ice. The features of his face slowly edged out of the black shadow as he turned slightly to sit on the bed near her waist.

"I forgot to tell you about our late departure tomorrow," he said. "After the incident at Seymour Waystation, we felt it was best to travel at night."

Anod could not ascertain the exact dimensions of Bradley's choice of the first person plural, we. Was it simply Bradley and Nick, or was it the majority of the Betan Leadership Council? One possibility meant a wider band of support. The other possibility would explain the new need for secrecy.

"What time do we leave?" Anod asked.

"We'll head down the hill at sunset. There should be virtually no citizens travelling in the direction of the Astral Mountains after dark."

Anod acknowledged Bradley's statement. She waited to see if the announcement was the limit of his thoughts. The Prime Minister of Beta did not move a muscle, not even a blink. The illumination of his brow and cheekbone highlighted the concentration in his eyes. What else did he have to say?

"Anod . . . I have something else . . . well . . . ," Bradley looked down at the sheets between them. "There's something else."

The Kartog Guards warrior felt a bit odd for some strange reason. There was no identifiable explanation. It was just a feeling – a delicate flower blooming full and bright in the middle of a desert – a strange, inexplicable feeling that was totally alien to her.

His eyes still looked down, as if he was waiting for some divine signal. Words were inappropriate, at the moment. Anod decided to change her position. She sat up raising her knees as a pillar for her arms. The sheet fell to the crease between her torso and legs. Bradley glanced up at her now exposed breasts framed by her outstretched arms, but did not reach her eyes.

Finally, he looked up directly into her eyes and spoke. "You may not fully comprehend this, but . . . I love you, Anod." His gaze was intense now. He searched her eyes for recognition. She shook her head ever so slightly which appeared to puzzle him.

"I may not entirely know what you mean, but I do understand that you have special feelings for me."

"Very special feelings."

"I am beginning to comprehend," Anod said as she reached up to gently touch his cheek. She felt the muscles of his face constrict to form a broad smile.

The kiss touched her heart, touched her down deep. She felt his hand softly touch her arm. He did not squeeze, or stroke, or move his hand. He simply wanted to make physical contact with her. His hand was warm, soft and caring.

Without breaking the intimate contact of their eyes, Bradley stood and let his robe fall to the floor. He stood just beyond arm's length. He was naked before her although the details of his body were still predominantly hidden in shadow. Bradley lifted the sheet covering her body to lie down beside her on the small bed without letting go of her eyes.

The feel of his warm, hard body against hers brought a new sensation to her expanding catalogue of experiences on Beta. Anod took his lead to return the gentle caress of his hand. The texture of his skin and the curves, creases and blending of his muscles were all fascinating and attractive to the searching of her fingers.

The exploration and enlightenment of each other, and the intimate, non-verbal communication between a man and a woman occupied the majority of the night. The enjoyment, pleasure, energy, connection and bonding between them climbed to a new, more pronounced level. For

Anod, the kaleidoscope of feelings associated with having Bradley close to her, inside her, took her emotions into distant, unexplored reachs of her consciousness. The surge and recession of their sexual tide inexorably passed as surely as nature's. The process of growing toward each other took long strides forward.

Chapter 11

The journey to the Astral Mountains took more than half the night. As expected, the train was empty except for Bradley and Anod.

The standing lights of Astral Waystation did not last long as the two humans began the difficult part of their journey over the mountainous terrain. The map provided excellent topographical detail for the trek from the train platform to their final destination. The starlight was sufficient for Anod as long as she didn't move too fast. The low ambient light was not enough for Bradley as he turned on a hand light.

"I can do better without the light, Bradley. Would you mind extinguishing the light?"

"It's black out here. I can't see a thing."

"That's OK. I can see for both of us. Put your hands on my shoulders, or my hips," Anod said with confidence. "I'll get us up there."

"Oh, yeah," he responded with a questioning tone as he switched off the light. The pressure of his hands on her hips produced a smile on her face. She enjoyed his touch for whatever reason.

Despite a few stumbles, progress was good. Anod's estimation placed them within a few hundred meters of their destination as sunrise approached. The soft, reddened glow produced an exotic blend of color with the green and brown of the surrounding trees.

Anod led Bradley out of the forest into a large meadow. Approximately a hundred meters across, the nearly circular clearing was flat and bounded by trees around most of the periphery. At the far side of the meadow, a sheer cliff of black rock rose sixty meters straight up. Even in the minimal illumination of twilight, they could see the dark, smooth, rectangular doors covering the mouth of the cave.

The twilight was also enough for Bradley. "We are here," he announced.

The retractable, black doors spanned the twenty-meter opening into the mountain. Anod quickly realized this was not a natural cave. The telltale markings of excavation were clearly visible around the lip of the cave as they approached. A small access hatch in the extreme left sliding door was the method of entry. Bradley quietly worked through a series of mechanical and electronic locking devices to open the hatch. The interior was black except for the narrow column of dim light passing through the hatch. Even Anod's exceptional vision could not see anything other than the floor and suspended dust.

Once the hatch was closed behind them, Bradley switched on the interior lights to reveal the secret they were protecting.

"Well, well, well!" Anod exclaimed as she surveyed the distinct shape of a Yorax interceptor.

The spacecraft was damaged in several areas. The long slender nose was missing the canopy. The characteristic burn marks of an ejection pod rocket motor surrounded the open cavity. The pilot must have felt the need to leave the craft in a hurry. The cause or reason for the separation of the pilot and his craft was not clear from the cursory inspection. The damage to the interior of the cockpit was also indicative of an ejection. The controls and displays of the interceptor cockpit confirmed the Yorax origin. The several jagged and mushroomed holes in the thruster wings and the rear fuselage were positive evidence of battle damage with an inferior opponent. A Kartog Guards fighter would have disintegrated the lightly protected Yorax interceptor.

The main engine propulsor nozzles were completely intact. There were no signs of damage to the propulsion system. The craft appeared to be flightworthy, if the cockpit and fuselage could be repaired, and there was no other significant damage. A very close inspection would be required.

The splendid image of space flight returned to Anod's frontal consciousness. The abused Yorax interceptor would not be her first choice of vehicles to launch herself into space, but it would suffice nonetheless.

"What do you think?" Bradley asked.

"With some repairs, it may be flyable," Anod answered without quantifiable data to substantiate her assessment.

"Do you think we can repair it?" he asked. "Will you be able to fly it?"

"First, I believe it is repairable. We will have to do a much closer inspection to establish the interceptor's specific condition. We'll need some help. Second, I haven't found anything I can't fly, and I know I can fly this . . . ," Anod smiled and looked directly at Bradley, ". . . this piece of junk."

"Good."

Anod placed her hand on the side of the craft just beneath the cavity in the forward fuselage where the pilot once sat. She acted as if she was taking the weak, but still present pulse of a living creature.

"What kind of help do you think you'll need?"

"We'll need a good special materials technician. Our androids would usually handle that task," she said with focused concentration on the prospective reconstruction process. "We'll also need a fabricator, someone who constructs things without plans." Anod paused still thinking of what might be required to repair the interceptor. Eventually, she shook her head.

"I don't think either of those should be a problem."

There was considerably more on Anod's mind. "Where did you get this thing?" came her rhetorical question. It was a verbal recognition of her withheld skepticism on their collective ability to successfully repair the Yorax machine. "What do you think the vehicle's status is?"

"None of our scientists understand the propulsion system," Bradley answered. "In addition, this vehicle is a weapon of war, a combat system. The Council has been very reluctant to acknowledge the presence of this interceptor to the population and to risk the exposure of our people."

"The Council is ready to accept the risk now?" Anod asked with definite concern for the change implicit in her presence at this place.

"Not exactly," he said with a coy grin on his face. "We'd like to know what can be done with the machine before we would allow it to fly."

"I see," Anod paused a moment for effect. "I'm sure you realize there is a real possibility the Yorax may detect the interceptor even in an atmospheric flight."

"Yes." Bradley's expression changed to deadly seriousness. "We are prepared to make that decision."

"Well, then, what's the plan?"

"We can assemble a team of our best experts to assist you. After a thorough evaluation, we'll need to provide further guidance."

"The conditions seem fair."

"Very good. Now, what other skills do you require?"

Anod specified additional technical disciplines including microcircuitry, chemistry, propulsion and computer engineering.

Bradley explained the process of assembling the necessary team of experts she would need for the repairs. It would take him several days to locate, notify and transport the correct people. Bradley added a few additional skills to the list of individuals to assist them. He also proceeded to show Anod the remainder of the hangar facility. Complete living quarters and supplies for a fairly large crew were available along with an impressive array of basic tools. There were sufficient beds for more than twenty people in two separate rooms. Men and women as indicated by the symbolic labels, Anod chuckled to herself.

"I thought your culture prohibited space flight," said Anod with lightness to her words.

The puzzled expression on Bradley's face lasted until Anod motioned to the extensive furnishings of the hangar. Bradley chuckled with his recognition of her intent. "We built this facility especially for this craft."

While they waited for the members of the team to arrive, Anod performed a more detailed inspection providing a running commentary on the attributes, capabilities and limitations of a Yorax interceptor. Mixed among the technical description floated anecdotal snippets to highlight several key elements. Anod's and Bradley's laughter echoed through the large hangar bay. The acoustics accentuated the volume of the interior that made the interceptor seem smaller than it was. The hangar could easily accommodate two of the slightly larger Kartog fighters.

Along with a midday break for sustenance, the two humans took a leisurely stroll outside. Anod suggested it as a respite from their technical task. In reality, she needed to reconnoiter the surrounding terrain for avenues of approach. The lack of any signs of human existence other than the hangar built into the cliff pleased Anod.

During their excursion, they came across a small cataract in a swift moving stream. The stream widened below the rocks into a deep pool. The temptation was too great. Anod suggested a swim, and to her surprise, Bradley quickly agreed. The refreshment of the cool water punctuated their mutual anatomical exploration and appreciation. The growing affection between them gave Anod the distinct feeling she had passed the point of no return. She simply enjoyed his touch too much to ever give it up.

The pleasure of their bodies amplified the multiple peaks each of them attained, both in the water and among the leaves under an expansive tree. The more physical pleasure she experienced, the more Anod wondered and questioned why the Society prohibited such human endeavor. The pangs of guilt she had felt earlier had nearly disappeared. The laughter and affectionate words became the testimony to the bonding between them. Anod began to understand what the simple word, love, meant.

The diminishing light of the late afternoon brought an end to their *au naturel* activities. The walk back to the hangar brought further discussion of plans and the future. Bradley would spend the night at

Astral and leave in the morning. The image of him departing produced unexplainable emotions of regret. Anod did not want him to go and it was quite obvious the feeling was mutual.

The words of emotion, *bon voyage*, passed both verbally and physically between them inside the hangar. Bradley asked her not to leave the hangar because of the security locks on the hatch.

A tear came to her eye for the first time in her life, one more manifestation of the latent human physiology and the coupling of deep emotions. The sensation made her feel good, and yet, so sad. She liked the new facets and dimensions of her being. Anod did not like Bradley's departure.

The following two days were spent fully absorbed in the completion of the detailed examination of the Yorax interceptor. After several attempts and spasms of sparks flying from various holes, Anod was able to successfully power up the spacecraft. To her surprise, the cockpit displays were still fully functional.

Sitting on a short stool where the pilot's seat had once been, Anod slowly worked her way through the vehicle's neural system evaluation. Most of the operational functions were still good although the lithium-carbon, referred to by the acronym, LiCa, plasma containment was out of fuel. The establishment of an operating power source was the largest obstacle to flight from Anod's perspective. Her lack of detailed knowledge regarding the intricacies of the LiCa propulsion system would have to be complemented by the Betans. Maybe between them, the problems could be solved and the obstacles breached.

Like a lightning bolt from a passing cloud, Anod remembered and missed Gorp. The faithful android would have been perfect, in his element, performing the evaluation and repair of this adversarial fighter. This was the time that slapped her with the reality of her own limitations and the capability of Gorp which had often been taken for granted, a reality of life no different from a heartbeat, or a breath of air. Another tear came to her with the memory of her lost friend, companion and guardian.

The more thorough inspection without the distraction of Bradley's presence revealed the principal damage. While the main propulsion system was intact with only superficial damage, the stability and control system along with the antigravity coils sustained serious damage. As the picture of the injury to the fighter became clearer, Anod could visualize the sequence of events.

On the basis of historical traits, the pilot was probably part of a marauding flight of Yorax fighters. Anod could see the flight of four fighters ambushing some hapless merchant craft that turned out to be not so defenseless. With the loss of control indicated by the damage and the elimination of the antigravity coils that guarded against the high accelerations of space flight, the pilot wisely elected to leave his craft. His comrades probably recovered him and left the damaged craft to the cold of space. The battle damage along with the collateral burn damage due to the slow leakage of the primary fuel logically accounted for the result standing on it's extended landing gear before her.

Anod tried to mentally catalogue and prioritize the repairs necessary to make the craft flightworthy. Most of the damage was repairable. The two elements she was the most unsure about were the plasma containment and the ejection seat. The potential for the fighter being irreparably damaged was real enough.

Nick was the first person to arrive at the Astral hangar. He opened the hatch locks and entered the hangar bay shortly after midday.

Anod was inspecting the right wing proton projector when she heard the small door open. The sight of the elder SanGiocomo brought a rush of warmth throughout her body and a broad smile to her face.

"Nick," she shouted as she ran to him wrapping her arms around him.

Somewhat taken aback by Anod's emotional reaction, he said, "It's great to see you, Anod."

"I didn't know you would be coming up here. When did you decide to come?"

"Yesterday," he responded. "Bradley stopped to brief me on the plan, on his way to find the technicians. He told me you were alone up here and would be alone until some of the team began to arrive. He thought it might take several days to find and assemble all the people you asked for."

"Good. We have much work to do before this machine will fly."

"Have you eaten?" Nick asked as he removed a small pack from his shoulders. Holding it up to indicate the presence of food within, he motioned toward one of the workrooms.

"No, I haven't. Did you bring some of your delicious cooking?"

"I don't know about delicious, but I did bring a small meal."

"Why is it you never seem to be far from food?"

His laughter confirmed the mutual levity regarding Anod's observation. "I suppose it's because I just like food."

The two walked over to the workroom moving two chairs to a workbench. While they ate the hand cakes and drank cold fruit juice, they talked about Anod's assessment of the Yorax fighter and the prospects for flight. They also talked about Anod's joy of flight, which was clearly an exciting anticipation.

Anod conducted a thorough briefing for Nick on the condition of the fighter as they walked around it. His avid curiosity was finally being satisfied. Countless earlier visits to this site and numerous technical conversations left so many questions unanswered. Access to someone who knew details about the craft excited Nick.

The power up of the cockpit displays was the culmination of the tour. Nick soaked up knowledge about the fighter like a human sponge. His avocation contributed to his fascination. Over the many years they had the machine, none of them had been able to turn the power on. For a long time, they hadn't even tried for fear of damaging the craft. Now, there was life returning to the mysterious space vehicle.

The questions from Nick and the discussions with him seemed to be an endless event that Anod enjoyed. The feeling of partial repayment of a large personal debt provided some satisfaction for Anod.

After a late evening meal, the two complementary teachers took two-foot stools outside into the dark of the night sky. Sitting in the middle of the open meadow under the brilliant canopy of stars, they talked about many topics.

Anod decided to let her inner curiosity out. "Nick, I have some subjects I would like to talk to you about."

"Please, what are your questions?"

The burning currents within her body and mind rapidly eroded the last vestiges of her heritage. Seemingly uncontrollable forces had been unleashed on Beta, and her conscious resistance was not sufficient to suppress the new feelings. "I would like to ask you about sex and love."

His body became somewhat rigid with her request. Anod noticed the change immediately and wondered why he reacted that way. "Did I say something wrong?" she asked with pure innocence.

Nick thought for a moment. "Well, no, not really. It's just, well, they are topics that are private. We learn about some things from our parents and experience. We don't really talk about them."

"Why are sex and love forbidden topics, and flight and propulsion are not?" she asked, again innocently.

Nick smiled and chuckled more to himself, but audibly. "I must say, you do have a point. So, let's see if I can put my prudishness aside and answer your questions as you have answered mine."

Anod conveyed to Nick all the physical as well as emotional feelings that had come to her since her arrival on Beta. She innocently described in detail the physical unions she had with Otis and with Bradley. The differences to her were subtle, and yet significant.

They talked about the physiology of sexual activities and the associated emotions that were indicative of love between a man and a woman. Anod listened with intense interest, much as a child might listen to her grandfather's revelations about past heroics long hidden in his memory.

The softly changing colors on the distant horizon offered physical proof they had talked through most of the night. They laughed and joked about the consequences of rampant curiosity and inquisitiveness as they finally conceded they must get some sleep.

As they walked slowly back into the hangar closing the hatch behind them, Nick wished her a good rest as he walked toward the men's living quarters on the opposite side of the hangar from the women's quarters.

"Would you make love with me?" Anod asked.

Nick stopped abruptly, held his two balled fists in front of him and stared at her with anger in his eyes. "Anod, I cannot. I am old enough to be your father."

"Why does that make a difference?" she asked, and then continued. "We have talked about the feelings between a man and a woman, and the higher communications between a man and a woman. I want to have those feelings for you."

Nick opened his mouth to say something, but he did not even expel a breath. "There is considerably more you need to learn about sex and love, but I am very tired. So please, accept my decline with love, but not rejection. I do love you, Anod, but I cannot make love to you."

Anod started to respond. She stopped when Nick raised his right hand toward her. Anod watched him walk to the men's quarters and disappear into the dark room. The thoughts racing through her brain confused and disturbed her.

The sounds of the opening hatch, footsteps on the floor and voices awakened Anod like a shot. Adrenaline raced through her veins. As she reached the door, the distinctive form of Bradley SanGiocomo and several other people calmed her physical reaction. Bradley looked around probably searching for her while most of the others talked and examined the fighter. For most of the visitors, this was obviously their first sight of the secret fighter. The almost childlike enthusiasm and excitement amused Anod.

She jumped into her pants, boots and loose fitting shirt, and moved smoothly into the hangar bay. Walking confidently toward Bradley, she was more than half way to him when he finally saw her. His smile beamed across the enormous room to join hers as they embraced and kissed.

The strange sensation in her groin was like an unsatisfied itch. Anod chose not to respond to the urge.

There were seven people in addition to Bradley, Nick and Anod, five men and two women, each a specialist in a particular discipline. Their ages varied from the youngest, a woman named Natasha Norashova, about thirty years old to the oldest, a man named Armand Bellier, who appeared to be a little older than Nick SanGiocomo.

After introductions of the team of people, Anod conducted a detailed briefing on her assessment of the damaged interceptor. She was somewhat surprised by an equal interest in her as in the spacecraft. Most questions, thankfully, were confined to the physical evaluation of the Yorax fighter.

The content of their questions, their enthusiasm for the science of the interceptor, and the interspersed explanations of their background portrayed the diversity and experience of the repair team as extraordinary. Natasha was the preeminent chemist on Beta. She possessed a sixth sense on new or exotic compounds. Armand was the principle structural engineer. George Robbins, the youngest male, brought his experience with microcircuitry to the team. George and Nick SanGiocomo utilized the unique language of molecular engineers. They seemed to be well acquainted with each other. Tim Bond was the propulsion expert whose most visible accomplishment was the high-speed train propulsion system. Most of the team members referred to Maria Verde as the computer doctor. She understood the science and art of computer construction and programming. Her ability to talk and listen to the complex devices was obviously highly regarded on Beta. Among the Betans, Gerald Oscarson and James Brown knew the most about energy conversion and projection systems. They were the closest the Betans had to weapons experts.

They worked through two meals, several technical discussions on the plasma propulsion system, and the proton projector weapon system. Late in the evening, Bradley collected everyone including his father for a planning meeting. A set of tasks, assignments and a schedule were presented, conferred upon and agreed to. With the plan, the day's activities were concluded.

Some of the team went directly to their respective sleeping area while a couple of the crew continued their personal inspection of the fighter. The machine definitely attracted most of the crew. An attraction that was difficult to put aside for some.

In the briefing room with its computers, writing screen walls, chairs and holographic projectors, Anod stood directly in front of Bradley and looked deep into his eyes. "I am happy you are back," she said softly.

"I'm glad to be back. I missed you."

Bradley leaned forward to kiss her gently on her forehead, then each cheek below the corner of her eyes and finally on her lips. The sensations of pleasure returned to Anod. She began to remove his clothes as they had done near the stream a few days earlier.

"No, not here," Bradley exclaimed as he withdrew from her.

Anod was confused by his rejection. "Why not? I want to make love to you right now."

"It's not something you do in front of others."

"We are not in front of others."

"We are in a common place. Anyone could walk in."

"Are you saying that making love is like nakedness? It is not something you should be proud of?" She searched his eyes for a response. "Why shouldn't sex be just like the human body, a celebration of life? People should be happy and pleased, if they saw two people making love to each other."

"Maybe so," Bradley conceded. "But, it's just not something we do in front of other people. It should be a private activity."

"When we made love by the stream, it wasn't very private."

An exasperated expression filled his face. "You're right, it wasn't. We shouldn't have done it there either," he said without much conviction.

"Why should something that makes me feel so good, makes you feel so good, and as you have told me, is natural for a man and a woman, be hidden?"

"I can't argue with you," he said giving in to her reasoning. "We'd better get some sleep."

"OK," Anod responded relinquishing her line of questioning.

Bradley kissed her then escorted her out of the briefing room. He kissed her again and left her to walk toward the men's sleeping quarters.

Many thoughts rumbled through her consciousness as she decided whether to say something or not. She did not want him to leave, even if it was to another room. "Bradley," she said stopping him about five meters from her. "Please just sleep with me. I want to be near you."

His hesitation acknowledged his consideration. "We can't, Anod. It wouldn't be right. I'll see you in the morning."

Anod nodded her head in acceptance although she still did not understand why her request was wrong.

The next morning began a series of days of concentrated effort on the part of the repair team. Each member of the team focused on his or her respective tasks.

Some of the superficial skin damage was fixed quickly although the application of the proper anti-ionization coatings would not be completed until the end. Several of the spots of damage were corrected, and then opened back up for access to the interior.

Once the repair process was adequately underway, Bradley announced his need to depart for government business. He would leave in the late afternoon with his father. Bradley instructed the team that Anod would function as the leader of the team. None of the Betan experts displayed any ambivalence toward the decision that was a relief to Anod. As a leader, she knew better than most people about the difficulty of people accepting the leadership of a stranger, and especially an alien.

Anod wanted to be close to Bradley before he left. The intensity of the work and the burden of leadership precluded the satisfaction of her yearning. The only intimacy they were permitted was a short kiss and hug prior to his departure. She also received a kiss on the cheek from Nick. Anod waited for them to disappear into the forest on the far side of the clearing before she returned to the task at hand.

The days seemed to all blend together. Without Bradley or Nick present, the repair of the Yorax fighter was the only focus for the humans at Astral. Missed meals and limited sleep were the norm rather than the exception for most of the team. Bradley had chosen well, Anod often reminded herself. The experts were intelligent, progressive, adaptive, capable and committed to the task. Anod's fractional descriptions of the thrill and wonder of space flight served as fuel and inspiration for the crew.

Gradually, additional systems were brought on line during the daily power up sequence. Several tasks still appeared as insurmountable obstacles to Anod. The difficulty of the remaining effort was never questioned.

Fortunately for Anod, the Betans assigned to the project contained their curiosity about her origins and background. Only an occasional abstract question would pop up usually related to some problematic technical task before them. There was also general acceptance of her traits and characteristics without objection. Anod recognized the subtle changes occurring in the team. Most notable was the fact that the two women who were becoming more outspoken and animated. It did not go unnoticed by Anod, although nothing was said, that Natasha had become less conservative and now slept without clothes. Even Maria Verde, who had displayed some resistance to the changes in Natasha, accepted the transition even though she chose not to alter her personal habits. Both women still marvelled at Anod's physical prowess and the intricacies of her morning exercises. A friendship of mutual respect grew steadily among the three women.

The rate of progress began to slow markedly on the fifth day. As Anod initially surmised, the propulsion system damage and refurbishment were the greatest problem. Anod had the most knowledge about the lithium-carbon plasma system, but none of them possessed all the requisite knowledge. The attention of the team began to concentrate on the plasma containment repair. They collectively spent more and more time in the briefing room struggling with the understanding of the damage and the potential repairs. The issue of how to test it once the repairs were completed entered their deliberations more often as their knowledge and understanding increased.

To help them understand the plasma containment system and how it operated, they performed several experiments. The key was now fuelling, initiating the fusion reaction and sustaining the containment. The resistance to faster progress was born in the lack of knowledge about the process and fear a mistake might injure someone and jeopardize the project. Despite the obstacles, they slowly and methodically made progress on the power system.

An additional few days passed before the team finally recognized and accepted reality. Two primary parts were irreparably damaged, and worse, they were beyond the fabrication capabilities on Beta.

The conclusion was conveyed to the Leadership Council via the rock communicator. After some protracted communications, everyone agreed they would seek the assistance of one of the merchant traders who occasionally visited the planet. Great care was taken, after Anod's admonition regarding the uniqueness of the required parts, to formulate the message to avoid arousing the suspicions of the Yorax, should they be listening. With understandable trepidation, the message was sent to the nearest merchant planet, Scorbion, in the Alpha Tau system. Potentially, a response would take a few weeks to return. With a beneficial intercept, they might know the answer in less time.

Waiting was never easy. This delay was even more difficult on Anod as she attempted to control her eagerness for flight.

With the majority of work completed, several members of the team were no longer being productively utilized. The team agreed they would disband while they waited for the necessary parts. Everyone who wanted to participate in the first flights of the vehicle created a recall list and personal code to notify each member of the team by the rockphone at the appropriate time.

James, Gerald and Maria decided to remain behind since there was more work for them to do. Anod agreed to wait for a small group of security personnel to arrive. Natasha and Armand departed first, receiving appropriate gratitude for services rendered. George and Tim left separately each with a simple wave of the hand as they passed through the hatch.

The sensitivity over the condition of the spacecraft was sufficient to warrant the extra attention to the safety and protection of the facility and the machine. Anod knew the gesture would be performed more to make the Betans feel good about every precaution being taken, rather than provide an adequate defense against an adversary as formidable as the Yorax. The minimal weapons capability of the Betan security forces would make a successful defense highly unlikely. The relatively simple proton projectors of the Yorax fighter they would be guarding could quickly overcome any resistance from the Betans.

In less than a day after the agreement to seek external assistance had been reached, a four-man security detachment arrived. Among the small group was the distinctive persona of Otis Greenstreet.

The reunion of Anod and Otis was considerably cooler than their last meeting. Although Anod displayed some excitement upon seeing Otis, he kept a stern, serious, distant expression. The security team performed rapidly and thoroughly as they completed their assessment of the area and the situation at the hangar. None of the four newcomers showed any interest in the space fighter resting on the hangar floor. It was not clear whether any of them had seen the fighter before, or they simply were not interested in such machines. With the security team finally settling in to a routine and the remainder of the team continuing their work, Anod was finally able to talk to Otis. "It is so good to see you Otis. I have missed you."

His expression did not change. There was little doubt. He was not excited to see her. "Why didn't you tell me you were involved with Prime Minister SanGiocomo?"

The chill in his voice puzzled Anod partly because she did not completely comprehend the meaning of his question and certainly because his tone of voice was almost hostile.

"I'm not quite sure what you mean by involved," Anod responded with appropriate seriousness. The distance between them seemed to be increasing rapidly with each passing moment.

"The prime minister is in love with you and has serious intentions toward you."

"I can appreciate the feelings. I share the same feelings toward him. I have no idea what you mean by serious intentions."

"He intends to marry you, to make you his wife."

Anod did not know what the words stood for, but she definitely did not like the image these words created in her mind. The implicit possessiveness of Otis' statement conjured up the image of imprisonment and loss of freedom. None of the aspects of the image were attractive or even pleasant.

The Kartog warrior wanted to respond strongly and negatively, however her lack of understanding for the local customs brought a measure of caution. "Your customs on Beta continue to be quite foreign to me. I largely do not understand why you do many things. Bradley has not indicated to me any change in our relationship. If your words are intended to indicate good feelings, appreciation and caring for him, then I agree," she said. Anod considered her choice of words. "What do my feelings for Bradley have to do with you? What is between Bradley and I should not affect the feelings I have for you."

A reaction of revulsion was quite evident on his face. "You can't do that," he stated emphatically. "You can only be with one man."

"Why?"

"It is the only proper way."

"This whole concept of love and relationships between men and women is confusing to me. Maybe I am beginning to understand why the Society prohibits intimacy between men and women. The emotions are too difficult to deal with."

"I can't explain it to you," Otis said with a noticeably more subdued tone. "That is something maybe Prime Minister SanGiocomo should explain."

"Then so be it," Anod said with an amount of frustration in her words. "I want you to know, Otis, the sensations I experienced with you were very special to me. They still are. I enjoy your company, your energy."

"High Cave brings back very good memories for me, as well."

"Why can't we just nurture those feelings we shared?"

Otis shook his head slowly. "I wish," he said. "But it would not be right."

Anod absorbed the futility with profound regret. The electricity she experienced during their union at High Cave still brought a smile to her soul. "I am sorry if I have caused any pain for you, Otis. What we did together is forbidden in my society, and I suppose it is not accepted here."

"You do not need to apologize. The mistake was mine. I should have known," he said as he lowered his head breaking eye contact. "The feelings were very powerful."

Anod moved closer to him leaning forward to kiss him on the cheek. Otis smiled, but did not look at her.

"I look forward to our next meeting, Otis. Until then, please protect our bird."

An expression of confusion rose up on his face as he looked at her inquisitively.

"It's an expression aviators use in reference to a machine that flies," she explained with a smile. "This bird will fly."

Otis smiled in return.

Without a word, Anod turned to walk toward the hatch.

"Where are you going?"

"I'm not needed here. I need to talk to Nick SanGiocomo. I'm going down to the train station."

"Wait, I'll go with you to make sure you get there safely."

Anod laughed inside without changing her expression. She also wanted some time to think and she did not want to talk to Otis until she had gathered her thoughts. "No, thank you, Otis. I will have no problem returning to SanGiocomo Waystation. Thank you, anyway. Until the next time . . . ," she said as she waved her hand as the others had done.

He returned her gesture with a look of disappointment on his face and in his eyes.

Chapter 12

Anod's disappointment with her reunion with Otis instigated a desire for solitude. The normal several hour walk to the train station had taken her parts of two days with a night spent under the stars. A renewal of freedom washed across her during the night with the thoughts of events to come and the future.

A folded route map in a small pouch at the Astral Waystation stimulated her curiosity. The high-speed trains made the circumnavigation of the planet relatively simple and effortless.

Anod decided to take the long way to SanGiocomo and see more of the planet. She figured the journey would take about five days, but she wanted more time to herself. She selected several stops at particularly interesting scenic areas. The longest duration excursion Anod took during her tour of the planet occurred at the Baikonov Waystation. For the first time in her life, she saw a body of water whose far shore was beyond the horizon. Part of a day and most of the adjoining night were spent in the exploration of the near shore, a frolic among the waves and sand, and listening to the sounds of the wind and water. Anod's only exposure to such geographic features was the scene wall at an outpost or the holographic chamber aboard one of the Society's starships. The splash of the waves against her skin and the motion of her body with the swells produced feelings of excitement and enjoyment.

The exhilaration of that night was provided by the proximity of an isolated atmospheric electric storm. The dancing of the jagged, occasionally multi-armed, shafts of light was painful to her sensitive eyes, but the dynamic image was irresistible. The rolling thunder was the audible evidence of the instantaneously fractured atmosphere. Anod's facial muscles were sore from the perpetual smile drawn across her face that night.

Stops in several towns and cities added to her appreciation of the Betan people. Her memory of the unfortunate events at Seymour Waystation substantially dampened the alacrity of her societal absorption. As a consequence, Anod constantly scanned the people and buildings around her for any sign of recognition, or compromise. The precautions removed some of the enjoyment, but the exposure was informative and worth the risk.

Early on the last day prior to reaching SanGiocomo Waystation, unusual new physiological reactions within her body reached undeniable levels. The initial symptoms had begun about a day after departing from Astral. Unexplainable nausea with flashes of hot and cold surged randomly through her body. The sensations seemed to be increasing in intensity although her awareness of the changes probably added to some of the increase. Some concern for possible illness prompted her to truncate the journey, and seek Nick's medical advice.

Anod arrived at SanGiocomo Waystation near midday. The walk up the hill was noteworthy because of the added measure of fatigue. She knew these symptoms were not familiar to a member of the Kartog Guards. She also knew she would feel better once Nick provided a medical determination.

The movement to Nick's cave took a little longer than normal. As she entered the clearing at the mouth of his cave, Anod made a quick scan of the area. A broad smile grew on her face when she recognized Nick sitting under the talking tree as they had begun to refer to it. His concentration on the reading material on his lap prevented him from noticing Anod's approach until she was within three meters of him.

"Anod," he shouted as he dropped his paper and rose to meet her.

"It is so good to see you, Nick."

Their embrace was strong and complete including a kiss on each cheek.

The smile drained from Nick's face. "Where have you been?" he demanded in a stern voice. "We have been worried to death something might have happened to you."

"Oh, I simply decided to take a tour of the planet."

"Otis sent me a message when you departed from Astral nine days ago," Nick began to explain. "When you didn't arrive the next day, I sent a message to Bradley. We couldn't alert all the security forces, so the Council assigned a team to look for you."

"No one found me."

"I gathered that." The frustration in Nick's words was quite evident. "I better tell Bradley you are here safely." He turned to walk toward the cave then stopped. "You are all right, aren't you?"

"Yes, I guess so," Anod answered with some trepidation.

Nick's expressions displayed vividly the rapid shifting of his thoughts. "Are you OK? Did something happen to you?"

"Yes, I am OK. I've just had some spells of not feeling well over the last couple of days. The episodes seem to be brief, and they do pass."

"Let me get this message off, then I will examine you."

Anod nodded her head that initiated Nick's departure to the rockphone communicator. She watched his retreating form with his robes flowing. A quick look around the area confirmed the normalcy of the clearing. A deep breath brought renewal of the delightful scents from the forest.

Nick was still concentrating on the rockphone communicator when she joined him. Without looking up, he listened and he transmitted several messages. After several minutes of effort, Nick looked up to her.

"I have received more information from Providence," he began. "The word from Scorbion indicates most of our requested parts have been located. Two items, the plasma pump and the flux generator, will have to be modified or remanufactured."

"That's pretty good news," Anod responded. "When do the parts arrive?"

"If everything goes well, one of the traders should arrive in a few days to about a week or so. Everyone agrees we should wait to see if the Yorax have recognized our project."

With a nod, Anod said, "Good."

Nick returned to the rockphone communicator to transmit Anod's consent. The conclusion of the conversation did not take long.

"That's it," Nick announced. "I'm hungry. Let's get something to eat," he said rising to walk passed her without waiting for a response.

Nick rambled on about events over the last few days regarding the search effort to locate her. There was a protectiveness building within some of the Betan people. Nick reported one of the ideas presented by Otis was to have an escort accompany her, always. The solution was not a particularly popular option for Anod.

This moment also presented the first opportunity since Anod's arrival at Astral for the two of them to talk without interference, or interruption. Nick took full advantage of the occasion to discuss several subjects he had been thinking about. The topic that occupied most of his interest was flight. The questions were continuous and detailed as he struggled to understand an experience that was only distantly familiar to him and was beyond his personal skill. Anod was all too happy relating the joys of flight and the excitement of being a Kartog Guards fighter pilot.

"Wait," he exclaimed upon a sudden realization. "Here I've been babbling on and I almost forgot about your health. Maybe we should find out why you are not feeling well."

"I'm quite all right now," Anod responded not wanting to stop their conversation.

"That may be, however I want to make sure nothing happens to you. Tell me about your feelings."

Reluctantly, Anod began to describe the occasional bouts of nausea mixed with rapid cycles of hot and cold sensations. Dutifully, Nick nodded to indicate he was listening as his mind raced through a series of possibilities. After several sensor scans and some bodily fluid analysis, the indisputable conclusion was reached.

"Anod, you are pregnant," Nick stated with a neutral expression of a detached professional.

The effort to fully comprehend Nick's statement was woefully incomplete. Anod quickly realized she did not quite understand what being pregnant meant.

"You mentioned that word, pregnant, many days ago when I was bleeding." Anod struggled with her memory and her thoughts. "Maybe you'd better explain exactly what pregnant means."

Nick did ask about and establish the paternity of Anod's child. There was only one possibility, given the facts. Anod carried Nick's grandchild within her. In addition, Nick expressed his concerns over her lack of appreciation for being a mother. Anod had no roll model from which to pattern her actions as a mother. A distantly latent instinct and near term training would soon govern her responses.

The explanation did satisfy Anod's inquisitiveness regarding her current physical condition. The possibilities of carrying a child within her, of birthing a baby and of raising an infant were alien to her, and yet mysteriously intriguing. Her inherent curiosity wanted to answer the questions, to absorb this new experience. The responsibility for the product of her curiosity was not fully appreciated.

"Maybe I should talk to Bradley?" Anod asked.

"That is a good idea, but I would recommend you come to grips with your own feelings, first."

"An excellent suggestion, I should think." She felt good. She felt new warmth within her. "We've got some planning to do," she added with effervescence to her words.

"We can wait until you decide what you want to do."

"No," she said with a laugh. "I mean we need to plan our actions once the parts for the interceptor arrive."

Nick laughed loud and deep in part for relief of a building tension within his heart, and certainly for his failure to recognize the subject change. "You're right, of course."

They immediately immersed themselves in the sequence of events for flight preparation, the risks associated with the initiation of the plasma field, and the potential ramifications of free flight and the exposure to the Yorax. Interspersed within the planning were the curiosity questions from Nick about the physics of the interceptor, atmospheric and space flight, and hyperlight speeds and communications. The technical nature of each personality played well against the necessity of the events before them.

Several days passed with the fundamental processes of their daily activities remaining virtually unchanged. The topics of discussion and the words between them changed radically over the span of time, but their routine was the same. They continued to wait for the parts to arrive.

Very few words passed between them regarding Anod's pregnancy despite several concerted attempts by Nick. He had a difficult time trying to determine if Anod's reticence was denial or withdrawal. More insistence would have been woven into the words if Nick had not trusted her reasoning and logic. He would wait for her decision, as well.

Anod asked several times about Bradley. Initially, Nick responded with the usual shield of governmental bureaucrats. He was very busy with government business. It took a little longer than it should have for Nick to realize Anod was probably feeling a need to talk to his son.

A series of messages to Providence confirmed his original presumption. Bradley and several members of the Council struggled with the societal question of what to do once the parts arrived and the interceptor became flyable. There was apparently not a clear consensus as indicated by the extended debate. Anod, however, felt an unexplainable, inner confidence they would reach the correct decision. In fact, it was the only decision from her perspective.

Then, for no known reason other than providence, Anod announced her decision. The location seemed appropriate, the shade of the large, talking tree with a cool breeze wafting the forest scent across them.

"I want to have this baby, if it is medically prudent and safe."

Nick simply looked into her green eyes and smiled the proud smile of a grandfather. "To the best of my knowledge, you are perfectly healthy and able to bear children." The smile washed from his face as he struggled with his thoughts. "Maybe we should have one of our best midwives take a look at you. She might see things differently than I do."

"Midwives?"

"A midwife is the principle facilitator for childbirth," Nick explained. "The midwife is a birthing expert, a well-trained, experienced technician."

"I see." Anod's concern was quite evident in her voice. After Nick's thorough description of pregnancy and childbirth, the apprehension about the physical reality of the process struck her with the potential consequences.

"You don't need to worry. The continual examination and monitoring events give us a virtually perfect picture of what will happen and what complications might arise."

"You did anticipate my questions quite well." Anod smiled. "Thank you."

"If I may ask a question . . . " Nick waited for Anod's gestured consent. "How have you resolved the conflict between your current physical situation and the Society's laws about intimacy and pregnancy?"

The question hit Anod hard. It brought with it all the trauma of her separation from the fold and the reality of her violations of Society law, her training and her heritage. "From my first coupling with Otis . . ." Nick's reaction to the words could not be controlled. "I have been beyond the law. The bombardment of my senses with all the experiences since my arrival on Beta has eroded my resistance." Anod paused looking down at the ground. "I must take the consequences." The finality of her conclusion took its toll on both of them.

Nick walked to a small bush pulling a broad leaf from the bush and placed the stem between his lips. Almost mumbling, he asked, "Can I send a message to Bradley about your decision?"

After a moment's thought, Anod answered. "I would prefer to tell him myself, Nick. I hope you understand."

Nick removed the leaf from his mouth. "Well, then, can I ask him to come, so you can tell him?"

"No. He has many important duties. When I see him again, I will tell him."

The expression change on Nick's face foretold the thought change. "There is a serious question in this." He looked at the ground and kicked a small stone into the forest. Like a determined opponent in a chess master's challenge, he returned to the stool near her and looked into her eyes. "With all the genetic manipulation by your scientists and the procreation prohibition by your government, why are you able to get pregnant?" There was an air of suspicion or doubt in his delivery of the words. "Why haven't they simply removed your reproductive and sexual organs?"

"I have never asked myself those questions. We've never discussed those issues. I don't know," Anod responded as Nick's questions triggered her own consideration of the issues.

"Doesn't it seem a little contradictory to you?"

"Yes, it does. I don't know why."

"With all that biomedical power, and certainly in light of what they have been able to do for you physically, it does seem strange that they would leave the capability in women, if they didn't want to use it. Maybe they wanted you to have the temptation, as a test," said Nick with a laugh.

The attempt at humor did not register on Anod as she considered the profound questions presented by her benefactor. A long list of facts and memories rumbled through her thoughts in an effort to understand the reality.

"I can only surmise that it may have been a form of insurance for the Society. If something catastrophic happened to our species, the societal obstructions could be removed to allow ancient reproduction."

Nick smiled. "Natural, not ancient," came the fatherly comment. "The coupling of a man and a woman to produce off-spring is the natural process of reproduction among humans."

"I concede."

"Weren't you ever curious about your sex organs and reproduction?"

"Not really."

"Why?"

"It never seemed to be important," Anod responded. "Remember, our societal stimuli were entirely different from what you have here on Beta. The human body, either male or female, is simply a tool or an apparatus for the execution of the brain's will."

"I know I don't understand the justification for such an approach or custom," Nick said shaking his head in disagreement. "It is such a mystery to me. Conditions on Earth must have changed drastically since my ancestors were forced from the planet."

The contrast between Earth and the Society, and life on θ27β continued to illustrate the conflict to Anod. She found it harder to understand the attitudes promoted by the Society. In addition, she also found it more difficult to talk about the discord within her.

The message arrived at SanGiocomo shortly after their morning meal. The merchant trader's spacecraft was forecast to reach $\theta 27\beta$ tomorrow. The message also stated all the requested parts were aboard. Nick's excitement vastly exceeded Anod's. The elder human expressed his excitement and anticipation of seeing the interceptor fly, even though it was a vehicle of destruction. The exploitation of the captured spacecraft was under their control. It was the first flight vehicle under Betan authority.

Direction received from Providence requested Anod travel to Astral in order to arrive no later than midday, the next day. Nick decided he would accompany her. The last of the series of messages indicated Bradley would join them in a day or two.

The journey to Astral was familiar and uneventful for Anod. The excitement that effervesced yesterday continued to bubble up during the hours of transit. Nick repeatedly called the events since Anod's fortuitous arrival as the dawn of a new era for his people.

The interceptor was just as she left it. Only half of the repair crew had returned. The security detachment remained.

A small, boxy shuttlecraft descended into the clearing in front of the hangar with a heavy hum, much like a magnified hummingbird. Anod observed the arrival of the craft from the rear of a gaggle of Betans collected for the event. The wide, web-footed legs of the shuttle's landing gear settled into the soft dirt and grass of the clearing. The quiescence of the shuttle took several minutes culminating in the opening of the clamshell doors at the rear of the vehicle.

A solo, large biped emerged from the dark interior. The individual had human male features mainly his head and general anatomical characteristics, arms and legs. His gait was noticeably mechanical as he moved in jerky, maybe even slightly off balance, motions toward the assembled audience. None of the Betans responded to the appearance of the new visitor. He was probably not familiar to them although he did not appear to be a threat, either.

Nick answered the question. "Alexatron, it's great to see you again," he said as he stepped forward to greet their guest.

"It is good to see you, Nicholas," came the coarse, deep, mechanical tone of the voice of Anod's rescuer. "I see your patient has recovered quite nicely," he said looking past everyone else, directly at Anod.

"Anod, come, meet the man who brought you to us," Nick said motioning for her to move forward.

She walked slowly through the group. As she neared him, his size became even more impressive. He was a good twenty centimeters taller than she was. His rough features became starker with the recognition that his arms and legs appeared to be mechanical which explained his movements. Alexatron's loose clothing, in shades of brown, reminded Anod of the rugged attire worn by the two bounty hunters at Seymour. She wondered if there was any significance to the comparison.

"Anod, this is Alexatron," Nick said with some pride extending his hand toward the latest visitor.

The Kartog Guards warrior shook his cold mechanical hand. "It is good to meet you." She knew there was more she had to say despite his foreboding presence. "Thank you for saving my life."

"You are most welcome, Miss Anod."

His gravelly voice continued to grate on her sensitive hearing. Her response to his persona must have been written in her eyes.

"Yes, Miss Anod, I am part biological and part mechanical. I am the product of several unfortunate encounters with hostiles, and the miracles of modern technology," Alexatron explained. There was pride, like a badge of honor, in his voice.

Wanting to change the direction of the brief conversation was foremost to Anod at the moment. "I understand you have brought us some parts."

"You are quite correct," he responded. "But, before we get down to business, are you fully recovered from your injuries?"

"Yes, I am fully recovered, thank you."

"I would like to ask you, what happened to you in space?"

"And, I would like to talk to you, however, I think we should first unload the parts you have brought us, so we can get the repair team working on the vehicle."

Alexatron bowed to Anod, motioning for some of the others to follow him back into the shuttlecraft. Anod mentally inventoried the parts as they were removed from the craft. She also took advantage of the opportunity to survey the simple, sub-light speed, shuttlecraft. The machine was probably more than fifty years old and definitely showing signs of extended service and maybe even a little abuse. The unloading process did not take long. Several of the team members went to work on the interceptor immediately.

"Now may we talk?" asked Alexatron.

"I believe so," she responded.

"May I listen in?" Nick requested.

"It's quite all right with me," Anod answered looking to Alexatron for his gesture of agreement.

The three walked toward the edge of the large clearing. A combination of a rock, a fallen tree trunk and a standing tree as a backrest served as their forum.

The ambush was violent, Anod recounted. Alexatron's time/date identification of his chance encounter with her slowly tumbling, damaged survival pod established the duration of her exposure. More than six days, one day greater than the specified lifetime of a human in a rescue pod, had elapsed from Zitger's betrayal to her rescue. Combined with the nearly three weeks of coma under Nick's care brought her unconsciousness close to a month. Anod could not remember any of her precarious life during that period, from the flash to her awakening. The one significant item that was not understood was the fact that she was left alive.

After the ambush, she was still alive although unconscious and adrift. The sensors of Zitger's fighter were more than able to distinguish her feeble life signs among the void of space. Why hadn't he finished his brutal task? Why was Alexatron even allowed to rescue her? Something must have distracted Zitger from completing his villainous deed. It couldn't have been a casual passing merchant vessel. He could have easily eliminated anyone, or anything, below the size or power of a starship. Alexatron was just as puzzled by the obvious questions raised by her survival. What was missing from the picture? What facts were they lacking?

The struggle with the ambiguity of her survival was eventually put aside, but not forgotten.

They returned to the hangar to find the repair team hard at work. Several of the necessary parts had already been installed. Work continued in the cockpit and on several parts of the power and propulsion systems. Anod walked around the fighter to absorb the progress and activity on the interceptor. With no major problems, the spacecraft looked as if it could be flyable in a day or two.

As she inspected the continuing refurbishment in the cockpit, Anod noticed, as she looked across the craft, a lone figure standing along the wall on the far side of the hangar bay. Otis leaned against the wall with his legs crossed and watched the activity on the machine. His distance from the craft and removal from the process troubled Anod. On occasional brief moments, she would recall with a smile their pleasure at High Cave. She still did not accept the retreat of young Otis Greenstreet.

After completing her inspection, Anod meandered toward her younger friend repeatedly stopping to look back at the interceptor.

"Otis, don't leave," Anod said as he tried to walk away.

He did not stop immediately. A few moments later he did. He did not look at her. There seemed to be something particularly intriguing to him about his black boots, or the floor beneath them.

"Why do you continue to avoid me?" asked the Kartog Guards warrior.

There was no answer as he persisted with his study of the floor.

"I still don't understand what I have done to you. What was so bad?"

"As I told you when you were here the last time, I cannot interfere with the relationship between you and Prime Minister SanGiocomo." The subject obviously pained the young man.

"Can't we at least be friends?"

"I wish we could, but every time I see you, I remember High Cave. The pleasure of that time makes the pain of realization more pronounced."

"What realization?"

"The realization that we will not be together again. I would rather pretend you are gone than be reminded I cannot have you."

"The possessiveness you portray is not a pleasant thought," Anod responded with some difficulty containing her resentment.

"I don't know what to say to you," said Otis. "I seem to never know what to say to you." There was an indisputable flavor of frustration in his voice. "What is, simply is, what is!"

"It is not my nature to accept any situation. If it is your desire that we not be friends, or talk to each other, then so be it. What is your wish?"

Otis shifted his weight from foot to foot as he averted her eyes. His hesitation broadcast the conflict within him. Fortunately, logic won over injured pride. "Maybe we could be friends. It's just we can't be together, physically I mean, while you and Prime Minister SanGiocomo are a couple."

"Otis, I have enjoyed your companionship since I first met you. Whatever conditions you want are fine with me."

"No physical contact," he said almost as a question instead of a statement.

"If you wish."

"Anod, excuse me. We need your help," asked Maria Verde, the Betan computer wizard. "George and I are having some difficulty getting the central processor to respond properly."

Looking at Otis, Anod smiled and said, "We'll talk later." The simple nod of his head conveyed his consent. Turning to Maria, she said, "Let's have a look at this machine of ours." The two women walked quickly to the interceptor.

George Robbins stood on a small stool buried to his waist into the bowels of sleek spacecraft. Maria began explaining the problem as a manifestation of a sequence of actions associated with activation of the interceptor's central processor, its brain and nervous system. Everything checked out normally, and yet some of the key outputs displayed in the cockpit were not quite correct.

The muffled and echoed words of the nearly swallowed Robbins provided further insight. "All the cross-checks and sample stimulations are absolutely correct. The frustrating element is, there are subtle discrepancies in a few of the output parameters displayed in the cockpit. I simply don't understand it, or know what to do."

"There are a couple of things it might be," Anod stated. Her words were sufficient to extricate George from his position inside the fighter.

Anod recounted the Yorax propensity toward believable, but false information as a protection technique. The Yorax being a large, rather Neanderthal species from the Yortreger planetary system assumed other genera were as gullible as they were. The thought was small, subtle errors would mislead or distract a pirate who may have commandeered one of their interceptors to use against them. The technique was known to be successful on several occasions. Distraction of an adversary was the key element. In the heat of combat, simply questioning the accuracy of presented information was usually sufficient to delay a critical action.

"Let's see what the cockpit can tell us," Anod said as she ascended the small crew ladder to the pilot's station.

The two scientists followed the Kartog pilot to the cockpit using a workstand on the opposite side of the interceptor's nose. With two non-aviators leaning over the sill of the pilot's station, Anod began to work the displays. The complex set of symbols and characters took some time to interpret and understand. Luckily, a good portion of the symbols were universal, virtually the same in every culture.

The process took several hours of concentrated effort and coordinated action by the repair team. They activated a variety of functions from the cockpit, and ran back and forth between several of the sensors distributed around the vehicle and the central processors. The frustration of the puzzle began to mount. Virtually, two more questions would be raised for every question answered. The key to the solution was born in the persona of Alexatron.

The Scorbian merchant pilot remained at a distance observing the activity around the spacecraft. As the frustration of George and Maria became more animated, Nick suggested to Alexatron that he add his experience to the solution. With the two Betans immersed in their own elemental tasks, Alexatron joined Anod at the cockpit. After some discourse on the findings, he provided several offerings, one of which triggered the idea to reprogram the processor to eliminate the ambiguity and disinformation.

Anod gained a better appreciation of the logic and technology utilized by the Yorax, although their capabilities were certainly less sophisticated than those of the Society. There was elegance to the simplicity portrayed by the interceptor. Anod was reminded of one of the principles she was taught in her youth. Learning was a continual process. Everyday she learned something new. The day you stopped learning was the day you ceased to exist.

The celebration for completion of the preparatory work was short lived. Everyone was anxious about the impending flight. They wanted to see their efforts transformed into physical performance. Several meetings were held over the next two days to consider the best course of action.

A methodical power-up sequence was agreed to. The risk associated with initiation of the plasma was real. Release of even a minute portion of the plasma would disintegrate this region of the planet, and probably irreparably devastate the remainder. Anod and Alexatron were more comfortable with the technology and the risk. Other alternatives were offered, discussed and ultimately rejected for one reason or another.

A suggestion was made to move the interceptor to space for the power up. However, Alexatron's orbitally parked craft did not possess a tractor beam. The shuttle did not possess enough power to tow the interceptor to space. Attempting to summon an appropriate vehicle presented the equally significant risk of alerting the Yorax.

Several times during the discussions, Anod wondered where Bradley was. The communications with the Betan Council had been prompt, accurate and expansive, yet succinct. Here, responses were not particularly timely which Anod attributed to the normal deliberations of a group struggling to arrive at a decision. She was accustomed to the autonomy of distance. Commanders, like Colonel Zortev, were given considerable latitude for decisions within the confines of broad directives. The distances of space were too great and the time required for communications even at hyperlight speeds was entirely too long for the immediacy of most decisions. Communication was the professional side of her concern, not the personal side.

Anod wanted Bradley's companionship. She wanted to tell him what was happening within her. The contrast with her heritage was never far from the surface of her consciousness, but the new facets were real nonetheless.

Finally, after the seemingly relentless onslaught of questions, answers, discussions and opinion, the reluctant consent was reached.

Tim Bond, the diminutive, round faced, black haired, Betan, propulsion systems expert agreed to stay with Anod for the power-up. Alexatron insisted on remaining with the two humans to lend his knowledge to the process. Everyone else in the team was given half a day to evacuate to a safe distance. Alexatron flew his shuttle over an area within 50 kilometers of the Astral hangar to verify the absence of human lifeforms. The time was upon them. Everything was ready.

With Tim looking over her shoulder and Alexatron observing from a short distance, Anod switched on the plasma vessel pre-heaters. While the temperatures rose to the minimum acceptable values, the related and ancillary systems were checked. Progress was good. With all parameters at nominal levels, mixing the volatile LiCa fuel began.

The pressure and temperature within the plasma containment vessel continued to rise. Anod watched the operating values approach the levels required for minimum power self-sufficiency.

The memory of Gorp flashed into her consciousness. The loyal android performed most of the routine chores, like powerplant start-up, for his leader. She missed him, but her focus had to be on this action. With a slight shake of her head, Gorp returned to her subconscious.

Anod looked at Alexatron, and then, Tim Bond. With a nod of her head, she moved the power lever on the left side of the seat to the start position.

The interceptor shuddered and was accompanied by a deep rumble as the catalytic initiator was injected into the fuel mixture. Temperature within the vessel shot up above 40 kilodegrees Kelvin while the pressure also rose dramatically above 150 kilograms per square centimeter. The blinding white light of a star did not envelop them. The plasma containment vessel held the intense heat and pressure. Anod looked back with a broad smile only to be greeted with comparable grins from her two companions.

Power was transferred to internal power. All the interceptor's systems were energized and checked through the central processor. All indications of activity stabilized. The craft was ready to fly. Anod considered asking Tim to open the hangar doors. The urge to fly was enormous. Reluctantly, the Kartog Guards warrior shutdown the interceptor. Small steps were prudent at this stage, Anod reminded herself.

"Yes! Yes!" shouted Tim. "We did it."

The broad smile with her brilliant white teeth and the nod of her head confirmed the assessment. "Yes, we most certainly did."

"Congratulations, Anod," Alexatron added as he approached the interceptor.

"Thank you, and thank you for your help, Alexatron. Without the parts you brought, we couldn't have done it."

"You are most welcome," he acknowledged. "I suppose we'd better notify everybody."

A simple message was sent via rockphone.

FIRE SUCCESSFULLY LIT AND EXTINGUISHED.

The response was appropriate, understandable and appreciated. The team would return for evaluation of the power-up and preparations for flight.

The remaining members of the refurbishment team arrived one by one. Each arrival triggered brief, but genuine celebrations that rapidly transitioned to tinkering with the craft. All the elements, parts, regions and bays were evaluated for damage or detrimental effects of the power-up. Everything was as normal as their knowledge was able to determine.

Anod noticed Otis approaching from the security room adjacent to the hangar door. "We received a message for you from Providence," he said with a subdued tone. "The Prime Minister and most of the Council will be coming to Astral. They will probably arrive tomorrow."

"Are they expecting anything special for their visit?" asked Anod.

"There was no indication in the message."

Otis turned to return to the security room. His head was lowered.

"Remember our agreement," Anod spoke loudly to his retreating form.

Looking over his shoulder, he just stared and eventually nodded his head in consent.

Anod watched Otis disappear into the security room. She considered the mood and thoughts of the young man. He was obviously still troubled by her relationship with Bradley. What was Bradley going to think about the news she held for him? Why hadn't she heard from him for so long?

No! Personal liaisons could not occupy her consciousness with the final preparations, she told herself.

"I have done all I know to do, Anod. I think this machine is ready," said Tim Bond, the propulsion expert.

"Does everything looks OK after the power-up?" Anod asked.

"Yes. There were no indications of leaks in the plasma vessel, and all the transfer coils are in perfect shape."

"Good," she answered. "Very good."

Activity on the interceptor began to look less purposeful and intense. It was time for the final assessment and agreement to fly.

"Attention everyone," Anod spoke with a firm, strong voice to ensure all members of the team could hear her. "I believe it is time for the decision. Can we meet in the briefing room?" The question was more a statement of direction rather than an interrogative.

Without acknowledgment, other than the muffled conversation among professional colleagues, the team migrated toward the room that had become the default site of their collective thought. The entire team plus several other interested people including Nick, Otis and a few of the other security guards were present.

Anod began the discussion. "I suggest each of us, in turn, provide an assessment of the vehicle's status." Everyone indicated their agreement in one-way or another. "Very well. Armand, would you begin with your assessment of the structural integrity?"

The structural engineer, Armand Bellier, moved to the front of the room. Using a large diagram of the Yorax interceptor, he began a systematic presentation of his assessment.

Armand was followed by each of the Betan experts. They detailed the problems encountered, the work performed to correct the deficiencies and their overall assessment. Anod concluded the discussion with her evaluation of the progress and the culmination of their collective efforts.

"If there are no objections, I shall consummate this endeavor with a pronouncement of readiness. Tomorrow, we fly," Anod stated in the collective plural even though she would be the sole pilot. "Let's outline the sequence of events for the first flight."

A thorough structuring of the first flight, a low altitude and low speed, atmospheric event, was also accompanied by an outline of the subsequent envelope expansion program. The conversation quickly transitioned from a professional interchange to avid technical curiosity as this group of Betan citizens was drawn into the fascination of space flight. They were ready. The briefing concluded with applause from the team, and congratulations and thankfulness for their accomplishments.

Chapter 13

The night had been sprinkled with several minute enclaves of excitement born in the crucible of a new era for the Betan pioneers. Discussions continued well into the night revolving around the wonders and responsibilities of interplanetary spaceflight. The simple pleasures of flight still eluded these travellers from a time three generations passed. That era rapidly came to a close and the words spoken between them conveyed the realization.

Activities on this momentous day began early. As part of the preparations and for the benefit of the other members of the team, the interceptor's plasma powerplant was restarted and shutdown after a complete systems checkout. Everyone was satisfied, to the extent of their knowledge, experience and intuition. The craft was ready for flight.

Anod advocated restarting the interceptor to allow the powerplant to idle for a longer duration until the Council arrived for the launch.

The consensus among the team was to the contrary. An inherent suspicion drew the Council to experience everything including the start-up for themselves. The decision to refurbish the fighter was not particularly popular as several of the team members stated. The simple presence of a distant relative, alien nonetheless, who longed for the freedom of flight, presented a real threat. The conflict for the Betans took on dramatic proportions. Anod recognized the inference.

A twinge of regret and guilt passed through Anod's thoughts with the knowledge her presence was changing the course of this microcosm of intelligent life among the diversity of space inhabitants. The rationalization was possible through the liberal application of chance, fate, karma or divine providence. The lone member of the Kartog Guards among these people had not chosen this planet for refuge. Certain events simply happened. Her presence and the course of actions associated with her presence were the natural evolution of *corpa vita*.

The constituent members of the Council began arriving shortly after midday. Greetings and introductions filled each arrival. Anod and the team tried to keep the technical explanations about the interceptor and their efforts to make it flyable to a minimum. It was more efficient to perform one collective description with concomitant questions and answers, but the excitement and protracted arrivals made the possibility difficult.

The Prime Minister was virtually the last to arrive with a short, rotund man with a bald head and dark complexion who was introduced as Bagiiwa Ashitrawani, the eldest minister. In addition to being a member of the Leadership Council, Mister Ashitrawani was also the Minister of Education for the Betan people.

Bradley informed the assembled group, a quorum of the council was formally constituted for a review of the flight project. After asking everyone to proceed to the briefing room, the repair and security teams along with their guests funnelled into the designated room.

"It's good to see you," Bradley said to Anod as they trailed the others to the briefing room. His words were delivered with the sterility of protocol.

"I was wondering if I was ever going to see you again," Anod returned sarcastically.

"The affairs of state are a heavy burden," came his response. "I have not been avoiding you. I have missed you and looked forward to this day."

"We have much to discuss, but it will have to wait until we have successfully completed our assignment."

With a nod of his head, he motioned toward the briefing room. "Shall we?"

The room was nearly full with an audience of attentive people from a variety of backgrounds. The Council members sat in the front row of chairs. A calm existed in anticipation as Anod entered the room and moved to the rear and one of the few remaining chairs.

"Not so fast, Anod," Bradley said motioning for her to return to the front of the room. "Ladies and gentlemen, for those of you who have not had the pleasure of meeting our distinguished guest, please allow me to introduce, Anod. As most of you are aware, she was rescued by our good friend, Alexatron, and brought to us in an unconscious state. Since her arrival, she has fully recovered from her injuries and has led the repair team working on this project." Turning to look directly at her, he continued, "I would like you to give the Council a good briefing on the status of your efforts."

Anod felt the strong sensation of *déjà vu*. A rerun of a scene she had recently been through. The details of the briefing were purposely kept at a fairly broad level, so as not to bog down the process. Numerous questions were asked and answered satisfactorily. The tone and content of some of the questions foretold the mood and leanings of the askers. Anod's assessment was the Council was generally positive. The most negative among the quorum was none other than Mister Ashitrawani. It was clear he did not want to relinquish the old ways for any reason.

The conclusion of the briefing brought a request for a closed-door caucus by the Council. The discussion took less than ten minutes with Bradley emerging from the room with a smile on his face. The expression on his face was sufficient to broadcast the result.

More than three meters from Anod, he spoke to her. "You have approval to fly. The Council requests you restrain your flights to the atmosphere until we can assess the risk. Are these conditions agreeable?"

"Yes," Anod responded. "The machine belongs to you. I am simply your agent."

"Very good. You are free to proceed."

Anod turned to the repair crew standing toward the rear of the interceptor. Giving them a broad smile and a thumbs up hand signal, she walked confidently to the left side of the machine. Ascending the crew ladder, the Kartog warrior settled into the pilot's seat connecting the harness that attached the spacecraft to her body.

The Yorax interceptor was not equipped with an ejection pod that meant her life was directly linked to the integrity of the spacecraft. The vulnerability did not escape Anod's awareness on the verge of her first flight. Simply stated, the risk was acceptable.

After signalling for her audience to clear the hangar and open the doors, Anod completed the start-up just as she had on the earlier occasions. All the indications in the cockpit appeared to be normal, as best she could determine.

The hum of the interceptor with its powerplant at an idle power level provided the pilot with a positive sensation. The harnessed stellar energy contained within the charged magnetic chamber about four meters behind her was the source of that power. The prospect of flight added the final ingredient to the mixture of sounds and feelings. The sensory rush missing from her life since her launch from Saranon, so long ago, returned to her body and soul, and she enjoyed it. Flight was one of those life sensations that was so difficult to describe. It was intoxicating, in fact, addicting.

With one last look to confirm a clear area, she looked down at the controls on either side of her seated body. The power levers on the left controlled the axial velocities and the anti-gravity field while the single grip on the right controlled the rotational velocities. The rotation controller provided the directional orientation desired for the primary thrust vector.

The time was now!

Anod slowly moved the gravity lever to the neutral position. The interceptor lurched somewhat as the gravity field generator created requisite counter force to cancel the local gravity vector. Anod nudged the controls to raise the craft off the floor of the hangar. The interceptor floated about fifty centimeters above the surface. Reaching with her left hand to the left side of the display panel, Anod raised the landing gear that retracted into their respective cavities within the fuselage.

Although she was now flying, the hangar still surrounding her inhibited the freedom of flight. The openness of the clearing beyond the hangar doors and blue sky above the trees beckoned to her. Slight pressure on the thrust lever moved the interceptor forward on its gravity cushion.

The heat and light from θ27 felt good through the transparency of the interceptor's canopy. Anod stopped the vehicle in the center of the clearing and increased the stabilized height above the ground to nearly seven meters.

Using the right controller, Anod rotated the interceptor about each of the principle rotational axes. The craft slowly rotating as if suspended by a cable above the ground stunned, awed and entertained the assembled crowd watching from the hangar. First, with the machine upright and level, she yawed the nose through 360° of heading change. The following motions were more difficult for the Betans to relate to. With the nose broadside to the audience, Anod commanded the interceptor to slowly roll completely through the inverted position back to upright. Even more surprising was the pitch rotation as she moved the machine nose down again passing through the inverted position. What the Betans did not know, yet, was Anod never felt the change in the local gravity vector. The rush of blood to her head or hanging in her harness while she was upside down were sensations eliminated by the anti-gravity field. The simple callisthenics assured Anod that she had full control of the interceptor and would not be subjected to the crush of the tremendous acceleration forces the machine was capable of producing.

Yes, Anod told herself, I'm ready to stretch my legs.

Looking to the still captivated stand of humans, Anod flashed a broad smile, an energetic thumbs up and a wave to her friends. The answered gesture completed her preparations.

The experienced aviator's instincts told her to move slowly. With due prudence, she commanded the interceptor into forward flight.

"It's great to be flying again," Anod shouted to herself.

The trees and rocks washed away into the multiple hued, seas of green and brown. The view was glorious, but the need for concentration was far greater. This was the first flight of a refurbished flight vehicle last flown by an enemy pilot. The requirement to control her speed as well as understand the nuances of the machine was ever present. A simple, slight indiscretion with the thrust controller while flying in the atmosphere could produce a tremendous sonic shock wave. While such an atmospheric phenomenon would be imperceptible to her, it would be devastating to most living creatures on the surface including humans.

From an altitude several kilometers above the surface, Anod maneuvered the craft through all the rotational and translational motions at progressively higher speeds. The process for centuries had been dubbed, envelope expansion. The phrase referred to the incremental exploration of the available and eventually the allowable flight envelope. The atmospheric restrictions were self-imposed to preclude unnecessary exposure to the inhabitants.

Anod thought about circumnavigating the planet. The thought passed quickly under the pressure of her discipline. That trip would come in time. Patience and deliberate caution were the watchwords on this maiden flight.

Her first flight since her rescue lasted a little more than an hour. It was a good flight with no detectable abnormalities. The craft handled surprising well in the atmosphere, which meant it would probably handle even better in space.

Upon her return to Astral, Anod decided to give the waiting Betans a brief demonstration of maneuverability. She performed a rapid combination of graceful aerobatics finishing in a steady hover in the middle of the clearing. Pointing the nose toward the hangar, Anod meticulously dipped the nose without moving from the spot in a traditional gesture of thanks, a bow with her machine. Anod could not hear the applause, but the smiles and motions were unmistakable.

Lowering the craft to within a few meters of the ground, she lowered the legs of the landing gear and moved the interceptor toward the hangar. Recognizing her intentions, the gathered onlookers parted like a diminutive curtain as she carefully moved the craft into the enclosure. Ever so slowly, Anod turned to face out and landed. The shutdown was quick and simple.

"Congratulations, Anod," came the distinctive voice of the Prime Minister as the canopy opened.

"How was it?" "Good show." "How did it feel?" "That was magnificent." "Was everything OK?" came the barrage of questions and congratulatory statements. The excitement was glorious and contagious with most of the crowd gathered around the interceptor in a pool of faces on either side of her.

A quick scan of the cockpit established the quiescent state of the former Yorax craft. Unstrapping from the seat, Anod descended into the assembly.

"Let's go to the debriefing room to talk about your experience and the plan," Bradley suggested.

Without any response, the group began meandering toward the designated location for their concluding discussions. Anod noticed several members of the repair team examining the interceptor for any evidence of adversity or malfunction.

Settling in their seats took longer than need be as Anod began to feel the surge of impatience. She wanted to complete this obligation. For some reason, the scents of the forest beckoned to her. She needed to smell the sweetness of the conifer trees, the delicacy of the flowers and the heavy, pungent aroma of the soil. The urge was strong and startling for a woman who was accustomed to the sterility of space and the associated *apparati*.

The debriefing took nearly two hours as the questions continued to flow essentially unabated. The discussions gradually transitioned from the specifics of the day's events to the experience of flight, in general. Anod was not accustomed to being the center of attention, especially as she was now. The brilliant light of notoriety was seductive, and yet awkward for a professional warrior. Anod was happy to conclude the debriefing.

Although she wanted to talk with Bradley, he was absorbed in dialogue with the other members of the Council. Extricating herself from the probing questions of the Betans, Anod walked alone through the hatch in the now closed hangar door.

Just as her imagination recreated in her thoughts, the scents of the forest beyond the confines of the hangar were a simple, relaxing pleasure. A moderate breeze dampened somewhat by the trees brought an array of clouds across the sky. In the distance, Anod spotted the telltale linear streaks and smears of rain descending from a large billowing cloud. The coolness of the air brought refreshment, relaxation and invigoration.

It was not until well into the evening that Bradley approached Anod who was standing at the treeline boundary of the clearing. She felt freer in the sanctuary of the dark, chilled air under the canopy of stars.

"I thought I might find you out here," Bradley said. "I suppose our fresh air and trees are growing on you." He touched her face with one hand and kissed her lightly on the lips, then stood up straight in front of her.

The thoughts of his extended absence and lack of messages filled her consciousness. "You are quite correct," answered Anod. She wanted to speak of her frustration, but reminded herself of wasted emotions.

"I know you have been waiting for this day and your return to flight," he said with a hesitation indicative of an undercurrent to his words. After a few moments of silence, he continued. "Now that you will soon have the means to leave this planet, have you thought about what you will do?"

The question surprised Anod somewhat. It was certainly not an interrogative she expected. "No I haven't," she answered. "There are too many things still left undone here on Beta."

"Like what?"

"I want to complete the testing of the interceptor, first. We've also got to figure out how to contact the Society without alerting the Yorax."

"Why don't you just take the interceptor?" Bradley asked innocently.

"I can't go very far with an interceptor."

"Oh yes, I suppose you can't," he said in recognition. "Insufficient life support systems for protracted space travel?"

"Correct. There is a small replicator programmed for the Yorax cuisine, which I am not particularly appreciative of, and other necessities. Realistically, the confined volume of the cockpit and limited fuel of the interceptor restrains flight duration to a few days at hyperlight speeds."

"There is Alexatron and his spacecraft," Bradley suggested.

"Yes, he could provide the transportation. However, with the Yorax still looking for me, the possibility of compromising Alexatron is simply too great of a risk. He is important to you and others."

"I know you want to get back to your people. We'll find a way."

"Maybe," Anod responded, quite subdued and tentative.

"What else is on your mind?"

"Let's go find a place to sit."

"It's pretty cool out here. Are you sure you want to stay out here?"

"Yes," Anod said as she walked off away from the hangar. Finding a large, flat rock outcropping, she motioned for him to sit beside her. "I've got something else I need to tell you."

His body and head motion conveyed his anticipation.

"According to you father, I am pregnant."

The expression of shock in his eyes was genuine. "Wha . . . wha . . . what?" he stammered. "Who . . . When did you . . . Oh my gosh. Are you sure?"

"Since I have no experience, nor prior knowledge of what pregnant means, I must trust your father's medical judgment."

"Am . . . am I, the father?"

"Again, according to your father, you are."

"Oh, my gosh," was all he could muster up. In a flash, Bradley's mood changed from astonishment to anger. "Why did you risk flying when you are carrying our baby?" he stated more than asked with tension and anger in his voice.

Anod smiled and released a slight chuckle. "Who else was going to fly the interceptor?"

"That's not the point," he snapped back. "I would rather not have initiated this project than risk the health of our growing child."

"The risk was minimal, certainly no greater than life itself."

"Maybe. I do not know." His mood calmed substantially. "It just seems like a lot more risk." Bradley rose from the rock. He started to walk back toward the hangar, then stopped and returned to Anod. "Can we go inside?"

"If you wish," responded Anod standing straight and proud in front of him. With an unexplained urge, she reached to him gently grasping his head with both hands and pulling him toward her. Slowly, Anod pressed her lips to his. As the electricity grew, their mouths parted to allow a deeper kiss. They embraced holding each other firmly and completely. The feeling, for Anod, was simply glorious. She wondered if the sensations were the same for him.

"I've missed your touch," Anod whispered to him. The long dormant feelings had captured her heart.

"As I have missed you."

"We can go in now. I just needed to feel you again."

"One more thing before we do go inside," Bradley paused to consider his choice of words, "this is not exactly the most romantic of times, but the essence is with us. Will you marry me, Anod?"

Anod remembered the earlier conversation with Otis. "I can only surmise the intent of your question, Bradley. What precisely do you mean by the word, marry?"

"The term, marry, refers to the age old tradition of institutional bonding between a man and a woman for the purpose of creating a family."

"Why is it necessary for an institution to intervene between the man and the woman? Why aren't the feelings and the children sufficient for this bonding?"

"Well, there is a long history behind the custom. The short version is, the process simply provides state recognition to the union which offers particular legal benefits."

Anod considered his words, but still did not like the image within her thoughts. "To marry, may be a Betan custom, but the meaning seems trivial in comparison to the feelings, I believe, we share. The changes I have experienced since my arrival on Beta have had and are continuing to have a profound effect on me. I do not want to unnecessarily detract from those effects. I have very strong feelings toward you, Bradley, stronger than I have ever experienced. However, I do not feel the need to marry, as you say, in order to lend institutional credence to our feelings."

"Let us go inside, then."

They walked arm in arm without words. Bradley blinked and squinted taking a few moments at the door to let his eyes adjust to the light of the interior.

The remainder of the evening was spent talking about the future in all its possibilities. Several members of the repair team and the Council periodically joined in the discussions. The content of some of the words between Bradley and Anod did not escape notice by several of their colleagues.

A few of them took the liberty of arranging a separate room with appropriate accoutrements for the Prime Minister and their pilot. Although they were not husband and wife, many began to think of them as a couple despite the customs of Beta discouraging cohabitation and premarital sexual relations.

As members of the assemblage began to dissipate into the recesses of the sleeping quarters, Anod and Bradley availed themselves of the privacy arranged for them.

"Who do you think should be trained to fly the interceptor?" asked Bradley.

Initially somewhat confused by his question, a few moments passed before Anod answered. "I haven't given that question any thought," she replied.

"Someone else is going to have to fly the machine now that you are with child."

"Your suggestion is not advisable."

"Why?"

"The craft may seem simple enough to operate. In many ways, it is, in fact, simple to manipulate the controls. The essential part which cannot be easily taught, or acquired, is what we call, air sense."

"What's that?"

"Air sense is an old term from the early days of human flight," she said choosing her words carefully. "The meaning is entwined with the responsibility of flight, recognition of the risks and fundamental knowledge of the capabilities and limitations of the vehicle."

"None of those elements would seem to be beyond the ability of our young men to assimilate," Bradley responded with an air of uncertainty.

Anod again hesitated to carefully consider her words. "You are absolutely correct," she responded. "However, the element of time and the means to train a few pilots makes the possibility impractical."

The subtleties of flight training were patiently explained to the Prime Minister in sufficient detail to achieve the desired result. With the realization came the fundamental issue, again.

"Obviously, your first child, our child, is growing within your womb. I am simply concerned about the risks of flight and potential for damage to our child," Bradley said solemnly.

"The risks are minimal as I have told you. We have a greater risk from the Yorax than from flight."

"Maybe so." Bradley fought with his own thoughts. "I want our child to grow to be strong and healthy."

"I understand your concern. I share your concern although I am more apprehensive about what is happening within my body than I am about the risks of flight." Anod's thoughts raced through the possibilities. "I know about flight. I don't know about pregnancy, as your father calls it."

"There is some time to provide you with the requisite information on pregnancy and childbirth," he spoke softly. "I suppose I must accept your assessment."

Their words gradually drifted toward the intimate language of lovers. Anod felt the renewal of the primitive carnal fires only recently ignited by her distant cousins. She enjoyed the pleasure, but still experienced the lingering suspicions of receding prohibitions. Tonight, however, Anod would be denied the fulfillment of their union and the satisfaction born from the rippling waves of physical ecstasy. The confusion associated with this denial and the lack of understanding for its heritage contributed to her frustration.

Although her desires were not quenched, Anod was still thankful for the enjoyment of his touch. They gradually descended into sleep without words.

Against Bradley's judgment and intuition, Anod continued the flights of the salvaged Yorax interceptor. Several of the most recent flights were flown more for the pure pleasure of flight.

The relationship between the physical and psychological sensations of the flight and her acquired taste for the sensuality of the human body did not escape her awareness and consideration.

The later flights enabled her to explore most the Betan planet, which was an incredibly diverse ecological system with widely varied terrain, weather and vegetation. Fortunately for Anod as well as the innocent citizens of Beta, the interceptor's masking field generator was fully functional permitting her to tour the planet without arousing the citizenry.

Anod liked to imagine she was observing the characteristics of the fountain planet that was ultimately the source of her very existence and yet not a location she had experienced.

"We are ready for space flight," Anod declared to the assembled group. Bradley and Otis were in attendance as well as most of the repair team.

"What are the risks?" asked Bradley.

"To me, none."

"I'm not sure I agree, but I was broadening the scope," he continued. "I was thinking of the risk of exposure."

"That risk is real. I believe we have several positive options." Anod stopped to consider the words she would say to carefully convey the content of her thoughts. "First, I can use the masking capability of the interceptor to . . . ."

"Wait!" exclaimed Bradley. "You said, masking capability. What exactly do you mean by that term?"

"The Yorax as well as the Society spacecraft are equipped with an electromagnetic field generators which recreate the inverse of the normal full spectrum, electromagnetic field. The result is an effective cancellation of the interceptor's broad spectral signature. The vehicle literally becomes invisible."

Bradley's eyes spoke of incredulity with his lower jaw dropping slightly. His response took some time to reach his lips. "You mean you can disappear?"

"Effectively, yes."

"Then we have the solution," Bradley stated.

"We have one of several solutions," answered Anod. "As is usually the case, there is a price."

The Kartog Guards pilot proceeded to explain the diversion of power to the electromagnetic counter-field generators reduced power available to propulsion and other systems. Anod also spoke of other alternatives like the use of Alexatron's shuttle and his interstellar trader spacecraft to shield the interceptor.

The questions began to flow from the other scientists, engineers and even a few of the security detachment. The technology of modern space flight stimulated their curiosity and concern.

Notably absent from the discussion was Alexatron. Probably not new subjects for him, Anod told herself. His distance from the human conversation and his continued presence at the site bothered her. He delivered his cargo and was paid for his services some time ago. Why was he still here?

After careful and deliberate consideration of the alternatives outlined by Anod, the decision was made and agreed to for the first of several space flights. The masking device would be utilized for the early excursions. Depending on the results, full performance of the interceptor could be eventually evaluated.

"When do you want to make the first space flight?" asked Bradley.

"With no additional discussion, I'd like to get started, now," Anod answered.

"It is nearing evening. Don't you think it might be better to wait until tomorrow?"

"No. I'm ready. The interceptor is ready. The first flight won't take much time. I will return before sunset."

"If you don't return before darkness, how will you find this place?" Maria Verde asked.

Not entirely successful in suppressing a chuckle, Anod smiled in response. "The navigation system remembers its starting point. I'll have no problem returning to exactly the same spot, and at a precise time, if that should be required."

"Then go with our blessing," Bradley said with sincerity.

"Thank you."

With a nod of her head in acknowledgment, Anod looked to each person, and was rewarded with a proud smile from Bradley. She also noticed Alexatron still standing alone at the rear of the room. What was the space merchant thinking? Why was he still here? The questions were present, but did not slow her down.

As she mounted the interceptor and settled into the seat of the cockpit, the thought of vulnerability floated through her consciousness intermingled among her efforts to prepare for flight. The Kartog Guards warrior was accustomed to the security of a flight suit designed to provide protection from the vacuum of space should the cockpit be breached. She would have to fly this flight without one. Her concern was her burden, which she did not want to share with the others around her.

Anod looked down at Bradley standing beside the craft looking up at her. "I'll see you in about an hour," she said with a smile directed solely at him.

The Prime Minister struggled to return the smile. "Be careful."

"Not a problem," she responded. "I'll be back before you know it. Since you haven't seen the masking system, I'll activate the device before I take off. I'll talk to you when I get back."

Bradley waved as she lowered the canopy and felt the locking tongs engage the railings. Anod watched as her audience retreated to the periphery of the hangar. The powerplant start up was normal. All the systems checked good.

The interceptor moved gracefully into the clearing. Anod turned the craft broadside to the hangar doors and the assembled crowd. If the Betans were to appreciate the full effect of the masking system, they needed a good view. Brandishing an enthusiastic thumbs-up signal in answer to the hand waving, Anod activated the interceptor's masking system with a simple touch of the displayed symbolic caricature of the craft.

Anod enjoyed the reactions of the observers, unmistakable even from the distance of twenty meters. Several members of the repair team advanced on the fighter thinking Anod had departed. Not wanting to allow what could be an unsafe situation by proximity to the operating interceptor, Anod moved the anti-gravity field lever next to the thrust controller. The height of the machine smoothly increased to more than fifty meters before she advanced the thrust handle.

Pointing the nose of the vehicle toward space above her, Anod increased her speed gradually to several thousand kilometers per second. The bluish-green planet disappeared behind her.

Anod performed a progressively, more aggressive set of maneuvers to evaluate the performance and handling qualities of the Yorax interceptor. The machine moved well, actually better than she expected, but certainly not as crisply as her former fighter. The turns and gyrations, accelerations and decelerations were smooth and predictable which was the best a pilot could hope for. Slowing to a stop, Anod checked her position from the $\theta 27$ star and its companion planets. Nearly 540 gigameters, thirty minutes at light speed, was a respectable distance. $\theta 27$ was just slightly larger than other stars that spanned the transparency of the interceptor.

"Let's see who's out here," Anod spoke aloud to herself. The Kartog Guards pilot focused on the various electromagnetic emissions detectable by the interceptor's sensors.

A variety of communications, some of them encrypted, were routine messages between individuals, organizations and locations. There were no indications of her detection by anybody. Normal sensor scans by merchants plying the void of space with their wares were received by the interceptor's systems.

"Whoa," exclaimed Anod.

The distinctive characteristic of the Yorax scanners washed over the refurbished interceptor containing their primary objective.

"The little buggers," a misstated euphemism, "are still looking for me," she told herself. A Yorax battlecruiser was quite some distance from her and in the opposite direction from Beta.

Anod rechecked the standby status of the active sensor probes. She was perfectly content to just listen with her passive sensors. There were no signs of detection. The masking system was fully functional.

The presence of the Yorax battlecruiser, even at great distance, did not make her feel particularly comfortable. The thought of an emergency broadcast message asking for help from the Society was strong, but suppressed. There was no reason, other than frustration, for risking the attempt. She still felt a dominant responsibility for protecting the Betan people. Her presence, if she did transmit, could easily be traceable back to the Betan planet.

The tactical display illuminated a vessel departing Beta. She watched the data presented about the craft. She also saw it accelerate to hyperlight speed and disappear from her sensor view. "That must be Alexatron. I wonder where he is going in such a hurry?" Advancing the thrust lever, Anod increased her speed toward $\theta 27\beta$. "Now, let's see how fast this machine can go."

The visual distortion of observable space confirmed her approach to warp speed. The warping of the time-space continuum was distinctive and unmistakable. The power required to sustain the cloaked condition prohibited the transition to superlight and hyperlight speeds. The smearing of the visual universe never ceased to impress Anod. The temptation to unmask and make the jump across the boundary her ancestors considered impenetrable was strong and inviting.

The interceptor handled reasonably well in the peculiar region of time-space near the light boundary. Anod was not particularly happy with the collision anticipation systems and her vulnerability at near light speeds, but the idiosyncrasies of the system were tolerable. Completing her control evaluation prior to reaching Beta enabled her to reduce speed, returning the stars to their normal discreet points in space.

The bluish-green colored orb that was Beta slowly grew out of the black of space. Anod found herself with thoughts of this minute occupant of the void as home. The feelings were different from those associated with her return to Saranon from a mission, or other places common to her service. Her thoughts of home were as intriguing as the others she had been exposed to since her awakening on Beta.

As Anod entered the atmosphere, the reddish-yellow glow characteristic of the gaseous interaction of the upper reaches of the atmosphere and the interceptor would make her visually detectable despite the masking system. She reduced speed quickly until the glow dissipated. The velocity of the interceptor continued to decrease to avoid generating compression shock waves in the lower, denser portion of the atmosphere.

The urge to make a quick trip around the planet prior to landing kept Anod in flight a little longer. The Astral Mountains were approaching the evening terminus and she wanted to land before dark.

Anod's thoughts turned to an appreciation of the pure beauty of the planet, the intricacy of rail and road networks and the telltale signs of humanity. The peace and serenity of the scenes below her had to be preserved, she told herself.

"I should get home," she decided to say aloud. The words had significance and inner meaning beyond their simple definition. Anod liked the ring of the sentence.

Making a low pass through the valley passed the hangar verified the lack of an appropriately attentive audience for her triumphant return from space. Anod knew how to gain their awareness.

Turning away from the hangar side of the valley, the accomplished pilot advanced the thrust level producing the associated rise in speed. Anod knew exactly how much speed she wanted to gain.

The loud report shook the doors and reverberated in the hollow cavity of the hangar. The shock wave startled all the inhabitants and scared some of them.

Anod extended her outbound leg and quickly decreased speed. She knew the sonic boom would arouse the spectators. The extension was just a matter of timing. They needed enough time to rush to the exterior to see what the commotion was. The sensors established the assemblage. She slowed the interceptor to 100 meters per second. As she approached the clearing and the hangar, Anod switched off the masking system and commenced a continuous rolling maneuver as she passed the hangar. Anod stopped the interceptor's rolling, and pulled the nose straight up. She added several more rolls to celebrate their accomplishment.

The crowd clapped and cheered generously although she could not hear them as she parked the interceptor inside the hangar bay. Once more the shutdown was completed without a problem.

"It's good to have you back once again," Nick stated for the crowd. He must have arrived while she was flying.

"What was that loud boom just before you landed?" asked Tim Bond.

"That was a sonic boom. A phenomenon associated with the compression of the air mass by the vehicle's velocity. The compression forms a shock wave. The sound is produced by the rapid expansion of the air behind the shock wave," Anod answered.

"I've never heard of such a thing," said George Robbins.

"It's in all the physics references," responded Nick, somewhat annoyed. "It's just been a long time since anyone generated such a spectacular event."

"How was your flight?" Bradley jumped in to change the subject.

"The flight went well. It felt so good to be back in space," said Anod with a broad smile. Her expression turned serious before she continued. "My sensors did pick up the Yorax. The signal characteristics indicate they are still looking for something, probably me."

"Did they detect you?" asked Bradley.

"I did not unmask from takeoff until my low pass," Anod answered. "There was no way they could detect me, and there was no evidence of detection."

"Let's get this debriefing out of the way. We need to hear the rest of Anod's experience on this flight."

As they all moved toward the debriefing room, Anod asked Bradley, "Where did Alexatron go?"

"He had to leave."

"I know. My sensor picked him up as he departed. He blasted out of here and into hyperlight immediately. He was going somewhere in a very big hurry. Why did he leave?"

"He said it was business."

"I see," said Anod. She considered the possibilities and implications, but decided to let it pass. There was nothing she could do about it, now. "As you said, let's get this debriefing done."

The formal debriefing was completed in short order. The discussions then moved through a wide variety of related topics. The enveloping curiosity about space flight began to make an impression within Anod's thoughts.

It was more evident to Anod with each discussion that the interceptor, her presence and the associated events were polarizing the Betan people. The size of each faction was impossible for her to determine, but their existence was not. Most of those around her were part of the space enthusiasts who had become addicted to the possibilities of space flight. Council member Ashitrawani was the most notable opponent of those familiar with Astral. Listening to side conversations certainly indicated a perception of popular support for the maintenance of the current norms.

The struggle within Bradley was also obvious, undeniable and dramatic. His post as prime minister placed him in an apparently untenable position of mediator across the growing chasm between the two opposed visions of the future.

Anod also recognized the additional burden she placed upon

Bradley. His feelings for her were not in question. The growing life within her womb was physical proof of their union. Anod's concern for her friend, lover and now mate grew along with the seemingly irreparable split within his community.

Maybe it would be better for her to take the risk with the interceptor and leave Beta. These people have found peace after so many years as nomads from Earth moving among the stars. The Society's strict rules of peaceful noninterference were clear, logical and unquestionable in their wisdom. And yet, here she was, the virtual center of this controversy and trauma to the Betan people.

The discussions among them along with the negotiations of the mediators were more than Anod wanted to hear. She knew she could not participate in the talks. She left the room and did not acknowledge the concerned expressions of some of the repair team as she walked out into the cool night air.

All the doors were closed and the light of the interior was sealed within the hangar. The light of the surrounding star field as well as the reflected light from $\theta27\gamma$, the third planet from $\theta27$ and the closest neighbor to $\theta27\beta$, was sufficient to illuminate the meadow, the trees along the circumference and the various objects within sight. The effect was just what she needed, her return to the stars. Anod could not ignore the sweet smells on the cold air. They were not confining. The realities of the senses stimulating her, amplified the attraction of the changes occurring within her and around her.

The cool dampness of the soil against her posterior as she leaned her back against a rock felt good. Anod closed her eyes to let the thoughts come and go as she considered the possibilities. Her meditative state was not sufficient to ignore the opening and closing of the small door behind her. The thought of identity passed quickly. At this particular moment, Anod wanted to be alone.

"Anod, where are you?" came the barely audible whisper of Bradley James SanGiocomo.

He called several times and did not receive an answer. She ignored his calls opting for her solitude. There was the possibility he might think she was in the forest and out of earshot. His voice gradually became closer and was mixed with the occasional grumblings over missteps, or bumped shins.

Anod did not look back over the rock. With his voice now only several meters away, she finally gave into his persistence. "I'm right here, Bradley."

"Where?"

"I'm sitting by the large rock to your right front," she responded. "Didn't you hear me calling? Why didn't you answer?"

"I wanted to think things out."

"Have you arrived at any decisions?" he asked with a certain tentativeness to his voice.

"No, but the situation is becoming somewhat clearer." The words sank like stones in a pond.

At first, he did not respond to the statement. "The disagreements of a parliamentary democracy are sometimes difficult to listen to," the Prime Minister told her.

"I am not a politician, as you say. I am a warrior. I deal with facts, realities and instinct." Anod hesitated as she arrived at the conclusion. "My intuition tells me it's time to leave."

"Why?"

"It's obvious my presence is tearing your community apart. I represent a definite threat to the well-being of your people."

"Life is filled with threats, Anod. If we are to live life with pride, we must face our fears." Bradley waited for a response or reaction from Anod while he wished there was more light. He wanted to see her face. The urge to speak overcame his patience. "It is human nature to resist change. The reaction by Ashitrawani and others is simply that resistance."

"That may be, Bradley." A pause punctuated her thought. "Nonetheless, your words and your philosophy do not change the facts," said Anod with strength to her words.

"What would you have us do, ask you to leave?"

"The thought has crossed my mind."

"Despite our parliamentary wrangling, I will not accept that option. You have brought much to this planet, and I know you have much more to contribute."

Anod rose from her seated position to look down into Bradley's eyes as he remained on the rock. She saw the sincerity in his eyes. Without a word, Anod turned to walk to the nearest tree. Touching the coarse and now damp bark felt good to the skin of her hand.

The answers to her questions were not clear. The right path, if there was a right path, was enveloped in a dense fog of doubt. The newly released sensations of her human heritage, her affinity for Bradley and the growing life within her made the decisions facing Anod even more difficult. She did not want to leave, and yet her presence and deepening involvement in Betan affairs were an unequivocal liability for these people. Something had to change. The question was what?

Chapter 14

Months passed as the desire to leave Beta continued to wax and wane. The bonding of Anod to her surroundings approached the point of irrevocability. The cause for the divorce from her past and the society she served for most of her adult life was predominantly the life growing within her and the father of her child.

Nick SanGiocomo, the father of the father and principle confidant to Anod, patiently and carefully answered the questions brought as much by her curiosity as by the reality of the changes within her body. The questions ranged from the growing streaks of pigmented skin rising from her pubic area, to her swelling breasts and darkening nipples, to the size, characteristics and phenomena associated with her distended abdomen. Nick prepared Anod well and complemented the extraordinary and personal efforts of the most renowned midwife on the planet, Mysasha Nagoyama. Her fascination with the human reproductive process was almost childlike, but her diligence with birthing preparations was unparalleled.

Anod's excitement with each noted phenomenon of human fetal gestation was celebrated with any handy audience and with exceptional effervescence. She enjoyed displaying her bulbous belly and brown vertical stripe, and much to the dismay of many an unwary visitor, she also enjoyed displaying her enlarged, ripening breasts. Anod's uninhibited, innocent nature was also changing those around her.

The celebration of life was being renewed in each visitor, each person who came in contact with Anod. There was always bewilderment when visitors realized the exuberant, expectant mother was also an exemplary member of the Society's Kartog Guards, and an efficient martial arts professional.

The flights of the Yorax interceptor continued on a sporadic basis over several months all under the veil of the craft's masking feature. Anod resisted the temptation to unmask and transition to hyperlight speeds. The last ten or more flights were flown with only one purpose, let Anod keep her skills honed with the pleasures of flight. All the systems had been evaluated, improved and certified operational within two months of the first flight. The offensive weapon systems and the biological sensor had been the most troublesome in achieving full effectiveness.

Anod's final acquiescence, to the insistence of Nick and Bradley

SanGiocomo and especially Mysasha Nagoyama, to stop flying came during the last trimester of her pregnancy. The Betans were cautious and conservative due to their lack of knowledge about the effects of high energy and space flight on the physiology of a mother and child. Anod knew there was no danger, but the combination of effects convinced her to agree with the concerns of her friends. Besides, her enlarged lower abdomen made the interceptor's seat harness more difficult to don and fasten.

Anod missed her flights including the rush of the images of speed and the expanse of space. It was approaching two months since her last flight. The urge was still present and strong, but the physical demands of her pregnancy, the continuing birthing education process and the preparations for the great day absorbed most of her interest and concentration. Anod also enjoyed the extra attention afforded her physical condition and the additional time Bradley spent with her. The reasons for the changes didn't matter. She simply liked it and enjoyed it.

On this particular day, the vigorous kicking of her unborn child awakened Anod. The motion of the child within her womb enthralled Anod beyond her growing imagination. She could feel each foot and hand pushing against different elements of her viscera as the baby stretched. The sensations of the burgeoning life within her body often brought tears to her eyes. Anod was not exactly cognizant of the reasons for her tears other than the flush of emotions associated with her impending motherhood.

Anod lay on her back in her bed and rubbed her distended abdomen. She marvelled with the feeling of each kick from the interior against her hands. The strokes of her own hands felt good on her stretched skin. Her breasts were swelling to a point of hardness in preparation for the approaching suckling of her child. All the knowledge she had been given by Nick, Mysasha and others contributed to her anticipation.

"Only a few more weeks," Anod said to her unseen child.

With some strange exertion, Anod rose to begin the day. The weight of her additional burden strained her back muscles. Every step brought an opposing motion of her enlarged abdomen and breasts accentuating the additions and changes to her anatomy. Her morning exercises were becoming progressively more difficult although Anod refused to concede to the difficulty. Several of her motions had to be suspended when the movement produced too much pain with the inertia of her heavy breasts and womb. The morning exercise period was important to her, even with the disruption to her normal routine.

The mirrors in the bathroom as well as the new ones she had rigged up in her room gave Anod a full view of her nude body. The changes in her anatomy continued to fascinate and captivate her. Incredible, that was the word she usually muttered to herself as she viewed her reflection.

Anod still enjoyed the water spray of the shower. It was a pleasure that was constant. The feeling of the warm water on her tight skin provided some welcome relief to the physical tension. The baby seemed to like the change as well. The usual kicks and punches calmed substantially as the sound and warmth of the water spray caressed Anod's abdomen.

Today was an occasion for her visit to Bradley in Providence. The plan included a midday meal with the father of her child and several other members of the Council followed by a visit to another medical technician for another checkup. Anod was not particularly excited about the medical event. She was perfectly happy with the information, advice and monitoring she received from Nick and Mysasha.

Anod accepted although she did not fully understand the boundaries imposed by Betan custom on their relationship, but she still wanted more from him. From all the talks and exchanges of information, Anod surmised the feelings they had for each other were probably the closest to father and daughter she would ever reach. It was times like this particular morning that brought out regrets for her heritage and wishes for more intimate human friendships.

Anod's departure this day was no different from any other since her arrival on Beta. She wanted to go, to enjoy the experience ahead of her, and yet she did not want to leave Nick. So, it was this day as it was so many times before.

The journey to Providence was uneventful by normal Betan standards, but to Anod every trip was an adventure although she had to admit the level of her alacrity was diminishing. She enjoyed watching the farmers tending their fields. Unfortunately, those scenes were only available at two of the stops along the route. Normally, the speed of the train blurred the near field visual scene even for her superior eyes.

"Whewee, you're gettin' ripe, lady," came the unusual vocal observation of an ordinary street vendor like many others she had seen before. "When you gonna drop that kid?" the man continued.

The peculiar modification of the language and the strange choice of words amused Anod. An option of not responding, of ignoring the question, was considered and rejected. Anod's ability to blend into the populace as one of the Betans was her primary protection. She laughed to acknowledge the man's greeting and stroked her bulbous anterior. "I have a little less than two weeks before the birth." she said parroting the information provided by Mysasha.

"Hallelujah. Are ya gonna name the critter after me?" the young man asked with a lightness to his voice and a boisterous laugh to punctuate his question.

The thought of actually naming the child had not entered her consciousness. An answer to his question was not readily available to the usually quick thinking Kartog Guards warrior. "I don't know. I haven't thought of that."

"Well, when ya do, how 'bout thinkin' a me."

"I will consider your request," Anod answered with a smile.

"Good. Good," he said with vigor. "I like that."

Anod waved her hand as she looked over her shoulder and walked up the street away from young street merchant.

"See'ya," came his adieu.

Anod did not respond as her attention refocused on the plethora of people moving up and down the street. She saw several people whom she knew and passed greetings. There were numerous other citizens who recognized her and offered their smiles and salutations. The thought was becoming more common to her consciousness; she was becoming one of them. It was a pleasant thought. The memories of her earlier life had not disappeared, but they were coming to her consciousness much less often.

The street made its characteristic turns and changes snaking among the city buildings. Anod still had time before she was supposed to meet Bradley. Taking advantage of the available opportunity, Anod looked in windows and entered several shops along the main street, or several side streets, to learn more about the people of Beta.

The sounds of the street changed markedly while Anod looked at various displays of clothing in one particular shop along the main street. The persistence of the alteration caught her attention.

As Anod neared the door, the character of the sounds became clearer. There was no sound to the right and a strange rustling sound to the left like muffled rocks rolling down a hill. There were no voices, which was the most notable change to the normally bustling and vibrant street traffic.

Looking first to the left to understand the nature of the changes,

Anod saw people moving quickly away from her. The people kept looking over their shoulders back toward her. Something was wrong.

Anod turned back to the right to check the other direction. Her heart skipped a beat as she almost ran into and now faced a Yorax trooper with his weapon drawn.

She froze at that instant.

His bile green eyes considered the woman standing in front of him. The strange bulge above her legs was not familiar to the trooper. This woman was very fat and not much of a threat, his expression indicated.

Anod surveyed the scene in a flash. There were three of them in sight. It could be a small patrol or the point of a larger group. The three troopers were practiced professionals. They remained alternately distributed on either side of the street about three or four meters apart.

For the first time since she had become pregnant, Anod wanted the extra burden in her womb to be gone. Under normal circumstances, dealing with this situation without a hand weapon would be difficult enough with the dispersed Yorax. It was impossible with the extra weight and expanded lower abdomen. There was only one choice. She had to bluff her way out of the corner she was in. She had to be as passive and nonthreatening as she could possibly be.

"Scuse me," Anod said trying to duplicate the young man's slang. She fought to control her urge to dispatch the ugly, foul smelling trooper within easy striking distance of her. The other two soldiers were not within striking distance, even if she was not pregnant.

"Who are you?" the leader asked with his coarse, guttural voice.

"Me Sara Johnson," answered Anod as she averted his eyes and lowered her head to appear subservient and make recognition more difficult.

"Why are you so fat?" the obnoxious entity asked. His gaze continued to alternate between the woman's face and her large belly.

Anod struggled with her logic. Was this a threat to her unborn child or simple curiosity? She had to take the correct chance, innocence. "I'm with baby," responded Anod. "Scuse me." Anod bowed slightly as she moved around the trooper. Her peripheral vision told her the leader was watching her, studying her. He obviously did not quite know what to think or do. She also recognized his struggle with the discrepancies in the image she presented. The ambiguity was her only salvation. She moved slowly, deliberately shuffling from side to side more like a duck waddle.

All three troopers watched her move with due caution. They had to be suspicious, but their hesitation told Anod they could not believe she was their target.

In fact, her knowledge of Yorax logic told her the balance of information they were considering was on her side. The Yorax usually responded to the slightest positive threat or condition. She continued to move slowly with an intentional waddle to her step. There was no reason to enhance their suspicion.

Anod did not look over her shoulder until she had moved more than thirty meters from the point of confrontation. The quick glance was sufficient to establish the status of her tormentors. They stood there like statues watching her. To the best of her skills, none of them had moved a muscle.

The distance remaining to the corner of the nearest intervening building was just over three meters. The past thirty meters and the next three were the longest in her entire life. The overwhelming sense of desperation raised its ugly head. Anod did not like the feeling and she still felt the strong desire to have her trim body back.

The corner brought some relief to the uncharacteristic anxiety. Another quick glance, this time through the windows of the corner store, confirmed the stationary position of the three dumbstruck troopers. The pregnant Kartog Guards warrior quickened her pace substantially when they no longer had a view of her.

Where were those tunnel entrances Bradley had shown her, Anod asked herself? There was no telling how many more of the Yorax were wandering about looking for her. The distance to the government buildings, she estimated, was about half a kilometer. As she walked the nearly deserted street, the paucity of people was threatening in itself. The citizenry was alerted, aware and absent. Her inherent suspicions tingled with intensity as she continued to consider the possibilities of other less accepting Yorax troopers.

The stimulation for Anod's extraordinary senses was still not sufficient to answer her incessant questions. Where were those tunnels? Anod wanted some terrain to neutralize her physical handicap and the advantage of her unburdened adversaries.

Why now? Why had the Yorax returned to Beta after so many months of absence? Had they discovered her presence and only now were trying to localize her? They knew what she looked like and she had not done anything to alter her appearance. The baby. It must be the baby.

The image contrast between her face and height, which were

confirmation, and her large lower abdomen, which was probably the key contradiction, must have been the source of their hesitation. The contradiction was the only plausible reason for the failure of the Yorax troopers to apprehend her standing right before them. They probably convinced themselves, in that moment, a warrior could never look like the distorted person they saw. Yes, that had to be the reason, Anod told herself as she continued to walk quickly with a consistent scan of the visual field. Her pregnancy, while a physical restraint to her martial skills, was her salvation. She wondered how much longer that would last.

The government plaza was around the next corner. Anod stopped, pretending to catch her breath, stretched her back and massaged her belly. During the respite, her eyes and other senses functioned in overdrive trying to comprehend the situation and assess her exposure. Nothing was behind her other than an empty street. The immediate area was safe.

With a casual nonchalance, Anod looked around the corner only to be presented with the worst scene she could imagine. The small square that linked several of the Betan government buildings was occupied by a substantial contingent of Yorax troopers. The large body of the Yorax leader she had seen during their last visit was the most dominant figure in the square. Anod quickly scanned the group. Most of the occupants were Yorax soldiers. Several Betans including two members of the Council were being questioned in the square directly in front of the Council building. The hostility of the Yorax leader was quite apparent with his raised guttural voice evident, but not understandable among the other voices and noise from the square.

To her relief, Anod could not see Bradley among the Betans being interrogated by the Yorax. The players in the square shifted positions exposing Anod's betrayer, the traitor, Zitger. The former Kartog Guards flight leader was much less animated than the Yorax commander, however he was deeply involved in the questioning.

Out of sight from the square, Anod pressed her back against the stone of the building corner. The cool stone felt good to the strain in her back, but did not help the pain growing in her abdomen. Oh please, Anod told herself, don't be birthing contractions, not now. She was not sure of the pains as a novice to childbirth. The words of Mysasha and Nick were clearly among her other thoughts as she considered the situation in the government square, in Providence and in her body.

A series of conflicts occupied her consideration of the next action she should take. Anod wanted to make sure Bradley was safe, and yet she knew refuge was the only protection for her child. She wanted to confront Zitger, and yet the threat was obviously too great and the possibility was out of the question.

The streets were deserted in every direction except for the small crowd in the square. The locations of the tunnel entrances still eluded Anod. Self-chastisement persisted for her failure to absorb her surroundings and remember the escape route location.

Anod's consideration of options was abruptly and rudely interrupted by another altered noise of a commotion and the scream of a woman. Quickly peeking around the corner, Anod saw her worst fears.

The Yorax had separated one of the Council members, Anod could not remember his name, from the others in the square. Zitger and the Yorax commander continued to question several of the other Council members including Bagiiwa Ashitrawani. The elder gentleman was showing unmistakable signs of stress. The intruders and the traitor were obviously not obtaining the information they wanted, despite their threats.

In an instant, the situation changed. The distinct and lethal, blue-green beam from a LASER rifle crossed the distance from one of the Yorax troopers to the chest of the separated Council member. The screaming woman slumped to her knees as the slain man crumpled in a heap.

The group of Yorax must have given up on their interrogation. They collectively walked toward Anod with the big commander leading the way.

Once again, the situation changed in a flash. Anod had to move, and move quickly. She started to run down the street with the excited pain of motion in her belly. The weight of her child felt like 25 kilograms hung from her chest.

The side street was eight meters away. The quick calculation told her she would not make the momentary refuge of the side street before the Yorax arrived at the corner. The door to the shop was locked. There was no time. A sharp blow from the heel of her right hand broke the lock.

Anod closed the fractured door behind her grabbing a small chair to jam under the handle. Did the Yorax hear the crack of the door, or understand what they heard? The answer didn't matter. Any time delay was needed at this point. A rapid scan of the store established it as a specialty food shop. There was nothing within sight that could be used as a weapon. She needed a door, an escape route.

Several additional scans were required to determine the purpose of the small curtain at the back of the store. It had to be a rear exit and she hoped it was not wishful thinking. She really did not want to know the answer to her earlier question about exposure. The rear door was behind the curtain. Unfortunately, the exit did not present her with a clear route of egress, either. The door led to a narrow, twisting alleyway with no observable exit other than several additional doors. An exit could be around any one, or none, of the corners. Without many options left, Anod decided she could not wait for the front door to come crashing into the room.

Finding a hiding place would bring her some time to think. Passing through a couple of other stores and walking along several back streets had taken her about 200 meters, she estimated, from the square. After evaluating several inadequate hiding places, Anod was able to find a well-protected, secluded room with two different egress routes available.

The periodic recurrence of her abdominal pain did not help her thought processes. Anod was concerned about the prospect of giving birth alone in the small room of her interim sanctuary. However, the most immediate issue was her extrication from the Yorax dragnet.

There was no way to tell if her presence had been betrayed, although the obvious change in Yorax tactics seemed to indicate something was different. Anod knew she had no choice but to assume she had been exposed. Now, everyone became a threat. Fortunately, the word of the more aggressive actions of the Yorax produced a rare, significantly reduced number of Betan citizens in Providence.

The correct decision did not take long for her to reach. Darkness. She needed an edge and the inevitable night might give her just enough advantage. Her best estimate of time placed sunset about 90 minutes away with full darkness 30 minutes after that.

There were no signs of life within the range of her senses, not even the distant sound of a barking animal, a passing human, or the smell of a meal cooking. The lack of clues from sight, sound or smell enabled Anod to focus her thoughts on other issues.

The pain in her back, her abdomen and her breasts began to subside somewhat. The baby was still. It took more than twenty minutes before Anod felt the first kick within her. The feeling brought a smile of reassurance to her face. The slight kick seemed to foretell the outcome of this particular ordeal.

Her precise location was not clear. The requirement to avoid capture by the Yorax overpowered the process of navigation. With the benefit of quiet time, Anod methodically worked through the possibilities of where she was and where the tunnel entrances might be located. The consideration of returning to SanGiocomo Waystation via the train came and went numerous times. She wanted to be with Bradley and Nick. She knew the birth of her child was near and she needed a safe place.

The majority of her thoughts sifted through the tactical situation and what might be going on beyond her sensory acquisition range. The possibilities were enormous. Again, her mind returned to the supposition that something had obviously changed. There was nothing in her memory that could, or even might, explain the change in the situation. Every action she and the Betans had taken was specifically oriented to avoid detection. There were no mistakes. Anod resigned herself to the warrior's common choice . . . assume the worst and do not be surprised.

One or more of the Betans may have succumbed to the pressure of the Yorax interrogations, or Alexatron may have compromised her. Until she knew what had changed, or had a clearer picture of the situation, Anod had only one choice. Everyone was a threat to her safety.

The extended duration of quiet and the dwindling light outside the shop convinced the Kartog Guards pilot to get some sleep. The rest would serve two purposes, preparation for a long night and passing of several hours of darkness. Anod found a secluded corner behind the service counter, a few work jackets and a blanket to make a soft spot to curl up in.

Anod could not immediately determine how long she had been hiding. Snippets of sleep had been punctuated by startled alertness with every little sound around her. Anod was not concerned about the time. Convinced she got the most rest she was going to get, Anod stood up with an ache in virtually every joint. Before venturing out onto the streets, each muscle was stretched and warmed. The strain of the extra weight would not go away. She could not change it. She just had to live with it, to adapt to the constraints imposed upon her. Convinced she was as ready as she was going to be, Anod made her way toward the door.

The suspicious instincts of a warrior, alone in a hostile place, dictated her actions from the long, deliberate looks up and down the street to the careful listening for any telltale sounds of people, any people. Satisfied the surrounding area was clear, Anod opened the door ever so slowly to avoid a squeaking hinge. There was still certain resentment over the conventional Betan doors. There was a greater elegance to the automated doors of her fading past.

The cool night air greeted her along with a new set of aromas. The scents of the city were different from the rural, agricultural environment, or the forest. The smells burdened the air while they were not offensive. They were likewise not sweet and rich as they were in the forest.

So far, so good, she told herself.

Her first steps on the street reinforced the rolling assessment. Still no sounds. Anod walked slowly with careful, deliberate steps pausing every five meters, or so, to listen and look. She was thankful for the absence of streetlights. Where were all the people, she asked herself? It was not particularly a question she wanted an answer to, although it did continue to nag at her.

The process of localization did not take long. Anod finally knew where she was. Now, the only problem was where did she need to go. Eventually, a few features and objects along the way began to trigger the recovery of her memory. The building she and Bradley had used those many months earlier was about fifty meters ahead on the left. The scene remained as it had been all night on her trek through the city.

Anod took a moment to lean against the wall adjacent to the entrance door. The gentle night was disarming. The chill of the stone against her back provided the same relief another wall had provided earlier in the day. Each roof, each window, each door, each element in every direction was analyzed several times in a purposefully casual manner. The walk from her hiding shop had taken a little over two hours and she had not seen another living creature. Less than a dozen windows had been lit along the way, but each window was covered with curtains or shades without any evidence of habitation.

A deep breath signalled her commitment to enter the building. The interior confirmed the correctness of her recovered memory. The series of specific doors lead Anod to one of the tunnels that made up the complex beneath the city.

Anod started down the tunnel and stopped as if frozen by an invisible beam. Bradley's words that earlier day returned to her with great clarity. The tunnel complex was specifically designed and furnished with the accoutrements of deception to confuse, disorient and otherwise befuddle any intruder.

"This is not a good idea," Anod said to herself. With a moment's additional consideration, Anod turned to seek a different route out of the city.

Less than half the night remained, there was no purpose to be served by procrastination. Returning to the street, Anod also returned to the methodical progression of search and advance. The destination was constant although the route and the means were still not clear. The Providence train station was not a feasible point of embarkation with the Yorax probably remaining in town.

The star field intermittently visible overhead and through breaks in the roofline on either side of her gave Anod the sense of direction she needed to navigate her way out of the city. Several options were available, none of which were exclusive or solitary. The most immediate concern was getting out of the city before dawn. Progress was good. Even her baby was cooperating.

The diminishing height of the buildings and the associated thinning of the constructed objects of habitation indicated the approaching limits of the city. Trees and shrubbery began to replace buildings and Anod still had about an hour of extant darkness.

Fortunately, the innocent inquisitiveness of her discussions with Nick and Bradley, as well as Otis, fulfilled her instinctive preparations for any eventuality. This was certainly one of those occasions. The maps Bradley and Otis had used to answer her questions of geography and demography now aided her egress.

The light of dawn was diffused by a mass of clouds, some dark and some light. The wind increased in velocity substantially with the rebirth of the day. The approximately ten meters per second wind pulled at her clothes and her hair as well as brought coldness to the air. The wind also reduced the effectiveness of her hearing and smell. This was not the kind of stimulation she needed or wanted at this moment.

The citizens of Beta also returned to view. She tried to be as casual as she could, as she watched each and every one of them for the first possible sign of recognition or betrayal. The fact that she did not see any abnormal response did not dull the edge on her awareness. Survival demanded all her senses, skills and instincts. Anod acknowledged to herself the extent of her vulnerability in this open country on foot without any weapons other than her body, which was seriously compromised by the grossly enlarged portions of her anatomy.

New India Waystation was an isolated locale in a small valley about 22 kilometers from Providence. Like Seymour Waystation, she and Bradley used earlier, New India was on a different line than the one serving SanGiocomo and Providence. Unlike Seymour, the New India line did not go through Providence at all.

The long walk to New India was more than she probably should do, but there was not much choice. As the morning progressed, the temperature did rise a little. The clouds persisted and released a few drops of moisture.

The peculiar snort of a horse, and the crunch of hooves and large wheels on the gravel road behind her were signs of an approaching farm cart. There were no voices that meant probably only one rider. The contrast between the transportation choices of the rural people and the modern Betan trains was sharp, but both were antiquated when compared to modern space vehicles. The Yorax would not be patient enough to use a farm cart when they had the modern implements of space travel. While not immediately threatening, the usual suspicions persisted.

The sounds of the approaching cart were about 25 meters behind her when Anod took her first quick glance. She confirmed the imagined picture. The closure rate was not particularly fast, but it was steady.

"Would you like to ride with me, ma'am?" an elderly man with thinning silver hair and rather rotund physique asked as he drew up beside her. "You're carryin' a pretty heavy load there."

Anod hesitated for a moment to consider the possible consequences. At face value, the benefits outweighed the detractors. If her judgment was wrong, Anod knew the slightest indication of ulterior motives, or the possibility of betrayal would give her no choice but to eliminate the possibility. "I'm going to the New India Waystation," responded the ambulatory warrior.

"Well, I wasn't planning to go to New India, but it's not too far from my path."

"I would not want to trouble you."

"Nonsense. It is no trouble. New India is about four kilometers from here and you shouldn't be walking that far when you are so close to the big day," the man said sincerely.

"That would be most kind."

The cart stopped. The reins to the horse were tied off at the horn on the left side of the cart. The man moved to the right side of the cart stepping partially down and extending his hand. "Here, let me help you up."

"Thank you," answered Anod as she grasped the proffered hand of assistance. Lifting her weight the one and half meters to the seat even with the man's help accentuated the twenty percent increase in her body weight.

A realization came to her. Women pay a serious price for bearing a child in the natural, biological manner. This is hard work carrying an unborn child in the womb, she told herself.

With both occupants seated, the man untied reins and flicked them across the horse's rump. With a trained response, the horse began to move with a slow gait.

"You have a very strong grip," the man said looking at her with a smile.

"Thank you," answered Anod, not sure whether the statement was a compliment, or not.

The man waited. The expression in his eyes and across his face asked for an explanation. Anod did not want to open up that particular line of questioning. She smiled in return. He took the hint.

"How rude of me! My name is, Youngoric, Gastron Youngoric," he said wiping his right hand on his brown pants before extending it to her.

Anod again gripped his hand although purposefully more lightly than earlier. There it was again, the same expression he displayed a few moments ago.

"Excuse me. I am Mary Smithson."

"Very nice to make your acquaintance, Missus Smithson."

Familiarity with the ancient titles of Earth and their common utilization on Beta helped Anod recognize the relationship between her physical condition and Gastron's choice of titles. Acceptance of the title on the alias was quite all right with Anod. No need to tempt fate, if you were a believer.

Gastron continued to ask questions to stimulate his desire for conversation. "Where you from?" he asked as an incomplete sentence. The unexpressed statement, you are not from this area, was obviously behind the question.

Anod's mind ran through a wide range of possible answers and conversational directions. She was thankful for the ride, but talking about personal information could only lead to trouble for her. "I am from Baikonov," answered Anod remembering her chosen false home was on the other side of the planet.

"You're a long way from home."

"Yes, I am."

"What are you doin' out in the country on this side of the planet?"

Anod knew this was the time to stop the discussion as gently as she possibly could. Before responding to his question, Anod tried to draw out a subtly pained expression. "If you will excuse me, Mister Youngoric, I don't feel particularly well. I am very grateful for the assistance you have offered, but would you mind if we do not talk?"

There was some surprise on his face. It was not immediately clear whether her request offended him. Anod preserved her calm, pained expression as she shifted her weight away from the man and mentally calculated the sequence for the singular blow that would send Gastron Youngoric into oblivion.

"I didn't mean to offend, Missus Smithson. I was just tryin' to make conversation." The hurt expression remained.

"Thank you, Mister Youngoric. I am sorry. I am just not feeling well."

His expression changed dramatically. "You're quite welcome and I'll keep my yap shut for awhile."

Anod nodded her acknowledgment. The slight personal abrasion was quickly cast aside among the trees along the roadway. The birds were alive with their unique songs. The sounds and smells of this agricultural area were rich and pleasant with an exotic combination of sensory stimulants that naturally played well together.

Thankfully for Anod, the population was sparse and not particularly concerned about a simple farm cart travelling slowly through the area with two people and farm goods. There was certain serenity to the glorious mixture of colors, browns, greens, blues, yellows, and reds playing on her senses in an even more glorious symphony of the sensations.

The baby must have finally become aware of the change in the level of her exertion. The stirrings were slight and gradual at first. Eventually, the pushes and kicks became more energetic and painful in a special way. Pressing her hands on her bulbous abdomen did not quiet the child's stretching. As if by some mystical signal, the muscular contractions began again. This particular series did not fail to bring back the words of Mysasha regarding the falsity of early birthing contractions as well as the ever-present possibility of confusing the false with the real contractions, and vice versa.

"You're not going to have your baby in my cart, are you?" The sentence was not presented as a statement, but the tone established his intention as an interrogatory.

"I am not certain, if you must know," answered Anod with true reflection of her inner concerns.

"Where is your midwife?"

"I am not sure of that either."

"This is not good," he said with compassion. "A woman so ripe with child should never be this far from her midwife."

"I suppose you are right."

"Of course, I'm right." Youngoric's agitation was unmistakable. "Is this your first birth?"

"Yes."

"No wonder you are out here in the middle of nowhere and don't know where your midwife is."

Somehow Anod felt like a child being lectured by a parent despite the fact that she had never experienced such an occurrence herself. She chose not to respond.

"What should I do?" asked Gastron Youngoric. The pained look on his face connoted his concern.

With much consideration, Anod knew the only option. "The best thing you can do is deliver me to the New India Waystation."

"I'm not so sure that's the best thing."

"I believe it is. The train will get me back to Baikonov the quickest way."

Gastron did not speak for many minutes as he considered her words and the situation. His lack of response foretold his confusion and inner turmoil. The concern of this stranger, this elderly gentleman she had just met, was an endearing characteristic for her. He did not have to care, but he did.

Finally, the sight of the elevated bed for the train came into view. The station was not readily apparent, but Anod correctly surmised, it was not far.

As if sensing the thought in her brain, he said, "We are less than a kilometer from the station."

The cart crested the ridge and descended into the shallow, narrow valley that contained the waystation. Anod discreetly scanned each segment of the terrain around the station out to the visible horizon. Gastron and Anod were the only humans in the area.

The cart stopped by the station. Gastron hurriedly jumped from the cart to help Anod down from the seat. Anod was once again thankful for his assistance.

"Thank you, Mister Youngoric. You have been very kind. I am in your debt."

"You're sure this is what you should be doin'?"

Anod nodded her head.

"Well, then, you're welcome." Gastron Youngoric extended his hand once again which Anod gently grasped. "Have a safe journey, Missus Smithson. Good luck with your birth. May your child be strong and healthy."

"Thank you again, Mister Youngoric."

The horse was directed to turn the cart. Gastron waved to Anod as he moved back the way they had just come. He was a nice man. She would have to get word back to him after the birth.

With the slow part of the trek behind her, Anod focused her attention on egress, exposure and translation.

The system route map posted on the wall confirmed her earlier analysis. Trains travelled in both directions from this station. She needed the one going to the right.

The sporadic cyclical contractions persuaded her to alter the original plan slightly. Instead of making three train changes for her extended return, Anod decided to make only one change to arrive at SanGiocomo Waystation from the direction opposite from Providence. The new route passed through relatively thin population zones with only one large city to transit.

Events continued to fall in her direction. The train had only three people on board when she embarked, none of whom showed any interest in the pregnant woman dressed in common clothes who walked slowly to the rear of the last passenger segment near the emergency exit.

The contractions eased somewhat until the train accelerated. The characteristic tug of the acceleration vector on the added mass of her body was more pronounced than she remembered from yesterday's trip to Providence. The baby reacted to the forces just as it had earlier. Thankfully, the contractions did not return.

Anod forced herself to concentrate on every piece of data she could acquire. The distraction of the physical phenomena within her was strong. The urge to find a quiet, safe place grew more definitive. She recognized the feelings from Mysasha's teachings as one small part of the natural human birthing process. The final sequence of the process was underway. It was only a matter of time now until she lost her amniotic fluid surrounding the infant within her womb.

The struggle to suppress the sensations became more difficult, but she knew there was no choice. She had to get back to SanGiocomo before the baby came, but the threat of the Yorax was constantly on her mind. The obvious change in Yorax tactics proclaimed a new dimension to her situation. The source of the change continued to jab at her concentration.

Every stop during her return journey brought a renewal of the warrior's tension. Everything and everybody combined to be a potential threat. On two occasions, Anod stood to position herself for the best response she could muster up. Fortunately, for her and for the approaching individuals, the threat never materialized.

There was no enjoyment of the journey for Anod. Her escape from Providence and the continuing vulnerability of her travel denied her the pleasure of the scenery and the absorption of the human diversity. The objective was singular, focused and exclusive. She needed a safe place. She needed to be out of reach of the Yorax.

Only a few more stops on the last leg of her trip gave Anod a sense of closure. Just as the warmth of proximate sanctuary washed over her for a few moments, the cold flash of instinctive realization brought an immediate end to her brief euphoria. Anod's suspicious mind clearly saw an undesirable tactical situation.

SanGiocomo Waystation was a relatively isolated location in a sparsely populated region of the planet. For reasons that are never known to anyone, the smell of a trap, an ambush filled Anod's immediate consciousness. The indicators were too close. The aggressive change in Yorax search operations, the focus on the Council building and the center of the Betan government, and the isolated train station close to the Prime Minister's father's abode were simply too many negative indicators.

Anod quickly scanned the wall route map. The tempo of her thoughts quickened as she considered the possibilities – the options – the choices. The most immediate task was to get off the train at the next stop. She couldn't get any closer to SanGiocomo Waystation. The next to last stop was the best she could do.

The stop in the small town was deserted much to Anod's relief. The distance to Nick's cave was more than 170 kilometers, too far for ground movement with the contractions continuing and becoming more uniform although still widely separated. The choices were not many.

The best alternative appeared to be backtracking on the train network to a station about 15 kilometers distance behind the High Cave area. The climb from the train stop, which was also an isolated station supporting several local families, would be arduous. From her memory of the terrain, the walk to High Cave would probably take 15 to 20 hours. There was no other viable choice in her situation.

Two train line changes and the remainder of the day were required to arrive at the proper waystation. Anod was thankful once again. The darkness of the night was her great ally. The thought did bring a brief, subtle smile to her face. Most creatures, human and others, would be asleep or preparing for sleep. The cloak of the night's blackness enveloped her to reduce the sense of vulnerability that had been with her for more than thirty hours, a day and a half, and gave her back some of the advantage lost with her distended abdomen.

Anod had never walked the ground from the backside waystation to High Cave. Her navigational abilities, especially with the availability of the discreet beacons of the star field, enabled her to move efficiently toward her intended sanctuary. The vestiges of habitation were behind her when the light of the θ27 star began to illuminate the sky above the forest. Progress was slower than she wanted. The pleasant scents of the forest were a welcome addition, making the physical exertion and occasional rest stops more tolerable.

Familiarity with the terrain, vegetation and geological features told her she was within two kilometers when the light of day came once again. Anod's continuing careful analysis of her perceivable environment reflected the lack of disturbance. The pristine character of the surroundings brought some comfort, but not relaxation.

Despite the debilitating fatigue from the relentless stress, physical strain and lack of sleep, Anod further slowed her advance on High Cave. There was no reason to lose her patience so close to her objective. The possibility of a compromise site was still real. Her diminished physical condition left her without many defensive options.

Once again, the darkness gave her some advantage. However, the canopy of the dense forest denied her most of the ambient starlight making even her superior low light vision more tenuous. The light reduction did not concern the Kartog Guards warrior. Progress was just a little slower and deliberate. Anod had to be more careful determining the adequacy of her footing in addition to minimization of the created noise of her movement.

Within two hundred meters of High Cave, as she reached the crest of the ridgeline behind the cave entrance, Anod froze every muscle in her entire body. She could feel her surging heart rate. The dim light reflecting off the trunks and foliage of several trees on the far side of the draw told her the situation was not good. Someone occupied High Cave.

Anod's analytical brain ran through the range of possibilities. Someone was waiting for her. Who could possibly know she was coming here? Someone could just be here by coincidence. Not likely. High Cave was not used often. The interior light could have been mistakenly left on. Once again, the utilization of the cave was very low, to near nonexistent, except for Anod. Animals? No, the light was artificial. Animals do not turn on lights. The bulk of the potential reasons for the light stacked up on the negative side of the equation.

The mouth of the cave was not visible from her observation point. Anod considered moving to another vantage point, but discarded the idea due to the risk of detection. The assessment of the area continued for a long time, probably an hour. Everything remained constant. Sight, sound, smell and intuition did not change, other than the background of the forest night.

The cold night air chilled her immobile body. The contractions of her lower abdomen became more frequent and consistent. They were also increasing in intensity verging on pain. There was not much time left. Something had to change. There were only two immediate choices. She had to retreat from the area and find another sanctuary, or she had to confront whoever was in the cave. The occupant was most likely to be a friend, or at least a neutral, but the possibility of a Yorax trap was also a reality. The remaining four hours of darkness and the gush of amniotic fluid wetting her pants convinced her to force the situation. Her choices were down to one.

Finding a fist-sized rock, Anod calibrated the mass of the stone along with the distance to the pond upstream from the cave entrance. With characteristic precision, Anod tossed the rock into the middle of the pond producing a loud kerplunk. The response did not take long coming.

Otis Greenstreet appeared in the light and quickly moved into the shadows with his weapon at the ready. He was a good soldier with good instincts and skills. His recognition of the ripples in the pond from the center told him the event was not natural. He methodically searched the surrounding area including several glances in the direction of Anod, but the light was too low for him to see the eyes watching him. Otis' reactions told her, he was alone.

Anod continued to wait hoping for Otis to call out. Although it would be a tactical mistake for him, an interrogatory from Otis would make her introduction less startling. After several minutes of patient, motionless waiting, Otis moved slowly toward the cave apparently convinced the pond disturbance was an aberration of nature.

Not wanting to take any unnecessary chances, Anod moved behind a large tree trunk. An instinctive reactionary response by a Betan with a LASER rifle in his hands could mistakenly injure her, or result in a more lethal consequence.

"Otis?" Anod asked softly.

His response was as predicted. The LASER rifle was instantly pointed toward the voice. He did not fire. He waited without speaking, frozen like stone.

"Otis?"

"Identify yourself," he demanded.

"Are you alone?"

Without the slightest change, he said, "Identify yourself."

Good response, Anod told herself. A professional would not offer information about his condition without confirmation of safety.

Before Anod could respond, Otis challenged his intruder. "Identify yourself immediately, or I will engage."

There was no point to continue the impasse. The indicators were sufficiently positive to warrant taking a reasonable risk. "Otis, it is me . . . , Anod."

"Why did you wait so long?" he asked with a touch of anger in his voice. "I was about to shoot."

Instinct held her in place. "My apologies, Otis." Anod paused before asking, "Is everything all right?"

"Yes, everything is quite all right. I am alone and I've been waiting for you to show up. Now, come on down here. You must be cold."

Descending the precipitous incline was slow and cautious. Otis waited patiently for her to make her way down to the cave entrance.

"My, my, but you must be about ready to give birth."

"From what Mysasha and Nick have told me, I'd agree with your assessment. I lost my amniotic fluid a short time ago, and the contractions are regular and increasing in frequency and intensity." She decided not to tell about the mounting pain.

The warmth of the cave's interior coaxed her muscles to relax. Anod sat down in the largest chair and spent several seconds twisting her body in an attempt to find the least uncomfortable position.

"We assumed you somehow became aware of the events in Providence." The nod from Anod confirmed his statement. "Prime

Minister SanGiocomo assigned several of us from the Astral security force to various locations to find you. As you can see, I was assigned to High Cave." The young security officer looked to Anod with a twinkle in his eyes, a solid grin across his face and wanting a response from her.

Anod smiled, nodded, but did not answer. The fatigue of her journey, the strain of her pregnancy, the now incessant contractions of her abdomen and the relief of this sanctuary eliminated any desire to talk.

Sensing the situation, Otis asked, "How close are you?"

"I have never done this before, Otis, so I don't know for sure. Based on what I have been told, I'd say the birthing process is well underway. I am probably less than a day from birth."

"They told me you probably would be close and they were right. We've prepared for this." Otis exuded confidence. "If you think you will be OK, I'll leave at sunrise to fetch Mysasha and Nick."

"That would be quite good." Anod did not feel up to conversation, but she did recognize the enthusiasm of her companion.

"Well, with that decided, where have you been?"

"I was at Government Square in Providence when the council member . . ." she stopped. Lowering her eyes with internal embarrassment and regret, Anod continued, "I can't remember his name . . . when he was assassinated. From that point until now, I have been trying to get as far away from the Yorax patrols as I can and find a safe place to have my baby."

"Then, you don't know what has been happening, do you?"

The tone and words of Otis' question told her events on the planet were greater than just the assassination in the square. "No, I don't."

"The Yorax say they have proof you are alive and on the planet. They have been systematically terrorizing the population all over the planet trying to get someone to talk. Prime Minister SanGiocomo is convinced someone who does not have immediate knowledge of your presence has betrayed you. There are only a handful of people who know about High Cave and fewer know you have used this place. We feel this is the place for you to have your baby."

Anod nodded her agreement and did not indicate the trouble within her thoughts. The possibility of these grotesque events had been with her since she regained consciousness over one year ago. Although the concern had diminished in recent months, the threat had always been with her.

"Have they injured more citizens?"

"Yes," Otis answered in a subdued tone. "They have selectively executed one person in each major city, so far."

"What are we doing about it?" Anod's choice of first person plural did not pass by either of them. She was somewhat surprised by her subconscious choice.

"We are doing what we always do, passive resistance."

Anod shook her head with the recognition of experience. "I don't think that will work this time."

"Maybe not, but it is the choice of our government."

Contractions caused Anod to pause for a few moments. The strength of the involuntary muscular contractions increased although they were not overlapping, yet. As the pain subsided, she wanted to know more.

"Are Bradley and Nick safe?"

"Yes."

"Have the Yorax been to Nick's cave?"

"No. We were concerned about the same thing. The Yorax seem to be focusing on the large cities. We've had a small security force in the area. They have also not visited Astral."

"It would seem the intruders do not have as much information as they would like. I agree with Bradley's assessment of their intelligence information."

Otis did not offer any additional comments.

"Where is Bradley?"

"He is travelling to the various cities hit by the Yorax and trying to bolster the morale of the population. It is what the prime minister is expected to do at times like these."

"Is he safe?"

"As safe as we can provide."

"How about Nick and Mysasha?"

"Nick is at his home waiting for notification of your location. Mysasha is also standing by at her home. They know you are close to delivery and will need their help."

"That is good," Anod said with a low voice more to herself than to Otis. Looking at Otis with a smile, she offered, "I need some sleep, Otis. I am very tired."

"Yes, yes, absolutely. It shall be light soon. I'll wait until you are soundly asleep, then I shall go."

"Very well. Please hurry. I fear I am close." Anod lay down on the bed. The smiling face of the protective Otis Greenstreet was the last image in her consciousness. Her sleep was fitful as the contractions continued to progress, but the burden of fatigue was heavy.

Otis waited dutifully as he watched slumber envelop the swollen form recumbent on the bed. The dim light of the rising star began to change the illumination of the interior when Otis pulled the door closed behind him.

Anod would not know, for some time, the physical risk Otis took that morning. He ran as fast as he felt he could sustain down the mountainous terrain. The dim light of morning contributed to numerous missteps and tumbles that fortunately did not seriously injure the young man. Time was of the essence.

Chapter 15

Nick SanGiocomo was the first to arrive although Anod was deeply into a quiet although brief period of sleep. Recovery from the debilitating fatigue was entirely too slow as the child within her began to fight for extrication. Nick recognized the characteristic signs of her physical condition. He had never seen her face with dark circles around her eyes and lines of pain and stress written across her face. While this was not peculiar, it was not a good condition to begin the struggle of childbirth.

Carefully and quietly, the elder SanGiocomo began to prepare the small cave for the impending birth. Most of the basic tools to protect the mother and child were brought up from his laboratory. Mysasha, in time, would also bring her kit bag.

The conflict within her body was evident in the cycles of pain that brought Anod close to awareness, but not to consciousness. Nick knew without asking that her body demanded rest to alleviate the fatigue of the escape, while the thriving child within her womb was ready to join the world on the outside. Several times during the hours of his lone observation, Anod's eyes opened briefly accompanied by deep painful groans with each sign of contractions, but she did not see. No one could see the slight signs of worry etched into Nick's face and eyes. Anod was obviously close to giving birth and she was precariously weak to help the birth as mothers have over the centuries.

The sounds of human movement diverted Nick's attention to the exterior of High Cave. He quickly exited the cave to brief the new arrivals.

Nick did not expect to face four armed men. The flash of surprise passed quickly with the recognition of Mysasha Nagoyama with her usual satchel.

Speaking directly to Mysasha, Nick began, "Anod is not in the best of shape to begin the delivery. She is quite fatigued, and probably malnourished and dehydrated. The contractions appear to be rhythmic and strong. I have not examined her yet, in deference to the need for her to get what rest she can."

"Well, I've been through worse I suppose, but my biggest concern is the lack of her cultural background toward childbirth."

"I share your concern, but that's water under the bridge, now."

"Shall we get started?" asked the experienced midwife, reflecting her characteristic no nonsense attitude.

"I have things essentially prepared," Nick responded. "Why the guards?" He motioned to the four security troops.

Mysasha demonstrated her lack of enthusiasm for the weapons. "This is someone else's idea." The frustration with state security was obvious. "I don't know who, but they will stay out of the way."

Otis volunteered a portion of their mission orders. "We will be in the area, Mister SanGiocomo. If there is any threat, we will divert them from this place. Before you ask, we have no indication of a Yorax threat other than the fact they are still operating on the planet."

Allowing himself to deviate briefly from the immediate task, Nick felt the need to ask, "How is my son?"

"To be very frank, Mister SanGiocomo, I am not sure. He has been following the Yorax who are still terrorizing our population. The last we heard from him was yesterday morning."

"Does he know about the impending birth of his child?"

"Yes."

"Very well," Nick responded turning to Mysasha. "Shall we see to our patients?"

Mysasha liked the sound of his question. They did indeed have two patients demanding their attention inside the small cave.

Mysasha indicated this was her first visit to remote High Cave. As would be expected, the diminutive medical practitioner made a quick assessment of the interior. "Well, this is not the best place to deliver a newborn, but it certainly isn't the worst either."

Placing her kit bag on the table already arranged by Nick, Mysasha carefully observed the resting form of Anod. Nick's brief description was quite appropriate. She had only known Anod for about seven months and there was no question the strain of her first pregnancy combined with her recent physical exertion had taken its toll on the larger woman. At least, she was sleeping peacefully at the moment. Mysasha gave Nick a nod of recognition and agreement, then proceeded to prepare for the approaching event.

The transition from quiet sleep to the alert focus of pain occurred in a heartbeat. Anod's head rose off the cushion as she grabbed her lower abdomen. The eyes of the warrior instantly accounted for her two unexpected, but welcome companions although she did not acknowledge their presence.

"Breathe, Anod," coached Mysasha.

Anod responded properly to the suggestion. The shallow, rapid breathing developed and utilized by humans for centuries to control the pain of childbirth seemed to come naturally to Anod. Her professional training and personal discipline contributed to her ease of adaptation. The pain of the moment was stronger than anything she had ever felt before. The breathing technique taught to her by Mysasha did not eliminate the pain, but it did reduce the intensity and sharpness to a certain extent. The pain subsided as the contraction ended.

Both attendants waited for Anod to regain her composure. Their patient took several deep, slow respiratory cleansing breaths.

Anod smiled a tired recognition of friends. "Welcome to High Cave," she said in a soft, tired, but clear voice.

"Thankfully, you were able to make it to a safe place," Nick said without really acknowledging the proffered greeting.

"I'll say," echoed Mysasha. "How do you feel, Anod?"

"Like I have been run over by one of the bulls in the agricultural fields," Anod answered with a feeble return grin.

"I'll bet. Do you have any specific problems, pains or concerns?"

"Well, let me take an inventory." A short chuckle did not convince either of them. "The general abdominal pain is as you described. The pain in my groin during the contraction is very intense like I am being torn apart."

"Welcome to the pleasures of childbirth," Mysasha laughed.

Another contraction gripped Anod as Mysasha reminded her of the pain control process. Both of her attendants noted the time from the last contraction giving each other concurring acknowledgment.

"We need to examine the birth canal," Mysasha told Anod after the contraction passed. A slight nod conveyed her consent. Gently, the two assistants helped Anod move from the bed to a makeshift, padded table set up by Nick. Once settled, the experienced midwife began to remove Anod's boots and loose fitting pants. Her clothes were wet and she had large beads of sweat covering her face.

"I am quite hot, Mysasha. Let's remove all my clothing, if you please."

"If you wish . . . no problem." Mysasha readily empathized with the taller woman, having given birth to three of her own children and having assisted in the birth of hundreds of others. "Would you like a sheet to cover yourself?"

"No, thank you."

"Much better. Thank you," Anod said. The beads of sweat rose quickly on her smooth exposed flesh. The moisture content of the cave virtually precluded evaporation.

Mysasha slowly lifted each of her knees. The examination confirmed her earlier rudimentary appraisal. Anod was only a few hours from delivery of her first baby.

"Based on the appearance of your cervical dilation, you've got a few hours of hard work ahead of you," Mysasha said as much for Nick as for her patient.

"Well, then, let's get on with it," Anod responded in a defiant tone.

The statement evoked a strong laugh from both Betans. "I'm afraid none of us have any control over this process of nature," said Nick.

The puzzlement on Anod's face transformed before their eyes into the concentration of a determined fighter as another contraction gripped her body. Anod knew the powerful muscular contractions were increasing in frequency as well as becoming more painful. The pain was not possible to suppress either with Mysasha's breathing technique, or her own force of will. Control of her body and mind passed from her grasp.

Between contractions as Nick and Mysasha tended to her body and their duties, an interesting thought came to Anod. Why was childbirth so important to the Betans? Surely, the first experience would be the last. Pain was not something normal people intentionally inflicted upon themselves.

Anod listened with distant detachment to the conversation between Mysasha and Nick. The birthing process was progressing at the normal rate and without complications according to the words she heard. They both took turns talking to her during the contractions, massaging her stretched and taught muscles, and tending to what relief they could provide. Although Anod had no standard with which to calibrate the benefits of their efforts, the effects were intriguing. The two Betans knew exactly where and how to touch her. They used several, pain-diminishing, herbal ointments in strategic locations on her tortured body. The mitigation of the pain enabled Anod to absorb some of the more minute events during the process. Everything happening to her seemed to focus on her groin. The center of her entire being rested on that region of her anatomy. Anod felt that the baby's struggle to leave the confines of the womb was dragging her entire viscera along with it. The indescribable heaviness between her legs added to the sensation of impending dismemberment. Anod knew her flesh was going to tear apart, if it had not already, under such great pressure.

Anod watched Mysasha and Nick move about the room. Mysasha's attention was almost completely directed to the site of Anod's existent being. Occasionally, the perspiring midwife spoke to Nick for coordination of their activities and spoke to Anod with words of progress and encouragement. Watching Mysasha specifically in the context of her own physiological reactions told Anod the arrival of her child must be near.

"The baby's head is close, Anod. You have one or two more hard contractions to go. I want you to push with your abdominal muscles, push the baby out."

The sound of the statement struck Anod as a bit odd, but she knew what she must do.

Another contraction began with a loud groan from Anod as she fought against the pain. "That's it, push," Mysasha encouraged her patient. To herself, she admired the physical strength, courage and will power of the naked and struggling woman lying before her. "That's it, Anod. Yes. Yes. Push. Push. You're just about there. Deep breath and one final push. Yes. The head is out. Looking good. Just a little more. Come on, pu . . ."

The command was truncated as Anod felt the gushing release of the pressure and tension in her groin. Both Mysasha and Nick moved quickly to tend to the baby while Anod dropped her head to the table with a thud. The contractions continued although they had a noticeably lesser force. With her eyes closed, Anod labored to control her breathing and the muscles of her traumatized body.

The first indication of the results of her labor was the cry of a tiny voice. It was not a loud cry. It was a soft cry, more akin to annoyance than protestation, or pain. Anod could not open her eyes to see the little person with the soft voice. She knew her child was in great hands.

The saturated, heavy blanket of fatigue was taking command of her body and mind. There was no fight left in her. Anod gave into the siphoning of the last vestiges of her strength.

Nick tended to the newborn while Mysasha tended to Anod. The probing efforts of the midwife to conclude the birthing process did not even register on the elevated threshold of her senses.

"Anod, you have a beautiful, healthy boy." Nick held the now quiet boy, so the exhausted woman could see her child.

Anod was barely aware of the jubilant words of her assistant. She still could not open her eyes nor could she move any part of her body. As her consciousness swirled into the oblivion of numbness and detachment, she could not respond.

"Are you awake, Anod?" Mysasha asked. There was no reaction. "Can you wake up to suckle your child?"

The words were drifting away from her. Shortly afterward, Anod felt a warm, almost hot, set of hands moving her legs and rolling her torso onto her side. Several soft objects were placed behind her.

Mysasha carefully laid the small boy, now swaddled in a light blanket, beside his mother guiding the young lad's mouth to the swollen breast before him. The natural process of transition from umbilical to active nursing did not take long for the newborn to take on. The phenomenal movement of the little jaw was positive proof the process was underway.

Anod's plummet into the darkness was brought to a halt. She knew something had changed. Slowly, awareness began to bring her back to reality as the fog of her weariness burned away a strange, but pleasurable new sensation emanating from her chest. Along with the rippling waves of pleasure came a rejuvenation of her inner strength. The heaviness in her eyes gradually began to lift as well.

Opening her eyes, Anod saw the tiny, pink face of a miniature person suckling at her breast. The feelings of reality, or at least elements of reality, returned. The wonderful relief of the child's sucking continued to draw the ache of her swollen breast out of her body. Anod worked to lift her arm and gently stroke the child's infinitely soft, warm head. Watching the child's instinctive activity with fascination, she wanted the relief for her unattended breast as she felt and watched the small stream of liquid moving slowly over her skin. The sensations, the feelings and the contrasts were beyond her years of galactic experience, the most monumental pain directly adjacent to some of the most absorbing ecstasy.

Eventually, Anod began to broaden her sphere of awareness. Her eyes refocused to the two humans beyond the small child's tranquil face.

"Isn't it wonderful?" Nick asked with the largest, all teeth, grin Anod had ever seen on his face.

Anod opened her mouth as she tried to speak, but accepted a modest nod to acknowledge the question. She wanted to laugh as the delightful, elder gentleman persisted with his grin and an odd gyration that might closely resemble a dance. Anod thought she could see all his brilliantly white teeth. He was a wonderful man.

"How do you feel?" Mysasha asked with an unusual smile of her own.

The new energy spreading from the infant's mouth throughout her body gave her sufficient strength. "Tired."

"I can tell from the complete set of physical manifestations of fatigue." Mysasha took another quick survey of the wet, matted hair, the dark circles around the drooping eyes, the chalk white pallor of her skin. All her normally taut muscles seemed to sag, dragging the joints of her sprawling body into an odd position. "Do you have specific pain?"

The inventory took longer than all of them expected. Anod was having some difficulty getting past the sensations at her breast. "No. I'm just tired. I'm so tired. I'm not sure I can feel pain." Anod smiled at Mysasha, then looked to her child. "Is this supposed to feel so good?"

Nick's expression dissipated as Mysasha laughed in recognition. "Yes, Anod, it is supposed to feel good. It's an essential part of life."

The tiny boy soon had enough nourishment from his mother. The infant was moved to a temporary cradle fashioned from a chair, two boxes and several blankets.

Mysasha and Nick helped Anod return to the bed, covering her with a sheet and blanket. Nick propped her up with several pillows so she could eat a few pieces of bread and some fruit. While Anod slowly ate, Mysasha explained the need and the process, and then extracted as much milk as she could from the new mother's unused breast. Anod was very thankful for the attention, the caring and expertise of her Betan friends.

"Now, my child, you must rest," Nick said stroking Anod's forehead and hair. "We will take care of everything. You must sleep as long as you are able. It will aid your quick recovery."

During the extended hours of Anod's sleep, the group of Betans were busy working on a variety of tasks. Nick and Mysasha shared the care of the newborn while the security personnel continued their careful patrol of the neighboring terrain. With Nick's insistence, several excursions were taken by various members of the militia to learn of outside events. The lack of a rockphone or radio isolated High Cave from the normal ebb and flow of information among the citizenry and governmental agencies. The information began to slowly trickle in from other parts of the planet. The Yorax were continuing their intimidation of the populace. The casualty list was also continuing to grow. Twenty-seven people, all adults, had died at the ugly hands of the Yorax troopers. There was no discernible pattern to their morbid activities that also seemed to highlight their frustration with the solidarity of the population. The Betan people were withstanding this latest onslaught to their generally passive nature. One of the security soldiers, a young man of moderate physique about the same age as Otis, reported a welling of resentment and anger. The emotions were directed at the perceived indiscriminate Yorax. Everyone knew, although none of them articulated their thoughts, the object of the Yorax intrusion, if discovered, could amplify and focus the latent emotions in a negative way.

The Prime Minister was keenly aware the popular response to this current threat was more by nature and custom rather than by coordinated, passive resistance. Very few citizens even knew of Anod's existence let alone her whereabouts. Many Betans had seen her and also had no reason to suspect she was anything other than a female Betan. Bradley was still safe, staying just out of reach of the Yorax. The new father was also informed of the birth of his son.

"When does he expect to arrive here to see his child?" Nick asked Otis Greenstreet on his latest return.

"I asked the Prime Minister, anticipating your question," answered Otis. "He wants to keep up with the Yorax. The containment of the exposure is vital to the planet, he feels. As soon as this reign of terror ends, he will be here."

"Well, I suppose that is how it should be. Everyone here is in good health, so there is no rush," Nick mused.

The baby boy, as yet unnamed despite his grandfather's inner choices, began a soft cry after an afternoon nap.

The two older experts moved into action. "It looks like I'll need to extract some more milk from his mother," Mysasha announced looking at Nick.

Nodding in acknowledgment of the implicit direction, Nick began to leave.

Otis did not move, apparently held in place by his own curiosity.

Nick returned from the threshold to grab the arm of the young soldier. "Come, Otis. Decorum dictates we must wait outside."

After an initial expression of objection, the younger man also nodded his reluctant agreement.

The experienced and gentle midwife slowly and delicately moved Anod's sleeping form to an appropriate position to allow convenient access to her now engorged and leaking breasts. Using a specifically designed light suction device, Mysasha patiently watched the tension on Anod's attractive breasts diminish as the full quantity of natural infant nutrients transferred from the human container to the temporary vessel.

Anod returned to her recumbent position without any indication of sleep disturbance. Preparation of the feeder did not take long. Mysasha thought Otis might like to take a turn with the feeding. After all, it was his break time.

"I'm all done," said Mysasha. Both men smiled. "Otis, would like to feed the baby?"

A touch of embarrassment flashed across his face. "Oh, I don't know."

"There's no problem. I thought you might like to give it a try."

"I really should get back to my patrol," Otis responded without much conviction.

"It's OK, Otis. Your patrol can wait. This won't take long. Come on, Nick and I have been taking our turns feeding the baby." Mysasha did not need any relief. She simply had a hunch, an intuitive sense, about the inner workings of young Otis Greenstreet.

"Well, I suppose I could, if it would be a help to you and Mister SanGiocomo," responded Otis.

Mysasha nodded her head then traded knowing smiles with Nick.

The absorption of Otis into his drafted duty was quick and merciless. The young man began to talk to the little person and seemed to be oblivious to everything going on around him. A natural father, Mysasha told herself as she performed other peripheral tasks around the room.

At the conclusion of the feeding, Mysasha suggested they take a short walk with the infant to give all of them some fresh air. Nick elected to remain behind to be available, if Anod should wake. The exhausted mother was approaching her nineteenth hour of uninterrupted sleep. She might awaken at any time. Nick did not want her to awaken alone.

The child was swaddled for warmth against the cold temperature and brisk wind. The adults thought the air was refreshing, but the small boy was still trying to adjust to the loss of warmth he enjoyed in his mother's womb.

Slowly, ever so slowly, Anod began the return to consciousness. The more than two days of immobility yielded new aches in her joints. The feeling reminded her of the not too distant recovery from her near-death betrayal. The dominant pain was clearly situated in her lower abdomen and groin. The strong, gripping sensation brought an instant and near continuous further reminder of the recent physical struggle.

"Where is my baby?" Anod asked softly in a somewhat coarse voice. The words were alien to the Society fighter pilot, and yet they flowed from her subconscious.

The answer began with a knowing and communicative smile with his equally expressive eyes. "Your new son, my grandson, is quite healthy and in good care," said Nick compelled to answer the unasked next question first. "Otis and Mysasha are taking him for a walk."

The image of his words made Anod consider the amount of lost time and the prospect of an advanced child, a child walking so soon after birth. The confusion passed quickly with the recognition of his figure of speech. Then, the presence of her initial lover fostered a new set of questions. "Otis?"

"Oh yes, he has taken to the child, actually."

"Why is he here?" The suspicion was unmistakable despite the normal strength of her voice. The memory of Otis' initial assistance upon her arrival was shrouded in the slow recovery from fatigue.

Nick wisely let the confusion pass unanswered. "We have had a security team in the vicinity of High Cave since we arrived. Do not be concerned. Everything is in a normal state."

Her eyes conveyed the relaxation. "Can I get some water?"

"Most certainly." Nick provided the cool water. Anod drank from the large goblet in one long drink.

"I'll get you some more water," said the gentle man as he took the vessel from her hand. "I am certain you are hungry as well. Can I get you something to eat?"

"Something to eat would be most appreciated."

Anod rose from the bed despite Nick's protestations as he prepared several items of food. The ache in her joints needed the benefit of several stretching movements to remove the stiffness. Before proceeding with her exercises, Anod took a quick survey of her body as Nick watched with the detachment of prior exposure. The skin over her lower abdomen made good progress toward returning to proper tension over her traumatized muscle wall. Her groin was still quite sore with the physical imprint of the recent pain. There were two small streams of fluid travelling down her abdomen. As she wiped up the silky fluid with her fingers, Anod became aware of the hardness of her breasts. Each touch brought even more milk along with a shot of dull pain.

"Your body is telling you, it's time to feed your baby," Nick explained with a fatherly smile. "Maybe we should suction off your milk to relieve the pressure."

"I think I would rather wait for his return, so I can feed him directly." The recent memory of those sensations was clear and fresh despite the earlier fog of fatigue.

Anod accepted the change at face value returning to her stretching, bending and twisting. Interspersed among the movements, she would eat a little, and talk and listen with her benefactor. Their discussions, as usual, ranged over a wide variety of topics from the experience of childbirth to the extant political and tactical situation with the Yorax. The combination of physical and mental exercises had the expected result. Anod felt better by the moment.

Anod's sensitive hearing detected the return of the two adults and one infant to High Cave long before Mysasha and Otis appeared in the entryway. The slight woman with short, black hair and a soft, yellowish tint to her skin seemed to command the presence. The child, however, took all Anod's attention as she reached for her newborn from the arms of Otis Greenstreet. She was completely unaware of the surprise on the face and in the eyes of both people.

Anod cradled the child as Mysasha had trained her. The little boy took in her nipple as naturally as the wind and rain to aid in his mother's relief and his nourishment. Their eyes did not separate and she was oblivious to the conversation around her. The intoxicating sensations returned with the sucking at her breast. Tears began to form and roll gently down her cheeks.

Several minutes passed before she felt the texture of the blanket Mysasha placed over her. It was several more minutes before she realized her protective midwife had directed the two men to leave High Cave while she was nursing. Anod did not care about why. She simply wanted to enjoy her child. The voracious tyke performed his task quite well releasing the pressure in both of his mother's swollen mammary glands. The grateful mother was thankful for the physical, mental and emotional relationship growing between mother and child.

Mysasha also provided counsel, in other ways, to Anod. She had heard brief, unconnected rumors about the societal differences from a distant, but related portion of the universe. Her experience, to date, with Anod had not been fundamentally different from those she had with other new mothers on Beta, especially those with limited exposure to childbirth around them.

"May I ask why you are not embarrassed to be seen without clothes in front of others?" There was a certain air of embarrassment of her own in Mysasha's words.

"I have explained all this to Nick and Bradley." The activity of the moment coupled with her frustration with the Betan customs did not lend themselves to philosophical discussions despite the caring of her friend.

"Excuse me, Anod," Mysasha said with resignation. "I was just curious."

"No. There is no need for regret." Anod paused to look at her son, and then returned to Mysasha's eyes. "I have lived in a society where clothes are a utilitarian complement for specific purposes, not a shield of arbitrary modesty. Among my people," the words seemed strangely odd to Anod at this moment, "the human body, in its entirety, is an instrument of the mind and a magnificent creation. In addition, as you may or may not be aware, the Society has gone to great lengths to deemphasize and essentially eliminate the cultural and societal differences between women and men. Within the Society, genital differences are the same as differences in hair and eye color, and the uniqueness of individual physiques."

"I see," said Mysasha. There was no strength to her response as she evaluated the words of explanation. She wandered around the room touching and moving slightly several objects on the tables or workbenches. "I suppose you are aware of the Betan customs?" she asked.

"Yes, I am. Sometimes I forget about the differences."

"There is something refreshing in your forgetfulness, Anod. Maybe there is room to reconsider our attitudes."

The first spoken acknowledgment of the possibility of change did not pass unnoticed, although Anod did not respond. It was good that people considered the possibility. Nick had changed, ever so slightly, but change was ongoing, as well. Bradley had changed. Anod also recognized the dramatic changes within her.

Over the course of the next few days as Anod recovered and

continued to bond with her child, news of events on the planet continued to arrive at High Cave. Events seemed to progressively deteriorate as the brutal intimidation continued. Anod felt the revulsion of the information, but it was a distant, somewhat less real, concern that could not compete with her altered biological state.

There was also good news, however small it might be. Bradley was still in good health, eager to see his new child and the child's mother. The security team also returned from a patrol with information on the untouched condition of Nick's home. Everyone agreed the local threat was minimal and the facilities of the larger abode were better for the new mother and child. As a result, the small group descended to the more spacious cave and settled into the more comfortable accommodations.

Anod took full advantage of the improved conditions. Cleaning her body with a small cloth and a basin of warm water could not compare to the pleasures of the hot shower. The baby, as yet still unnamed, also was given the benefits of a larger basin and additional medical evaluations. All the tests established the excellent health of the youngest human.

For Anod, the changes that came with the birth of the child in many ways were just as amazing and intriguing as the wonders of the environment of Beta. Everyone displayed some level of personality change all for the better. Nick had always been talkative, but now he was categorically effervescent. Anod had not experienced the true, unabashed inquisitive of the Betans toward her as much as she had with her new child. The energy of all those around her seemed to be enhanced. Even her relationship with Otis improved substantially. Anod had seen the young soldier more in the last few days than she had since their first meeting at High Cave, and his warmth finally returned. She liked the changes, within herself and in those around her, the child brought with him into the world.

The newness of her motherhood faded into routine and supplanted a longing for Bradley. Anod became more aware of her need for the assurance of his presence. Her thoughts filled with so many contradicting considerations. His well being, the situation with the Yorax, the frustration of the invisible umbilical to her child, among so many other thoughts, flooded her consciousness. For the first time, Anod felt the need to give her child a name. The requirement was not foremost in her mind as long as Bradley was not present to contribute to the process. The urge gave her yet another reason for wanting his return.

Mysasha was a great help not only with the care of her son, but also with Anod's continuing education regarding the suppressed characteristics of the human body. In a growing number of ways, Anod resented the denial of her biological heritage by the leadership of the Society.

There was recognition and acceptance of the necessities of the customs and living rules imposed by the Society. However, the sacrifices for the common good simply appeared to be too great in comparison to the abjured phenomena of the human experience. There was also a clear acknowledgment that a better method of societal fulfillment must be possible, had to be possible. Strangely, the realization of the metamorphosis she had undergone first dawned on her during the time spent at Nick's home. Anod knew she could not return to service for the Society in the Kartog Guards, at least as it was currently defined.

The routine of life slowly evolved and returned to the inhabitants of Nick SanGiocomo's cave. The educational and inquisitive questions of the new mother began to diminish resulting in the inevitable departure of Mysasha Nagoyama. Anod felt a loss, but also understood Mysasha had her own life, her own family and other births that needed her expertise. The sense of loss was genuine and surprising as she watched Mysasha leave the clearing with one of the security guards toward the train station.

The resiliency and recuperative powers of Anod's body were again demonstrated to those who were aware of them. The morning exercises, callisthenics and martial arts routines tightened up her stretched muscles and distended flesh. The completeness of her return to normal was absolute except for the heaviness in her breasts that came and went between feedings. The marvels of the human physiology amplified, broadened and focused her experiences on Beta, and especially the entire sequence of events from conception to the nurturing of her young boy.

A fresh appreciation of life came to Anod with each passing moment and new experience. There was also a certain curiosity about the denials of her past and the potential of what might be. Anod's mind began to consider other options, actions and objectives. A strange sense of loss also accompanied her thoughts of consequences and possibilities.

Eight days passed before local events were altered by a new arrival. Anod absorbed the movements of her son lying on his back in a small cradle. She was aware of two people entering the room, but did not feel the need to identify the arrivals.

"How is my boy?" The words were clear and distinct. There was no doubt about the identity of the speaker.

Anod turned and ran into his open arms. There was no thought given to the uncharacteristic exhibition of emotion, as she felt his arms close around her. It was so good to see, feel and smell Bradley again. This particular day was entirely too long in coming.

"Well . . . ," Bradley said with expectation.

"The baby is excellent. He gets stronger and more alert by the day."

"Let's take a look at the little fella."

They walked together, arm in arm, to the cradle. The child seemed to sense the significance of this moment as he cooed and gurgled. His eyes were bright and absorptive. The flailing of his arms and eyes accentuated the excitement.

"He is so beautiful," said the father as he lifted the child from the cradle. Bradley held his boy close kissing his head several times. Looking to Anod, he continued, "How are you?"

"I am quite fine. My body is still adjusting to nursing the baby, but I feel great."

"You have fully recovered from the birth experience?" asked Bradley, not entirely sure he knew what the norm was.

"Yes, certainly."

"Ah, yes, the now famous regenerative capabilities of our Miss Anod," Bradley acknowledged with a broad grin and nod of his head.

Nick entered the room with his son, but remained at the threshold choosing to stay silent. Watching his growing family in their reunion was enough to convince him to leave.

"What name have you given him?" asked Bradley.

"I have not given him a name. I wanted to wait for your return and contribution."

"Well, then, let me think." Bradley cradled his child in his left arm freeing his right hand to touch and play with the tiny hands and fingers. "Do you have any suggestions?"

"The name that has come to me is, Zoltentok," Anod stated with pride and enthusiasm.

The somewhat stunned expression on Bradley's face conveyed the true emotion of his reaction although his words were controlled. "Why did you pick Zoltentok?"

"It is the name chosen in recognition of our most renown space pioneer, Admiral Zolten. He was also one of the most accomplished interstellar diplomats in Earth history, as well as an accomplished warrior."

"I see." The intonation of Bradley's simple response did not necessitate further explanation. The pause gave him time to consider his own suggestion. "I had almost forgotten about the propensity of the Society toward symbolic distinction. I suppose I was thinking of something more traditional, like Nicholas James."

The combination of elements from both his full name and his father's name did not lessen an inner hurt Anod felt at the rebuke. The instinctive defensive response fortunately did not manifest itself in any physical manner.

"Your reaction is lamentable since you did not know Admiral Zolten. He was a great man filled with ideas, compassion, energy and an unbounded appreciation for interstellar exploration," Anod said in her defense and in recognition of the importance of her deceased mentor. "This child was not born in the ways of my culture, however I feel he was born with the virtues of Admiral Zolten."

"I don't know," responded Bradley. A little voice in the back of his consciousness told him to change the subject. "You mentioned the rank of admiral. I just realized I have never asked you, what rank you are?"

"I have the rank of lieutenant."

"And if I recall correctly, you referred to your betrayer, Zitger, as a captain. Am I right?"

"Yes." Anod was somewhat irritated with Bradley's rather obvious attempt to change the topic of discussion.

"If my recollection of history and the military ranks of past earth practice are correct, you are using the naval as opposed to the field ranking structure."

"Actually, no. If you must know," Anod began to answer with growing annoyance. She paused to regain control of her emotions. "If you must know, nearly a hundred years ago, it was decided to combine the naval and field ranks into one system. The field ranks are for the junior officers while the naval ranks are used for the senior officers."

"How interesting."

"Now, can we return to the principle topic of discussion?"

"Maybe we should let it rest for a while," suggested Bradley.

Anod knew she had to let her frustration pass. Her life, until the instant of the ambush, had been characterized by orderliness, structure and stone cold logic. In her past, problems were always addressed straight ahead until their eventual resolution. However, she was still their guest although she found the relationship was fading with time. "As you wish," Anod answered.

"This also may not be the best time to bring this up, but it has been on my mind since I first heard the news of the birth of our baby. Have you reconsidered the issue of marriage?"

"If you mean, marriage, as the noun version of the verb, marry, yes, I have reconsidered, but the answer is still, no. My feelings have not changed since you first asked me to marry you at Astral."

"I see," Bradley responded. "Is there anything that I can say to change your mind?"

To Anod, the question was quite shallow and lacked conviction. Maybe now, he was feeling some of the frustration that had been present with her for so long. "No," answered Anod. "The logic remains true to the best of my knowledge."

"I see."

Anod wanted to let the words hang in silence since he was obviously at a loss of words to deal with her logic. Then, with some empathy for his situation, Anod decided to shift to another neutral topic. "You have not mentioned anything about the Yorax. What is the status?"

"So, now, it is your turn to change the subject."

Anod smiled in silent acknowledgment.

"Well, the Yorax have departed although we are convinced it is only temporary. Debriefings of several of our citizens lead me to believe they have definitive information, although not conclusive, that you are alive and in hiding on Beta."

"If the Yorax believed I was alive and on Beta, they would systematically destroy the planet until I was relinquished to them."

Both of them considered the possibilities. Something had changed in the consideration of the Yorax. They also both knew, from past performances, the Yorax would show no remorse over the total destruction of the Betan planet and its population, if it suited their purpose.

Anod continued the thought. "I can only surmise from the evidence they have stronger suspicions and they want me alive. The latter portion of the hypothesis is based on the hesitation of the Yorax toward wholesale destruction."

"I would tend to agree with you."

Anod did not particularly want to hear the answer, but she had to ask the question. "What does the Council want me to do?"

"Your status has been discussed at length as you can well

imagine." Bradley paused to choose his words carefully. "As I am sure you are also aware, there is natural disagreement within the Council on the appropriate action, however the majority opinion is to hold our course and try to weather this particular storm."

"Is there a plan for the worst case?"

"Yes. Only a handful of people are knowledgeable of this plan. Alexatron and several of his friends are prepared to signal the Society, if the situation deteriorates. We have established a code word to activate the plan."

"Alexatron is prepared to compromise the neutrality of his people to help us?" Anod inquired a bit suspiciously.

"Yes. Other than that, we still intend to wait for a Society spacecraft to pass within our region to transfer you back to your people."

The thought brought a recurrent internal struggle to the forefront of Anod's consciousness. Part of her did not want to leave this place and these people, and yet, her alter ego wanted to remove the threat of her presence and return to the life she was violently wrenched from by the traitorous Zitger.

"With the support of the Council, however tenuous it might be, we shall stay the course, then," Anod responded.

"It is our desire," Bradley said with a warm smile.

"How much damage did the Yorax do on this visit?"

"They indiscriminately executed 32 of our citizens and burned several buildings."

"I am very sorry for the misery my presence brings to your planet, Bradley."

"Nonsense. You have brought much to us and we are not particularly impressed by intimidation. It is a characteristic of our heritage."

"Thank you. I am thankful for your fortitude."

Chapter 16

Ten days of relative peace were a welcome respite from the turmoil and violence of the most recent Yorax visit. Bradley was able to spend more time with his newborn son. The laborious process of selecting a name for the infant took three days of fragmented discussion between the parents and the prodding negotiations of the child's grandfather to finally settle the issue.

Everyone was still warming up to the strange combination of new and old, alien and familiar. Zoltentok James was the compromise. As would be expected from their respective heritage, Anod chose to refer to the infant by his given first name. Nick and Bradley used the contraction, ZJ, to offset their difficulty with the child's full name. Several of the Betans made a strong effort toward the transition using both of the child's given names.

The resolution of the child's name also brought out the recurrent discussion of marriage between Anod and Bradley. The shedding of her past indoctrination was not easy, plus Anod was not convinced of the necessity and logic behind the Betan custom.

Zoltentok was in good health and continuing to progress well. Both mother and child learned their respective rolls and mutually complementary tasks quite well. The lessons provided by Mysasha were sufficient to help Anod over the initial uncertainty of her new responsibilities.

Another not so dormant instinct began to return specific thoughts to Anod.

There was an absolute certitude to the inevitable return of the Yorax. Although their actions to date were not entirely within character, probably due to the influence of Zitger, there was no doubt, based on their most recent foray to Beta, the Yorax would be back. The next visit would most likely be more violent than their last sojourn. It was time to hone the edge of the sword.

Anod's physical recovery from childbirth was nearly complete. Her body returned to the lean, well-toned form she possessed prior to the birth of Zoltentok. Nursing a growing child kept her breasts quite pendulous that necessitated a few adjustments in her exercise routine, but other than the physiology of motherhood, Anod felt tight. Although she was pleased with her physical progress, there were other skills in need of sharpening.

"Nick, I need to go to Astral," announced Anod. Bradley was on a two-day trip to Providence and several other cities.

"Well, then, we'd better make some arrangements. What do you want to do with ZJ?"

Anod discussed several alternatives relative to the activities she wanted to pursue. Anod wanted to make four to six flights with the interceptor. More importantly, it was time to exercise the weapons system of the interceptor that required her to travel about 20 to 30 hours at near warp speed. Firing the weapons could, and most probably would, be detected by the Yorax. With these activities, they agreed Zoltentok should stay at Nick's place. After consultation with Mysasha, a wet nurse was contacted to perform as a brief surrogate for Anod during her absence. The substitution of another nursing woman was an old process, Anod learned for the first time. Parts of the human process were so simple and ingenious, and yet there were elements that did not sit well with her.

Anod's temporary surrogate, an older, dark skinned woman named Guyasaga, arrived with the newest of her four children. Guyasaga's other three children were under the immediate care of her husband, a farmer. Her deep, strong, gravelly voice, inner self-assurance and take charge attitude produced mixed feelings with Anod. The thought of leaving her child with another woman was not comforting, however Guyasaga seemed to be quite accommodating and amenable to taking Zoltentok to her breast as her own. The decider was the recommendation from Mysasha.

After spending some time with Guyasaga observing the larger woman's handling of her own child as well as Zoltentok, Anod gained some confidence of her own. The knowledge that Nick would be available during her absence provided the remaining measure of confidence she needed to leave her child for a few days. Bradley would also visit at least once until her return to SanGiocomo.

Prior to her departure for Astral, Anod and Nick had several communications with Bradley, who was on the other side of the planet, and with the security forces. Most of the concern was for the immediate protection of Anod, although there was also concern for the interceptor. It was agreed that another detachment of four security personnel would stay at Astral until she completed her flights. None of the names were familiar to Anod. She would not see Otis this time.

"Be careful and don't take any unnecessary chances," Nick said as Anod walked across the clearing toward the waystation.

As she reached the edge of the forest, Anod turned to take one last look at what she was leaving behind. Nick waved with a smile on his face and sadness in his eyes. Guyasaga stood next to the elder SanGiocomo holding Zoltentok in one arm and her child's miniature hand in her other hand. The voice of her conscience asked Anod if she truly wanted to leave this idyllic place and the pleasure of her son. The urge to stay and withdraw into the immediate dimension of her child and her new friends were excruciatingly strong. However, the call to duty tipped the scales of conflict with the thought her greatest chance to protect Zoltentok and the Betans lay with the expert use of the interceptor. Anod was the only person with the skills and rudimentary tools to stand between life and destruction.

Nick knew in an instant why the accomplished warrior hesitated at the treeline. It was a good sign. The thoughts rolling through his head as he watched Anod disappear into the mesh of bark, leaves, branches and mottled lighting were of the dramatic changes he had witnessed in the year of Anod's presence on Beta. A human being, a woman with extraordinary innate sensory performance, incredible control of her bodily functions and almost no personality, whom was now a mother softened by the once latent and suppressed emotions of her species. The changes were indeed startling and certainly to his liking.

"So that is the famous woman Mysasha told me about," stated Guyasaga. "She looks perfectly normal to me except for leaving her newborn behind, but that's not particularly uncommon either, now is it?"

"You must get to know her better," responded Nick. "She is an absolutely amazing person with an astonishing number of contrasting characteristics."

"In what sense do you say this?"

"I'm not sure it would be proper for me to cover all the details. Let it suffice to say she was not born on this planet. She is a child of another world and a vastly different culture, and yet she has not entirely lost the essence of her biological heritage."

"Well, I am not exactly sure what you mean, but I think I understand what you are trying to say." Both of them remained silent as they returned to the interior. Then, Guyasaga added, "I look forward to learning more about her."

"You shall," said Nick. "You shall. Please remember, though, she is a very special individual who must be protected."

Guyasaga burst forth with a strong, deep laugh. "Somehow, I don't get the impression she needs to be protected."

With that comment, Nick sat down with Guyasaga after Zoltentok was asleep in his cradle to explain a portion of the background behind Anod's existence. Her round face and large dark eyes told Nick she did not entirely understand why she was so special. The inadequacy of Guyasaga's comprehension bothered Nick since her knowledge added one more element of potential exposure, a threat, to Anod's existence. He was content to let the situation simmer a bit. After all, he had at least a couple of days with this woman and her child before the concern could be translated to reality. There would be more opportunity to enlighten the caretaker of his grandson.

The journey to Astral was uneventful. Anod's sweep of the forest around the hangar cave established the security detachment had not arrived and was not in the area. She decided to proceed with her activities without the guards. Opening the access door with its coded lock presented no problem for her clear memory. Anod locked the door behind her.

The checkout of the interceptor also proceeded quickly with no detectable deficiencies. The bird was ready to fly and Anod was eager to launch into space.

With the heightened hostility of the Yorax and the lack of long range sensors to establish their absence from near space, Anod wanted to start and mask the interceptor before she opened the hangar doors to eliminate any possibility of detection. Unfortunately, there was no way for her to accomplish this task by herself. She had to wait for the security unit.

Several communications passed between Nick and Anod on the status of the planet, to make sure the Yorax had not returned yet, on Zoltentok and on the whereabouts of the security personnel. The planet was quiet. Bradley was at a Council meeting in Providence. Zoltentok, as well as Nick and Guyasaga, were doing quite well. Now, quiet moments always brought thoughts of her son. The security people were enroute and should arrive within an hour.

With one last glance at the interceptor, Anod went through the access door to the exterior. It was a cool, but bright day with scattered cloud formations leisurely travelling across the sky. A quick assessment of the terrain proved to be negative. The large meadow and hangar doors did not provide much cover. The warrior tactician within her told her to seek a more neutral arena for a rendezvous with armed people. Anod headed off into the woods.

The shadows of the forest and the addition of the wind, even though it was light, made the temperature cooler than Anod had felt at first. Evening twilight approached and the warmth of the θ27 star waned.

She was more than 500 meters into her first sweep of the immediate area when she realized she was not adequately attired. Her physiological response made her consider returning to the hangar to find additional clothing, however the challenge of detecting the security people overrode her personal comfort. The discipline of her mind kicked in to blank out the effects of the air. There was an honest recognition that the distractions of life on Beta took some of the edge off her martial skills. With that recognition came the inner dedication to renew and polish her *répertoire.*

The distant thrashing of an animal caught her attention as an uncommon sound within the forest. The smell of processed leather and artificial fragrance followed shortly by muffled, unintelligible words established the ingress of humans to the area. Anod needed not quite a minute to determine the general location, direction of travel and rough speed. Only two entities could be detected which meant two of the four expected security personnel were more careful with their condition, or there were two unknown humans approaching. One small consolation was the lack of any identifiable signs of the Yorax, not that she expected them.

A rapid evaluation of the surrounding terrain, vegetation, lighting and wind direction helped her identify an observation point. Anod moved with prudent and deliberate speed like a large cat in its natural habitat. A small, inconspicuous outcropping of rocks and bushes was her intended vantage point. Downwind, in the shadow of several large trees and possessing two egress routes, the location was acceptable to observe the intruders.

The first one came into view. He was dressed as a Betan security officer, then another. Number three was off to the far side. Where was number four? The first two were not being particularly careful. They were much too close together. Number three was a good twenty meters beyond and slightly behind the first two. Where was number four? If he was as good as number three, he should be closer to her position and possibly within detection range. Anod scanned quickly. There he is, she told herself, right where he should be. There were no signs they were aware of her presence.

"Ya'know, I hear she is some kinda freak," the first trooper said to the second.

"What do you mean?"

"She can see in the dark, hear anything and she doesn't bleed."

Anod found some amusement in the exaggeration of her persona.

"She's human. She must bleed," said the second trooper.

Neither man paid much attention to where they placed their feet. The two complacent men were the most unprofessional of the Betan security personnel she had seen since she had become their guest.

"Maybe she's not human," suggested the first Betan.

"Forget it, Jonas. It doesn't matter what she is. We are supposed to protect her."

"Yeah, well, maybe I ought to find out what she is."

Anod's concentration on the four Betan security men was broken by something out of the ordinary. Additional faint sounds that were not of the forest were intermittently detectable among the distractions passing before her. Something was definitely not right.

As the four security men moved away from her position toward the hangar, Anod was able to focus her senses on the new targets. The processes of location and vector determination took an agonizing five minutes. Time always passed too slowly when you waited for something, especially danger.

Anod's observation position was still adequate. The new intruders followed the security unit. Were they additional security men? It would be logical for situations like this to have a rear guard. They were human, which meant they were not Yorax. There were two of them based on the pattern of sounds from their movement. Were they adversaries? Anod's memory immediately jumped to Seymour Waystation those many months earlier. They could be mercenaries using the security men to get to her.

Anod's mind worked at a feverish pace evaluating the increasing sensory data she was receiving as well as a series of contingency plans to deal with the intruders. The intervening terrain between her present position and the meadow in front of the hangar was not particularly good for a stealthful approach, or a close quarters ambush.

There they were, right in front of her, not 40 meters away among the trees. They moved with appropriate caution considering the dried leaves on the floor of the forest. The two trailers were considerably more deliberate than the first two security men assigned to protect her, which is probably why the two careful men did not detect their trailers.

These two unwelcome intruders were dressed as Betan farmers. Their attire was quite common. It was what they were carrying that gave her the most problem. The two rather large men were heavily armed, LASER rifles, neuron pistols and large knives. They also had large packs on their backs. They were well equipped for long periods of independent operations and several possible situations.

After considering a variety of possibilities, Anod decided on the conservative course of action. The two trailers were hostile and had to be neutralized, the pleasant word for eliminated.

There was no easy way to get to the security detachment and let them deal with this situation. The risk of exposure was too great. In addition, judging from the ingress technique of the security unit, Anod was not confident they could deal with the two trailers.

Several factors were on her side. She knew the terrain probably as well as, if not better than, the two trailers. She was already downwind not that she was particularly concerned about the Betan's inferior sense of smell. More importantly, once again, the last vestiges of daylight were rapidly disappearing. The only detractor to the lighting was the growing overcast that would remove even more light, potentially negating Anod's low light vision.

When the two men were about 100 meters beyond her, Anod slowly rose from her secluded position. She began to move in a parallel direction toward the hangar meadow. Each step was carefully tested, then placed. Stopping every five meters or so, Anod scanned everything around her focusing all her senses on detecting the slightest abnormality. The intruders moved faster than she was, thus opening the distance between them. Anod was perfectly content with the situation since she preferred caution to parity, plus she needed more darkness.

The last confirmation of her assessment would come as the security men entered the hangar on the far side of the meadow. If the trailers continued across the meadow, then maybe she was wrong and they were actually friendlies. If they stopped in the forest and settled into observation positions, their fate would be sealed.

In the distance, unseen through the trees, Anod could hear the hangar access door being opened. A very faint yellow glow identified the location of the hangar and provided some additional lighting in the forest. She was now less than 80 meters from the edge of the forest. If the two trailers were waiting, they would be about ten meters, plus or minus a little, from the treeline. Anod slowed her advance even more, moving only several steps each minute. She had no weapons and once again she was trying to deal with several heavily armed men. No matter how casual the situation, it was never a condition to be taken lightly.

"I wonder where this woman is?" was a very faint question asked near the hangar.

"I don't know, but she must be around her somewhere," came the equally faint reply.

"She's an accomplished warrior with extraordinary senses and we are at a distinct disadvantage out here," were the words of a new voice. It must have come from one of the other two security men, since she had not heard either of their voices, yet.

The metallic sound of the door closing accompanied by the elimination of the yellow light established the return of the security men to the interior.

Movement was now much slower than earlier. The clouds overhead obscured the stars taking away the only light source. Anod was forced to wait for relatively long periods for breaks in the clouds to give her sufficient light for quiet movement. The two trailers would not be able to see anything other than a few slivers of light emanating from the seams of the hangar doors.

The suspense of the unknown was always difficult to deal with especially when a good portion of your senses was rendered useless and the specter of death was about. The additional annoyance of the increased cold of the night air added more challenge to be suppressed.

It took Anod more than three hours to move the 200 meter distance to the perimeter of the meadow. A purposeful offset placed her further downwind from the intruders. Anod resigned herself to the time consuming and laborious task of clearing most of the meadow fringe. The process had taken entirely too long, when her heart stopped in midstep. Anod had to struggle to keep from sucking in an enormous gulp of air.

There, barely eight meters from her, was a dim handheld light illuminating a map and a small notebook as well as the two men. Several hand signals passed between them. They were definitely professional hunters who, fortunately for Anod, had made one fatal mistake. They had seriously underestimated the capabilities of their quarry.

Anod carefully considered the possibilities. The attraction of the two of them in proximity to one another was not great enough for Anod to give up the benefit of the darkness. She wanted their light out then she would wait for a break in the clouds, or morning twilight, whichever occurred first. If these two were as good as they appeared, they would probably be five to ten meters apart, as they watched the approaches to the hangar.

While she waited for the optimum moment to strike, Anod considered a number of other elements. Why hadn't she smelled them? The natural scent of a human was distinctive in the forest. The wind had shifted a little, but not enough to explain the absence of any scent. Were these two, Betans or outsiders, possibly androids or automatons, brought in by the Yorax? The former was probably correct in light of the Seymour Waystation incident, but the latter was also quite plausible. Zitger was smart and cunning. From a distance in low light, the identification of non-humans was virtually impossible. The use of mercenary human trackers, to be less obvious, was certainly within his capability and consistent with the information available to Anod. The use of the handheld light. The hand signals. If her adversaries were non-biological, they would have no need for the supplemental tools and techniques. They must be Betan.

Being so close to the threat did not make Anod very comfortable. However, even gradual withdrawal could compromise her position. She knew she was committed, now.

Moments of minimal light enabled her to see one of her stalkers and occasionally his companion, but the lighted periods were not sufficient for an approach. Being frozen in space in the cold air was not helping her muscles and joints. Anod used a common technique learned by her distant ancestors in situations like this; she flexed her muscles in isometric contraction without moving. The process gave her some warmth and stimulation for the muscles, but could not help the stiffness building in her joints. The patient warrior calculated the probable compensation for her diminished physical capacity.

Anod continuously scanned the entire volume of space around her especially searching the sky above her through the trees to catch a break in the clouds. Nothing changed except the growing ache in her joints. Immobilization in an erect position under stress was simply not good for humans.

Is Zoltentok resting quietly? How was his first day apart from his mother? The thought of not seeing her son again did not enter her consciousness. However, the frustration of the distractions also grew with the pain in her joints.

This is one of the detractors of human intimacy, Anod told herself as if to justify the distraction. Yes, she had experiences, incredible new feelings and emotions that made her feel much more alive. The price for that pleasure was the drain on her concentration and focus of her body and mind. The struggle against her emotional thoughts was real and substantial, reflecting the contrasts in her life on Beta.

A combination of events altered the status quo.

The clouds broke allowing the first extended period of starlight as the first rays of light were refracted by the upper atmosphere adding slightly to the ambient light. Now was the time. Anod had barely 30 minutes to accomplish her task before the light would be sufficient for her human targets.

Anod winced at the pain of her first movement, fighting with each motion and concentrating on the placement of each step. Both men were located now. Both men appeared to be awake, maybe not alert, but awake. She had to assume they were both at full capability, which made her movements more cautious.

Seven meters.

The first one would have to be neutralized as silently as possible. There would be some sound. The snapping of a human neck made a horrific crunching sound similar to a breaking branch of a tree. Anod had to hope there was enough confusion in the darkness to cause his companion to investigate the sound.

Six meters.

If it did not work, she would have to resort to weapons fire. The alternative was not particularly desirable. The deadly tongue of light from a LASER rifle could be detected at fairly long distances. In addition, the energy could easily start a small fire in the forest.

Five meters.

Why didn't the security force conduct a perimeter patrol? They should have, at the very least, understood the immediate environment. Anod might not have been in this position, if they had been a little more conservative. They were not a martial people, Anod reminded herself, but do not underestimate them.

Four meters.

The first man's concentration remained on the hangar door as if a momentary glance away might miss something important. It was obvious he did not have the slightest suspicion about the violence that was so close to him. Yes, he had to be human. There was no other explanation for the inability to sense Anod's presence.

Three meters.

From this distance, she could lunge for a destablizing blow followed quickly by the *coup de grâce*. The event would probably require weapons fire. The sounds of her assault would be unmistakable. The only mitigating factor was the darkness. The other man would not have a clear target, should be quite sensitive to the presence of his cohort, and would have no way to know of his demise.

Two meters.

One more step would place Anod in perfect position to disable her would be captors. The man still had not sensed her presence. She could almost feel his warmth. Then . . .

Crack.

A small twig broke under her descending foot.

The man's face initially turned toward her with an inquisitive expression. The curiosity was instantly transformed into terror as, even in the dark of the early morning, he recognized the shape of a human as the source of the telltale sound. His LASER rifle began the short move toward her, but never reached its target.

Pivoting on her left leg, Anod swung her right leg in a wide arc rising toward his head. Her torso descended to balance her ascending leg as her eyes concentrated on the precise spot for her blow. The ball of her foot contacted the man's head slightly forward and above his left ear. The energetic shock stunned his brain causing him to collapse instantly into a jumbled pile.

Anod was fairly certain the blow had not been fatal, but it did render the man unconscious for a sufficient period. She would deal with the conclusion after she dispatched his companion.

As expected, the other intruder knew something had happened and it probably was not good. Anod heard the other man's first steps toward his fallen comrade.

"George, are you all right?" called the voice in a very low whisper from a distance of about five meters. There was a touch of anxiety in his words.

No response brought him a few more steps toward her. The light was still quite low. A quick assessment led Anod to the decision to remain exactly where she was in order to avoid making any sound that might confirm her adversary's suspicion.

"George," he whispered again as he continued to close the distance.

There was no question the hapless person did not realize the fate that awaited him in the dark. There was also no question his weapons were at the ready and he was prepared to shoot at the slightest provocation. Only a few more meters, now. Anod could clearly see his face and the agonizing look in his eyes. Even though the man probably had many years of experience as a hunter, Anod told herself, he was not equipped to deal with this situation.

At the exact moment, Anod sprang from her semi-crouched position leading with the right hand toward his still passive face.

"Geo . . . ," came the incomplete gush of a word intended to be his friend's name at the instant the heal of Anod's right hand struck him between the eyes. The bodily tremors of a fatally wounded man were his last testament.

Once again, Anod faced a life or death decision regarding the fate of the still unconscious man. The light level increased and the colors began to come out. The browns and grays of their clothing to the black sleek chiselled shape of their LASER rifles. She would allow him to regain consciousness to determine why they trailed the security force and why they were hunting her, and then turn him over to the Betan security personnel for incarceration. She could also close the task right now. These two men represented the third and possibly the fourth Betans to die trying to capture or kill her. The root question was, did the Betan's possess an adequate capability to isolate and silence a man such as this?

The information to answer the question was too ambiguous. The risk was too great. Interrogation would satisfy her curiosity without altering the ultimate conclusion.

"So be it," Anod whispered to an imaginary partner.

The surviving intruder was bound, hand and foot, to ensure immobilization and maximum resignation. Anod's attempts to revive him took longer than she expected, but were eventually successful.

"Wha . . . ," came the recognition of his condition. The terror in his eyes was absolute. He knew exactly who stood above him.

"Who are you, and why are you here?" Anod asked.

A crooked, sneering grin came across his face along with his silence.

Anod cocked her arm for a final strike at his head. "Then, you shall die," she spoke in a calm, quiet voice.

The grin did not leave. "You can't do that. It is not allowed."

"That may be," Anod responded with her hand still raised above him, "but, there is no one here to observe your fate, now is there." Anod did not move and the man did not answer. "Do you know who I am?" "You are the woman from old Earth."

The light of day, even dispersed by the clouds, brought the terminus to the interrogation. Anod knew what she had to do.

"And, you are a mercenary cajoled by the Yorax to capture or kill me."

"Now, why would you think that?" the man said rhetorically.

"Your actions from trailing the security personnel to this place, to the vigilant observation of the doors across the meadow leave little doubt about your purpose here."

"My, aren't you the perceptive one," he said sarcastically.

"Once more, who are you?" asked Anod with the patience of a dominant position.

The bound and prostrate man chose not to answer.

"Well, then, George, you shall die in silence as your fellow conspirator did," Anod said. Glancing over to the stiff, bloody and graying hulk, then back to George, Anod twisted her torso to prepare for the thrust with her weight to add force to the blow.

"Wait. Wait. I'll tell you," said George gathering his words before continuing. "My name is George Rimstone. We are looking for an alien woman which I do believe is you."

Without acknowledging his assessment, Anod pressed for the connection. "Why are you looking for this woman? Who sent you?"

"The Yorax, more specifically a human with the Yorax, asked us to find you."

Anger filled the entirety of her thoughts at that moment. A man who had been her partner, whom she had lived with and flown with for nine years, was now her hunter, her nemesis. The realization meant Zitger and the Yorax were fairly certain she was on the Betan planet, but it also meant Zitger must be restraining the Yorax from their typical response for some reason.

"Why would you do this? The Yorax are not your allies."

"They offered five kilos of gold," the man answered with the cold words of his prostitution.

"You would betray your people for a paltry reward," Anod said half as a statement and half as a question.

"First, it is not meager to me. Second, you are not of this planet. You are not one of us. You, in fact, are a serious threat to the safety of Betans."

Anod, again, did not acknowledge George Rimstone's, if that was his true name, assessment. The faint, but distinct sound of the hangar access door opening brought a conclusion to the discussion. The strike was lightning fast and the consequences were instantaneous and final.

One of the security men stretched, and enjoyed the early light of day. Anod waited for the man to return to the interior of the hangar before she moved from the place of death. They would remain as they had fallen except for the removal of George's bindings.

Anod's entry into the hangar was met with incredulity, amazement and awe. These new Betan security men had never seen a woman with such presence and confidence. The reaction redoubled with the explanation of the night's activities and the subsequent discovery of the remains of her effort. Rapid communications with Providence established the record of the events and the identification of the two deceased bounty hunters.

While the Betans struggled with the aftermath, Anod decided a flight would be best for her. Initially, the Betans resisted Anod's intentions with the typical response of a police officer faced with a potential crime. Reassurances and affirmations reduced, but did not relieve the resistance. A level of antagonism marred the conversations between Anod and the Betan security unit, although it did not alter the activities.

Settling into the cockpit, Anod began the preflight procedures as she discounted her lack of sleep and mounting fatigue. There was also the added reminder of her biological heritage. Her swollen and hardened breasts were now leaking fluid intended for her child. The verity of the changes in her life was unmistakable and undeniable. As the interceptor came to life, Anod wondered what the future held in store for her and the Betan people, and what the conclusion to the constricting noose might be.

With all four security men looking on, Anod commanded the interceptor to lift off the floor, retracted the landing gear and switched on the masking feature. The process was the signal for the hangar doors to be opened.

The Betans, at first, did not respond as agreed, as they stood dumb struck by the waving scintillation of the masking device observed at close range. The slight imperfections of the technique were more obvious when viewed in proximity. To the Betans, the space where the interceptor had been was now filled with a strange, seductive distortion as if someone, or something, had smeared a transparent jelly across the image before them.

Anod waited patiently until one of them realized they had a necessary task to perform. With the doors now open, the interceptor slowly moved to the middle of the meadow. The passing shadows of the thinning clouds produced an errie mutation of the otherwise tranquil scene. With a distance approaching fifty meters, the scintillation diminished substantially rendering the interceptor nearly invisible to the still awed men.

The billowy shapes of the clouds were an irresistible play field for a young pilot returning to the sky. Anod flirted with the manifest portrayal of condensed atmospheric moisture as she darted in and out between them. The rush of their passage gave Anod the exhilaration that was the opiate of all pilots since the beginnings of human flight. Recognition of her purpose eventually caused her to pull back on the controller hurling her into the void of space.

Anod accelerated out to 0.9 warp speed, the maximum velocity of the interceptor while masked. The twisting and turning of a pilot testing her wings filled most of the first hour of the flight.

The time for further envelope expansion brought a few moments' hesitation as Anod considered the sequence of events in her plan against the consequences. The detectors on her spacecraft indicated no unusual activity in her sector as well as no Yorax units. The threat must be present although Anod thought the risk was relatively low. She had no way of sensing a masked Yorax battlecruiser.

Deselecting the masking mode, Anod advanced the throttle to maximum, accelerating the small craft to nearly ten times the speed of light. The warping of the time-space continuum, which gave rise to the unit of velocity measurement, also produced the characteristic streaking of the sublight visual field.

Anod held the maximum velocity for only twenty minutes. It would take more than three hours to return while masked. The sensors of the interceptor found an appropriate object for her purposes. Decelerating to sublight speed, Anod targeted the roving rock and fired her microarray proton projector gun. The bright blue beam of coherent light bridged the distance to the asteroid in an instant vaporizing the hapless rock into an enormous burst of energy. Several other quick tests yielded the same results. The interceptor was in full operational order.

Masking her craft once more, Anod began the long journey at

sublight speed back to Beta. There was no choice. The extraordinary warp speeds took her a great distance from her temporary home. The last detectable vector had to be away from Beta. Any one of a number of space travellers could have detected her jump to hyperlight speed dash and weapons discharge. A vigilant Yorax battlecruiser could have been one of those travellers.

The return to Beta was ponderous and boring. Anod passed the time with a multitude of thoughts of Beta. The most prevalent image was that of Zoltentok which also produced a recognition of her painful breasts. The sensation of her suckling child brought a smile to her face and a warm wave of pleasure along with more wetness on her chest. Bradley's face and body elicited a different, but equally pleasurable set of feelings and a longing for his touch. There were also the words and actions of her growing sphere of friends, Otis, Nick, Mysasha and the others whom she had come to know since the ambush.

As a good pilot, her personal cogitation was sufficiently interspersed with observations, analysis and evaluation of the variety of sensory inputs from both the interceptor and her own that continuously streamed into the cockpit. The communications and sensor portions of the electromagnetic spectrum were as normal as any instant in time. Events were never the same, but they were similar.

The little interceptor identified the signals of what could have been a Society starship. The signals indicated it was near the far side of the adjacent sector that would place it about 10 light-years away. The temptation to herald her brethren was real, although not great. The traces of the Society finally flushed her with waves of guilt, an emotion she had rarely felt. Virtually all of her conscious thoughts were now of Beta, not of her comrades in arms. Versions of a recurrent question continued to come to her. Had she irrevocably separated from the Society, from her heritage? The answer was not immediately forthcoming.

There were no signs of the Yorax over the last several hours since she began her flight. The recognition of this lack of information was gradually raising her awareness and suspicion. Thoughts of the time prior to the ambush intermixed with her current evaluations. Routine communications, although not intelligible, usually meant routine operations. No communications often meant one of two possibilities. Either the Yorax were not in the enormous detectable volume of space around her, or it was the quiet before the storm, another ambush.

If a Yorax battlecruiser was in the area, their ever-watchful sensors would have observed her dash to hyperlight speed. The realization of the possibility had the expected effect. Personal thoughts were essentially banished from consideration. Anod began a series of maneuvers utilizing her sensors to look for the unusual, the abnormal. The more she looked, the more suspicious she became. Her usually reliable sixth sense, her intuition, began to tell her something was wrong. The Yorax had been too close for too long to disappear from this region of space. They were out there waiting for her to make a mistake. Anod also confronted the possibility that a simple error on her part could cost the lives of many innocent people in the fires of retribution.

Anod strained to see the slightest potential indication her suspicions might be overstated – too conservative. There was no information with which to refute, or confirm her thoughts. If she could not disprove the prospect, then she must assume it was true. With less than an hour to Beta, Anod began to consider a set of response contingencies.

The remainder of the flight was devoid of markers, events in common time, which might forewarn of an impending attack, or ambush. The lack of indicators did not relieve Anod's suspicion. Instead, her tactical mind was reinforced with conviction.

Fatigue from the previous night's events on Beta, the tedium of the prolonged flight and the tension of her instincts had not reduced the concentration of the warrior. Anod was consciously thankful for the restoration of her resiliency. Her senses were still at full performance that fortunately did not alter her acquisition of amplifying information.

The hues of green, brown and blue with the smattering of grays and brilliant white were the familiar visual character of Beta. A brief feeling of safety, of warmth, of completeness came to Anod as she watched the size of the sphere grow. The realization that the planet could be the bait for a potential ambush, doused the pleasant thoughts. She knew she had to reach the protection of the hangar without detection. The approach would take longer to avoid the luminescence of atmospheric heating that was inescapable with a high-speed reentry. A gravity wave descent would take ten times longer than a conventional reentry, but the benefit of the interceptor's masking system could be fully retained.

As Anod approached the planet, she slowed her small spacecraft in preparation for the gravity descent. The central processor programmed and initiated an acceptable descent profile.

Nearing 100 megameters, Anod noticed a very slight change in the reflected light from the planet directly in front of her. Natural curiosity and inquisitiveness attracted her attention to what the distortion might be. As the size of the distortion and the scintillation associated with the phenomenon increased, Anod recognized what she was approaching. She was very close to a masked spacecraft and she was on a collision course. More importantly, it could be and probably was a Yorax battlecruiser.

Anod instantly commanded a vector change as she decelerated to decrease her turn radius. As she passed within several hundred meters of the nearly invisible ship, Anod rolled the interceptor inverted to observe the characteristics of the masking system on a larger vessel from her proximate observation point. There was a detached appreciation of the technology and capability of the Yorax. The masking technology had not been perfected to this degree by the Society, yet.

Returning to her descent profile, Anod watched the sensor displays in the cockpit for the slightest possible sign her interceptor had been detected and would be engaged. Nothing changed. Anod rotated the craft several times as she continued, to watch the distortion fade away completely.

Anod's calculating mind briefly considered what might have happened. If she had not been watching the planet at the proper time, it is doubtful she would have seen the battlecruiser in time. As it was, she barely missed an inadvertent and probably fatal collision with the considerably larger battlecruiser. Luck was often good enough, Anod reminded herself, and what might have been, is not what will be.

The interceptor's velocity and altitude continued to diminish reducing the passage of terrain beneath her and increasing the size and detail of the surface. With the near miss of the masked and lurking battlecruiser, Anod altered her descent target to a large body of water on the opposite side of the planet from the battlecruiser's probable position. Once the interceptor was within a kilometer of the surface, she would fly at a moderate subsonic speed to avoid atmospheric condensation and the acoustic disturbances associated with the shock waves of supersonic flight. The precaution would add another 90 minutes to the flight allowing her to arrive at Astral near sunset.

Watching the activity on the surface, the innocent people and creatures unaware of the menace above them, made Anod feel both happy to be back and troubled by the threat. A few scenes brought a smile to her otherwise stern and focused expression. Several times during the transit, Anod rolled the interceptor inverted, although the only indications of attitude were the visual images outside the canopy and the symbols on her displays, in order to observe an object of interest passing directly beneath the interceptor.

The shadows of the trees and the familiarity of the increasingly mountainous terrain were both signs Anod approached Astral. After one last check of her sensor displays to ensure the threat was minimal, Anod manipulated the controls to make the final approach to the meadow, stopping the interceptor in a hover above the plush, green grass.

The hangar doors were closed and there were no signs of the security team. Anod waited for happenstance to alert the men inside to open the doors. The communications device would compromise her location and unmasking in the open was simply too big of a risk, especially with the battlecruiser somewhere in space near the planet. The realization of futility along with the perpetual assessment of the situation helped Anod arrive at the only conclusion. She would have to land the interceptor and get out. Opening the canopy would present some brief exposure, but there was no other way. Anod did some quick calculations based on the limited data she had in an effort to predict the location of the Yorax spacecraft. Several possibilities were determined, one of which was still within line of sight of Astral. The possible location would pass beyond the horizon in a few more minutes. The sky was beginning to darken rapidly, so while she waited, Anod turned off all the electromagnetic emitters in the cockpit to virtually eliminate the detectable energy emanations once the canopy was opened.

A few more minutes were added to the passage of the potential threat before Anod took a good look around the area and cracked the canopy. She felt the winds in her face and hair, and smelled the wondrous aromas of Beta, titillating her senses. The pleasure of the moment could not be enjoyed because of the exposure.

Anod quickly closed the canopy to remask the interceptor. Bending and stretching her body helped her recover the muscle tone and function lost in the hours she was confined to the small cockpit. A quick, but thorough scan of the area with her physiological senses did not detect even a hint of danger.

The security team again was not being particularly security conscious as the four of them sat around a table in the food area consuming their evening meal. Anod's entrance froze the four men for a moment.

"A Yorax battlecruiser is orbiting the planet looking for me and the interceptor, I presume. We must perform a coordinated recovery to secure the interceptor without compromising our location," Anod said in a calm, confident voice.

None of the men could answer as they considered her presence and her words. The blank expressions did not contribute to diminishing Anod's blooming annoyance.

"Is there something I should know about?" asked the returning pilot. Still no answer. "Is everything OK?"

"Why were you gone so long?" asked one of the men without answering her questions.

This delayed reaction did not appease Anod, however tolerance was the emotion of the moment. "I had to make a hyperlight dash and a sublight return, as well as evade the battlecruiser." Anod knew the latter portion of her answer did not add appreciably to her return time, but she wanted to add some stimulus to these rather poor examples for soldiers.

After a few more nonessential questions, Anod focused the conversation on the instructions for the recovery of the interceptor into the protection of the hangar. The plan called for Anod to use the interceptor's sensors to scan the sky above for the remote possibility the battlecruiser could be detected. In addition, she would use the continuing calculations of probable positions to find the optimum opportunity. One of the men would stand close enough to the interceptor to observe the indentations made by the craft's landing gear in the soil. The interceptor would lift off to a hover allowing the light breeze to move some of the grass and leaves under the legs. At that moment, he would signal the others to open the door. The light of the hangar and the scintillation of the masking system would be sufficient to confirm the position of the interceptor fully inside, and the doors would be closed.

Anod needed to explain in lay terms how the anti-gravity field system on the interceptor worked and the inherent safety associated with being in proximity to the hovering craft. Skepticism eventually replaced acceptance. An additional series of explanations was also required to satisfy their concern to the potential danger of an orbiting battlecruiser. They wanted some assurance their actions would not contribute to the detection of Astral and engagement by the enormous firepower of the Yorax craft, or deployed troopers. Satisfied at least to an acceptable level, the four men consented to assist with Anod's plan.

Upon returning inside the waiting craft and safely enclosed in the cockpit, Anod systematically checked the now dark and stellar illuminated sky for the slightest movement, reflection or other sign of an orbiting spacecraft. The calculated positions had two possible, line of sight tracks, one descending and the other ascending. There was less than a minute remaining of exposure from the retreating track, but more than ten minutes of exposure from the approaching track. Anod used the time to perform several passive sensor scans in a futile attempt to acquire some information. Patience was the key although the man assigned to observe her lift off was beginning to show signs of impatience.

With the last potential exposure track beyond the horizon by an adequate margin, Anod commanded the interceptor to a height of three meters. After some hesitation, the man using a small handlight confirmed the liftoff and signalled for the doors to be opened. The remainder of the plan proceeded without any further complications.

Once the interceptor was safely in the hangar, the doors completely closed and the power secured, Anod opened the canopy and descended to the ground. It was not until she sat down in the food preparation and eating room that the crushing waves of fatigue began to take away the precision of her mind. A quick, small portion of food, though she was not particularly hungry despite not eating for so long, and some instructions to the security men for notification of the Council on the events in space concluded her professional activities. She also asked them to send a short message to Nick and Guyasaga regarding her safe return. She resigned herself to waiting for news of her son. Convinced she had fulfilled her obligations and personal requirements, Anod withdrew to the separate room arranged for Bradley and her those many months earlier.

Anod's evanescent thought about a shower was just as quickly transformed into the simple acceptance of the pleasure of the cool, soft sheets of the bed. The pleasant feelings were not even partially appreciated, nor enjoyed, when the mounting weight of fatigue took her once again into the virtual world of unconsciousness.

Chapter 17

The urgent rockphone message solidified for the security detachment at Astral the image created by other subterranean communications from elsewhere on the planet. The Yorax had initiated a broad, general purpose attack on Beta, nearly a half day ago. After some discussion and one clarification message, the leader of the security unit decided to carry out his instructions and wake Miss Anod.

The return to consciousness took far longer than the guard thought it would, based on the reputation and exploits of the mystical woman lying before him. The next few moments would add substantially to her reputation.

Eventually, Anod became aware of the hand shaking her shoulder that probably produced a realization someone was close to her without her knowledge. She literally sprang from the bed into a coiled position, prepared for combat, knocking the man backward onto his rump.

The man was startled and shocked partly due to the violence of Anod's awakening, but mostly due to the nakedness of the woman. If he had not been confronted with the threatening posture, the man would have been more admiring of the beautiful, well-sculptured body standing above him. Embarrassment for himself and the intrusion into Miss Anod's privacy compelled him to quickly leave the room without any words of explanation.

Anod brought all her senses to full performance and dissipated the adrenaline with several deep breaths, she stretched all her muscles and moved all her joints to assist her return to normalcy, despite an incomplete sleep. The wetness on her bed sheets and the pain in her breasts reminded Anod once again how her life had changed and what she was missing.

While she showered, Anod massaged her hardened and painful breasts, and marvelled at the quantity of milk she was able to express. As her breasts softened, the pain eased. As she dressed, Anod finally got around to wondering why the guard had awakened her in the first place. Had she been asleep so long they were worried about her health, or was something wrong with Zoltentok?

Entering the dining room with her usual confident demeanor added to the respectful distance the four men gave her. The security team leader recounted the story of Anod's awakening as they watched her take some fruit and drink. This was obviously not a woman to be trifled with came through the tone of his words.

Sitting down at the table with the four men, Anod asked, "Why did you wake me?"

"We were instructed to wake you, Miss Anod. A Yorax battlecruiser has been attacking Beta and . . . ."

"How long has this been going on?" demanded Anod.

"About eight to ten hours now."

"Why didn't you wake me earlier?"

"You needed to sleep and we had no instructions to disturb you," the leader answered.

"Then, why couldn't you tell me this when you woke me? Why did we waste this additional time?"

"Well, Miss Anod, you were not dressed. You needed your privacy."

Anod exhaled a strange agitated laugh with some resentment and contained anger mixed in. She checked her frustration before she issued an admonition on their prudishness. "What is the plan?"

"The Council has asked you to contact them by rockphone to discuss the plan," the leader said. The other three men continued to remain quiet and inanimate.

Anod walked immediately to the communications room without finishing her small meal. She was quite hungry, but duty called. Numerous messages were sent both ways to bring Anod up to date on the situation and discuss the plan of action. Anod liked the plan devised by the Council although she knew that events had been irrevocably set in motion.

Duty drew her inexorably to space and the battle yet to be fought. Other thoughts came to her as she donned her flight gear and prepared to launch the interceptor. This time it was not going to be a routine flight. One lone interceptor with no additional support against one, or more, battlecruisers was not the kind of situation that was conducive to long life. The gravity of the confrontation did not and could not alter the necessity for it. There was simply no other choice. The Yorax had decided, for some reason, to start the wholesale destruction of this peaceful planet and its people because of their unconfirmed suspicion a Society warrior had sought refuge there.

The sequence of the previous flight was repeated with the exclusion of the frivolity of the cloud dodging. The ascent was routine although the smoke from the still burning fires of what was once a tranquil agricultural community was unmistakable and added poignancy to the task at hand.

The battlecruiser was either masked, or on the other side of the planet, as Anod left the atmosphere of Beta behind her. A thorough visual sweep of space around her confirmed what the interceptor's sensors had already told her. The presence of the Yorax command ship, or lack of same, did not affect the plan.

Anod pushed the throttle forward accelerating the small fighter to reduce the travel time necessary to cover the short distance to Gamma. The Kartog Guards pilot expertly brought her craft to a hover about 50 meters above the surface at a point furthest away from Beta. The third planet from the parent star was a barren lifeless place with no atmosphere. It gave her a cold feeling although her temperature was perfectly normal.

The sensors still indicated normal space activity without any sign of the Yorax in any form.

With the touch of a finger, Anod unmasked the craft. Repeated passive scans continued to be consistent. Still, no immediate threat. Anod reminded herself she had only ten seconds to complete this part of her mission. If the Yorax were on their toes and had mutual support somewhere in the hemisphere of the universe above her, they would be able to detect her transmission and react accordingly.

Anod took a deep breath and exhaled as she keyed the transmitter and committed to the plan. "Mayday, Mayday, Mayday," she spoke the ancient distress call of mariners and aviators, "this is Society Lieutenant Anod issuing an emergency distress call from the Theta 27 star system. The planet Beta is under attack by a Yorax battlecruiser. Urgent assistance is required."

Anod instantly checked the time. "Thirteen seconds, much too long," she said aloud.

The interceptor was remasked immediately and the throttle jammed full forward accelerating away from Gamma, Beta and the θ27 star.

The instant the light of the star illuminated her cockpit her sensor displays erupted with a multitude of information. Fortunately, the plan continued to work. A Yorax battlecruiser that had been tormenting Beta was right behind her. She looked over her shoulder down the long slender back of the interceptor to see the plasma projectile fired from the battlecruiser impact at the spot she had just departed.

There was also something new to add to the tactical equation. Now, three battlecruisers were within sensor range on the tiny interceptor. All of them were unmasked and converging on this sector of the universe. As she maneuvered the fighter to keep track of her three giant opponents, the realization she was virtually alone in this struggle came to her in the silence of no response to her distress call. The lack of an acknowledgment probably meant there were no friendly listeners in the area. The antiquated radio message might take days, weeks or months to reach a friendly listener, and the arrival of assistance would take longer.

The power cell of the interceptor would only last about three to ten days depending on what actions she had to perform. At present, the Yorax pursued a shadow. Their failure to engage her was implicitly confirmed her masking system was working. Even their sensors were unable to detect the essentially undetectable craft. Anod also knew their pursuit would not last long. With no quarry to stalk, one or more of the behemoths would return to their mission of destruction.

Two of the three battlecruisers were within weapons range, but she waited. Only her distress call provided a sign she was in this area. There were no indications her interceptor had been acquired, or were there any signs Beta was still under attack, at least not yet. Anod maneuvered her craft to an optimum position out of the paths of the approaching cruisers.

Her spacecraft's sensors intercepted an extensive series of encrypted communications, but Anod was unable to manipulate the communication system controls to translate the messages. The number of subspace communications seemed to suggest a change of plans. Anod knew there would be virtually no discussion, if the Yorax were simply faced with executing a plan.

To further contribute to her assessment, the three Yorax cruisers conducted a rendezvous. Several shuttlecraft passed among the three battlecruisers, which puzzled Anod. The Yorax had matter-energy converter transporters. Why weren't they using the capability? Several transporter activations were detectable by Anod's sensors, but the shuttle traffic was unusual.

Anod remained at a sufficient distance to avoid any detection including minor positioning to ensure there were no stars behind her. The scene before remained unchanged for nearly an hour. There were still no signs of any response to her single distress call. Anod told herself, partially as wishful thinking, it was the time required for the radio signals to travel to an appropriate listener. Her actions would have to be predicated on no assistance from any distant friends or Samaritans.

Anod was perfectly content to loiter in the vicinity of the three battlecruisers and watch from a safe distance. There was no doubt the situation would change, but most probably any change would mean more risk and danger for her and the Betan people. She could not imagine the Yorax not increasing the intensity of their pressure on the Betans, now that they had their first substantial evidence she was alive and in proximity to the θ27 star system. It was only a matter of time.

The interceptor's sensors continued to register routine space communications and the three cruisers. There were no other spacecraft within sensor range, not even a merchant trader. Anod still kept an ear to the communications, wondering when, more than hoping for, someone would answer her distress call.

"Well, this should be interesting," Anod spoke aloud to an unseen companion as the scene before her began to change.

The original battlecruiser turned and began to move toward θ27β while one of the enormous spaceships turned to depart in the opposite direction. The third initiated his masking system.

Anod recognized instantly her only hope for tracking the masked cruiser was to move close to the craft in order to pick up the proximate visual field distortions. Her instincts told her the Yorax were trying to set up a classical bait and trap ambush, and her best chance would be to keep track of the masked cruiser, the hunter, visually while her sensors followed his companion.

The situation continued to change as the lead cruiser accelerated to hyperlight speed directly toward θ27β. A quick estimate of the velocity and distance relationship told the lone defender of Beta she would probably be able to maintain sensor contact with the lead battlecruiser on the trip back to Beta. The destination was an assumption, but an obvious one.

Anod's agile interceptor travelling at maximum speed while masked left no maneuvering margin as she tried to maintain a close left wing formation position on the battlecruiser. She concentrated on the wavy visual distortion, but the black void of space occasionally took even that sole indicator away from her. As they neared θ27β with the increasing ambient light and number of reflecting celestial bodies, Anod was able to regain visual contact for the approach.

As the leviathan and its undetected companion passed a range of two gigameters from Beta, the sensors in the small interceptor detected the distinctive signature of a plasma projectile detonation on the surface of Beta. The evidence grimly reminded her the senseless attack on Beta had begun, again.

The urge to take the offensive was strong, but the distance was too great. Any action from this distance would be futile. An unmasked, hyperlight dash to engage the attacking cruiser would provide a perfect target to the other cruiser waiting to spring the trap. Attacking the masked cruiser would allow the assault on Beta to continue. She had to wait until the range was substantially less and the second battlecruiser had begun its deceleration to orbit. Another few minutes should do it, Anod thought.

The objective of this portion of her mission, Anod reminded herself, was to distract and preoccupy the two Yorax warships, and to prevent further attacks on Beta. Agility and timing were the keys to her survival. Anod was not certain whether these two cruisers carried their own complement of interceptors. She knew some of the Yorax battlecruisers did carry up to six interceptors although most did not carry any, if the Society's intelligence was correct. Adding six interceptors to the equation would make her mission considerably more difficult and the odds of success even more remote, but there was no alternative. Anod's success would determine the duration of the respite given to the Betans. There was always the possibility of a few lucky shots and no interceptors that would enable Anod to return to Beta, to Zoltentok, to Bradley, and to Nick and the others. The longer Anod could hold off the Yorax, the longer the Betans had to survive and the greater the probability help might arrive to answer her Mayday call.

The masked battlecruiser began to slow allowing Anod to pull away to intercept its sister ship that was currently behind the planet. Anod directed her fighter to the right of the planet to come from the stern of the battlecruiser. She drove toward the edge of the planet being particularly careful to remain above the atmosphere. At her present speed, about 0.9 Warp, she would ionize a trail of molecules and identify her position as clearly as if she were unmasked. Nearing her chosen orbital insertion point 500 kilometers to the right of the planet, Anod applied the appropriate commands to maintain the desired height and slow the interceptor to a quarter of her speed. She did not want to overrun her target.

As the craft settled into the commanded trajectory, the sensors detected, localized and identified the unmasked battlecruiser ahead of her. A quick calculation established the optimum intercept point that would probably be in view of the other battlecruiser, the one she could no longer locate. Estimates would have to be sufficient. Several possible scenarios were considered. Anod decided to wait until the next projected obscuration, a short period of about one minute when the two battlecruisers would not be observable by each other with the planet between them.

Several kilometers separated Anod's tiny interceptor from the enormous craft directly ahead of her and well within her weapon's gate. She scanned her sensor displays for some subtlety that might identify the location of the unseen cruiser.

The surface of Beta passed beneath her as serenely and alluring as a beautiful picture, but Anod forced herself to avoid the attraction and concentrate on her target and her plan. The scene around her from the displays and control of the cockpit to the majesty of an object as big as a Yorax battlecruiser gliding above the planet brought thoughts of regret that the situation had deteriorated to this level of destruction. There was some solace in the lingering feeling there was no other way.

A sequence of changes to the peaceful conditions broke the solitude of her contemplation. The electromagnetic shield surrounding the unmasked battlecruiser vanished. The reasons could be many, but were probably one of two. Either they were preparing to fire on the planet again, or the enormous craft would soon mask. Anod advanced the throttle to close the distance hoping it was the latter and not the former reason. She quickly considered firing on her target to begin the diversion and prevent further damage to the planet, but the possibility they might mask kept her right index finger from depressing the trigger.

Action was decided for her when the bright tail of a plasma projectile descended toward the planet. Anod did not wait for the impact. The result was a reality she could not change. Her window of opportunity, a strike at the vulnerable stern of the battlecruiser, would soon close.

Quickly, Anod unmasked the interceptor, fired a salvo of shots at the unprotected propulsion section of the cruiser, remasked, slammed the throttle forward and pulled back on the controller. The intensely bright white light of a horrific energy release confirmed the accuracy of her shots. Although Anod would not know for some time, her engagement of the battlecruiser had nearly destroyed its propulsion system leaving the craft immobile and drifting in space while the crew frantically tried to save their spaceship. The vessel was severely damaged, but not mortally wounded.

Anod maneuvered the fighter through a series of random trajectory changes to preclude any degree of predictability for the sister ship of the floundering battlecruiser. She had stung the Yorax. They were now a much more formidable adversary. They were alert, prepared and probably very angry.

Turning the interceptor back toward Beta, her sensors quickly established the condition of her target. The information was neither particularly clear nor absolute, but the indications led Anod to assess the craft as unable to maneuver or fire her weapons, at least for the time being. Now, the problem was the other cruiser and the situation was considerably more dangerous. Neither Anod's physiological senses or instincts, nor the expansive reach of the interceptor's elaborate passive sensors could determine the immediate location of the other battlecruiser.

Anod slowed her craft and established a casual orbital insertion trajectory while she continued the search for the now poised cruiser. Several orbits of the planet yielded nothing. She accelerated and slowed to change her orbital frequency in a routine search pattern. She also passed the wounded battlecruiser several times giving it a wide berth to avoid chance detection by the crew. Fires were still burning. Anod was tempted to scan the craft for life, but an active sweep would also divulge her location for the still lurking sister ship.

The game of cat and mouse, or hide and seek as some would say, continued for hours with no changes. For all she knew, the other battlecruiser could have departed. The possibility was highly unlikely with a severely damaged companion still orbiting Beta. The fires were just about extinguished, which indicated either a successful damage control operation by the survivors or a lack of combustible material.

As the hours continued to roll on, Anod knew the status quo would not be maintained. Something was going to happen. There were many potential scenarios to consider. Most of the event sequences were certainly not advantageous to Anod, or the Betans she was trying to protect. Whatever was going to happen, Anod wanted the course of action to be at her direction and initiative rather than dictated by the Yorax. Anod reminded herself, one of the principles of warfare over so many centuries of conflict was, the best defense is a good offense. The odds were not in her favor, but waiting for someone else's action would only make the odds worse.

What would the Yorax do in a situation like this? Anod asked herself that question over and over again. The thought of another Mayday call from the backside of Gamma was tempting especially since no response had been received, yet. The lure worked once, but probably would not work again. If the Yorax commander was smart, she thought, he would probably have an interceptor or two stationed in the vicinity waiting for just such a move.

Fatigue began to take its toll again on Anod's thought processes. There was no immediate danger, which meant she could not rely on her own adrenaline to stimulate her tired mind and body. Anod recognized the effects of a lost night's sleep and an incomplete rest period along with the stress of combat. She thought about returning to the surface for some rest. She was also considering trying to sleep in the cockpit of the interceptor. The latter choice would certainly not be as restful as a bed, but it would be relatively safe for her and the Betans. Then, a cold realization came to her.

If she assumed a reasonable portion of the battlecruiser crew survived the explosion of the propulsion section, the worst case would be restoration. The wounded cruiser could regain some mobility, possibly enough to return to a repair facility. The reality rested in the inevitable retaliation by the Yorax. One of their prize warships had been seriously damaged in the vicinity of a less than cooperative planet. As Anod's mind laboriously worked through the possibilities, a chill shuddered her body in the warmth of her cockpit.

The remaining cruiser was probably positioned to protect its sister ship. Undoubtedly, reinforcements were enroute. The patience of a waiting warrior could only be explained by the need to strengthen their position. Once additional warships arrived, the wounded cruiser would probably be withdrawn, and then a systematic obliteration of Beta would commence. Anod knew she had to make something happen while there were any odds left. She also had to hold on for help to arrive, if it was coming.

Her course of action was now clear. The wounded cruiser had to be finished off, and the other cruiser had to be drawn into a running battle away from Beta. She had to buy time for Beta.

With her plan established, Anod wisely decided she should get a good rest prior to the execution of her plan. Nothing had changed in more than six hours, and Anod believed nothing would happen for possibly a day or two. The warships were not communicating, at least no detectable communications, which meant they were probably performing to a contingency plan designed for such situations.

The recovery process back to Astral was identical to her earlier returns. The security detachment at Astral had been supplemented by several of the scientists from the renovation effort, Tim Bond, the propulsion systems expert, and Maria Verde, the computer technician. The additional people were simply good planning on the part of Bradley and the Council.

"Welcome back, Anod," said Maria with a gentle, warm smile on her face. "We weren't sure we were going to see you again."

"So far, so good," was all Anod felt like saying.

"Was that you that caused the battlecruiser to explode?" Maria asked.

"Yes. I was able to fire a quick salvo before her sister ship could respond."

"That was magnificent," added Tim.

"I'm afraid this was only the beginning. The Yorax will be back in force, and I've got to move the fight away from Beta."

"How?" Both scientists spoke in unison.

Anod did not feel like initiating a long discourse about the probable Yorax actions, or her plan. She knew the Betans deserved to understand and accept the plan since it was their safety that was at stake.

Gathering all the Betans in the briefing room, Anod explained quickly what had happened so far, what the likely Yorax response was going to be, and what her plan was to stop them. Questions flowed from the astounded audience, but Anod cut off most of the interrogation. If her plan was going to work, she had to get a good rest. Anod asked for them to inform the Council of her plan. She also left instructions for them to wake her, if the situation changed.

Anod desperately wanted to see Zoltentok, to feel his touch and to know he was all right. The strange attraction, like an enormous undetectable force of nature, pulled at her consciousness, her logic and her thoughts. She also wanted to feel Bradley, but the attraction to him was distinctly different. Anod missed her son, his father and grandfather, but the mission was simply too important to risk the additional time. If she was unsuccessful, there would probably be no tomorrow to enjoy the companionship with her new . . . what should she call them? Friends, companions, or family as the Betans called such groupings of people. The philosophical questions were not an issue for today. Her rest and rejuvenation for the fight ahead were now the only objectives that mattered at this moment in time. Her success in space was the only positive way to protect her son and the others. The shielding of the anthratite cave and the remoteness of Astral would not stop the eventual, relentless onslaught of the Yorax.

Anod granted herself the relaxation and pleasure of a hot shower and took the opportunity to tend to her swollen breasts, once again. It was midday at Astral when Anod passed into a nearly unconscious state of sleep. Bone aching fatigue was certainly a contributor, but it was her trained mind that was the true enabler.

As Anod slept peacefully under the protective shield of the hangar's anthratite rock and her Betan friends, the subterranean messages passed almost non-stop for hours as the information provided by Anod was transmitted to the Council for consideration. Messages were also sent to and received from SanGiocomo, the essence of which would be waiting for Anod when she awoke.

There was a genus of inner rejoicing among those who knew her. Some had witnessed the dramatic events above their skies as confirmation of her skills although they had no direct evidence of her involvement. They were all relieved by word of her safe return, although they also knew the threat of the ominous craft drifting around their planet was not gone.

For those, the majority of the population, who did not know of Anod, the interceptor, or the facts surrounding the events they bore witness to, were nonetheless impressed by what they saw or heard. The destruction of their planet by unseen forces had been stopped, even if it was only temporary.

"Should we sue for peace, Bradley?" asked Nick of his son during the Prime Minister's short visit to see his father and his son.

"No, Father. I am afraid I agree with Anod's earlier assessment. The Yorax will not rest until this confrontation is concluded. I am relatively certain they have direct evidence of her survival and presence."

"Have we received any help from beyond?"

"No."

Nick looked around the rooms to ensure they were alone. There was no need to alarm Guyasaga any more than she already was. "Are we likely to get any?" he whispered.

"We have no way to know," was Bradley's somber and succinct answer.

"Then, what do we do? What is the plan?"

"The plan remains unchanged. Anod will fly as long as she can until she runs out of fuel and will do her utmost to defend us. Our only hope at this point is someone else comes to our defense before it is too late."

"How have the other council members reconciled themselves with the violence we now condone?"

His father's question burned into Bradley's sole touching a vein of anger. He understood the precipitation of his Father's almost rhetorical question, however the elder man's distance from the issues of state deepened the incision of his words. No purpose could be served by the admonishment of his inquisitor. "The Council is not unanimous. The majority cannot see another way."

With a calm, fatherly tone, Nick spoke. "Our people have survived all these years of hardship with a conviction to peace, passivity and diplomacy. Has Anod's presence and her ways so affected us that we are willing to cast off our heritage in difficult times?"

Bradley continued to win the internal struggle with his own emotions although the conflict became harder to suppress. "No, father. We have not abandoned our principles. Our decision was predicated upon our nonparticipation in the fighting and the distance from Anod's efforts." Bradley said the words that reflected the Council's mood and position, however they left a hollow, sickening feeling in the pit of his stomach. The implication of surrogate defense as applied to the woman he loved and the mother of his only child was not what he wanted to believe. The remembrance of his mother's removal from his life came rushing back to him. Would ZJ have to grow up as he did?

"Some would say in the House of Justice, we are guilty by association. We are coconspirators," Nick responded simply.

"I will not argue this point with you, Father." The interior of his father's spacious dining room began to close in on Bradley. He knew the direction his father was headed with his questioning, but the suffocating, burdensome feeling that came with the questions only grew worse.

"If we cannot discuss these issues, then what have we become?"

Suddenly, Bradley felt an overwhelming burden beyond his experience. For the first time since he became Prime Minister of Beta, he wanted the weight to be removed. He wanted to rest.

Sebastian Nicholas SanGiocomo recognized the stress his only child was under as he watched the younger man sink into a chair and lower his head to his hands. The desire to relieve his son of the ladening of leadership was strong, but the requirement to temper the metal for the fight ahead was greater. "We must know our actions are correct and in the best interests of our people, Bradley. We simply must believe we are right."

At first, Bradley did not respond, sitting motionless before his father. Bradley knew his progenitor was correct. As the words were absorbed, he drew strength from them. "You are quite correct. The Council has agreed with our plan although not without serious dissent. Anyway, the dye is cast."

"No, it is not," Nick said strongly, nearly shouting. "If the Yorax believed we were hiding Anod, the bombardment would have been much more severe, I should think."

"Then, what do you suggest?"

"I am not suggesting anything," his voice calmed. "I only want you to be convinced, beyond any reasonable doubt, our plan is the right one and best for our people."

The reference to our plan, as opposed to your plan, did not escape Bradley's awareness. The realization his father was only testing him did not lessen the weight, it only made it slightly more tolerable.

Nick continued, "I have grown to love that child almost as I love you," referring to Anod and motioning toward ZJ. "She has born us a wonderful boy, even though she has given the lad a strange name." Nick smiled to his son, as if to transmit a deeper message. "She is part of our family, now."

"Yes, she is," responded Bradley. "I want to keep it that way."

"That very well may be, and I tend to agree. However, you cannot ignore the simple fact her presence places this whole planet in danger and her aggressiveness has altered our chosen course of passivity."

"Once more, you are correct. The changes are real," Bradley said with a low, subdued voice.

"Are they right for us?"

"Time will tell, and history will record the answer to your question."

"Yes, but are you convinced?"

"These answers are not clear and you know it, Father. We have no way of knowing with certainty, but I am sure this is the right way."

"Then, you must confide in the people. They must know what they are being asked to endure, and why," said Nick.

"We cannot take such an action at this juncture. Our situation is too precarious to risk the debate."

"You are forgetting your heritage, my son. We are a people of ideas, of opinions, and of the fundamental right to debate and decide."

Bradley considered his father's words. "You are absolutely correct, but you also recognize the need for the leadership to act in the best interests of the people in difficult times." Bradley paused to choose his words carefully. Nick waited patiently. "A public debate would only accomplish what the Yorax have been trying to do since her arrival. Confirm Anod's presence and condemn her to their hands."

The elder man rose to walk around the room several times with his son's eyes following him through each step. "Then, so be it," Nick said turning to face his only child.

"Thank you for your blessing," responded Bradley with respect, and yet a touch of sarcasm.

Bradley remained at the SanGiocomo cave for several more hours to eat a meal with his father, Guyasaga and his son. Holding the tiny person was everything he knew and hoped fatherhood would be. The pride, the dreams, the plans, the future were all removing the burden of state from Bradley. Zoltentok left his father's arms only long enough to suckle at Guyasaga's breast. The boy was well taken care of and was in excellent hands. The reassurance renewed Bradley's confidence and conviction. Success was not a question.

After a reluctant farewell, Bradley left SanGiocomo for his next destination, Astral. The infant was making the affairs of state easier and strangely more difficult. Bradley knew they must eliminate the present threat somehow with a minimum of sacrifice. He was, to an even greater extent, convinced the future of the Betan people lay in the skills of Anod.

Chapter 18

The scene at Astral gave no indication of the turbulent times outside, or the hope within. Bradley felt an unexplainable sense of reassurance as he completed the several kilometer walk from the station to the hangar. Contact with the security detachment had been completed about 500 meters from the clearing with some subtle admonition to the Prime Minister for travelling alone. Although there was some annoyance over the rebuke, Bradley was thankful for the concern.

Bradley gathered his citizens together for a quick explanation of the situation, as best he knew. The comparisons with Anod's reports provided a more solid picture, although there were considerable unknowns. Most notable among the questions was, what did the Yorax intend to do? It was a question none of them could answer.

"How long has Anod been asleep?" asked Bradley.

The commander of the security unit answered, "Nearly twelve hours now."

"We will let her get as much sleep as she can."

Everyone nodded their heads in somber concurrence.

"What is the condition of the interceptor?"

"Well, Prime Minister, we think it is in very good shape although we could use some more fuel," responded their propulsion expert, Tim Bond.

"Can we get any more fuel?"

"It appears our only hope for more fuel is to capture another interceptor."

"Not likely. What about importation by one of the traders?"

"It is possible, Prime Minister. However, if such an effort were discovered by the Yorax, there would be no doubt what the purpose of the fuel would be."

"I see," Bradley said as he looked at his boots and shuffled his feet as if the actions would help him to consider the possibilities. "We might have a way, if we are lucky. We'll have to see what we can do. What type of fuel and how much do you need?"

"I'll write it down for you," said Tim as he retrieved a piece of paper and a pen from the briefing room desk.

"How much operating time can she expect with the fuel remaining?" asked Bradley.

"My best estimate without talking to Miss Anod is about eight to ten hours without firing the weapons. Maybe as low as an hour or two, if she must fire the weapons extensively."

"I see," Bradley repeated his simple response without conveying the grave assessment Tim's answer brought. The odds were long enough as they were. Without Anod's distracting maneuvers in space, the destruction of the planet and the people leading to their eventual demise would be even closer to reality. Another realization came to Bradley in the solitude of his own thoughts. Even if they could get more fuel, one lone interceptor against an armada of Yorax battlecruisers was not exactly an encouraging situation. To make the dire condition worse, it was the woman he loved who was the pilot of their last hope.

Without further conversation, Bradley left the briefing room to look in on Anod. Very carefully, he opened the door to the sleeping room. Despite the gravity of events around him, the sight of her peaceful body brought a pronounced smile to his face and a single tear to his eyes. He enjoyed her simple beauty even more with each renewal of their meeting.

Her rich auburn hair had been dulled somewhat by the confinement of her flight helmet, but the soft rosy white color of her skin shown brightly against the pure white of her pillow case. The only thing missing from the recumbent image before him was the emerald green sparkle of her eyes. In time, that too would return. The urge to touch her cheek, to feel her soft skin, was almost more than Bradley could bear, but the need for a well-rested pilot was even greater. Bradley left Anod as he found her.

The security detachment commander and one of the guards were in the communications room when Bradley entered. There was not much activity other than a few of the colored lights blinking and changes on the displays.

"Has there been any change in the situation?" asked Bradley.

"No sir," responded the commander. "The fires on the damaged battlecruiser are completely out and there are signs of repair work going on from the reports we have received, but the situation remains essentially unchanged."

"Thank you." Bradley worked through his possible actions without confiding in the security people. "Please try to reach, Miss Natasha Noraskova, by rockphone. I need a few questions answered." The commander acknowledged the Prime Minister with a nod of the head that

Bradley did not see. "I'll be outside the hangar. I need some fresh air and to feel the wind."

The task took longer than Bradley expected, but he was thankful for the extra time outside in the warmth of the θ27 star and the fresh scents of the afternoon breeze. Confirmation of the desired contact was passed to him by one of the guards. Bradley hesitated to take one last deep breath of the stimulating air before returning to the communications room.

"We found her, sir. She is waiting for your message," the commander said.

"Very well. Please ask the following question. Is there some method to communicate our need for LiCa complex matrix fuel without alerting the Yorax?"

The message was keyed into the machine and sent. The response took nearly ten minutes to return as Natasha considered the question.

"Sir, the answer is, she does not think there is. The Yorax would most probably understand any scientific notation or alternative description. It is a fuel they are quite familiar with."

"I see," Bradley said aloud although more to himself than to the faces turned toward him. His mind continued to grind away on the grist of possibilities. "Ask her if we could ask for the components and make the fuel ourselves."

The response took less time than the previous one. "No," was the succinct answer delivered by the communicator.

"Please tell her this, I am certain you know why I ask these questions. Do you have any suggestions?"

The communicator laughed when the answer came. "Yes, I am, and no, I don't, she says, Prime Minister."

"Well, it was worth a try," Bradley said with a chuckle. "Please send my thanks."

"Very well," responded the young man at the console. Almost before he sent Bradley's message, he received another. "She asks, if her presence is needed here?"

"No. Thank her for her offer." Bradley looked directly at the communicator sitting at the console. "That didn't work. Let's give Councilor Ashitrawani a try."

"Do you have a message, Prime Minister?"

"No. Just raise him, first."

The task took only a few minutes and the oldest of the current

Council members was standing by at his home more than 2,500 kilometers from Astral. With the acknowledgment, the communicator looked back to Bradley SanGiocomo.

"Ask him if there is a method of encryption which can by understood by Alexatron, but not by the Yorax?"

The response was quick. A method did exist. A series of messages passed through the subsurface rock of the Betan planet to establish a plan. Bagiiwa Ashitrawani would assist in the construction of a message request to Alexatron or one of his cohorts. The fuel would be mixed in with other items to be transported to Beta. The reply surprised everyone.

"According to Councilor Ashitrawani, Alexatron is about a day out with the fuel. Apparently, he anticipated our need and is willing to take the risk of delivery."

"I'll be damned," exclaimed Bradley.

"What's going on?"

Bradley turned to the voice he recognized. "Anod, it is so good to see you."

"It is good to see you, too, Bradley," she answered, not quite sure what she should do.

Bradley solved the dilemma for her as he walked toward her. After a warm embrace, Bradley touched both her cheeks as they kissed as if no witnesses were present. He felt the warm rush of their renewed bond.

At the first available moment, Anod resumed the conversation. "So, what is going on?"

"It appears Alexatron has taken it upon himself to bring us some fuel for the interceptor."

"That is good news," Anod responded. "If I heard correctly, he is about a day away."

"Correct."

"What is the situation with our friends in orbit?"

The facetious reference to their antagonists was not readily understood. Anod misinterpreted the hesitation by Bradley as a sign of grave consequence.

"What has happened while I've been asleep?"

"The only detectable activity has been some repair work on the battlecruiser you damaged," Bradley answered.

"Has there been any sign of the other battlecruisers?"

"No. Why?"

"I expect it is only a matter of time before something is going to happen. My guess is, once they have the repairs sufficiently along, the Yorax will reinstate their attacks in an effort to force the situation. The other cruiser will wait for a reaction from us."

"Do you want to wait for the additional fuel?" asked Bradley.

"Good question," said Anod, "I don't think so. I need to prepare a response, if the Yorax decide to attack. If they start an all-out attack, there may not be enough time to react. The best thing we can do is, get the fuel from his normal landing site to Astral and wait for the right time to refuel."

Bradley didn't like the answer because he knew what it meant to him, personally, but he also understood the wisdom. He did some quick mental calculations to determine the earliest arrival time for the fuel as Astral. If Alexatron made it past the Yorax, landed at the expected site and the rail system was still intact, the fuel could be available to Anod within two days. The time seemed very long in their present situation. It could be a lot longer, if any element of the sequence changed. Even though the time seemed long, Anod confirmed Tim Bond's estimate.

"When do you want to launch?" asked Bradley despite the fact he did not want to hear the answer.

"I'd like to get something to eat, then take off as soon as possible."

"Very well," Bradley acknowledged with a subdued tone. "Let's get you something to eat and we can talk."

The others let the pair retreat to the dining room. There was no small measure of empathy for what each of the pair must do.

Anod and Bradley took what could be their last opportunity to be together. Each carried an enormous responsibility, and although they both desired a more intimate connection, they had too many subjects to discuss. The burdens of the present obscured the thoughts of the future.

Among the intricacies of the contingency plans and a review of all conceivable scenarios, Anod did manage to get in a few questions about their son. She missed the infant mentally, emotionally and physically. The reminders were with her constantly and were unmistakable.

All too quickly, their brief reunion was concluded with the knowledge that destiny awaited them both. Bradley watched Anod climb into the cockpit of the interceptor and prepare the craft for flight. The stealthful launch sequence utilized previously was executed with the perfection of practise. Bradley was once again alone with his thoughts among the band of Betans remaining at Astral. With some final words of encouragement to the others, Bradley left the hangar at Astral to return to Providence.

The colors of the planet fell behind her as she ascended into the blackness of space on a trajectory to intercept the orbit of the battlecruisers. Neither of the Yorax spacecraft was within her sensor's field of view. Anod took advantage of the rendezvous time to roll the interceptor inverted to observe the splendor of the planet. A sensation of tranquillity, a soldier's calm before the final battle, compelled her to absorb the beauty of the celestial body above her head. She was content to remain in an inverted attitude until the damaged battlecruiser was detected. The milestone did not take long to achieve.

With the first indication from the IR/visual/UV broadband scanner followed shortly thereafter by the telltale neutron flux signature of an unmasked Yorax battlecruiser, Anod rolled the interceptor. Anod placed the planet beneath her and refocused her attention on her adversary. The damaged behemoth was still beyond visual range, but the interceptor's optical sensors brought the craft clearly into view.

Anod studied the image as she continued her slow closure with her target. The Yorax had made good progress on the repairs. Activity around the warship was quite evident. A slight sense of relief came with the scene on her display. As long as exterior repair work was underway, the battlecruiser was not likely to attack anyone although it was probably capable of its own defense. The vessel was still immobile, a good sign, and no defensive shield was present. It was an easy target. A few well-placed shots could inflict the *coup de grâce* for final destruction of the wounded craft – a temptation but an unwise endeavor.

Although there were still no signs of other Yorax warships in the detectable volume of space, the damaged battlecruiser was just a little too vulnerable, perfect bait for a careless hunter. Anod was persuaded to an even greater extent the other battlecruiser was still waiting for her to take the bait. It was now time to focus all of her efforts on trying to find the jaws of the trap. The exterior repair work gave her confidence and patience for the search. Even if the other battlecruiser was not in company, the process would still leave her in a good attack position when the time came.

A methodical search sequence was laid out and initiated. Anod was thankful for the long rest she was able to complete allowing her the foremost concentration and consideration. The plan started at a range of maximum practical engagement where the volume of potential ambush positions was quite large. Anod told herself several times she had to move slowly even though the distances were relatively great. She would need sufficient time to maneuver to avoid collision with the masked battlecruiser, if it was out there.

Hours passed with the only detectable, on orbit, activity being around the wounded battlecruiser. The continuing repairs sustained her patience. Several times, events on Beta distracted Anod.

Traditional radio communications between different locations provided a constant reminder of the Betan concerns about their situation. There were no official *communiqués* between the Betans and the Yorax. It was all interplanetary traffic among worried citizens. There was also considerable discussion of a routine, business-as-usual, nature that was an encouraging, although possibly naive sign. Occasionally, surface activity could be detected visually, like a moving train or a large boat on a body of water. The planet seemed so peaceful, so fragile, and so vulnerable – even more vulnerable than the damaged battlecruiser.

When the detectable exterior activity around the Yorax battlecruiser began to decrease, Anod's attention was inherently drawn toward it. The implications of the change could be benign or dangerous. The shields were still down, but once the shields went up, her task would become substantially more difficult. Anod knew she had to find the other battlecruiser before the shields on the exposed craft went up, if it was out there with her.

Anod increased the speed of her search, well aware of the significantly higher risk. She lived her life with the often-teetering balance between risk and the necessity of the moment. The pragmatic view was, this was simply another test of her skills. Anod approached this task as she had the innumerable preceding situations with a calm, surgical precision.

Indications on her sensor displays told her the propulsion system on the larger craft was at least partially functional. The assessment was confirmed when the craft slowly increased its orbital height.

Still no shields, but where was his companion? She instantly sensed the other cruiser had to be out here somewhere.

Anod quickly reexamined the possibilities. She ran out of ideas and began to convince herself the other battlecruiser was probably not covering its still struggling cohort. Her instincts told her to never assume away a threat.

Then, a wiggle in the visual field to the right side of the interceptor caught her eye. There was nothing unusual on her sensors and there was nothing visually out there. Anod quickly turned and slowed the interceptor to return to the suspected point. Was she imagining something? Was it simply wishful thinking to make her task easier?

The search grew agonizingly slow as she attempted to carefully and methodically confirm, or deny, her instinctive suspicions. It was times like these that made the weak grow weaker, and the strong lose some of the edge. The still exposed battlecruiser stopped its orbital transfer. There was no discernible activity around it. The signs were pointing toward a return to full combat capability. Time was not on her side, at the moment. She needed to attack the battlecruiser before its shields went up, it masked, or began bombarding the planet. Her target was certainly closer to that point than she was comfortable with allowing.

Just as she made the control inputs to initiate her attack, the visual wiggle passed her again.

Anod stopped the interceptor. As she rotated the craft, the wiggle became more pronounced. She moved closer. The image distortion passed her, again. The companion battlecruiser's enormous bulk could not be masked at such close range. He was in a less than optimum, but certainly adequate, position to protect his brother ship. After marking the location of the leviathan, Anod accelerated to a position astern. This was not going to be easy. She was now dealing with two alerted and probably ready Yorax battlecruisers, and most likely several unseen interceptors waiting for her move.

She commanded the interceptor's weapons to lock on to the marked location. The appropriate response was provided. There was no target, but the command had been fulfilled. As her right index finger began to tense upon the trigger, the flash of a plasma projectile descended from the damaged, but now functional, cruiser. The Yorax attack on Beta had begun.

Anod unmasked and fired a calculated string of shots at the invisible Yorax warship. She was rewarded with an enormous detonation. Instantly, she commanded the shields up only to be rocked by the shock waves from the explosive release of the plasma field. Her body was thrown around the cockpit, temporarily stunning her despite the restraining harness she wore. The energy from the explosion hurled the interceptor several kilometers before Anod was able to regain control of her craft.

The flash of a LASER cannon shot a destructive beam of high energy, coherent light only a few meters from the cockpit. The fortunate miss was an instant reminder that while her shields were up she was visible to all sensors. Anod jammed the throttle forward, waited an instant to ensure she was not engaged, switched her shields off and initiated the masking system. Several more shots were fired at her including a plasma projectile. Anod slammed the control to the right quickly, then pulled back hard to change her trajectory as rapidly as the tiny interceptor could perform the commanded maneuvers. As a good pilot flying defensive jinking maneuvers, Anod concentrated on random flight path changes in frequency, direction and velocity. Several more shots were fired in a broad spread designed to cover the maximum volume of space, any one of which could destroy the unprotected interceptor. Luck was usually better than skill. Fate could easy dictate the luck of the Yorax might win this game of chance.

For an instant, Anod reminded herself there was no ejection pod in her spacecraft. Any damage to the cockpit would probably prove to be fatal. The thought passed. There was no value in worrying about things she could not control.

Anod turned back toward Beta. Her sensor displays told her four Yorax fighters were now searching for her. Their patterns were coordinated and methodical, but they were searching for a phantom. The lone battlecruiser was still orbiting Beta with no change in its trajectory. The repairs might not be as far along as she earlier thought. Her immediate threats were the four vipers trolling for her in the empty expanse of space. Anod considered going after the still vulnerable battlecruiser, but the odds for success with at least the four visible interceptors in near space were not large enough.

The path of the right wing of the Yorax formation was the closest to Anod's present position. Anod slowed her spacecraft to allow her new target to pass. She maneuvered in behind him. His shields were up making him easily visible. Her target was an interceptor identical to her own. With the shields up, only a full force shot at very close range would be able to penetrate the resilient shields.

The distance between hunter and prey was now less than 500 meters. Anod made a quick mental calculation to evaluate her ability to inflict a lethal shot against the survival of her own craft so close to a detonation. The sequence of actions would have to be quick and precise. She needed to unmask, fire, raise her shields and maneuver to remask. With a brief confirmation of the positions of the other three interceptors, Anod fired.

The brilliant flash confirmed the hit on her target, but there was no shock wave. Her shot had not penetrated the shield. The pilot would probably be stunned for a few seconds, but his companions were now very angry and focused. Anod fired a quick spread of shots at her converging tormentors. None of them hit anything, but they bought her just a few seconds of time.

Anod slammed the throttle forward commanding a leap to hyperlight speed directly toward the incoming fighters. Most of their coordinated shots narrowly missed her as the craft accelerated.

Another brilliant flash accompanied by the tremendous shock was the physical evidence her shields had been hit nearly head on. The interceptor's central computer detected no damage. The energy of the hit and the violent trauma to her body blurred her vision for a few moments temporarily disorienting her. The interceptor continued to accelerate. A few more shots missed. The inaccurate firing of the Yorax would not last much longer.

At the instant she passed among them, Anod commanded a maximum deceleration, pulled hard on the controller to change her flight path, switched on the masking system and reverse her turn. She knew the Yorax interceptors were turning hard to reacquire her. Survival depended on disappearing and gaining some distance to avoid the inevitable searching shots.

As her sensors reacquired her adversaries, the continuing shots by the Yorax missed by greater distances. The tactic appeared to be working. Anod straightened her vector using every bit of her maximum speed, while masked, to open the distance. The spread of shots from the Yorax would soon widen substantially.

Anod took a deep breath to release some of the tension of combat as she considered her next move. A quick scan for the battlecruiser orbiting Beta confirmed what she hoped for . . . no change. She had to get these pesky interceptors off her back. Her heart skipped a few beats as she recognized the changing situation. A new capability was initiated and being employed methodically.

The Yorax interlaced a broad diffuse LASER shots. They were now using the energy of their weapons to probe enormous volumes of space instead of to destroy. Reconnaissance by fire, her ancestors had called the technique. The surprise was their technical ability to precisely spread the beam of energy.

The pattern was carefully planned and executed as the searched volume was rapidly expanded. They moved out from her last known position. The numbers of shots took considerable energy, but obviously they were not as concerned about fuel state as she was.

One of the broad fanned shots would probably not damage her unshielded interceptor, but the impact of the energy would certainly illuminate the craft despite the cloaking system. Once illuminated, targeting for a high-energy shot would be only moments behind.

The growth of their search volume was greater than her maximum speed under the veil of the interceptor's masking system. It was only a matter of time and there did not appear to be much of that. She had to take the offensive.

While they were firing, their shields were down. Anod thought she might be able to get one, or maybe two, before the others could engage, but they would know where she was and the range was too great for a repeat of the masking maneuver she used earlier. This was going to be a very risky engagement.

Anod turned to attain an adequate engagement position based on the projected flight paths of the four interceptors. As she considered the possibilities, she also chastised herself for not eliminating the one interceptor she hit earlier. The odds would be better now, if she had, but the past was the past. Anod maneuvered and evaluated, trying to find a location where she had the maximum chance to fire a rapid salvo to hit more than one of the Yorax interceptors.

The broadening bands of probing shots from the Yorax were getting closer. There was no good angle. These were experienced, well-trained warriors who clearly knew their craft. The task before her seemed to become more formidable with each moment.

"There's no sense postponing the inevitable," Anod said aloud as she made her engagement decision. "Let's get on with this," she added to her spiritual companion.

Anod established a good lock-on to her first target and programmed the sequence of shots at the other fighters. She would have to maneuver quickly to bring her weapons to bear. For one last time, Anod rehearsed the sequence in her mind. She would not be able to see the results on her targets directly, nor would she truly be able to see her subsequent targets. The commands on her displays would guide her to the proper positions she had planned. There was confidence she had done all she could do. The outcome was now in the hands of fate.

Sucking in another deep breath to clear her lungs, Anod unmasked and fired her first shot, pulled to the next marker, fired again, rolled and pulled hard, to the next shot, and fired. Flash. Hit, she thought. Anod ignored yet another flash as she settled the interceptor on the last mark and fired. A quick jink and Anod commanded maximum hyperlight speed to pass between the last two targets. Two more flashes were markedly different from the first two. The last two were probably shield hits, Anod thought.

Three shots passed her vessel just as she jumped to superlight. Anod moved the controller to change her flight path at the maneuvering limits of the interceptor's superlight speed. As the craft passed five times the speed of light, hyperlight speed, she would no longer be able to alter her flight path. She would be on a perfectly straight and predictable course.

There were no more immediate shots and she knew there could not be any more at these speeds, but she was certain the Yorax would be predicting her track and trying to follow her. As her velocity continued to build toward the limit of nine times the speed of light, Anod recognized this was not a winning maneuver. It would only be a matter of time before she would no longer have sufficient fuel to sustain these speeds, plus she was rapidly moving farther away from Beta. If she was going to die, she wanted to be on or close to the beautiful planet she was defending. A reversal was the only answer.

Anod switched off her propulsion system permitting time-drag to decelerate the interceptor as the time-space warp of hyperlight travel began to return the craft to sublight speeds. There was no reason why she should not take full advantage of the momentum her powerful engines had generated. With her expected pursuers at hyperlight speed, they would overtake her in a few minutes. Her principle exposure time would be the period of sublight speed. A linear reversal directly back at them would require only a few seconds. A turning reversal would add more time, although use less fuel, but the added exposure was just too risky with two, maybe more, Yorax interceptors closing on her.

As she approached light speed, Anod switched on her engines again commanding maximum acceleration. When the craft entered the sublight speed region, Anod made a quick scan to find the Yorax. An exterior flash of light along with a capture target confirmation on her displays established the presence of two small spacecraft travelling at speeds greater than the speed of light. The reversal worked, but they would also know exactly what she was doing.

Anod waited until her fighter slowed to sublight speed before making her course correction to Beta. The Yorax would have less time and precision in their tracking of her flight path. Her interceptor continued to decelerate. Checking the navigation display provided the sobering reality of her situation. The tiny spacecraft did not have enough fuel to make it back to Beta at warp speeds. The chase would be over before Anod could see the elegant colors of her haven.

Options were formulated, considered and ultimately discarded as the facts of her condition began taking on an ominous form. Recognition of the only real option took several minutes. Anod was simply not willing to concede defeat. The face of little Zoltentok came to her as vividly as if she was holding her child – survival – that was her sole objective now.

Her hand was heavy and resistant to movement as she reached for the throttle, pulling it back to idle and then switching off the propulsion unit. Anod would allow the interceptor to coast down toward sublight speed. As the craft continued to decelerate past warp five, Anod initiated the masking system. Her only hope now was for some momentary lapse in concentration or attention on the part of her pursuers. If they did not detect her deceleration or her disappearance, they would not know where to begin their search. The new broadband, recce by fire, search technique demonstrated by the Yorax could localize her in an instant, but the volume was too great.

The brief flash on her display established their overshoot, passing her at hyperlight speed. Anod's sensors confirmed the warp nine speed of the two interceptors. Luck was on her side, again, with their apparent complacency and missed opportunity. Near the limit of her passive sensors, Anod detected their deceleration. They finally discovered her disappearance. If the Yorax remained predictable, they would retrace their steps to the last known point they had their target. These pilots would be relentless in their search since they would not be able to admit their failure from a moment of complacency.

The small cockpit felt even smaller now, confining actually. Anod knew she was virtually defenseless. If she did not change the trajectory of the interceptor, or fire the weapons, she would have about ten hours before the masking system failed due to low power from the plasma reactor. Failure of the life support systems would come another five hours after that. The clock was now ticking toward her demise, although Anod refused to accept her approach to the edge of the abyss. A fight was never over until it was over.

Anod had no way to know about the small successes that were occurring despite the ominous signs. Unfortunately, the Betans and their new visitor did not know about her situation either. The interstellar commerce center six kilometers from Providence was also the welcoming site for the new arrival.

"It is good to see you again, Alexatron," Bradley said upon seeing the merchant trader. "I was excited when I received the news of your arrival, especially under such difficult conditions."

"I would like to say it is good to see you as well, Bradley SanGiocomo, but these circumstances present a serious risk to all of us."

"I thank you on behalf of my people for your efforts. We recognize the risk you have taken."

"Yes, well, I expect to be amply rewarded for my skill and risk."

Bradley nodded his concurrence. Business was business, no matter who the practitioners were, or how risky the endeavor might be.

"It took me a while to understand what was happening here, and a little longer to realize a Yorax interceptor has a relatively small fuel supply. I was about a day out of Scorbion when we received your cryptic message. I slowed down anticipating I might have to go back for something until we figured out what you were asking for. The implicit message embedded within the words was, you were in trouble." His coarse, gravelly voice added to the sense of defiance in his words. "Anyway, here I am, and I have two fuel pods for you."

"We are most grateful."

"Certainly," the merchant trader acknowledged as if he were swatting an insect. "Now, where is Anod? Everyone heard her distress call."

Bradley lowered his eyes and swallowed hard. "She took off nearly a day ago and she has not returned. We have seen signs of her battles with the Yorax, but nothing for the last eight hours."

"Is she alive?"

"We don't know."

"This is not good," Alexatron spoke the obvious. He had taken a liking to the smaller Society female ever since he rescued her injured and unconscious body inside the battered ejection pod. "Is there anything I might be able to do?"

Bradley responded with a dry, tense laugh. "No, not unless you brought a battle fleet with you to eliminate the Yorax and find Anod."

Alexatron did not appreciate the attempt at sarcastic humor. He would have to continue to tolerate these strange humans.

"Wait," Bradley continued. "Maybe there is something you can do." Alexatron did not react or respond. "Can you get away from here and send a hyperspace *communiqué* to the Society, or anyone willing to help us with the Yorax?"

At first, Bradley was not certain Alexatron either heard his question, or understood the meaning. The Betan Prime Minister waited patiently for the Scorbion merchant to react.

A slight smile finally grew from the scowl that was the norm as he matched up Anod's subspace distress call with Bradley's request. "Ah, yes. Now, I see the relation. But, conventional radio takes a very long time to travel such distances. Why didn't she use hyperspace?" Alexatron asked in reference to the time-space distortion system utilized for interstellar communications.

"Probably because it did not work on the interceptor, I suppose. I don't really know. I saw her only briefly after this latest phase began, and we did not talk about the communications medium of her message."

"Whatever! Anyway, I did receive her message and I talked to my brethren on Scorbion. As you can imagine, we, as a neutral merchant people, were not particularly enthusiastic about entering into this confrontation between you and the Yorax. We trade with the Yorax as well, you know."

Bradley nodded his understanding even though the words produced a nauseous sensation deep within him. It was a fact that he did not like and often tried to ignore. Bradley nodded again.

"I called in a few favors from a good friend of mine. He departed Scorbion in his ship and transmitted the distress call in hyperspace."

"Did he get an answer?" asked Bradley almost not wanting to hear the response.

"Yes. A Society starship is on the way. The last word we received was, it should enter the θ27 star system in about a day or so."

"Do you think the Yorax know?"

"Probably not. We used an intermediary and tried to keep the message routine without antagonizing the Yorax."

At that moment, a messenger burst into the control room. He was gasping for air having run some distance from somewhere. "Oh good." he said struggling to regain his breath. "I have found you," he paused again. "I have a message from Providence," once again a pause as Bradley was getting impatient. "The Yorax have begun a wholesale bombardment of the planet."

"Thank you," Bradley said to the messenger. Turning to Alexatron, he said, "I must return to Providence immediately."

"Most of Providence has been destroyed," the young man said with sorrow in his words. "I am surprised you did not know."

Bradley was somewhat ashamed he did not know, but he knew he could not be everywhere at once.

"I am afraid I must be going," said Alexatron with obvious reference to his reluctance to get caught by projectiles from the Yorax battlecruiser.

Bradley acknowledged the assistance. "Safe journey," he said.

Alexatron waved a response as he was already eight steps on the way to his vessel. He would launch in the first window of opportunity presented by the battlecruiser.

Bradley turned to the messenger. "Has the Council survived the attack on Providence?"

"Most did not. Those that did are making their way to Fortisco."

"I would like you to personally take a message to them. Tell them, we have the fuel pods and I am going to Astral. Can you do that?"

"Yes, sir. I am on the way," the man said as he left the room.

There was no way to know if the fuel pods would ever be used, but Bradley knew he had to get them to Astral just in case Anod was able to return. He thought about a quick stop at SanGiocomo to see his father and his son. The idea was dropped as quickly as it came. There was simply no time now.

Chapter 19

The Prime Minister of Beta could only travel the distance to the outskirts of the destroyed capital city. The train track was severely damaged. With the aid of another passenger, Bradley unloaded the two fuel pods placing them in a small room of the station house.

Fires still burned from the attack on Providence. A large crater had been gouged out by a Yorax plasma projectile and now occupied what was once the center of their capital city. The characteristic fused soil at ground zero was highly reflective and virtually iridescent under a thin veil of vapors as it continued to cool. The tremendous heat of the plasma literally melted whatever it contacted. The ejecta from the impact explosion had damaged almost everything within a kilometer of the crater. Several large chunks of molten material had landed on portions of the elevated track taking a large bite out of the bed. Why hadn't he felt or heard the explosion? The buildings at the official, spacecraft, landing site were not that good. What was I doing when this happened, Bradley continued to ask himself?

People wandered aimlessly in a state of ambulatory shock. Some had serious injuries. The less severely injured tried to tend to those less fortunate individuals still alive.

What people could be so cruel to render such destruction of innocent people? Bradley knew the answer, but even he was surprised by the wanton disregard for life. This was low even for the Yorax. This was also the price to be paid for the earlier decision to protect Anod. Walking among the rubble of what was once the largest city on Beta, Bradley considered the price of principle, of correctness. It was the sight of the devastation that made Bradley think about their decision to use passive resistance instead of offensive power. The magnitude of death around him was more than he could bear. Tears of sorrow fell from his cheeks as he bore witness to the failure of his decisions.

Maybe it was the approval of Anod to initiate the strike against the Yorax that had brought such destruction and misery to his people. Maybe it would not have been so severe, if they had not allowed Anod to fly against their tormentors. Maybe, when they realized the controversy around the woman, they should have asked her to leave, helped her to move on.

"Prime Minister SanGiocomo," was the call from a male voice he did not recognize at first.

Bradley looked around him only to see destroyed or damaged buildings, merchandise strewn among the broken structures, and blank or pained faces of people trying to grab a shard of flotsam before drowning.

"Prime Minister SanGiocomo," came the call once more. This time he caught the speaker. It was Otis Greenstreet kneeling beside an injured woman tending to her wounds.

The distance of eighteen meters took a few minutes to traverse due to the circuitous route required to avoid the debris. The woman Otis was helping needed more than the limited assistance the security officer could provide.

"Otis, you're wounded," Bradley said upon seeing the torn clothing, wounds and blood.

"I'm OK, but this woman needs help."

"Where are the medical teams?"

"There are only a few who survived the explosion and they are doing the best they can."

"Has the call for more help gone out?"

Otis looked at Bradley with an expression of frustration and disappointment. "As far as we can tell, they are all committed at other damage sites," Otis explained.

The burden of leadership became even heavier as Bradley realized he was even less aware of the change in events. Mingled among his immediate concerns for the welfare of those around him were several thoughts about Anod, about ZJ, and about his father. Were his son and his father safe and unharmed? Oh God, he hoped so. That hope could not be so strong for the woman he loved. The more violent and frequent attacks probably meant Anod was no longer alive, thus allowing the Yorax to concentrate on rending Beta with their revenge. His heart sank with his descending realization.

Among all the destruction, Bradley SanGiocomo thought of Anod's beauty, her soft, curly auburn hair, her emerald green eyes and her rosy, milky white skin. She was truly a beautiful woman who was probably drifting lifelessly somewhere in space, or was returned to the elemental compounds that once defined her body and mind. They were not pleasant thoughts. He pushed them out of his consciousness. The present and future demanded his attention.

The two men discussed the possibilities as they completed the bandaging of the woman's wounds and tried to make her as comfortable as conditions permitted. The fuel was needed at Astral in case Anod was able to return, and yet Bradley felt an understandable compulsion to tend to his wounded nation. The Council had to be reconstituted with the survivors. The task seemed almost futile in contrast to the physical reality before him.

"Otis, I have to ask you to take the fuel pods to Astral," said Bradley.

"What?"

Bradley looked at the conscious woman. "We have fuel pods for our friend."

"Good, but there are so many wounded citizens who need our help."

"Quite true. They also need our help to ensure our only defense can still fly, if she's still alive."

"I suppose you're right," answered Otis.

"Of course, he's right," the wounded woman said with surprising strength as she lay between them.

Otis laughed more with relief than in humor. "Then, so it shall be."

"Are you capable of the journey?" asked Bradley with sincere concern.

"I believe so. Maybe I can find another of my compatriots to assist me."

"That's a good idea," Bradley responded. "I'll take care of this," he added looking around at the devastation. "The fuel pods are in a small room at the train station. You should have no problem finding them."

"Very well."

"Good luck, Otis. Please give my love to Anod when you see her," Bradley said with a note of optimism not fully formed within him.

"Thank you."

"Yes. Good luck, and thank you for helping me," the woman said with a smile on her face and in her eyes.

Otis Greenstreet nodded his acknowledgment and departed.

"Are you really, Prime Minister SanGiocomo?" the woman asked.

"Yes, I am, and I am terribly sorry all this has happened and especially your injuries."

The woman's facial expression turned quite sour. "Why have

you done this to us?"

Bradley faltered with the sudden change in his constituent. He struggled to gain control of his thoughts, to find an answer to her challenge. "What do you mean?"

"You've brought this destruction to us."

He knew exactly what she was talking about, but a sense of indignation grew rapidly within him. "The Yorax have done this!" Bradley said strongly motioning to the grotesque scene around them. "Not I!"

"The Yorax are looking for that alien woman. You and your father are protecting her."

Bradley refused to acknowledge the implicit threat. The topic of this discussion had to be changed. Small medical treatment teams began to appear to care for the injured. He had to try to bright face on a difficult situation. "The medical technicians are here to treat the injured. We'll get help for you promptly," the Prime Minister said vigorously motioning for the technicians to assist the irate woman. "We'll do our best to end this senselessness. You have my word." Bradley released the woman to their care, but not until he knelt beside her and kissed her bandaged forehead as if he were withdrawing the pain.

Fortunately for all, the woman quickly turned her attention to the medical treatment and needs of others around her. Bradley used the moment to extricate himself.

Otis found another member of the security force. The man's name was Anton Trikinov. He was a large, well-muscled man with dark brown hair and eyes, and a thick moustache. Anton also had several wounds that had been bandaged, but otherwise looked fit. The two men located the fuel pods exhibiting some curiosity as to their content, but did not question their assignment. With the rail system damaged at least at Providence, they had to construct a makeshift sled to pull their cargo out of town. Their plan was to move along the elevated rail line to find an undamaged, functional vehicle and hope the rail system was still operable to Astral.

The speed of the interceptor had slowed to a mere 0.2 warp, 60 megameters per second, as a result of her final maneuvering and trajectory refinement. The cockpit was very dark with the light from only one small display. The confines of Anod's environment felt so cold even thought the temperature remained near normal. Of all the times she had flown in space, this was the most alone Anod had ever felt. The isolation and sense of futility were overwhelming and difficult to deal with. Anod refused to recognize the terminus of the descending spiral she felt was consuming her. It was her grip on hope that sustained her – an unwillingness to concede defeat or failure despite incomprehensible odds.

The lone display showed:

FUEL:	10.2hours
WEAPONS:	NONE
TIME TO SUSTAIN:	
MASK:	0.7 hours
ENVIRONMENT:	4.5 hours

The words on the screen were sterile, impartial and carried a hard finality to them. Anod gained little satisfaction from her invisibility to the searching Yorax interceptors. One of the identically shaped, but definitely hostile craft passed a mere two kilometers from her without detection. The Yorax were not using their recce by fire technique, probably due to their own low fuel state. The urge for one final strike at her tormentors surged strong, but there was not enough energy left in the power cell to fire even a single shot.

The environmental control of the interceptor's cockpit would fail in less than five hours and she would be about three gigameters from θ27β, a little less than one minute's distance from her son. The sad part was, despite the proximity to Beta, she did not have enough fuel to slow the interceptor to make a landing on Beta. Reentry into the atmosphere, an attempted landing, would simply result in a fiery streak across the Betan sky. It was the latter prospect that produced the final trajectory correction to literally hit the planet, if the Yorax did not intercept her first. Her incineration, upon atmospheric reentry, would be an appropriate funeral pyre for an elite pilot of the Kartog Guards.

There was no hibernation capability on board the tiny fighter. The only way she could extend her time was to use less energy. She had to relax to the greatest extent possible. Sleep, Anod told herself, sleep was her only choice. There was nothing else she could do.

With the solemnity of a disciplined warrior, Anod began the mental and emotional process of clearing her mind to sleep. It was not what she wanted to do, but it was what she had to do. It would not be a deep sleep, but her control was sufficient to bring on the diminished capacity of a tranquil twilight. A soft, warm blanket of acknowledgment enveloped her gently. Whether or not she would ever awaken was no longer in her hands, her control.

Otis and Anton with their precious cargo were only half way to their destination after nearly half of a day's effort. The two men labored without any knowledge, or even an inkling of the events transpiring in space.

The entire journey should have taken half the time, however the Yorax had performed their mission well. The primary transportation system had been broken in several places. Hundreds of kilometers of the elevated rail system were still intact although no transporters were on that portion of the system.

Numerous citizens, without questioning them on their mission, had helped them along the way. A farmer and his family carried them in his cart. Others shared their food and water.

A young boy used his levitation scooter, probably traded or commandeered from a Yorax soldier or a merchant trader, to shuttle the two men, first Otis followed by each of the fuel pods and then Anton, as far as his tiny craft would allow. The rocky terrain made the further use of the scooter impossible.

The Prime Minister found a merchant's home whose dwelling was only slightly damaged and his rockphone was intact and operable. It took numerous messages and some miscommunication to locate the surviving members of the Leadership Council and determine the extent of damage to the planet. The seismic shock of each impact had been duly recorded with the rockphones. Each impact also destroyed portions of the messages travelling through the subsurface rock at that moment.

The bombardment by the Yorax battlecruiser continued as it indiscriminately fired plasma projectiles at the planet. The Yorax had the capability to locate and target specific pockets of people, but there were no signs they were taking that approach. In fact, there was no discernible pattern at all to their bombardment.

Numerous queries from various regions sought advice on the actions they should take to protect themselves from the merciless horror of the Yorax attack. The dispersal of the population kept the loss of life quite low although the damage to the transportation system and other elements of the societal infrastructure was extensive. Years of labor would be necessary to recover from the destruction, if they survived to begin the repairs.

The renewed attacks continued. With each reported explosion, Bradley faced the double trauma of injury to his people and planet, and further confirmation something had happened to Anod. There was no doubt in Bradley's mind the Yorax would not be firing at Beta if Anod had a functional interceptor. Each impact brought the additional pain that he might not ever see Anod alive, again. None of the thoughts associated with the current events were pleasant. He wanted this to end. It had to end, soon.

Anod awakened to the warbling alarm tone associated with an uncommanded unmask. The power cell of the interceptor was no longer able to sustain the masking system. It was only a matter of time now until the Yorax detected her presence and converged on her for the final stroke. The last functioning display now showed:

FUEL:	10.8 hours
WEAPONS:	NONE
TIME TO SUSTAIN:	
MASK:	NOT ATTAINABLE
ENVIRONMENT:	5.6 hours

There was some satisfaction in her significantly lower metabolism while sleeping. Anod, with her efficient physiological traits, used less oxygen that the Yorax troopers the interceptor was designed for. Simply, Anod placed much less demand on the environmental system increasing her safe endurance. The energy in the power cell was still not enough to reenter the Betan atmosphere, but it was sufficient to enter a sustainable orbit letting the planet's gravity do the work. Anod quickly made the necessary mental calculations and the very slight course correction to achieve orbit instead of the *sepaku* of a fiery impact.

The likelihood of reaching orbit with the Yorax still attacking Beta was essentially zero. Once again, the warrior-pilot's instinct for survival and the recognition no one could yet predict the future told her to make every attempt and never assume away a survivable option.

The θ27 star, positioned in her forward canopy, was clearly growing in size. Her trajectory was well to the right of the star on a path gravity would direct to an intercept with the second planet of the θ27 system, Beta. Although the planet was not visible and her sensors were no longer functional, there was no doubt in her mind Beta was exactly on its predictable path to the intercept point.

Anod knew the odds were against her, but miracles had saved space travellers in worse shape than she was. She also knew the key to maximizing her odds was to continue conserving her very limited, dwindling power. She might awake to the sight of the beautiful planet filling her canopy, or she might never awaken as her final instant is met with the flash of vaporization from the proton projector of a Yorax interceptor. What will be, will be, Anod told herself as she drifted off to sleep once more. Her energy consumption had to be the lowest she could possibly make it.

With only a few exceptions, the path of the train system was a clear, passable route. The third cataract of the Astral foothill's rocky terrain persuaded the two security officers to take the risk of travelling along the elevated rail bed. They had not seen an operating train since the damaged rail forced them to dismount for overland travel. The semi-circular arc of the guideway, even though the large holes in the bed were constant foot traps, provided an even avenue for the two men and their cargo. If a train was operating at full speed, which was not likely with all the damage, they would have a few fractions of a second to react. They might be able to jump off the guideway taking their chances with the fall, but there would be no way to save the fuel pods. The long, metallic cylinders would be obliterated by the momentum of the train and would detonate as a result of the spontaneous, high energy, release of the fuel. If the train did not get them, the explosion surely would. Both men agreed they simply had no other choices. Otis accepted at full value and faith Bradley's statement that the fuel pods were the highest priority. The risk was justified.

The task of lifting the pods to the guideway was going to be difficult and would take time. Otis and Anton were quite fatigued despite their brief naps along the way. The decision to rest prior to lifting the pods was an easy one. Once the two men and two pods were on the guideway there would be no time to rest. They would be committed to their movement until they reached Astral, another break in the rail or an unlucky meeting with an operating train.

They ate a modest meal of protocarb biscuits, and then slept for an hour before they continued their efforts. Rigging a makeshift lifting device and then getting the pods up to the guideway took another few hours. The two accomplished security men labored in the quiet solitude of their own thoughts with an unspoken feeling any words would be wasted effort.

The tension of carefully placing every step to avoid stepping into one of the lightening holes and yet keeping all their senses alert for an approaching train was taking its toll on their concentration. The slippery surface of the guideway enabled the skids supporting the fuel pods to move easy, but also provided ample opportunity for two humans to misstep. By the time they had travelled ten kilometers, their bodies displayed the evidence of the arduous task.

"Otis, we can't keep this up," Anton protested after a particularly painful stumble. "We've got to do something to keep us out of these holes."

"The guideway is slippery enough, maybe we can make up some rudimentary skis or something."

"Good idea, but that might be harder than it sounds," responded Anton although he thought Otis's idea was about their only option.

"We don't have much choice," Otis stated. "We're getting so banged up, we won't make it to Astral."

"Let's get to it, then."

They decided to leave the fuel pods in the guideway. Climbing down a pedestal ladder to the ground was a very welcome change for both men. They agreed to split up with each taking one side of the rail pathway and searching outward for the required material.

Otis heard Anton's shout of discovery. The join up process took several minutes in the rugged, thickly vegetated terrain. Anton had found what appeared to be an old hunting cabin, long since abandoned. There were no signs humans had visited the site in probably ten years judging from the extent of the overgrowth.

Using their large field knives, the two men fashioned a pair of crude, ski-like, foot boards from the cabin walls and bound them to their feet with strips of forgotten hides. They also cut several saplings to use as poles for movement over the slippery surface of the guideway. With both hands and feet soon to be devoted to propulsion, Anton and Otis combined the remaining strips of hide with vines to make a simple harness to pull the fuel pods behind them.

Both men returned to the guideway and tested their new travel aids. Although not ideal for the task, the footboards at least kept them from falling through the holes in the guideway.

After arranging the harnesses and securing the pods behind them, they were ready for the final stretch to Astral Waystation.

"Isn't this a fine way to make a living?" Anton asked rhetorically. "Here we are relegated to being pack animals."

"Isn't that the truth?"

"I'm sure these fuel pods are important, as you say, but I don't want to ever do this again," Anton added.

With the brief exchange, the two men set out to complete their mission. The movement was much easier now, both physically, as they slid over the surface, and mentally with the elimination of the concern about the holes. They advanced at more than four times the rate they had been able to travel prior to the addition of their transport accoutrements.

The air was fresh, heavy and sweet smelling as it usually was in the agricultural regions of Beta. Except for the unavoidable memory of the current situation and an occasional waft of smoke tainted wind from a distant fire, Bradley felt the invigoration of the cool evening breeze. The messages were too depressing and he needed the brief moment of rest and distraction.

The merchant whose home he was now a guest in, a large gentle man named Dahar Gibritzu, was kind enough to stay with the rockphone monitoring the message traffic and noting the impact reverberations. His wife, Naomi, and their five children were quite caring and generous.

"Mister SanGiocomo, we just received a report from Osterdike," announced Dahar. The city was on the edge of the largest body of water on Beta, and was on the opposite side of the planet and on the far side of the sea from Baikonov. It would be approaching morning for the residents. "They say the Yorax warship has departed."

"Did they observe its departure?"

"Yes. They saw it grow smaller as it left orbit overhead."

"Do you know when the last impact was?" Bradley asked Dahar in an effort to determine what was happening.

"I'll go check my records," Dahar responded.

"No. Just tell me what you recall."

"If my memory serves me, it was a little more than an hour ago," he answered.

Bradley thought for a moment. Several possibilities came to mind. The reason for the change did not matter as far as the respite from the bombardment was concerned, however temporary it might be. The change did bring a glimmer of hope that the cause might be Anod. It could be her, although he knew her fuel had to be extremely low, if what she had said was true. Whatever the reason, the incessant bombardment of Beta had ended for a short time, at least.

After asking Dahar for a map, the Prime Minister located each of the surviving councillors and tried to find a good meeting place. They needed to reconvene the Council to consider their next actions, if there were any actions to be taken. As the map showed, the little village outside Providence appeared to be the best place. Bradley issued the message requesting the Council be reconvened the next day. With that done, he retired to the small cot provided by the Gibritzu family to get some much needed rest.

Each of the Yorax actions were clearly noted by the captain of the Society Starship Endeavour, the renowned Colonel Zontramani, one of the most highly regarded Starfleet officers. Zontramani had flown fighters from various bases throughout the galaxy as a young lieutenant and captain, which was where his exalted reputation began to grow. It was his tireless exploration and skillful negotiation with native peoples that truly brought him fame.

Past accomplishments and accolades were of no value, now, as he prepared his crew for battle. The bridge of Endeavour was a paragon of technology and efficiency. The automation embodied by Mostron, the main computer, was the perfect complement to the adaptive logic and instincts of the human portion of the crew.

"Full shields, battle alert," commanded Zontramani. The peculiar warbling of the klaxon accompanied by the characteristic red light flashing in every compartment and passageway on the starship was the unmistakable warning of impending danger.

"They know we're here," observed Astrok, the Endeavour's first officer.

"Right you are. We'll maintain our state. Let's see what the buggers are going to do," the captain stated with a serious, but confident tone. "Conduct full sensor scans of the region. Let's see what else is out here."

"Aye aye, sir," responded the science officer, Major Astridag.

"Mostron, what information do you have on this star system?"

"This region of the galaxy has not been explored by the Society, or its allies," came the calm, clear voice of Mostron. "According to Society records, this is a void system. θ27 is a class three star with no known satellites."

"Well, we can change that information right now," reported Astridag. "Sensors indicate four primary planets, all solids, with, at least, twenty secondary objects. According to the sensor data, the second satellite is a category E planet, a high grade category E, in fact."

"Any higher order lifeforms?"

"Numerous," came the simple answer from Astridag.

"Have you developed any profile on the population?"

"It appears to be humanoid."

"I'll be . . . Have we found yet another caldron of life in our prolific galaxy?" asked Zontramani.

"It's too early to tell," answered the science officer.

"Do we have any other vessels in the area?"

"No. At least, none our sensors can detect," an obvious reference to the effectiveness of the Yorax masking system.

"Lieutenant Anod's distress call, as I recollect, indicated Beta, presumably the second planet. It does correspond with the classification of the second planet as a class E," stated Colonel Zontramani.

"That would be my assessment, as well," added Astrok.

"Wait," interjected Major Astridag. "Sensors have just detected a small craft in orbit and coming out from behind the second planet."

"Slow to half warp. Maintain your trajectory to the last known position of the Yorax battlecruiser," commanded Zontramani.

The manifestation of pride in the Society's premier starship maneuvered as it was commanded. The existence, location and intentions of the Yorax battlecruiser were on everyone's mind although not spoken.

"Sensors confirm the vessel as a Yorax interceptor adrift," reported

Astridag.

"Maintain a continuous sensor scan of this region. We will remain at alert status," Zontramani commanded with his mind working in overdrive in an attempt to anticipate the next move of the Yorax. "Stay sharp," he added to the bridge crew, "the Yorax are still out there and I suspect we have not seen the last of them."

The crew moved methodically through their assigned and familiar tasks. The tension among those working at their stations was evident although their seasoned experience enabled all of them to remain calm.

"Lock on to the interceptor and prepare to engage upon my command," the Endeavour's captain ordered. No one thought twice about the reasons behind the command. "Maybe if we threaten their straggler, we can flush the parent out of hiding," Zontramani said more thinking aloud than offering a comment to any one of his crew.

The massive, but graceful starship moved past θ27 and its planets on guard against the unseen threat and very much in the hunt. Zontramani knew that once the threat diminished substantially they would be able to investigate the events that had transpired in this system as well as explore the new solar system. The θ27 star was falling further behind the slowly moving starship.

"Should we engage the interceptor?" Astrok asked as she watched the range opening up to the only potential Yorax target they had.

The hesitation of the captain conveyed his calculating mind and purposeful thought. A hasty response was not called for with their only detectable threat being a non-maneuvering interceptor. "Hold," was his only response to ensure the crew and the starship maintained their vigilance over the interceptor.

"What is your concern, captain?" asked Astrok.

Zontramani stared off into the distance of the visual image of space ahead of them, then glanced at the large situation display before responding to his first officer. "There is something not right about this situation."

"What do you mean?"

"I don't know, but it's just not right."

The bridge was quiet while the two senior officers as well as several other members of the bridge crew contemplated their own versions of Zontramani's instinctive supposition. The pensive atmosphere did not last long.

"Yorax battlecruiser unmasked astern," stated the tactical officer.

"Hard about," commanded Zontramani with a calm, but determined voice. "Place us on an intercept course. Standby to engage." "Weapons ready."

Then, in an instant, the starship captain recognized the situation at the same moment the tactical officer announced, "They are engaging their own interceptor."

"Fire a volley between the battlecruiser and the interceptor," Zontramani said with unusual urgency. As the command was carried out, he turned to his science officer. "Astridag, scan that interceptor for lifeforms."

The Yorax pressed on toward the interceptor ignoring the obvious direct threat from the Endeavour.

"Why are they attacking their own craft?" asked Astrok.

At the same instant, the tactical officer announced, "The battlecruiser is firing on the interceptor."

As the plasma projectile shot from the Yorax warship toward the tiny interceptor, Zontramani instinctively knew the correct action. Turning to his tactical officer in a flash, he ordered, "Destroy that projectile!"

The LASER blast from the Endeavour's enormous projector caught the Yorax plasma projectile at nearly three quarters of the distance to the defenseless interceptor. The detonation illuminated the sky for a brief moment saving the interceptor from oblivion. However, the explosion also produced a shock wave of expanding gases. The wave hit the interceptor causing it to shake violently for a few moments. Although the impact of the shock wave did no damage to the interceptor, it provided sufficient force to change the trajectory of the small craft into a decaying orbit that would shortly and ultimately result in the fiery consumption of the craft.

"Engage the battlecruiser. Fire the LASER," commanded Colonel Zontramani as he was forced to focus his attention on the menace before him.

Several more LASER blasts lept out to the battlecruiser, only to be dissipated by their shields. The Yorax vessel turned toward the Endeavour and attempted to mask. Their powerplant was not performing adequately as the characteristic wavering image seemed to sputter and vary.

"Fire again."

The command was carried out quickly. The blast from the Endeavour's large LASER was sufficient to penetrate the last vestiges of the Yorax shields vaporizing the entire forward portion of the vessel. Minor explosions and huge bolts of electricity fanned out from the damaged craft as it began to break apart from its own energy. Fortunately, the propulsion reactor was not breached since the Endeavour passed close abeam to the fatally damaged battlecruiser.

"Let's keep a good watch on this beast," Zontramani stated motioning with his head toward the visual image of the damaged battlecruiser.

As the intensity of the engagement began to subside, the science officer, Major Astridag, reported. "According to our scan, there is a human on board, and apparently near death. Life signs are weak and diminishing."

"That certainly is strange," observed Astrok. "A Yorax battlecruiser bombarding an apparently defenseless category E planet with multiple plasma projectiles and engaging one of their interceptors with a human at the controls."

"That may be the reason they were trying to destroy the craft," observed Colonel Zontramani.

"While we contemplate the possibilities, the human is dying," Astridag stated forcefully. "In addition, the orbit of the interceptor is decaying rapidly. The interceptor and its human occupant," she said with particular emphasis on the word, human, "will reenter the atmosphere in 97 seconds and will burn up within four minutes."

Colonel Zontramani knew what had to be done. "Is there any reason we should not bring the human aboard?"

"No," responded Astridag.

"Very well. Transporter, lock on to the human lifeform in the Yorax interceptor and bring it aboard. Shuttle, retrieve the interceptor for examination. Medical, report to the transporter room to receive a critical patient."

"Aye aye," came the unison responses from all three groups.

The task took only a few seconds to complete. As the body materialized on the platform in a seated position, it fell to the floor of the transporter. The two medical technicians immediately scanned the body to determine its condition.

Reporting the findings for themselves and their captain, the senior technician, Captain Amdorona, the medical officer, said, "We have a human female in gaseous deprivation although there are some indications of a hibernative state."

"Can you save her?" asked Zontramani from the bridge.

"It is not clear, yet. We must try to stabilize her first, then move her to the clinic for a complete evaluation."

"Carry on."

The two human medical technicians, with the transporter room operator watching, worked with the skill of practiced professionals. The cardiovascular stimulation provided by the technicians brought the desired reaction. The vital signs of their patient began to slowly respond although the serious oxygen deprivation of the nearly depleted environmental system left most cerebral functions absent. She was in a coma.

With the patient stabilized and securely restrained on a lifting slab, they guided their floating patient through the security hatches and passageways to the medical clinic. Neither of the two on-duty technicians required words to communicate the actions needed to help their patient. What their medical scanner discovered surprised both technicians.

"Colonel Zontramani, this is Amdorona, in medical. We have completed most of our evaluation. I think you should come here while we try to complete the identification."

"What have you found?"

"I'd rather have you see this for yourself, captain."

"Very well, on the way."

It took Colonel Zontramani less than a minute to travel the 80 meters from the bridge to the medical clinic. The identification was still on going when he entered.

"Look at this," said Amdorona motioning to the scanner display wall.

The device displayed all vital functions simultaneously including most of the important physiological parameters. Hemoglobin density, blood oxygen, uric acid level, synaptic frequency and a multitude of other values were presented in an ingenious graphical display for ready reference, comparison and cross check.

"Obviously a human," observed Zontramani as he continued to absorb the plethora of data on the wall.

"Yes, but look at these particular parameters."

"My, my . . . It would appear we have one of our own on the table. This could be our missing Lieutenant Anod," the captain said as he watched the characteristically designed responses struggling to keep the body alive.

"Mostron, do you agree with our assessment of this human?"

"Yes."

"Can you identify this patient?" came the quick question of interest from Colonel Zontramani.

"Please standby," said Mostron. The central computer processed the genetic patterns of their patient. "Yes, with a 99.99% confidence factor," came the direct response. Without the need for the next question, Mostron continued, "The female on the examination table is human. Her name is Anod, Starfleet lieutenant of the Society's Kartog Guards."

"Send an immediate message to Central. We have found Lieutenant Anod. She is in critical, but stable condition. Yorax threat considered imminent."

"Very well."

Zontramani looked directly at his senior duty medical technician. "Let's take very good care of her, Amdorona. Complete your evaluation. We need to know how much damage she may have sustained."

"We will do a complete analysis of her, captain. Do you . . ." Amdorona's question was terminated by the virtual simultaneous bonging of the attack alarm and the shudder of the entire ship. Endeavour was under attack, probably from a Yorax battlecruiser.

Without speaking, Colonel Zontramani promptly left the clinic to return to the bridge. As he entered, he immediately recognized the maneuvering of the warship to respond to a rear quarter attack. Astrok was issuing a series of commands preparing the weapons array. The ship shuddered again.

"Captain, it would appear we have more than one Yorax battlecruiser in this fight," stated Astrok.

"Damage?" asked Zontramani.

"Minor local damage. Shields holding," reported the security officer, Captain Zalemon.

"Good. Helm, accelerate to warp two," commanded Zontramani. "What is your heading?"

"253 by minus 172," responded the helmsman with the azimuthal declination associated with their present track.

"That should do. Maintain heading. Let's get this fight away from the star system."

A sequence of two rapid impacts occurred from opposite directions.

The Yorax would not be able to match speeds with the Society starship as long as they were masked.

"Send to Central, under attack by multiple Yorax battlecruisers. Request assistance." It was quite unusual for Colonel Zontramani to ask for help, however he knew this situation was well beyond a normal exchange between the Society and the Yorax. Precaution was always a good choice in conditions of threatening and unknown dimension. The communications officer performed the task without reacting to the command.

After an appropriate span of time, Zontramani was satisfied the separation distance had opened enough. He ordered, "Slow to warp point nine five. This ought to give them sufficient bait."

The bridge crew continued to perform their duties with almost detached precision and calm despite the prospect of the recent, rather rare, battle engagement with a hostile adversary.

"Prepare for a rapid engagement sequence. Rotate 180 degrees," Zontramani commanded. Holding the trajectory constant, the warship was turned so that it was now travelling backwards at the same speed. "As soon as they fire, we'll have to drop the shields, fire a broad conical spread around their firing point and raise the shields before impact. If the engagement range is less than two point five seconds, hold the shields." In space, distances were often measured in time.

"Aye aye, sir," answered Zalemon.

The waiting portion of combat was always the most difficult no matter how big or powerful the participant. A warrior's mind had time to consider unknowns, alternatives and consequences. This engagement was no different. One rarely is afforded the foreknowledge of precise timing. Modern technology could predict an adversary's response once an array of facts, directly or indirectly, associated with the threat was available. There was no technology capable of precisely predicting the response of higher order beings. The Yorax were begrudgingly classified in that category.

"Slow to warp point eight," commanded Zontramani.

Before the large craft could complete the deceleration, two points of light appeared at some distance along with the wavering image of a Yorax battlecruiser partially unmasking. The cruiser was not fully unmasked before it disappeared again.

There were no words spoken and the multiple shots from the Endeavour extended out to the now invisible Yorax warship. The impact of the plasma projectiles from the Yorax on the restored shields caused brilliant flashes as they disintegrated on the force shield and a rumbling shudder in the starship. A few moments later, Colonel Zontramani and his crew were rewarded with a miniature supernova, as the pursuer became the victim.

"Rotate 180 degrees and accelerate to warp two." The crew responded. "We don't need the punishment of his shock wave." The Endeavour would outrun the rapidly expanding shock front and white-hot gases characteristic of the breached, plasma reactor containment.

The laborious process of moving the fuel pods to Astral neared completion after two days of exhausting effort. Otis and Anton arrived at the Astral Waystation on their skis. They were more relieved by the removal of an oncoming train threat than they were by the relief from pulling the fuel pods. The makeshift skis and poles fulfilled the expectation of the two men making their job easier. Only a short portion of the journey remained.

Otis suggested, since he was more familiar with the provisioning at Astral, they leave the pods at the waystation to search the hangar equipment room. Otis thought there must be some piece of equipment they could use to make the last segment of the task a little less arduous.

Their arrival at the hangar stimulated a whole series of questions from Anton. Otis told him about the hangar's general purpose and what had been done from this location. Anton's curiosity was difficult to contain, but Otis was patient with his explanations. There were also words of caution regarding the sensitivity of the site and the need for secrecy. The connection to the violent actions of the Yorax was fortunately beyond Anton's sphere of concern, and Otis did not volunteer the information regarding Anod and the interceptor.

Otis tried not to show his surprise and apprehension with the absence of any Betans, or other people for that matter, at the hangar. Eventually, Anton found a handwritten note explaining the departure of the people. The messages and observable evidence of the Yorax bombardment were more than they could reasonably bear with no apparent mission other than waiting with their families exposed to such danger.

The equipment the two men did find, for one reason or another, was simply not usable as cartage for the fuel pods over the rough terrain between the waystation and the hangar. They resigned themselves to the brute force approach.

The remainder of their mission took a few hours to complete. With the fuel pods safely stored in a small room off the rear of the hangar bay, Otis Greenstreet and Anton Trikinov had no desire to find any residual strength to eat or clean up. Both men virtually collapsed into the beckoning beds of the dormitory. They were unconscious before their bodies completed the descent.

Bradley noticed the series of bright flashes near the horizon toward the rising dawn. Maybe Anod was still alive and able to inflict yet another wound on the Yorax. If it was her, it was a major victory. Whatever exploded so far out into space had to be big, he told himself.

With the message of the warship's departure from orbit and the lack of any impacts on the planet in more than eight hours, the signs of relief, a respite from the carnage, looked more positive.

"I should be on my way, if we are to reconvene the Council this morning," Bradley said to Mister Gibritzu. The sky continued to lighten. It would be a clear, pleasant day.

"You are welcome any time, Mister SanGiocomo."

"Thank you and your entire family for the gracious hospitality you have provided. You have made a difficult situation easier to bear."

"It has been an honor for us, Prime Minister."

"Have a good day. Hopefully, this day will be the beginning of our recovery."

"We hope so as well."

The Prime Minister waved his hand as he walked down the road toward Providence. The village for the Council meeting was between the Gibritzu home and the devastated capital city. The journey would take about four hours walking.

Bradley SanGiocomo's thoughts returned to the might-have-been in an effort to see a clear direction toward the future. The task was not simple, nor easy. With Anod possibly lost the void of space, maybe the correct choice was to acknowledge their involvement to the Yorax and acquiesce to their wishes. In essence, they should sue for peace.

There were also thoughts of ZJ and his father as Bradley walked in a somewhat oblivious state down the country road. The sounds of the animals and birds along with the smells of life did not register with him. The couple of messages from SanGiocomo established the well being of his son and father.

Although Anod's absence simplified their problem slightly, Bradley missed the mother of his only child. He enjoyed Anod's natural, unadorned beauty, her strength and confidence, her courage and most of all her innocence. There was something uniquely attractive to Anod's almost boundlessly absorptive mind and lack of practical human life skills. He still could not imagine how anyone could grow up having so many common, every day, and tasks done for them. Her education was his pleasure.

The little village was untouched by the Yorax and if it was not for the repeated questions from the citizenry, one would think this particular day was just another pleasant day on this peaceful planet. The council members gathered at the tiny town hall within an hour of one another. The usual greetings were mixed with the news of lost comrades. The mood and tone of informal discussions were somber and yet resilient. They and their ancestors had survived societal traumas of this magnitude before. They would survive this one as well. It was simply a matter of their collective will and problem solving capabilities to achieve the objective.

This Council meeting was decidedly less stormy than previous conclaves. Although the Prime Minister did not offer his observations, he took a mental note and was thankful for the change. The sometimes-raucous debate was replaced with a purposeful resolve to find the solution.

After nearly an hour of problem definition and solution determination, Bradley's dreaded questions arose. What had happened to Anod? Was she still a factor? Was she still alive?

Bradley mustered all his control and tried to be the impartial leader his people needed. With cool, clear detachment, Bradley James SanGiocomo, Prime Minister of Beta, provided his assessment. Anod had not returned from her last sortie. By her calculations, the fuel in the interceptor should have run out more than eight hours ago. The extra fuel pods were safely at Astral and available, if she was able to return. There was a remote possibility she could still be alive by some miracle.

The avoidance of an answer to the question of her involvement in the future course of events was duly noted. The question was reoriented and represented. For the first time in an official capacity, Bradley acknowledged his connection to Anod, the mother of his son, and hopefully, his future mate. The news came as a surprise to a few who were more distant from him personally. Even more surprising was the apparent sense of relief by most of the Council at the recognition of her importance to Beta. She was now considered a *de facto* citizen of Beta and, as such, should be afforded the same benefits. Bradley was astonished by the change, the acceptance of the woman he loved and also the person who had brought such destruction with her presence.

"Did you notice the explosions in space," asked one of the council members.

"Yes, I did," answered Bradley. "They were rather far away. I thought they might be a result of Anod's efforts to protect us."

"Yes, but did you notice the smaller one much closer to us?"

Bradley's heart stopped. Smaller one . . . Closer to us . . . The words sent ripples of internal agony through his body and mind as well as an overwhelming deflating sensation that sapped his strength like a vacuum pump.

The interceptor was the smallest object he knew of in space near their planet. Tears of sorrow and deep personal loss began to well up in his eyes and stream untouched down his cheeks as he fought with his own emotions. He desperately wanted this not to be true.

Several of the council members moved to him placing their hands upon his shoulders to provide their prime minister some strength. Bradley slowly regained his composure, acknowledged the gestures of understanding and enjoined the Council to proceed with their business.

With a new conviction, the Council decided to maintain their course. They would walk a very thin line disclaiming any involvement with opposition to the Yorax, and yet they would not compromise Anod's existence, if she ever returned to Beta. There was a sense of inner peace among the surviving councillors. Bradley felt better about the future despite the looming prospect of his personal loss and the still present storm clouds that were the Yorax.

"Initiate a general broadcast on subspace communications. Request a conference with the Yorax before this goes any further," directed Colonel Zontramani.

"Very well, sir," came the response of the Endeavour's communications officer. The answer from the Yorax did not take long to arrive. "We have contact with the Yorax Battlecruiser Gortekon, General Barbaronstrek commanding."

"Open the conference channel."

The communication screen filled with the disfigured face of the Yorax leader. "Why have you violated Yorax space?"

"General, there is no basis for this region to be classified as Yorax space."

"Let me assure you that this is Yorax space. In addition, you have violated the peace by destroying several of our battlecruisers."

"The loss of your ships was regrettable, however we were attacked and simply defended our vessel."

"You have initiated a war. Either you leave this region, or there shall be war," the Yorax general continued to press their typical offensive stance.

"The Society has no interest in war, General Barbaronstrek. We responded to a distress call from one of our missing pilots," Zontramani said with no change in his expression.

"We have heard no distress call," the Yorax leader lied. "Have you found your pilot?"

"We are still searching," Zontramani evaded the question without a falsehood. "We would like to proceed with our search and investigation."

"No!" Barbaronstrek shouted. "You have no right to search this area."

Colonel Zontramani remained calm although he felt the urge to challenge his deceitful adversary. "Let me restate our intentions. We are on a simple rescue mission. We do not desire combat, however we will do what we must to retrieve our pilot and ensure peace for the people of the second planet."

"Then, if it is a fight you wish, then it is a fight you shall have."

"We do not . . . ," Zontramani said to a blank screen at the same instant the starship shuddered violently from multiple impacts. "Accelerate to warp three on course 245 by minus 175."

"Aye aye, sir," responded the helmsman.

"Captain, Central has dispatched Avenger and Kamakani to assist. Avenger is three days out and Kamakani is five days away."

"Well, that gives us some time to deal with our attackers," Zontramani said with a chuckle. The starship was again shaken by a plasma projectile as the vessel passed warp one with the characteristic visual field distortion of the jump into time warped travel. "At least, they got one last shot off while they could," the captain said sarcastically.

"One of the battlecruisers has unmasked and accelerated to warp speed for intercept," reported Captain Zalemon, the security officer.

"Time to intercept?"

"Two point three minutes."

"Accelerate to warp seven point eight," Zontramani commanded.

"Let's see how many pursuers we do have?"

The high speed, interstellar chase lasted nearly two hours and covered trillions of kilometers across space. There were now three Yorax battlecruisers in the pursuit of Endeavour. The Yorax deployed in a typical and appropriate battle spread, and were travelling at their maximum speed of warp nine. Zontramani had purposefully held the Endeavour's speed down to seven point eight allowing some closure for the Yorax to keep them in the chase.

The calculations and tactics worked. They headed directly toward Centauri 47, a decaying, solo, red, giant star. The tactical plan called for an adequate separation between Endeavour and the Yorax, which they had, and the use of the approaching star's gravity field and size. Passing through the outer fringes of the star's atmosphere would distort Endeavour's track and the star's size would mask the starship's maximum deceleration. The result would be an overshoot by the three Yorax pursuers. The timing would have to be perfect. Endeavour would be out of view for only a short time and the track distortion was predictable by the Yorax, if they considered it.

The crew of Endeavour performed the difficult maneuver with impeccable precision – a space version of an ancient aviation tactic called the lag pursue turn and reversal. Two warships passed on the right side and the other craft passed on the left. The engagement was conducted with blinding speed and precision. Two of the three battlecruisers were destroyed partially by Endeavour's projectile impacts, but mostly by the tremendous speeds involved in the engagement. The third Yorax warship, the lead ship, was able to get beyond weapon's range although it was now pursued by Endeavour.

"Maybe our adversary will yield to a graceful departure," Colonel Zontramani thought aloud.

"It is worth a try," responded Major Astrok. "This could last a long time since we have been opening on Avenger and Kamakani. They should be able to deal with the $\theta27\beta$ situation when they arrive."

"Quite right, Astrok." The captain turned to the communications officer. "Hail the Yorax captain."

General Barbaronstrek's image appeared on the communications screen again. "You continue to commit violent acts against the Yorax people," he shouted with almost amusing animation. "You shall pay for your transgression."

"We are not interested in further injury to your people." Colonel

Zontramani spoke with a calm, almost sleepy, diplomatic tone. "We are only interested in recovery of our missing pilot and bringing peace to the θ27 star system."

"Now, it is the θ27 star system as well," the Yorax leader grunted.

"We want peace." Zontramani spoke the words although his instincts told him the Yorax did not feel the same.

"What do you propose?"

The Society starship captain offered a discrete withdrawal with the commitment from the Yorax not to visit this region again and let the people of the second planet live in peace. The discussion occasionally flared into harsh words from the Yorax leader, but eventually the objective was achieved. It was the consideration of losses and the prospect for a further increase in the toll that brought the conclusion.

With an informal agreement between warriors, the Society Starship Endeavour decreased speed to allow the Yorax Battlecruiser Gortekon to continue its withdrawal. The warship would eventually return to the Yorax sector of the galaxy and claim victory over a Society starship. The lie would probably not be discovered for several years.

"That was an interesting bluff, captain," Astrok observed with the negotiations concluded.

"It seemed to be the best tack to take and we were fortunate this time. I am certain this is not the last we shall hear of Yorax aggression." Colonel Zontramani paused for a moment in thought. "I do wonder what caused this incident?"

"Maybe our young Lieutenant Anod will have some answers," said Astrok.

"Yes, maybe, if she ever regains consciousness."

First Officer Astrok turned to the communicator. "Send confirmation of the conclusion of this engagement and the recovery of Lieutenant Anod. Also report, she is in critical, but stable condition." Astrok looked back to her captain. "Destination, captain?"

"Let's return to the θ27 star system. We should investigate the condition, origin and intentions of the inhabitants."

"Very well. Helm, set course for the θ27 star system, warp five," Astrok spoke the routine commands now that the tactical engagement was over. "Shall we call off Avenger and Kamakani?"

Zontramani thought of the possibilities. "I should think not. We should leave that to Central. It might be an appropriate show of force for three starships to remain in the area for a short time."

After several communications with Central Command to ascertain the specific situation and conditions of the local commander, the starfleet command group agreed to Zontramani's proposal. Messages were sent to the other two starships allowing them to stand down from combat alert and reduce speed to a more prudent warp five, hyperlight velocity. As the tensions of combat dissipated and on board activities returned to a more normal tempo, Colonel Zontramani as well as other members of the crew allowed their thoughts to return to the characteristics of an unexplored singular star system. Why hadn't the inhabitants of the star system shown up on the Society's population charts? What was their heritage? How had Lieutenant Anod, a star fleet officer and pilot of the elite Kartog Guards, wound up in this place? What had happened at the 2137M19 star system that caused her to be displaced so far?

The questions seemed to be endless as Colonel Zontramani thought of events surrounding this incident. Combat was always regrettable although it seemed to be an inherent element of space travel. One bright spot among the destruction was the continuous learning process that each experience brought to the humans. They all knew they were soon to learn much more.

Chapter 20

"What is our estimated arrival time at the θ27 system?" Colonel Zontramani wanted to refocus his attention on the task before his crew instead of the idle meanderings of a fertile mind.

"Three hours, forty two minutes to θ27β, sir," responded the helmsman.

"Amdorona for Colonel Zontramani," came the voice of the chief medical technician over the intercom.

"Yes, Amdorona."

"Captain, if you have a few moments, I think you should see the results of our evaluation of Lieutenant Anod."

"On my way," Zontramani answered.

The thoughts of the accomplished commander raced through numerous possibilities. Was she irreparably damaged? Did she contract some exotic disease? Was she altered by her captors? None of the considerations were positive, however they were the normal preparations his warrior instincts allowed him.

"What do you have?" he asked as he entered the clinic.

"First, she has not regained consciousness, or cognitive functions. We have not attempted stimulation, yet. She has no musculoskeletal damage although there are indications of recently healed wounds and trauma. There is a remote possibility she has suffered asphyxiation and synaptic injury to several higher regions of her brain although we cannot determine the extent, if any, until we initiate cerebral stimulation. She will require a day or so to regain her proper blood chemistry after her near fatal hibernation experience."

"Are her recuperative powers still active?"

"Yes. Her body appears to be quite normal except for the blood chemistry and coma, and a few other parameters." Amdorona paused to consider how to approach the subject of the data she had collected.

"Well?" the captain led his medical chief.

"All the parameters our instruments can test point to a couple of significant changes." Again, the medical expert paused. This time Zontramani waited with her, continuing to wonder what was so dramatic. "I haven't seen anything like this in my entire career, not even in training.

The instruments tell us Lieutenant Anod has borne a child."

"That's impossible," exclaimed Colonel Zontramani. His trained and experienced logic knew never to consider anything to be impossible, however his surprise at the news brought the reflexive choice of words. A new series of possibilities filled his mind. As he filtered and classified those possibilities, he considered the consequences of Amdorona's discovery. Turning to the other two assistants in the clinic, he commanded, "What you have seen, I am designating as, state secret, and will be protected accordingly. Do you understand?"

Both technicians nodded without fully understanding why.

Zontramani added, "Please leave us. We will call you when our conference is concluded." He waited for the clinic to be cleared. Looking directly into Amdorona's eyes, he continued, "You do realize the seriousness of your findings?"

"Yes, I do, Colonel Zontramani," Amdorona said with slight irritation at the paternalism in his question and tone.

"What evidence do you have?"

"Well, let me show you," Amdorona said as she touched several positions on the scanner display wall. A full color, three-dimensional, holographic image of Anod about one meter high appeared and began revolving on the platform adjacent to the display wall. "Here is Anod as she is now." Amdorona touched a few more positions on the wall. Another image appeared to the left of the first form with exactly the same orientation and rotation rate. "This is the last full body scan conducted by the central computer on Saranon, her duty station."

Zontramani examined the two images closely. The obvious differences between the two representations were the longer braided hair, noticeably larger breasts and darker areolae of the right image. "The right one is her current condition?" asked Zontramani.

"Yes."

"How old is the Saranon scan?"

"About one year. It was recorded the night before she disappeared."

"The difference in physical appearance is quite apparent. What other anomalies are there?" asked the Endeavour's captain.

"Several key hormones have been activated probably due to her removal from our environment. The specific hormones allowed her to be impregnated." Amdorona touched several additional positions on the wall. The layers of skin and muscle vanished from the lower abdomen of each hologram exposing the viscera of both images. With several additional commands, the snaking tubes of the intestines disappeared as well. "As you can see," she said pointing to the lower abdominal organs of both images, "her reproductive organs, here and here, have been distended and are still in the process of recovery." Amdorona enlarged both images so that only the stripped away lower abdominal areas were now the projected one-meter height. "They are quite enlarged in the current image. The older image shows the normal subdued state. In addition, she is lactating which is consistent with the hormonal alternations, and does account for her swollen breasts."

"Pardon me, Amdorona. I am not familiar with the term, lactating."

The medical chief returned both holograms to their full exterior shapes. "It means her breasts are engorged with milk as you can see." Amdorona pointed to each of Anod's breasts circling her finger to highlight the swollen glands of the right image. "She is apparently producing milk to feed her newborn infant. According to the medical references, it is an ancient physiological response for a female after gestation and birth of a child through the ancient bodily process." Amdorona recited the information provided by Mostron earlier.

"Did the Yorax do this to her?"

"Not likely. It is possible, but not likely. The year old injuries, which correspond to the time of the incident at M19, could be torture. However, there are no collateral indications of torture, or force. The other alterations are probably part of some natural process."

"Then, she has violated Society law," stated Zontramani, more aloud to himself than to his medical officer.

"It would appear so," she answered. "However, we must withhold judgment until we understand what has happened to her during her captivity." It was Amdorona's turn to be superior.

"Quite right, Amdorona," he answered without reaction to her words. "Can you stimulate her to consciousness?"

"Yes, although the nature of her coma dictates a slow and cautious process."

"How long?"

"It will probably take about an hour."

"Then, let's begin," said Colonel Zontramani.

"It is a critical procedure and I will need the assistance of my technicians."

"As you wish, however, I ask you to caution them on the need for the utmost restriction on any information derived from Lieutenant Anod, or associated with her treatment."

"Understood."

"Begin when you are ready and let me know as soon as she becomes coherent." Amdorona nodded her consent. "Mostron, all information, directly or indirectly, linked to Lieutenant Anod will be classified as, State Secret."

"As you command," answered the faithful and diligent computer. Zontramani began to leave the clinic for his quarters. "One more thing, how many people know of her condition?"

"My two duty assistants and the two of us," Amdorona answered.

The meticulously slow process of cerebral stimulation took the specified time to accomplish the desired result.

Anod opened her eyes, but was not immediately aware of her new surroundings. At first, she thought she was on a Yorax battlecruiser. However, the room did not look like the crude heavy construction typical of the Yorax. She definitely was not on Beta. About the time Anod began to consider she might be on a starship, an attractive woman slightly older than her and dressed in a starfleet uniform came into the room. It was also at that moment Anod realized she was suspended ten centimeters above a table without the touch of the clothing she had become accustomed to on Beta. She was in the medical version of an isopod. It did not have the protective covering of a personal isopod. An exactly identical gravity field held her in place above the table with an equal, imperceptible force over her entire body.

"Where am I?" asked Anod.

"You are aboard the Society Starship Endeavour," responded Amdorona.

"Where are we?"

"We are enroute to the θ27 star system to investigate what happened there and who the inhabitants are?"

"What about the Yorax?"

"We have destroyed three battlecruisers and another has been allowed to return to their sector in order to preserve the peace."

"They were looking for me and they were destroying Beta and its people," Anod stated.

Without responding to her statement, Amdorona spoke to their invisible companion. "Mostron, intercom." She waited a moment then said, "Colonel Zontramani, Lieutenant Anod has regained consciousness."

"Very well. I will be there shortly."

Anod realized the bioscanners would have already established her identity and undoubtedly her altered physical condition. There was no sense trying to hide anything, or be ashamed of what she had done. "Colonel Zontramani is commanding this ship?" asked Anod. She had heard many stories and read numerous mission logs about him, but she had never met the legend.

"Yes, he is."

The captain of the Endeavour entered the clinic. When Anod saw his uniform, she attempted to rise in recognition of his status, but was restrained by the progressively resistive force of the medical isotable.

"Not so fast. You just lie still for the time being," the medical chief said.

"I am Colonel Zontramani, Captain of the Society Starship Endeavour."

"I am Lieutenant Anod, right wing, Section Three, of the Saranon Detachment," she responded. The words flowed from her mouth as naturally as they had a hundred times before, but for some reason, they did not sound correct this time.

Zontramani bowed his head slightly in acknowledgment, and then looked to his chief medical officer.

"She is fully cognitive with no detectable synaptic damage," Amdorona explained without being asked the expected question. Again, Zontramani gestured his acknowledgment of the information.

"We rescued you from a drifting Yorax interceptor in a decaying orbit around the second planet of the θ27 star."

Anod nodded her agreement although the recognition of a decaying orbit meant something must have happened while she was unconscious.

Captain Amdorona continued, "How did you arrive there? What were you doing there?"

The anger of the not too distant past instantly returned to her thoughts. It was her former friend and compatriot who had brought all the change and pain to her life. "My section was betrayed by Captain Zitger and ambushed by the Yorax." Anod stopped with the expression of shock on Zontramani's face. She wanted him to say something as she realized she was probably the only citizen of the Society who knew of Zitger's betrayal. "I was apparently rescued by a Scorbion trader, by the name of Alexatron, who brought me to Beta, the second planet of θ27." Anod did not want to continue without some reaction from Zontramani.

The captain of the Endeavour took his cue. "You have made a very serious accusation, Lieutenant Anod. I trust you have facts to substantiate your allegation against a deceased officer."

Anod could see the tension in his eyes. She quickly made an assessment of the mood. Continuation of the discussion was not a clearly advisable choice.

"What evidence do you have?" Zontramani pressed for an answer.

Anod related the sequence of events from the Section Three launch from Saranon to investigate a suspicious set of events to the flash that destroyed her fighter. Each step clearly and concisely recounted. The disintegration of Zarrod's fighter rekindled the anger spawned from their betrayal. Her mood changed dramatically as she articulated her memories of Beta and the information provided by Nick and Alexatron about the history associated with her protracted coma. Anod purposefully avoided discussing the forbidden fruits of her time on Beta. There seemed to be no purpose served since the medical scanners certainly provided all that data. The history of the Betan people, the culture and society were also presented in a general sense.

Zontramani asked numerous questions about her activities on Beta although he likewise avoided any direct reference to her violations of Society law. One of his many concerns that he approached from several different directions was her apparent failure to communicate her existence and status to the Society. Her explanation and reasons were consistent although difficult to believe. He remained quite skeptical of her story and resistive to any compassion until Anod spoke of the Yorax, their activities and their collaborator. The physical sighting of Zitger in the Betan town of Providence as well as the escalating violence of the Yorax began to, at least, raise questions about his own doubts.

"Bridge to Colonel Zontramani."

The Colonel did not answer immediately as he watched Anod's eyes as if he were trying to find some revelation in her soul.

"Bridge to Colonel Zontramani."

Again, there was no response to the hail of his crew. Finally, he broke eye contact. "Yes, what is it?" he answered.

"My apologies for disturbing you, captain. We have arrived at the θ27 star system."

"Very well. Assume a standard orbit about the second planet. Conduct a passive probe of the planet. Initiate no contact until I return to the bridge," he commanded.

"Aye aye, sir."

Zontramani's eyes returned to Anod who was in turn watching him intently. "I would like you to rest. You have been through a great ordeal. You need the rest."

Anod did not agree. She still sensed the suspicion and thought he could see in her eyes. "I need to return to Beta, Colonel," she said with conviction.

"I don't think that would be a good idea, just yet."

"I have many friends who are apprehensive and concerned about me and the situation with the Yorax. They need to know."

"Then, we shall tell them," he responded with some irritation with the young lieutenant's obstinance. "Who is their leader?"

"The Prime Minister of Beta is Bradley James SanGiocomo," answered Anod.

"I will let you know how our investigation proceeds."

The word struck her like a bolt of lightning. Investigation. She was being investigated. They would soon know, if they did not already, exactly what she had done on Beta. Anod did not like the sound of Zontramani's words although it was his reputation as a wise and fair leader that persuaded her to relent. Zontramani left the clinic to be replaced by Amdorona and an assistant. They wanted to run a few more tests and discuss medical specific topics about her condition. Amdorona expertly worked her way toward the topic of most interest to her professionally. The chief medical officer called up the same images she had for Colonel Zontramani and provided a similar explanation of their findings. She wanted to know more of the details surrounding her pregnancy, birth and nursing.

The sensitivity of the topic made any discussion with a starfleet officer, even if it was a medical officer, impossible. The detailed clinical information provided by the two full body scan images appeared to be quite conclusive and undeniable. Her silence could not confirm nor refute the medical findings. As she listened to the physiological facts and the persistent questions, Anod's thoughts went to Zoltentok, her son, the one person she missed the most. She wanted the feel and smell of her infant son. She needed him probably more than he needed her since the little boy had Guyasaga's breasts for nourishment. Anod wanted to tell everyone about Zoltentok, about how proud she was of the child and about the joy surrounding his existence. She also missed Bradley's touch.

"This is Colonel Zontramani, Captain of the Society Starship Endeavour, calling Bradley James SanGiocomo, Prime Minister of Beta." The call was repeated several times as they orbited the planet. A response took nearly thirty minutes to return and it was an ancient voice radio signal with no visual component. Zontramani added that simple fact to the accumulation of details associated with Lieutenant Anod.

"This is Bradley SanGiocomo."

"Bradley, it is my understanding you are the leader of the people on the second planet from the star, θ27. Is that correct?"

"Yes."

"Very well. Can we be of any assistance to you?"

"Yes, you can, Colonel, if you have not already done so. We have been repeatedly attacked by the Yorax."

"We have taken care of that menace, at least for the time being," answered the starship captain.

"A woman who was instrumental in saving us from more extensive destruction is missing. Can you find her? She is in an Yorax interceptor which is probably out of fuel and adrift." The concern in his words told Zontramani a great deal about the connection Anod had made with these people.

"We have recovered a pilot of the Kartog Guards, Lieutenant Anod."

"Oh, thank God." Bradley hesitated not really wanting to hear the answer to his next and obvious question. His words were enveloped in timidity and fear of the answer. "Is she alive?"

"Yes, she is, I am happy to report. She was near death when we found her and she is recovering quite nicely."

"Will you be returning her to us?"

The question from the Betan prime minister sounded so strange, and yet, it also added to the growing impression of what happened here. "Prime Minister, I do not fully understand the intent of your question." Zontramani had strong feelings and a clear hunch about the man's question, although presented ignorance often led to further revelations.

"We know where she came from, but she has become a very important part of our community," Bradley stated.

"Prime Minister, Lieutenant Anod is a member of an elite unit called the Kartog Guards. She is a very important member of the Society. We appreciate your caring for her, but she belongs with us."

Bradley did not want to press the issue especially since his counterpart held the strongpoint. "Would you, at least, let her return to say good-bye to her friends on Beta?"

"She is resting in the care of our medical staff. We will discuss her visit at a later time." The bait incentive was always important to a successful negotiation. "I would like to discuss the facts associated with Lieutenant Anod's arrival on your planet and her stay under your care."

"I would be happy to discuss the topic with you, Colonel."

"Can we transport you aboard the Endeavour?" asked Zontramani.

"You will return me to Beta in the same condition?" Bradley asked before speaking his agreement.

"Yes, certainly."

"Then, I will accept your invitation, if I am permitted to see Anod."

"That will not be a problem. Are you ready, now?"

"Wait. Let me tell my family and colleagues what I am doing. Give me a moment." The pause lasted several minutes presumably for him to complete the task. "I am ready," stated the Betan prime minister.

"Transporter, bring Bradley SanGiocomo aboard." commanded Zontramani as the captain proceeded to the transporter room.

The process of establishing the location of Bradley James SanGiocomo without a communicator beacon, locking in his biogrid, and then activating the transporter took a lengthy time, allowing for the Captain to arrive for an official greeting. "Welcome aboard, Endeavour, Prime Minister. It is a pleasure to have you with us," Zontramani said with the diplomatic precision and polish of a seasoned emissary.

"Thank you," Bradley answered somewhat tentatively. "That was my first experience with a transporter." He looked himself over and felt a few parts. "I suppose I am the same man I was before this experience."

Zontramani chuckled with the common reaction. "We can assure you, there were no changes. The process is virtually fail-safe." The captain motioned toward the door. "Shall we go?"

"I would like to see Anod before you begin your interrogation."

Colonel Zontramani did not like the choice of words although he understood the defenseless position the Betan leader was in. "As you wish," he responded as he led Bradley toward the medical clinic.

When they entered, Bradley appeared to be fascinated and enthralled by the treatment tables, medical consoles and other items of medical technology. Bradley was introduced to Captain Amdorona and her staff as they entered. Amdorona led the Prime Minister into the subdued light of the treatment room. The six tables held only one patient, Lieutenant Anod.

Colonel Zontramani noted the expression on Bradley's face as they entered the room. The visitor's eyes said much more about the connection between Anod and the Betan people. The senior warrior had never seen the expression before and did not know quite how to categorize the response.

Zontramani and Amdorona followed Bradley as he walked slowly toward Anod. They did not know what to expect, wanting to ensure no harm came to their comrade.

"Shouldn't she be covered up?" asked Bradley without looking away from Anod.

Both observers looked at one another not knowing what the Betan prime minister was concerned about. "What do you mean by covered up?" asked Amdorona.

"She has no clothes on. She is completely exposed. Everyone can see her body," Bradley said without taking his eyes off Anod's quiet face.

"You are quite right. That is the whole point. This is common practice to ensure the absolute best, error free, treatment of our people," offered Amdorona, still not certain she was answering Bradley's concern.

Anod opened her eyes and smiled when she saw Bradley. Her lips moved although no one other than Anod herself could hear the words. Bradley reached to Anod, but could not pass the invisible protective curtain.

Amdorona moved promptly to the control panel for Anod's isotable when Bradley spoke. "Why can't I touch her? Why can't we hear her?"

"There is a protective force field around her which can allow or deny any penetration of the region around her," explained Amdorona.

"There," Amdorona announced as the force field commands were altered.

Anod reached out to grasp Bradley's hand. "It is sure good to see you, Bradley," Anod said with a soft, quiescent and weak voice.

"We were so worried about you. I am so glad you are OK. Everyone on Beta is all right," said Bradley knowing Anod would understand without compromising her status with her rescuers.

"It would appear I am making a career out of being rescued just in the nick of time," she added. Anod became somewhat confused, or concerned, or curious. "Why are you here?"

"The Captain asked me to come so we could talk about what has happened to you during your stay on Beta." The look in Anod's eyes conveyed the anxiety within. "And, I needed to see you." Bradley smiled. "I see that you are all right."

"I am in good health, now, although I am a little tired."

Colonel Zontramani interjected. "You should rest, Lieutenant. The Prime Minister and I have much to discuss." Anod nodded her head and squeezed Bradley's hand as if to say, be careful.

"I'll come back to see you when we are done," Bradley added before leaving the treatment room.

The discussions with Bradley were cordial, professional and expansive. An hour of question and answers could not be exhaustive, but they were informative. Zontramani had essentially forgotten the banishment of the Betan ancestors from the Society of Earth. When the interview was complete for the day, he would consult the history files in Mostron's possession to refresh and expand any latent knowledge of that era of the Society.

Several times, Colonel Zontramani touched the subject of Anod's physical condition without success. Bradley purposefully avoided talking about Anod's experience. After several attempts, the two men finally agreed that Anod should tell her story and no one else.

Zontramani began to develop a picture, however misty it might be, of the relationship between the Betan prime minister and the young Kartog Guards lieutenant recuperating in the clinic. He could send an investigative team to the surface and collect relevant information about the stay. Somehow he knew, the option did not have any teeth. Although he had no substantive information to corroborate his hypothesis, Zontramani suspected the two new arrivals aboard his vessel had a stronger relationship than guest and host.

"Captain, if you will excuse me, I would like to conclude our discussions, for now. I would very much like to talk to Anod alone, if you don't mind," requested Bradley.

"I certainly have no objection. You are welcome aboard Endeavour anytime and for as long as you wish."

"Thank you."

"Do you remember the way to the clinic?"

"I believe so, thank you." Bradley departed the meeting room.

Upon arrival, he asked for Amdorona, but she was elsewhere on the ship. Bradley told the duty technicians of his request and the captain's permission. Neither person objected. Bradley heard them check with Colonel Zontramani as he entered the treatment room. The splendor of the sight in front of him grabbed Bradley's complete attention as he stopped and then slowly walked toward Anod. Her entire face smiled at him. Bradley realized, at that moment, the naked form of the woman he loved, suspended several centimeters above the table, did not embarrass him, or make him the slightest bit uncomfortable. She looked warm, smooth, soft, content and ever so peaceful. To Bradley, Anod was the most beautiful woman he had ever seen and her nakedness, for some strange reason, seemed to accentuate her beauty. "Can you hear me?" Bradley asked as he reached for her.

"Yes. Perfectly," she answered as their hands joined.

Bradley tried desperately to ignore her nakedness and concentrate on her eyes and lips. She looked so peaceful lying there totally unsupported by anything visible. "Can we cover you up?" he asked with a grimaced expression.

"I know you are not comfortable, but this is quite normal here. Would you like me to turn over so you will only see my backside?" Anod said with lightness to her voice. As she started to move, he shook his head. "Just try to ignore it," she added.

"How do you feel?"

"I am OK although I feel exhausted."

Nodding his head, he continued, "I asked to talk to you alone. I wanted to hear, from you, what you want to do."

"I don't know," she said averting his eyes for the moment. "I just don't know."

"We want you back. I want you back."

"I know." Anod paused.

Bradley could not believe she might actually consider any other option.

She continued, "My decision may be made for me."

"You mean because of ZJ?"

Bradley could sense the conflict within her between the old and new, between the modern and ancient. There was no clear choice he could see for her. He knew how important space flight was to her, and yet he also thought he recognized the instant blooming of a long suppressed instinct to mother her child.

"If you stay here, what will they do to you?"

"I don't think I will be allowed to stay. Unless an exception is made to Society law, I will either be imprisoned, or banished."

"If you are banished, you could stay here."

Anod looked as if she thought of the prospect for a moment. "Possibly. However, I think banishment, to the Society, will be to one of several forbidden zones."

"Why are your people so rigid?"

"We have talked about all this before, Bradley. I don't think it is a question of rigidity. It is essential for survival."

"It is simply beyond my comprehension why Earth has come to such an inhuman set of rules."

"I'm not sure that is fair, Bradley. The Betans are similarly rigid about the human body. Each culture has rules, customs and strictures."

"Maybe."

"The alternative for me is life on Beta. While the environment and people are very delightful, I cannot see Betan society accepting the essence of what I am."

"Your ways are different, but I think we are more tolerant than the Society," he said. "We want you to stay with us. Our son is here."

"When you say we, you cannot include all Betans. I have no doubt you, Nick, Otis and our other friends would not object to my presence, but . . . ."

"No, Anod," exclaimed Bradley. "The people will accept you once they know you." He spoke the words he felt from the heart, not the words of an impartial leader.

Anod chuckled at the veiled emotion behind the words. "Bradley, I understand and appreciate your motive, but I also know you cannot agree with your own words."

He stood up straight still holding her hand. He knew she was right, but could not accept it.

"I am a warrior, bred for one purpose, to protect and serve the Society. My capabilities are a threat to many people although I have not threatened them. I am afraid my presence in your culture would be a rending influence."

Bradley faced his own internal conflict. The woman whom he

had grown to love and whom had borne him a beautiful child displayed in all her glory before him. She personified the good and bad, the strong and weak in the human species. He knew her words were true, he simply refused to accept the conclusion they were leading to.

"You should rest. We do not have to decide the future at this moment. I will return in eight hours. That should be enough time for you to rest. Should I bring Zoltentok back with me?" It was the first time since his birth Bradley James SanGiocomo referred to their son by his given name.

The smile on his face was recognition of the event. Her smile faded. "No. It would not be a good idea. As much as I want to see him and feel him suckle at my breast, it is a violation of Society law and would not be permitted."

"Then, I shall return alone."

"No, Bradley. I want to come to you. A good rest should satisfy the medical requirements. I will see you on Beta." Anod thought for a moment. "In fact, I will meet you at SanGiocomo in eight hours. OK?"

"Are you sure they will let you come?"

"I am not a prisoner, yet," she said with a slight smile. "Yes, I am certain."

"I will go and let you rest. I will tell all your friends on Beta you are well. We will see you shortly at my father's home."

"Yes. Thank you."

Bradley nodded his consent and left the clinic. He spoke one last time with Colonel Zontramani to thank him for the hospitable visit and inform him of the agreement Anod and he had reached. There were no objections since Endeavour would be in orbit for some time, at least until Avenger and Kamakani arrived. A security plan had to be established.

The medical isotable worked its magic to complement Anod's recuperative ability to restore her to full performance. Amdorona ran numerous additional tests to ensure Anod had completely recovered before releasing her from treatment.

Dressed now in a starfleet uniform, a more neutral less utilitarian attire than her Kartog Guards flight suit, Anod was more thoroughly debriefed by a committee appointed by Colonel Zontramani and chaired by Major Astrok. All the questions and discussion focused on the professional events surrounding her last mission from Saranon to her arrival aboard Endeavour. None of the questions, yet, delved into the personal aspects of her time on Beta.

Colonel Zontramani interrupted the inquiry proceedings at the appropriate time so Anod could meet her appointment on Beta. Anod was thankful for his understanding and acceptance, although her unspoken concern for future action against her was irrepressible. The Captain of the Endeavour granted Lieutenant Anod an unrestricted, contingent leave of absence for her to remain on the surface until a departure time was set for the starship. Anod agreed and thanked him for his permission.

The familiar rock's and vegetation of the SanGiocomo cave snapped into view as the transport process completed the reconstitution of the molecules that defined Anod. An instant smile came to her face and her heart. The thought of seeing her son was foremost in her mind, but it was Nick who was first to meet her.

He stepped toward her, then stopped, turned his head and shouted into the cave. "Anod is here." The elder SanGiocomo moved quickly to embrace Anod and kiss her on both cheeks. "It is so good to have you back."

"It is this place and its people who kept me alive. It is good to be back."

Several other men and women who she did not recognize came out and greeted her as if they had known her for many years. There was some confusion with all the commotion, but it disappeared in an instant when she saw Zoltentok in the arms of Guyasaga. Sound, movement, smell, everything vanished as her attention narrowed to the swaddled child being carried toward her. Guyasaga carefully handed the sleeping child to his mother.

Anod cradled him in her arms looking only at his small face. Anod was totally unaware of the emotion welling from deep within her as she sank to her knees and felt tears descending her cheeks. Several of the drops of what she would learn was love fell on Zoltentok's face startling him. He grimaced in preparation to cry. Mother and son joined with their eyes as Anod touched his face to wipe away the fallen tears, but more to feel his skin, to feel his warmth. The infant's expression changed in a flash to the smile of simple pleasure. Anod smiled so hard her face hurt and the tears would not stop coming. There were no other words, or faces, or existence beyond what she had in her arms.

The urge to complete the connection she had dreamed about so many times in the solitude of space overcame her. Anod opened her tunic to offer her breast to her son. Zoltentok took her breast without taking his eyes off hers. Anod could feel the union between them as the tiny boy drew the life fluid from her. The sensations were stronger than she ever remembered pulling from every extremity into his suckling mouth.

A hand grabbed Anod's shoulder eventually shaking her into awareness of the people gathered around her. "Anod, you should not do this. It is not proper," said Guyasaga.

Anod moved her eyes toward the voice, but never saw Guyasaga. She was lost in her own discreet world and everything beyond it simply did not exist.

It was Bradley who knew what was happening and reassured his son's caretaker that the events before them were all right. She was entitled to a little indiscretion by their customs.

All time stopped for an indeterminate duration. All the danger and risk Anod had taken to protect those she had come to love was worth this particular moment in time.

When her son was sated, Anod slowly returned to the reality of where she was. No one was in sight. She and Zoltentok were alone in the clearing before the SanGiocomo cave. Anod rose only to recognize the pain in her knees from the protracted time she must have been kneeling on the rough soil.

The reunion in the interior of Nick's cave was more subdued than her initial greeting, but was nonetheless friendly, warm and caring. During the course of conversation, they each shared the events of the last days of trial. Each of them saw the events from a different perspective. Despite a few voices of passivity, all were awed by Anod's courage, energy and sheer will power.

Zoltentok lay still in her arms looking only at his mother as she talked in a less animated fashion. Her eyes shifted from Bradley to Zoltentok with only an occasional glance at the others in the room. There was a sense of satisfaction and tranquillity associated with the warmth of the room and its occupants.

Eventually, the conversation worked its way around to Anod's situation and status. Bradley withdrew from this part of the discussion, not wanting to hear an answer he refused to accept. Nick was his usual curious, gentle self and was quickly satisfied with her answers. It was Guyasaga and the others who were the manifestation of interrogation. They wanted to know all about the subjects she had been over so many times before. She remained patient and accepting as if the protracted conversation would solve the problem above her, or prolong her stay on Beta.

The absence of Bradley motivated Anod to excuse herself from the room and search him out. She found him seated on one of the tree stumps near the edge of the forest where they had talked in a time that seemed so long ago. He was looking at some indistinguishable point in the woods and did not look at her as she approached.

"What's wrong?" Anod asked feeling certain she knew the answer.

"I don't want you to leave," he responded without moving.

"Actually, I don't want to leave, but I'm afraid the solution is beyond my wishes."

"I don't understand why. Can't you simply resign your position?"

"I don't know. I have never known anyone to resign from service in the Kartog Guards. I don't know if there are any rules regarding such actions."

"Isn't it worth a try?"

Anod wanted to say, yes, but the thought of relinquishing her wings, the ancient symbol of flight, kept her from speaking the answer. Once again, she felt lost, caught between two worlds, similar and yet so much different. The law of the Society had been broken, partially due to ignorance and the remainder the product of curiosity and desire. The experiences of Beta had irreparably altered her life. Her presence among the Betans was a foreign influence that the community might not be able to assimilate. Anod was confident, not self-conscious, aggressive, uninhibited and strong. She felt welcomed on Beta although she knew the population would never accept her. There was so much more to life beyond a surface existence, no matter how pleasurable it might be.

"I suppose your silence has answered my question," Bradley said with a subdued voice.

Anod looked into his troubled eyes and smiled. A tear formed in her eye to move slowly down her cheek. "Bradley, I have never known such good feelings. I have learned so much, seen and felt even more, while I was your guest on Beta. I want to stay. Zoltentok . . ." She hesitated to absorb the presence of the child sleeping in her arms. "Zoltentok has brought a new dimension to my life." Anod again looked into Bradley's waiting eyes. "You must admit, I am an oddity here. I don't fit in and I am not sure I am able to change. There are pleasures of flight and space that cannot be experienced on the surface. Those are equally powerful forces within me. I feel like I am straddling a chasm which continues to widen and I cannot jump in either direction safely." Night was coming to SanGiocomo. The darkening sky enabled both of them to see the distinctive shape of the Endeavour passing overhead. The object of interest was a reminder of Anod's impending decision, if she was allowed to decide. The prospect was definitely not a certainty.

"I understand the contrast and the conflict," Bradley began. "In many ways, I share your paradox, although I was not wrenched from my world," Bradley said with calm sincerity. "In more ways than I can state, I feel responsible for your conflict." He paused to gather his thoughts as if the next words he would say might change his life forever. "If I had kept my distance, if Zoltentok had not been conceived, this decision would be much easier and seemingly less final than it is now. I must apologize for my contribution, however I am thankful beyond words for the times we have shared and the life we have created."

"You are not to blame," Anod said with thoughts of her first experience with intimacy at High Cave with Otis. "I certainly do not hold you responsible for my actions. I chose to take the path which has brought me to this day of judgment."

"Why don't you two come in and eat?" Nick shouted from the mouth of the cave. "It's getting too cold out here for the baby." It was indeed dark and the temperature had fallen substantially.

The couple smiled at each other, then Bradley turned and said, "Coming father." The discussion was not over, but the available words were dwindling. Maybe a good night sleep together would help convince her, Bradley thought as they walked into the cave.

The first task, now a temporary peace had been restored, was to understand and resolve the issues associated with the events surrounding Lieutenant Anod, Colonel Zontramani told himself. The circumstances and consequences demanded immediate attention before rumors began to spread among the crew. The more insidious and traitorous deeds of Captain Zitger, alleged by Lieutenant Anod, would be the subject of an exhaustive and laborious examination by a starfleet tribunal.

"Major Astrok, the subject we are about to discuss I have classified as state secret," Zontramani stated emphatically in his ready room.

"Understood."

"The medical scan of Lieutenant Anod has revealed a grievous violation of Society law." The first officer maintained her attentive expression, waiting for her commanding officer to continue. "While she was on Beta, the data indicates she was intimate with a man and has borne an infant. Her body, and probably her mind, have been irreversibly changed."

"How can this be?" Astrok said with genuine surprise. "She knows the law and the consequences."

"I am sure she does. There may be other circumstances which were beyond her control once she was no longer under our protection."

"Yes, but she knows the law," repeated Astrok.

"Our choices are rather few which is what I wanted to discuss with you."

"How many others are aware of Anod's condition?"

"Captain Amdorona and two of her technicians, and they are aware of the sensitivity and classification of this subject."

"What do you have in mind?"

"First, I would suggest we conduct a discreet inquiry on the surface once Avenger or Kamakani arrive, to determine the cause and involvement in this transgression. Depending on the results, the law is quite specific, banishment or rehabilitation."

"Are you certain there has been a violation?"

"Absolutely. I have reviewed her previous and current full body scans with Amdorona. The data are accurate, corroborated and conclusive," Zontramani responded with an air of frustration in his voice. Actually, he desperately wanted the medical data to be wrong. He knew from the Society records Anod was an exemplary officer with considerable potential for future command. Her loss, while only one pilot, would be significant for many more reasons than the loss of her skills. Anod represented the future of the Society. "I would like you to head the inquiry. Select four other officers of appropriate rank, conduct the investigation under state secret guidelines and report back to me upon conclusion. I would also like your recommendations at the proper time."

"Very well. I shall proceed with the preparations and we will review the medical data until Avenger or Kamakani arrives."

"Thank you, Astrok. Take care, be thorough and return safely." Zontramani paused as his mind considered additional words. "Let me know if you need any assistance."

Major Astrok performed her task with characteristic precision. The review of the medical scans along with questioning of the cognizant medical personnel took nearly a day to complete.

Avenger arrived first and the inquiry team transported to the surface of Beta after notification of and permission for the visit was granted by the Prime Minister of the colony. The process took several days with the investigation team returning to their residence, Endeavour, after each day's proceedings while Anod chose to remain on Beta through the inquiry. Anod freely described the events surrounding the purpose of the investigation including the feelings and thoughts that came to her during the periods of intimacy. The description of her pregnancy, birth and postnatal care of her child was provided in vivid detail without reservation. Anod knew the significance of what had happened, the seriousness of the consequences, but her nature required full, unqualified disclosure and precise accuracy in reporting the details. To her, this event was no different from debriefing a long patrol.

Numerous Betans were also interviewed with a spectrum of cooperation. Bradley understood more than most why the proceedings were so important to Anod and the Society board of inquiry. He also stood to lose the most, but Anod had convinced him it was in hers and his best interest to offer complete testimony. Otis Greenstreet was the most resistive. The probing of strangers into the private experiences of individuals and especially regarding the subject of intimacy shocked young Otis. Major Astrok and her team were patient, tolerant and persistent.

The citizens of Beta who participated in the Society inquiry were, as a whole, confused, flabbergasted and resentful of the investigation. To them it was an invasion of privacy. Outside the official events, Astrok was well aware the Betans talked about the potential results and returned to the history of their people, the reasons their Betan ancestors had separated from their common predecessors on Earth. The renewal of the separatist fervor was strong and infectious. The intrusions by the Society brought back suppressed emotions regarding past events. Although the questioning was directed at a visitor, a foreigner, to their planet and a citizen of the Society, the action was repulsive by its very nature. Betans who had never known or even seen Anod soon became inflamed with the reaction to the external stimuli.

With the Yorax, the Betans seemed to be more accepting since there was no veil of justice or righteousness. They wanted something and they did not care what they had to do to get it. They were evil that was easy to deal with. The Society board of inquiry was conducted, as a proper and legal proceeding that was not particularly palatable, especially when they shared common genetic lines.

The deliberations of the board took three days to complete. Major Astrok delivered the findings of their investigation to Colonel Zontramani personally and privately. The Captain of the Society Starship Endeavour rarely was presented with simple problems to resolve. This one, an errant starfleet officer of exceptional potential, was the most difficult and personally traumatizing. Colonel Zontramani summoned Lieutenant Anod to his ready room.

The flight uniform of a Kartog Guards pilot felt good on her body and to her mind. She knew the purpose of the summons. The pride and confidence given to her by genetics and training helped to hold her head high and walk with dignity from the transporter room to the Captain's ready room passing several starfleet officers in the passageways. The presence of a Kartog line pilot on a starship was rare.

"Lieutenant Anod, reporting as ordered," she stated standing in front of Colonel Zontramani's austere desk.

"Lieutenant, as you are aware, a board of inquiry was conducted by Major Astrok into the events surrounding your stay of the planet Beta of the θ027 star system." He spoke the stilted words to the official, permanent record retained by Mostron. "The facts associated with the ambush of your flight and your subsequent bravery in combat with the Yorax are not in question. In fact, I offer for the record nothing short of the highest praise for you, as a pilot, and for your contributions to the protection of innocent people. However, specific events occurred on Beta which have drawn your ancillary actions into question."

Colonel Zontramani carefully read each of the findings of fact from the record of the investigation. The picture being created by the words did not match the feelings Anod retained in her memory. The facts were methodically correct, accurate, complete and thorough, but there was no discussion of the feelings, the sensations or the stimulation associated with those facts. Without the perceptive elements of those events, they seemed so ephemeral, so basic, so degrading. Anod did not like the image unfolding in her mind with the brush strokes of Zontramani's words. He was not talking about the same events.

"All the evidence collected, and especially the facts which have been corroborated by physical as well as testimonial evidence, establish the fact that you have violated several of the most sensitive and important laws of the Society, the body of collective laws prohibiting intimacy between humans," the starship captain said with such finality.

Anod knew she would eventually have to face this action. There were not many officers she would rather stand in front of to face the law. She thought of Colonel Zortev. It had been so long since she had seen her mentor. She was glad she was not standing in front of Zortev; it would have added embarrassment to the regret. Zontramani was a good leader and a fair officer.

"Do you wish to refute the findings of the board of inquiry?"

The question came as a slap across her face and it stung with the same sharpness. She knew all this effort would come down to this one question. Despite all her preparations, Anod was not ready to answer. She wanted this pain to end. She wanted the comforting touch of Zoltentok and soothing hand of Bradley and Nick. "No," Anod responded in a quiet, soft voice almost submissive in nature.

"Mostron, stop the record."

"The record of the board of inquiry conference with Lieutenant Anod has been suspended by Colonel Zontramani," the faithful servant reported.

"Anod, you can't do this." Zontramani's voice wavered with uncharacteristic emotion as he bore sole witness to her demise. "Your record is too good. You have demonstrated such impressive performance and your potential is irreproachable. You've got to respond to these charges regardless of whether they are correct, or not."

"I appreciate your words, Colonel Zontramani, and I thank you for them. However, my violation of Society law is undeniable. I cannot plead ignorance of the law. I just want to get this over with."

"But, you can't let this happen. You have the opportunity to explain why, to offer mitigating circumstances which affected your actions." Zontramani paused to gather his thoughts and form his words. "Maybe it is time for a change. For a new precedent."

"I appreciate what you are saying, but I have violated, for whatever reason, one of the most fundamental laws of the Society. If we draw the foundation of our community into question, then what is the basis for our system? I am not asking for a change."

The accomplished starfleet officer considered her words. He searched his mind for a way around this fissure. Zontramani appeared to be facing a sensation he had never felt. Here he was performing his duty as a judge with the accused standing before him, and he looked as if it was he who was the accused, as if he was on trial. "Mostron, we shall return to the record," he commanded with solemnity.

"The record of the board of inquiry conference with Lieutenant Anod is reinstated."

"Do you wish to refute the findings of the board of inquiry?" Colonel Zontramani repeated his earlier question.

"No," responded Anod.

"Very well. I have no choice, but to find you in direct and unqualified violation of Article 7, Section 16, points 4 through 10, of the Society Code of Conduct. You are to be removed from the rolls of the Kartog Guards and stripped of your citizenship. Your only choices are banishment, or imprisonment for rehabilitation. Do you understand the choices you have?"

"Yes." Anod knew in the abstract what the choices were. She had never experienced either. What she did know was, imprisonment meant the relinquishment of her freedom in return for the basic amenities of Society life. At this point in her life, freedom was far more important than comfort and protection. "I choose banishment."

The finality of her words now hit Colonel Zontramani like a rogue asteroid hurtling through space. The disappointment and disgust of the seasoned leader erupted across every facial muscle like a red-hot lava flow. "Very well, then you are hereby banished from the Society and, since Beta is the closest inhabitable planet, you will be transported to the surface."

The words washed over her like a warm wave of enveloping fluid. The words meant an end to the life she had known, but it also meant she would not have to be without Zoltentok and Bradley. The judgment was also more than she would have expected. She would not have to plead for a modification.

Anod nodded her head to avoid speaking which would only confirm the tremors reverberating thorough her body and soul. Her pride kept her head high and her eyes clear. She would not give in to the humiliation.

"You are dismissed. You will proceed directly to the transporter room. These proceedings are concluded," Colonel Zontramani said with considerably more detachment than at any time since she first saw him in the clinic.

Turning crisply, Anod walked toward the ready room doors that opened upon sensing her approach. She stopped before passing through the opened hatchway. A small, flickering flame of strength returned to her. Anod turned back toward Zontramani taking several steps forward allowing the doors to close. "I have a favor to ask."

The impartial, defensive eyes of the warrior returned to Zontramani. "What is it?"

"I would like to depart in the Yorax interceptor you found me in. It should still be in your hangar bay."

Zontramani thought about the request and all the consequences of his consent. The Society knew the capabilities and limitations of the small fighters. The craft was of no use to the Society. "I see no problem. Your request is granted. Mostron, summon Captain Zalemon to escort Anod to the hangar bay."

The lack of her rank before her name was an instant reminder of what had just happened in this room. There was a sense of relief with the removal of the cloud over her. "Thank you, Colonel Zontramani."

The orders were executed explicitly. Zalemon carried out his instruction with the sterile, impersonalness of virtually every starfleet security officer. Her interceptor had been fully fueled and prepared for launch.

Anod carried out the launch sequence with her usual skill. She made two circuits around the Endeavour to take a close up look at the elegant and graceful starship before departing for the surface of Beta. This was the end of the beginning she told herself as she descended into the atmosphere of her new home, however tenuous it might be.

Cap Parlier

Author of *Anod's Seduction* and *Anod's Redemption*

Cap and his wife, Jeanne, live in Andover, Kansas, along with Cap's mother, four dogs and a bowling ball with legs otherwise known as a cat. He is a graduate of the U.S. Naval Academy, a former Marine aviator, Vietnam veteran, experimental test pilot and successful manager who currently serves engineering manager for an aerospace company. Cap is a former director of the National Marrow Donor Program and director emeritus of The Marrow Foundation. Cap helped a Soviet test pilot who was a hero of the Chernobyl disaster and needed treatment for his radiation exposure obtain a bone marrow transplant in the USA, and Cap told the story of these heroes of Chernobyl in his book, *Sacrifice*. He brought his aviation, engineering and intelligence experience to *TWA 800 – Accident or Incident?* when he joined Kevin E. Ready to co-author the detailed assessment of the 1996 tragedy. Cap has numerous other projects completed and in the works including screenplays, historical novels and a couple of history books. He has remained an outspoken and fervent advocate of manned space exploration, as well as inner space exploration.

Interested readers may wish to visit his website at <http://www.parlier.com> for his essays and other items, or subscribe to his weekly on-line "Update from the Heartland." Cap can be reached at: cap@parlier.com.